GORGEOUS VILLAIN

USA TODAY & WALL STREET JOURNAL BESTSELLING AUTHOR

CHARITY FERRELL

Visit my website at www.charityferrell.com
Cover Designer: Lori Jackson
Cover Model Photographer: Wander Aguiar
Editor: Jovana Shirley, Unforeseen Editing, www.unforseenediting.com
Proofreading: Editing4Indies

ISBN-13: 978-1-952496-79-0

These violent delights have violent ends,
And in their triumph die, like fire and powder,
Which, as they kiss, consume.
—William Shakespeare, *Romeo and Juliet*

PROLOGUE

GIGI

I fell in love with my family's enemy.

And now, he's holding a priest and me at gunpoint while forcing me to recite the vows that'll make me his wife.

You think you know me, but you have no idea.

I'm Gigi Marchetti, princess of a notorious Mafia crime family.

And Antonio Lombardi's pawn.

1

GIGI

I'll blame my death on a large vanilla latte and a small bladder.

Along with my older brother, Benny, who parked his Range Rover behind a sketchy warehouse twenty minutes ago and instructed me to stay in the car until he returned. He should've remembered I carry the attention span of a squirrel and can't be left alone in weird places for long.

No one has entered after him, and as the daughter of a Mafia boss, I'm certain illegal activity is happening inside. Anything from corruption to murder falls within those parameters.

But it's something my bladder and I will have to risk.

"I'm kicking your ass if I get E. coli, Benny," I mutter while stepping out of the SUV.

The New York wind whips against my face as I stomp toward the building.

Hopefully, there isn't Crime Scene tape blocking off the restroom.

Or I don't die, of course.

I tug at the door, finding it unlocked, and invite myself right in.

The scent of harsh cleaning solutions hits me.

Fingers crossed they also used that in the restroom.

"Ben—" I'm cut off by a scream.

"Please!" a man desperately begs. "Let me go!"

Instead of fleeing like a rational person, I tiptoe toward the noise. Crouching behind a row of barrels, I peek through the narrow gap to find a beat-up man bound to a chair. Three men dressed in black suits surround him. Swear to God, it's like a scene plucked straight out of *The Sopranos*.

I blink, inching closer, certain one looks familiar.

A suited man steps toward the restrained one and punches him in the face. I wince at the loud crack when he rears his fist back for another hit. Blood gushes down the tied-up man's nose.

"Antonio, please!" he howls in pain. "Let me speak with your father. I'll explain—"

Antonio.

As in Antonio Lombardi—son of notorious crime boss Vincent Lombardi.

He's considered the sane one in his family, but that doesn't mean he isn't as corrupt as the others. From the rumors, he just does a better job of hiding his ruthlessness behind his charm and smooth talking.

Another fun fact about the maniac? He's also a cold-blooded killer.

"Speak with my father?" Antonio spits. His calculated timbre sends shivers down my spine. "You think he'd speak with a rat who talked to the police, Norman?"

Oh man, a rat?

Norman is doomed.

Antonio backhands him, and Norman doubles over in agony.

I creep closer while Antonio digs two black gloves from his pocket and slips them on. A brawny man drags a blanket off something in the corner to reveal an animal carrier and brings it to Antonio.

"Do you know what eats rats, Norman?" Antonio opens the carrier with a click.

"Uh …" Norman kicks his heels against the concrete, pitifully attempting to break free.

Antonio removes an animal from the carrier.

I wedge my head between two barrels to get a clearer view.

It's a snake, for fuck's sake.

Norman realizes this at the same time. He thrashes his body from side to side, desperate to break free. The chair teeters and braces on three legs. The snake is calm, allowing Antonio to hold it as if it's a pet he's raised since it was a pup … or whatever you call baby snakes.

Reminder: Google that later.

"Now, Norman"—Antonio circles him like the predator he is—"meet our Lombardi mascot, Ace. He teaches our *rats* lessons."

Norman attempts to lift his arms, but the tape restraining him is too tight.

Antonio hums and smirks. "Ace is a saw-scaled viper, the most venomous snake in the world."

"I'll do anything," Norman cries out. "I'm begging you! Please don't let him bite me."

"Bite you?" Antonio tsks. "I'd never make Ace stick his fangs into the likes of you." He pets Ace. "Ace had his venom removed, so I'm injecting it into you. He'll kill a rat without even having to touch it."

One of his men opens a cooler and extracts a syringe, and Antonio takes it from him.

Norman sobs when a man behind him grips the back of his head and exposes his throat. Antonio plunges the syringe of venom into Norman's neck, and he screams.

Oh my fucking God.

I clutch a hand over my mouth to muffle my gasps.

Seconds later, Norman falls silent, his face covered in sweat as if processing what happened. Or searching his brain for any known facts about what happens to the body when injected with snake venom.

Reminder number two: also Google that.

"What should we do with him, boss?"

"Wait here until he dies." Antonio removes one glove and shoves it into his pocket before checking his watch. "It should only take about twenty minutes."

That's my cue to slither on out of here.

Forget about peeing.

I'm not about to become snake food.

I slowly back up, turn … and then my foot smacks straight into a bucket, knocking it over. The sound echoes through the warehouse like an alarm. Antonio's focus shifts to me, and he charges in my direction.

I'm about to die, all for a pee break.

I circle the barrels to escape but am too slow. Antonio captures my wrist and swings me around to face him so forcefully that I knock over a barrel.

Raising my gaze, I find him staring down at me, his face stolid.

I shiver as his brown eyes, enigmatic and alluring, search mine. The longer I gaze at him, the deeper he draws my soul into his darkness.

People mistake his manipulativeness with charm, but I see right through him.

My father has done business with his family for years, but I've never seen him so up close to appreciate how gorgeous he is. He doesn't give me a chance to do it either.

"What's a princess like you doing here?" His question oozes with intimidation, his own form of venom.

His voice.

It's smooth, like my favorite lattes in Paris, yet callous at the same time.

And oh my God.

It makes me feel my heartbeat in my clit.

I should be worried about him and his snake, but here I am, lusting over this murderous psychopath.

Norman starts screaming again in the background, and Antonio grins as if it's his favorite lullaby.

"Girls like you shouldn't linger around the devil's dungeon unless they're asking for trouble. So why are you here?" He tightens his hold on me, knocking some sense into my brain.

I struggle to release myself.

"If you don't answer me in three seconds, I'll provide you the same fate as Norman."

"I'm certainly not injecting people with lethal toxins, *like you*." I provide a forceful jerk with my last two words.

His solid body doesn't move an inch during my struggle. "Norman betrayed my family."

I shudder when his glove-covered hand rises to curl around my face. He mercilessly digs his fingers into my cheek. My skin feels like it's being scorched by an invisible flame.

No big deal. Just breathe, Gigi.

It's not like he was just holding *the most venomous snake in the world* in that hand.

My muscles tighten, and I know I should pull a Norman and scream. Benny is somewhere in the warehouse and will come to my rescue. Then, he'll murder Antonio for laying his snake-handling, Norman-killing hands on me. But I stupidly don't.

"Why not just shoot him?" I ask instead. "Grant him a quick death. It's the humane thing to do." I'm fully aware that murder in any form isn't humane. It's semantics at this point.

"If a man is worthy of a humane death, he'll receive it. Norman isn't."

"Let's hope I never marry a man with your mindset."

"If your husband isn't a killer, he won't remain your husband for long, *Giana*."

I stop my fighting. "How—"

"Oh, princess." He tsks like how he did with Norman. "You thought I didn't know who you are?"

My tense shoulders soften an inch. "Knowing who I am

means you won't kill me." I smugly clasp my free hand around his gloved one.

"Someone's name has never deterred me from killing them."

"How would you kill me then, *Antonio Lombardi*?"

The shock factor of knowing his name isn't what I hoped for. Instead of appearing fazed, he looks almost entertained.

"Let's hope we don't find out." He abruptly releases me and retreats a step.

"Gigi fucking Marchetti!"

Looking past him, I spot Benny storming toward us with a black duffel bag slung over his shoulder. A duffel that no doubt has money or weapons inside. Raul, one of my father's men, is behind him.

"I'd recommend keeping a tighter leash on your sister," Antonio tells Benny, sliding his glove off and not looking away from me. His voice carries a layer of annoyance, like he's a teenager stuck babysitting a toddler.

"I told you to stay in the car," Benny scolds. "Come on." He holds the duffel up. "Pleasure doing business, Antonio."

Antonio narrows his cold eyes at me without bothering to reply to my brother. I struggle not to glance back at him as Benny pulls me out of the warehouse.

During the ride home, I squirm in my seat, still needing to pee.

"You need to start listening to what I say," Benny lectures. "Whatever you saw in that warehouse, you keep it to yourself."

I ignore him.

Antonio Lombardi consumes my thoughts.

My face warms when I run my hand over the same cheek he touched.

Then, I smack myself in the face.

Not bitch-slap-style, but with enough force that there's a slight sting.

Raul whips around from the passenger seat. "What the fuck?"

"Just slapping some sense into myself," I say with a smile.

Antonio Lombardi is bad news.

Next time he touches me, I'll scream.

And he'll die for it.

FOUR MONTHS LATER

I'm well acquainted with death. It seeps into my bones, oozes into the walls of my home, and hangs like rotting branches on our family tree.

Funerals always remind me of my mother. I was six when I stood in the cemetery, eyes flooded with tears, and said goodbye to her one final time. Since then, I've lost count of the number of funerals I've attended.

Today, I'm paying my respects to Edda Bova. She was a gentle soul, and like my mother, she was killed in a drive-by shooting.

Poor Edda wasn't the target. Her husband, Remo, was. Unfortunately, a wife paying for her husband's sins is common in my world.

After the service ends, I offer my condolences to the family. When my father waves my bodyguard, Bruno, over, I sneak out of the cathedral in need of fresh air. I pass cars and people lining the sidewalk before turning the corner into a back alley.

"If it isn't Princess Marchetti."

Spinning around at the taunting voice, I nearly twist my ankle while finding Antonio casually walking toward me. My heart races—a warning signal mingled with a twinge of excitement.

Even though he's the one following *me*, he looks pissed off at my presence. His malevolent expression matches the one he wore when telling Benny to keep a tighter leash on me in the warehouse.

I hold a hand above my brow to block out the sun as he approaches.

Antonio lacks a smile or any warmth, dressed in an all-black suit and leather loafers. I want to trace the rugged lines of his stubbly cheeks with my fingers. His nose, while perfectly shaped, is slightly off-center, adding character to his face. Blinking, I make out the small scar on his forehead—kinda Harry Potter–style, but less lightning bolt and to the right.

Knowing he has the power to unleash total destruction, anyone with brains would run away from him.

Me? I want to dive in headfirst.

"Sorry for your loss," he says. His voice holds no sympathy as he stands in front of me like an eerie castle.

"Edda was a sweet woman." I sigh. "She didn't deserve to die like that."

"If it makes you feel better, your father will murder every man responsible."

"That won't bring her back, though."

"It'll soothe the family's soul."

Will it?

My father wiped out the entire organization responsible for my mother's death. It didn't bring her back. Sure didn't *soothe our souls.*

"Why's the solution always murder? Maybe we should offer them a therapy gift card or a one-way ticket to the psych ward? I feel like you'd do especially well with a vacation there."

The corners of his mouth turn up. "Murder is our therapy, princess."

Goose bumps ripple along my skin.

Princess.

I never thought I'd be turned on by such a simple name.

A name I hate anyone else calling me.

"Therapy is supposed to help with your problems," I say. "Murder leads to more problems. There's no reward."

"Knowing they'll no longer breathe is the reward."

"I think you're a legit psychopath."

"And you're in la-la land if you think talking about my feelings will ever cure the madness embedded inside me."

"How's your pet snake?"

"Ace is doing well." His facial muscles relax, releasing a tiny bit of tension. "Would you like to visit him? Maybe he'll listen to this therapy you speak so highly of. I heard he's a great listener." He clicks his tongue against the roof of his mouth. "Can't promise he's not a biter though."

"Visit him so you can kill me next?"

"*Kill you*? You're untouchable, princess." The statement rolls off his tongue with ease and familiarity, like he was taught that at a young age.

My pulse elevates. "No one is untouchable."

"No one *but you.*"

"What do you mean, *untouchable*?"

He raises his large-knuckled hand and separates his fingers. "It means that if even one of my fingers touches you, your father will kill me, my family, and, hell, probably even my fucking snake."

My thoughts wander to the warehouse, remembering how he touched me, fully aware of who I was. That didn't stop him then. It doesn't stop him now either as he reaches out and presses his palm over my racing heart.

His touch doesn't soothe me.

It sets me aflame.

He mirrors the smug look I gave him moments ago when he feels my heart running wild beneath his hand. "Do I make you nervous?"

"No." I glower at him. "And for someone who claims I'm so *untouchable*, you can't seem to keep your hands off me."

"I like testing my limits." He smiles viciously.

"Test your limits somewhere else." I silently beg my heart to chill the fuck out.

"Where's the fun in that?" He runs his hand along my chest, and there's an ache for him to return when he pulls away.

"I'm not a limit, Antonio. I'm a death sentence."

"Death is so pretty to me though." He chuckles. "See you around, princess."

I wait until he turns before saying, "Hopefully not."

He peers back at me, those dark eyes of his promising me he will. "Now, wouldn't that be disappointing?"

2

ANTONIO

It takes all my willpower to walk away from Gigi in the alley, but too many people are around. I'll find another way, somewhere more private, to corner her next time. Biting into my lip, I grin at the fact I'm about to become a major problem for her.

Even if I have to become a stalker, I'll see her again.

There's a chance I can die for it though.

Every man understands a few certainties in this life will lead you straight to your grave:

Betraying your family.

Disobeying orders.

Touching Cristian Marchetti's daughter.

While I'll never be stupid enough to commit the first two, I know my desire to fuck Giana Marchetti is inviting death to my door. Prior to the warehouse incident, I hadn't paid her much attention because I knew the history of men who'd wanted her.

A man who'd once grabbed her ass was found decapitated in a gutter. Another, even though he was a member of an allied family, drunkenly and publicly announced he'd *fuck the shit out of her*. No one has seen him since. You don't fuck with Monster Marchetti's daughter and live to tell of it.

So my take was, why stare at the forbidden fruit you know

you can't taste?

That was why I always ignored her.

But then she had to sneak her ass into the warehouse and tempt me.

Now that I've seen her up close and touched her, I can't get her out of my mind.

Can't stop imagining how her thick black hair with random strands of purple would feel knotted between my fingers.

I want to rip off and destroy that veil of innocence on her angelic face.

The moment she smart-mouthed me, I knew she was mine. Now, I need to make that happen before Cristian marries her off to someone else for some business deal.

Fuck, the things I want to do to her.

Pin her against the cathedral wall and fuck her like a god.

Hear her moan my name as I thrust inside her.

Dirty up the Mafia princess.

My cock jerks in my pants at the thought.

I'm a man known as the problem solver in my family, so I'll figure out how to own her.

Then, I can touch her however I want.

Fuck that sharp mouth whenever I want.

Claim her as mine.

As I turn the corner, I nearly collide with my older brother, Vinny, who decides to remind me of my fucking problem.

"As much as I'd love for you to piss off Cristian Marchetti by fucking his daughter, it's risky." He shakes his head and lights a cigarette.

I raise my brows. "Who said I want to fuck her?"

"Don't insult my intelligence, brother." He takes a hit. "You're the only person I trust in this family, and I don't know if I can take over without you by my side. Don't cash out your chips on me over a woman."

I scrub a hand over my face and ignore him while walking toward my car.

"Funerals fucking suck," Vinny rambles, taking long strides to catch up with me. "You think I give two fucks this bitch is dead?" He blows out a puff of smoke. "Wrong place, wrong time. It happens."

"The Marchettis are allies. It's our duty to attend these."

"Our obligation is done then. Let's get the fuck out of here." He tosses his cigarette to the ground and snubs it out with his loafer. "Plus, I have some info on your newest obsession that you might not be happy about."

I whip around to face him. "Elaborate—*now*."

He jerks his head toward my black Bentley along the side of the road. As soon as we're inside, he starts talking. "Leandra called, and guess what she told me."

Leandra is Vinny's preferred prostitute who works at his favorite brothel. I appreciate him picking her well, because she always has information for us.

Since I'm not a fan of guessing games, I glare at him impatiently.

"Eddie Polorono took a call while waiting for his whore in a room. He told whoever was on the other end that he'd pay ten thousand to anyone who brought him the pussy you were drooling over minutes ago."

There's an urge to elbow him in the face for referring to Gigi as *the pussy I was drooling over*, but the desire for more details stops me. "How reliable is Leandra?"

"Her word is as good as she sucks dick, and since she's the trainer for sucking dick at the brothel, I'd say it's pretty damn reliable." He arches his lips.

I remain quiet, waiting for his next words, and merge onto the street. While Vinny takes pleasure in talking, I'm more of a listener, mentally noting every detail.

"Eddie is out of hiding," he continues as I drive. "And he's running his mouth about seeking revenge on Cristian for killing his family. He plans to use Gigi as his means of revenge."

Everyone knows Gigi is Cristian's weakness, but no one is

stupid enough to risk their lives and use that against him. We witnessed his wrath on the Poloronos after they murdered his wife. He nearly slaughtered every member of Eddie's family involved. Eddie was a teen then, so Cristian spared his life. What a mistake that was.

My family, along with three others—the Marchettis, Cavallaros, and O'Connors—are the top crime families in New York. The four of us hold a mutual understanding of respect and never cross each other. If you do, the other families join to eliminate you.

And while we're dangerous, the FBI deemed the Marchettis the most notorious in the country. Even the cartels fear Cristian. He's the Grim Reaper who surfaces out of nowhere and sends you to your death.

"Eddie would be stupid to try." I grind my teeth.

Vinny tugs his vape from his pocket, playing with it in his hand. "Desperate people do desperate shit."

Making a right, I enter the rear parking lot of Lucky Kings, our family's casino. "We need to tell Cristian."

"The hell we do." Vinny violently shakes his head in disapproval. "Cristian Marchetti needs to be pushed down a notch. He believes he rules the city and controls everyone. He'll lose his shit if something happens to his daughter dearest, and it'll only make our family stronger." He squares his shoulders. "Hopefully, Eddie is smart enough to take out Cristian and his son too."

Do I care if Cristian or Benny dies? Fuck no.

Like Vinny said, it'd strengthen our family. We'd reap the benefit of less competition.

Do I care if Gigi dies? For some reason, yes.

The possibility of Eddie killing Cristian or Benny is nil. Eddie has a lower IQ than the rodents swarming the city's alleys. He'll die, and Cristian will stay in power. But that doesn't mean Eddie won't get his hands on Gigi before Cristian discovers his plan. I've heard a bodyguard follows her everywhere, yet she was alone during both our run-ins.

"Fuck the Marchettis," Vinny says, raising his voice.

My brother is reckless. Not as much as Eddie, but still reckless.

I dread the day he assumes control when our father dies or steps down. Since Vinny is the eldest, the family will fall under his control. Having him in charge will lead our men to early graves.

Our father became don of the Lombardi family decades ago and worked hard to restore our reputation after my grandfather tarnished it. His alliance with Cristian and the other families is the best thing to happen in decades.

"Is it Luna's brothel?" I swing the car door open.

We pay Madam Luna a substantial bonus for any reliable information brought our way from clients who frequent her business. Lucky for us, she has no issue discreetly planting cameras in the rooms.

Vinny cracks a smile. "Are you asking me to hunt down Eddie or because you want your dick sucked?"

I glower at him. "Just tell me which brothel."

He levels his glare on me. "Luna's, obviously. Like I'd go anywhere else."

"Talk to Leandra and find out when Eddie will be there next."

"I'll need to go with you."

Even though it'd earn me favor with Cristian if I informed him of Eddie's plan, I want more than that.

I want his daughter.

And Eddie is my ticket to her.

Despite having a shit ton to do, I've spent all day tracking down Eddie, my prey for the day. I can't wait to get my hands on the sleazebag.

I grab my phone when it rings, and Vinny's name flashes on the screen.

"Leandra called," he says as soon as I answer. "Eddie is at the brothel now, but we're short on time. He's panicking because someone told Cristian about his little plan."

I jump up from my chair, snatch my pistol, and speed-walk out of my office at the casino. If Cristian knows Eddie wants to hurt Gigi, he'll find him soon, so I need to beat him.

The melody of slot machines plays in the background as I charge toward the exit. My uncle Sonny attempts to stop me, muttering bullshit I can't make out … nor do I care.

"Not now, Sonny." I wave him away and ignore him while he continues talking behind me.

"Where are you?" I ask Vinny.

"Just pulled into the parking lot," he replies. "Meet me at your car."

I've developed an unhealthy obsession with Giana Marchetti. And Eddie will die for it.

An armed man wearing slim glasses approaches my car. When I roll down my window, he crouches to get a better view inside.

"Sup, Maurice?" Vinny raises his chin.

Maurice calls out, "Good to go!" before granting us access into the underground parking lot. Cars that cost no less than six figures occupy the spaces.

I park, and a second guard stands at the entrance. Like Maurice, he doesn't give us any hassle once he sees Vinny.

Luna's brothel caters to the wealthiest and most influential citizens of New York City. It's reputed for its discretion and top-level security.

Even though we pay Luna for information, Vinny usually delivers the payments to her, so this is only my second time visiting the brothel. My first was on my sixteenth birthday when my father, Vinny, and Sonny took me. I fucked an escort named Janie who faked moans and called me Daddy too many times.

"The Lombardi men," Madam Luna welcomes from behind the counter. Her gaze cuts straight to me. "Antonio, darling, it's been way too long."

"Yeah," I mutter, wanting to get Eddie and leave this place.

She claps her wrinkled hands. "Now, what are you looking for today?"

"Eddie Polorono." I possess no patience for small talk. "What room is he in?"

She hums in disapproval, tapping her red nails along the counter.

I ease five hundred-dollar bills from my blazer and slap them in front of her.

Luna shakes her head, staring at the bills as if they were roaches that just scattered.

I add another five hundred.

Not one fucking word leaves her lips.

I add a thousand to the pile, snarling, as I'm normally not one to negotiate.

Nothing.

"Name your fucking price, Luna," I snap, slamming my palm on the desk. "And if you don't in the next thirty seconds, I'll decorate this brothel with your brains and search every room my goddamn self."

"Three thousand." She stays composed. "*And* if anyone asks, you snuck in and found Eddie yourself. I can't have clients concerned with my confidentiality."

I toss another thousand on top.

Luna collects a key hanging from a hook and hands it to me. "Last door on the right."

I smirk cunningly and walk in that direction.

"Antonio, what the fuck?" Vinny asks behind me. "This'd better not get me banned from here."

I don't bother looking at him. "Luna will always take your money."

Luna knows Vinny will kill her if she attempts to turn down his business. She made a deal with the devil when she granted him access.

"You mind if I have a turn while you take care of Eddie?" Vinny asks as we walk toward the room. "I won't be long."

"No." I face him when we reach Eddie's room. "Keep your ass right here until I need you."

He throws his head back. "Fuck, you always kill my fun."

Cracking my neck, I wiggle the doorknob before unlocking it. When I walk in, my stomach twists in disgust at the sound of theatrical moans and pathetic groans. The escort springs forward when she sees me. Eddie's dick slips out of her as she snatches a blanket and wraps it around herself. I step aside, giving her space to leave the room.

"Why are you crashing my party, Lombardi?" Eddie's kneeling on the bed, covering his dick with one hand.

"Get dressed, Eddie." I kick a pile of clothes that reek of cigarette smoke and BO by the foot of the bed.

He removes his hand from his weasel dick to flip me off. "Fuck you."

I smirk.

Eddie stupidly assumes he's safe at Luna's. Unfortunately for him, Luna always sells to the highest bidder. And that sure as fuck isn't Eddie's broke ass.

Eddie's arrogance calms when I drag my pistol from my waistband. When he screams for help, I round the bed and press the gun barrel against his skull over his greasy hair.

"Scream again or try to fight, and I'll blow a hole through your brain," I warn.

"Why …" he stutters. "Why are you doing this?"

"Because Gigi Marchetti is mine." I push him forward. "Get dressed."

Eddie whimpers while grabbing his clothes.

I call for Vinny, and he joins us, resembling a kid coming to finish their chores. He pulls zip ties and tape from his pocket and helps me restrain Eddie.

Eddie doesn't fight us while we drag him to the back door, where Leandra waits by her car. She pops the trunk and helps us roll Eddie's body into it. He stares at me with wide, pleading eyes and a taped mouth right before I slam it shut.

"Thanks, baby." Vinny hands Leandra a stack of cash in exchange for the car keys.

"Anything for you." She kisses his cheek.

He smacks her ass, and she squeals before strolling into the brothel.

"It would've been easier for us to just shoot him," Vinny comments as we drive to the warehouse.

"Killing him won't get me what I want," I reply.

My pitiful pawn can't die yet.

Just because I can't kill Eddie yet doesn't mean I can't beat the shit out of him.

Eddie sits in a chair, shoulders slumped, whimpering like a child in time-out in the same spot Norman did. His gaunt face is covered in blood, his front tooth missing, and his stained shirt is ripped down the middle, exposing the letter L that I carved into his chest with my switchblade.

When I finally call Cristian, he answers on the third ring.

"I have something for you," I tell him.

Vinny, standing in the corner, lowers his phone and tells the person on the other line he'll call them back.

"What's that?" Cristian asks, unimpressed.

I look at Eddie, who's struggling to hold himself up. "Eddie Polorono."

"Bring him to me." It's a demand, not a request.

"Before I do that, we need to discuss business. A thank-you for my service."

"Quit wasting my time and name your price."

I lick my lips. "I want a contract."

"Elaborate."

"A marriage contract."

"A marriage contract?" he repeats slowly.

"Yes, like the contract you signed with Severino Cavallaro."

"Unfortunately, you're too late. My contract with Severino marries Benny to his daughter, so *he's* unavailable for marriage."

"Gigi is available, correct?"

"No." There isn't a second of hesitation from him.

"At least consider it, Cristian. It'll be good for business, especially given we're allies."

"I'll die before forcing my daughter to marry a man for the sake of business. Gigi is off the table. Name another price, or if you want to be such a great *ally* to my family, bring Eddie to me as a show of respect."

I brush my bloody knuckle along my cheek in frustration. "With all due respect—"

"The answer is no. It'll be no tomorrow and no for the next fucking century. While I appreciate you finding that Polorono piece of shit, my daughter is off-limits. Are we clear?"

"Crystal." I chuckle arrogantly and hold out my phone so Cristian hears me shoot Eddie in the head. "Eddie is dead. Consider it an IOU."

Eddie's body jolts backward in the chair, his head snapping back before his body drops onto the concrete. Blood spills from his skull, running onto the plastic we laid underneath his chair earlier.

I end the call, snap a picture of Eddie's dead body, and text it to Cristian. He might believe I can't have his daughter, but he underestimates my determination. I'll find another way to claim Gigi.

3

GIGI

"I can't eat another bite," Aunt Helena says, relaxing in her chair and rubbing her stomach.

"Me neither." I groan but can't resist having *just one more* nibble of my pasta.

"Sucks for you two because I'm ready for dessert." Aunt Celine wipes her mouth, careful not to smudge her deep maroon lipstick.

Aunt Helena and Aunt Celine are my father's sisters. Like me, Aunt Helena grew up as a Mafia boss's daughter. She married Lorenzo, a man who works for my family, and they had Luca, who is now involved and moving up in rank.

Aunt Celine, on the other hand, is a result of one of my grandfather's many affairs. My grandparents treated her as such. My grandfather left a demand in his will that Celine marry Santos, his attorney's son. If not, she'd lose her inheritance and protection. After my grandfather's death, she married Santos, forever binding them to us.

"I mean, I could go for some cheesecake," I comment before gulping down my vodka cranberry, setting my napkin on the table, and standing. "Order me something. I need to use the ladies' room."

Their conversation shifts to talks of their husbands as I leave our private dining room. I pass a guard blocking a door to a room with a man screaming inside. I quickly glance away and pretend not to hear anything. A server waiting with a drink tray in his hand does the same.

L'ultima Cena, the restaurant we're eating at, translates to the *last supper* in Italian. This place is known for concealing crimes and homicides—turning meals into a man's literal *last supper*.

When I leave the restroom, the guard and server are no longer in the hall. I stop when the door that was blocked off earlier opens. Antonio emerges, cleaning blood from his hand with a napkin. My heart races, and I press my back against the wall, watching him wipe each finger carefully. His white button-up shirt sleeves are rolled to his elbows, and specks of blood linger along the collar.

I draw in a breath of courage and stroll in his direction, pretending not to notice him.

My strategy is to stare at the floor and *accidentally* bump into him as I pass.

I should've planned it better because as soon as I reach him, he shoves my shoulder, driving me backward. I gasp when my elbow collides with the wall, nearly causing a *Mona Lisa* replica to fall.

"If it isn't the Marchetti princess." Antonio steps closer, invading my personal space, and stares down at me.

Shutting my eyes, I catch my breath while also inhaling the smell of cinnamon on his lips, alongside … *metal?*

No, blood. Definitely blood.

Opening my eyes, I peer into his wicked ones. "If it isn't the Lombardi villain."

His pupils dilate like I'm his next victim to bloody up. "You shouldn't wander around alone. You never know who's hiding, ready to snatch you up."

"I think I'm safe in a restaurant."

"You're not safe anywhere." There isn't an ounce of humor in his tone.

"Anywhere or *with you?*"

A cynical smirk tugs at his lips. "*Especially* with me."

My gaze gravitates to the hand he was cleaning blood from. "You'd never hurt me."

It's a ballsy statement. Deep in my gut, I feel safe with him. Maybe my desire for him cancels out the insanity, but if I had the privilege of choosing a husband from a lineup of men, Antonio would be my first choice.

I don't flinch when he raises his hand to roughly trace his callous thumb along my lower lip.

Dark thoughts … *erotic ones* … about him overwhelm me.

"You're right." He slightly nudges the tip of his thumb between my lips. "Which is why I killed a man for you last week."

"What?" I gulp down the aftertaste of cranberry.

He lowers his voice and dips his head forward, making it easier to hear him. "A man wanted to hurt you, so I killed him before he could."

"You're lying," I whisper, failing to hide the tremble in my voice.

"I don't lie."

"Why didn't you tell my father?"

"Princess, your father knew." He glides his thumb across the surface of my front teeth. "But I found the man first."

I brush my tongue along his thumb. "Why?" My question is partially muffled behind his finger.

He drops his mouth to my ear. "I wanted to gift him to your father in exchange for you."

Ex-fucking-cuse me?

The man thinks he can just … buy me?

Like I'm a carton of eggs, just chilling in the grocery aisle?

I wrap my hand around his wrist and yank his thumb from my mouth. "What the fuck does that mean?"

"I don't know how much clearer I can make it. I killed a man because I want you as my wife. Your father declined my request." He licks his lips and then smirks. It's too confident, too cunning, and it pisses me off. "And I'll keep killing men until you're mine."

I blow out a long breath, processing his words.

He frees his wrist from my hold to trail his hand along my cheek. "Unless you'll let me own you without that permission?"

Antonio has been on my mind nonstop since the funeral. He's so different from other men around me. He doesn't handle me with care, isn't afraid to rile me up or cross lines, and doesn't view me as the untouchable Mafia princess. And apparently, we need to add that he isn't scared to kill someone as a proposal gift.

His eyes sear into mine like an inferno that'll never burn out while he waits for me to reply.

"Gigi Marchetti!"

I jump, losing our eye contact when Aunt Helena calls my name.

Antonio withdraws a step, and I already miss the heat of his body so close to mine. I look around him to find Aunt Helena suspiciously eyeing us. This reminds me of what happened with Benny in the warehouse. My family always interrupts, like they intuit I'm in the presence of evil.

"Time to leave," she demands.

Antonio fixes his intense stare on me, not bothering to look back at her.

"I need to go," I whisper.

"Shame." He clicks his tongue against the roof of his mouth. "I'll give you a warning before you do. Don't pretend to bump into me again unless you want me to do something about it. I won't be so gentle next time."

He steps back and clears a path for me to walk past him.

My father seldom calls me into his office.

It's his personal space, where he does business, and unless invited, it's strictly off-limits.

Fifteen minutes ago, he called and told me to bring my ass downstairs before abruptly hanging up.

As I descend the winding stairs barefoot, I trail my fingers along the intricate staircase railing, and silence greets me when I land in the foyer. My father's office door is open—another rarity. I roll my shoulders back to calm myself, and the silence is haunting when I enter.

He's regarded as one of the most notorious crime bosses in history. He runs the family with an iron fist and doesn't offer second chances. He's called evil, a killer, a menace to society.

To me, he's a loving dad, my protector, and a man with a massive weight on his shoulders. He took over the family at a young age after the murder of my grandfather. And even though he attempts to keep me in the dark of his evil deeds, the older I get, the clearer they get.

He sits behind his desk, and Benny stands near the bar cart across the room. Both of them wear black suits and similar looks of disappointment.

The office hasn't changed since the mansion was built, except for *one* thing. He replaced the portrait of my grandparents, Aunt Helena, and him with one of Benny, him, and me. Everything else—from the refined oak finishes to the fireplace and wood floor, selected by my deceased mother—remains.

My gaze drifts to the portrait.

To my sixteen-year-old self.

I hate what I see.

A lost girl. Lonely. So unsure of herself and if she'd ever have a life of her own.

It's sad that I still feel the same even a decade later.

My father clears his throat, and I straighten my skirt before taking the seat across from him. Benny stands taller but offers me a slight smile, easing some of my tension. With each passing day, he evolves into a carbon copy of our father with the same black hair, heavy jawline, permanent scowl, and all-business demeanor. My father hardened Benny, trained him for cruelty, and educated him on business. He wants him prepared for the day he takes over our family.

"Care to explain why you were whispering with Antonio Lombardi today?" My father props his elbows on his desk.

Nausea rolls through my body, and the pasta from earlier threatens its way up. I should've known he'd find out about our little run-in.

When I don't answer, he clears his throat again, more impatiently this time.

"We randomly ran into each other." I shrug.

He continues to stare, unsatisfied with my bullshit answer.

"What?" I throw my arm out, my Cartier bracelet nearly falling from my wrist. "I'm not allowed to share friendly conversation with people?"

"No," he clips.

"Seriously?"

"I don't care if the motherfucker's head is on fire. You don't speak to any men outside our family. Do you understand me?"

"All I said was *excuse me* and asked if it was still raining outside because I didn't want to get my hair wet."

I hate lying to my father for two reasons:

I want him to trust me.

He can always tell when people are deceitful.

"Don't bullshit us, Gigi," Benny says.

"I'm not bullshitting anyone," I argue. "Do you think I'm dumb enough to just hang out with a Lombardi in public?"

They exchange glances, and I scrunch my face, offended.

"Do it again, and it won't be *you* who suffers the consequences," my father warns. "It'll be him."

Damn Aunt Helena.

She for sure ratted me out. Her intentions were pure—I know that—but it still sucks she didn't speak with me first to give me a little heads-up or the opportunity to beg her not to tell my father.

I bite into my lip, tasting where Antonio's thumb lingered, and debate on asking my father if what Antonio told me was true. That he killed a man for me and then asked for my father to trade me like I was a prized horse or something.

I can't now. It'll confirm I'm a liar.

"Do you understand?" my father repeats, breaking me away from my thoughts. "No speaking to other men, *especially* a Lombardi."

"What's wrong with the Lombardis?" I ask. "Aren't you civil with them?"

"Civil? Yes. But I don't trust them."

"And once Vinny takes over, the Lombardi family is fucked," Benny adds.

My father nods in agreement. "We've kept our distance from them, and when Vinny gains control of their family, we'll have nothing to do with them."

My stomach knots.

Do the Lombardis know that?

My guess is no.

"Can I go now? I promise to keep all words to myself," I say with too much sarcasm.

"Lose the attitude." My father works his jaw. "You can go."

I stand, ready to leave, but stop. "What happens when I want to marry?"

I've never mentioned marriage to my father, mostly out of fear of giving him the idea that I want him to choose a husband for me. It's one of those conversations that dangles in the air, yet neither of us wants to grab it.

Benny pours himself a drink.

My father falls silent.

My cheeks redden.

"Get some sleep," he finally says. "It's late. We'll save that conversation for another time."

I leave his office without another word.

My mind races as I walk through our home, known as the Marchetti Mansion. I grew up in this home, where Benny, my father, and I have private wings. While some call it intimidating, almost castle-like, it's my sanctuary.

My mother designed it, meticulously selecting every detail. It's what I'd refer to as Gothic romantic if that were an actual term. The limited natural lighting reminds me of late nights in a historical library. It's just … *comfortable*. People are always in awe of the massive marble staircase. When I was a little girl, I'd imagine I was climbing it up to heaven to visit her.

My head is nearly spinning when I reach my bedroom. When I was born, my mother made my father promise never to marry me off. Unlike her, she wanted me to find my own love, not be forced into it for the sake of a business contract. Her wish was for me to experience the fairy-tale love she wasn't allowed.

Just because he promised her he wouldn't select my husband doesn't mean I get to choose him either. If I come home one day and tell him I want to marry a cop, that cop will mysteriously die in a random crime.

A member of a rival family? He'll go missing.

Sure, I can love someone, but it's clear my father has the last say. And if what Antonio told me was true and from our conversation in the office, my father will never allow me to marry Antonio. Whether I want to or not.

Tonight is the Mayor's Ball.

My father was invited, but since he loathes public events, he always sends Benny in his place. The problem is that Benny also hates them.

Unlike the men in my life, I love public events, so I'm always Benny's plus-one.

Benny's goal tonight is to keep Mayor Miller in power. The mayor turns the other cheek to Marchetti crimes and gets rid of anyone who questions our name. He's already fired two prosecutors who publicly swore they'd clean the streets of organized crime.

Morons.

Did they not realize they'd become target number one on organized crime families' hit lists?

There are two types of politicians:

Ones who want to get rid of crime and end up dead and corrupt ones who are paid off by my father.

I've witnessed many of them come to my father with requests to commit crimes for them.

But I like Mayor Miller. He keeps my family out of prison, invites me to balls, and always compliments my dresses.

As a man should.

When we enter the ballroom, I loop my arm through Benny's. A soft melody from the orchestra radiates through the packed event. I'm surrounded by money—men wearing expensive tuxedos and women donning lavish gowns and expensive jewelry that cost more than the average New York income.

"Let's get this bullshit over with," Benny grumbles.

"I love your enthusiasm," I reply, patting his chest. "Such a fun time you are."

We only ever stay long enough to show our faces and for Benny to complete whatever business my father instructed him to do. When he's finished, we leave. There's no lingering, engaging in small talk, or sipping bubbly champagne. It's all business, all the damn time.

The mayor compliments me when we reach him, and Benny slips me a pointed look, telling me to stay within view yet not close enough to hear their conversation.

"I need to use the restroom," I whisper to him.

"Come right back."

I weave through people, and luckily, there's not a line. When

I walk inside, a group of women stand in front of the mirror, touching up their makeup and debating on which eligible bachelor has the largest net worth. I cringe when one mentions Benny.

"I'd risk my life to spend a night with his psycho ass," the woman says, bumping her friend's hip with hers. She slaps a hand over her mouth when she notices me in the mirror's reflection.

I enter my stall, and they're gone when I step out to wash my hands. As soon as I leave, someone grabs my arm and swings me around the corridor corner. A cold hand clasps over my mouth, and I elbow the man's stomach while he draws me away from the party, shoving me into a dark room.

No, a closet.

He shuts the door, and the lock makes a resounding click.

"What the fuck did I tell you about wandering around alone?"

The light switches on, and Antonio comes into sight.

My body relaxes. This man might've pushed me into a closet, but I can't stop my lips from twitching into a grin. I didn't know when I'd see him again.

Antonio doesn't return the gesture. "Don't smile at me, Giana. I don't appreciate disobedience that can get you killed."

"Why do you care if I *wander around alone* when it seems that every time I do, I fall straight into your mouse trap?" I squint at him. "Speaking of that, do you have GPS on me?" Anytime I'm alone, *boom*, Antonio appears.

"No." He runs a hand over his jaw. "We could arrange that if you'd like though?"

"No, thank you." I cross my arms. "The fewer crazies who know where I am, the better."

He smirks. "You think I'm crazy?"

"I don't think so. I *know* you're certifiable."

"Certification is always preferred in trades, so I'll take it."

"Is that trade *stalking* me?"

"I'd love to stalk you. Unfortunately, you make it hard."

"That's not creep level one hundred or anything."

I back up when he advances, and my body smacks into a shelf. Cleaning bottles tumble on the floor, and Antonio kicks one away from my foot.

His eyes lock on mine before roaming down my body like I'm an expensive item he's debating on buying.

Shamelessly, I do the same to him.

We haven't had a single encounter where I didn't find him the most gorgeous man I'd ever seen—not even when he was ruthlessly torturing a man. Everything about Antonio is seductive, but my favorite part about him is that even though he's handsome, he hasn't made it his entire personality, like so many attractive men do.

Tonight, he replaced his suit with an all-black tux.

He inches closer, lowering his head to nudge his nose against mine.

My heart vibrates in my chest.

Antonio possesses an angelic charm, but deep down, his soul is no angel. It's desolation, one that'll drag you to your ruin. As I stand there, cornered in the shadowy closet, I wonder if I'll face that same fate.

He nearly confirms it when he says, "I think our run-ins are fate, princess."

I gulp. "Fate has no room in my life."

Antonio might call me princess, but my life is no fairy tale.

"Your brother paid me a visit." He clutches my chin between two fingers and pulls it toward him, so I'm looking straight at him. "He warned me to stay away from you … something about it being wrong that we shared a conversation about the weather."

"You said it yourself. I'm untouchable. You should've expected the repercussions of cornering me. You lay a hand on me, a Marchetti will brutally murder you." My muscles tighten at the thought. "You think venom is a crappy way to die? It'll be nothing compared to dying at the hands of my father."

A chilling laugh leaves him. "It's funny you assume I fear death."

"What do you fear then?"

"People I love dying."

I catch my breath, and my knees buckle when he skims a finger down my bare arm.

"Another fear? I'll lose my mind if I don't fuck you soon."

I moan, grasping that I'm as mentally disturbed as him.

Antonio doesn't want to love me.

To marry me.

He wants to *fuck me*.

Plain and simple.

I'm forbidden, and men love nothing more than to bite into forbidden fruits. Ask stupid-ass Adam with the apple lodged inside his throat.

But unfortunately for me, I want all those things with Antonio.

Love.

Marriage.

Fucking.

His eyes linger on my lips as if they were ready to spill my family's biggest secret.

He places the pad of his thumb on my lower lip and whispers, "The things I want to do to you, princess."

"Tell me." He pops his thumb into my mouth, sliding it along my teeth. "*Show me.*"

My request surprises us both.

I forgot where we are.

Who we are.

About everything but *us*.

"I could break every rule," he hisses, gathering saliva from my tongue and coating his thumb with it. "Throw all my fucks out the window and feed your pussy my cock *right here*. And I bet you'd let me."

I stutter for words. They'd come out unclear against his thumb even if I had them.

"Has anyone ever touched this cunt, princess?"

Even though I want to lie, I can't. So I shake my head.

He removes his thumb. "I knew it." Intrigue rolls off him like a scent. "My plan for when I saw you tonight was to rub your spit all over my cock and fuck you against this wall, but now, that's changed." His sensual voice overpowers my thoughts. "You have no idea what that information just opened up inside me. Pandora's fucking box."

I chew on my lip. "What do you mean?"

"You thought I was a *stalker* before." His voice changes, coaxed with a hint of malice. "My obsession with you has just begun."

"Your obsession is your death wish, especially when I find a *real* husband."

"I own you, princess." A tight-lipped smirk stretches across his face. "You ever let another man even talk about making your sweet pussy come, I'll cut off every organ he can use to make that happen. His hands." He snatches mine, interlaces our fingers, and rests them on my chest. "His lips." He bows his head to brush his lips against mine. "His *cock*." Our entwined fingers lower to his erection, pressing against it as he shoves his hips forward.

A rush of emotions crashes through me. I shiver, and my mouth drops open, allowing his tongue to grace the entrance of it. He runs our hands over his cock before swiftly grabbing my wrists and bracing them against the wall. He thrusts his hips against my core.

"This body is mine," he groans. "You might bear the last name Marchetti, but you're the property of a Lombardi."

I gyrate my hips into his, growing wetter and wetter between my legs.

His eyes are stormy as he smashes his lips to mine, kissing

me roughly like he wants to leave a stain of himself on my mouth, a weapon that'll hurt any other man who ventures there.

"Antonio," I groan.

He inches his mouth away, and his lips brush along mine as he says, "That's right. Say my name." His head lowers as he sucks on my neck. "You are mine, Giana Marchetti." Another suck to my neck, this time harder. "The princess doesn't always end up with the prince. Sometimes, it's the villain. There's no pathetic knight in shining armor in our tale because I'll kill him."

Another suck.

He withdraws a few inches. "But good news. The villain will do dirtier things to you."

I don't care who he is. I want this man.

I push myself off the wall and smash my lips into his.

"Fuck," he mutters before wildly kissing me back.

His tongue slides into my mouth, dancing with mine, and he grabs my waist, holding my body against his.

This is it.

I'm ready to lose my virtue in a closet with a man I might never speak to again.

"Take it," I gasp into his mouth. "Take me. Be the villain who tears me apart."

That doesn't happen.

Reality shatters through the closet when a knock on the door interrupts us.

"Hey," a masculine voice calls through it. "Someone is looking *for their keys.*"

I'm smart enough to know that's the code name for something.

Antonio pulls away, and I nearly lose my balance when he spins around and stalks toward the door.

He cracks it open and holds his hand through the slit. "Give me your burner."

"Huh?" the man replies.

"Your burner. Give it."

Something lands in Antonio's hand, and he slams the door in the man's face.

He holds up a flip phone. "I'm the only person who knows this number. I'll call you tonight. My name is under Murphy."

"What am I supposed to do with that?" I ask. "Carrying it around won't look suspect or anything."

I shudder when he lowers my gown bodice and sinks his hand under my strapless bra. His thumb grazes my nipple before he drops the phone into the space.

He straightens my bodice and retreats a step. "Talk soon, princess."

And just as quickly as he whisked me away, he's gone.

I allow myself a moment to catch my breath before leaving the closet and rush into the restroom to readjust myself.

Thank God I did because as soon as I walk in, a girl takes one look at me and says, "Damn, looks like someone was thoroughly fucked. Attagirl!"

I ignore her and hurry into a stall to deal with Antonio's burner. Flipping it open, I see one contact—*Murphy*—and text it.

> Me: IDC if it's a burner. I don't trust it. If you want to talk to me, find a way that won't put my family in possible danger. You can find this in the women's restroom trash.

I hit Send and stash the phone in the trash can before leaving.

As much as I want to take it, I can't. Electronic devices always pose a risk and potentially contain trackers, explosives, or recording devices. My father doesn't even allow his men to carry their phones into the mansion without his approval.

"Where the fuck have you been?" Benny asks as soon as I walk out.

Bystanders stare at us. One woman even gasps. *Cue eye roll.* Benny doesn't care about the audience.

Blushing, I motion toward the restroom and am proud of my steady voice. "Exactly where I told you I was going."

"You were in there for a long time." He eyes me skeptically.

"I started my period and had to track down a tampon. Sue me."

His voice softens some. "Do we need to stop on the way home for something?"

I shake my head. "I'm all stocked there. Let's go."

As we leave, I peer over my shoulder, searching for Antonio, but I don't find him.

A hint of regret hits me for ditching the burner. It could mess with our fate, but if we're so destined to be, Antonio will find another way to see me again.

4

ANTONIO

I pay a janitor a hundred dollars to block the women's restroom for maintenance so I can retrieve the burner from the trash can. Gigi's little stunt is more impressive than infuriating. Sure, it's annoying I can't communicate with her through the phone, but it shows she cares about her family more than herself. Cristian taught her well.

"You're playing with fire," Vinny warns when we leave the gala. "No, you're playing with *death*. Cristian rejected the marriage offer, which means Gigi is off-limits to you."

Earlier, we were mid-conversation when I spotted Gigi enter the restroom.

"I was talking business with a Marchetti—that's all." I smooth out my blazer's collar.

My shirt carries Gigi's scent, serving as a reminder of how good it felt to touch and kiss her.

I want a repeat.

I want *more* next time.

"Business." He snorts and fake wipes something off his cheek. "Did you use red lipstick to seal the deal? It seems you forgot some."

I don't wipe my face. No way am I removing a trace of Gigi off my skin.

"My *business* doesn't concern you."

"She's the most off-limits woman you could want."

I shake my head and hand him the burner. "No one is off-limits to me."

I exist in a world steeped in corruption.

A full circle of crookedness.

My great-grandfather founded Lucky Kings in 1946. It's our *legal* business—a clean paper trail to keep the IRS off our backs.

The Marchettis own their club, Seven Seconds, to make themselves appear legit.

The Cavallaros have a line of alteration shops and laundromats.

We have Lucky Kings.

It's the largest and most profitable casino in the state, and my father expects us to help it run smoothly.

Now, that's not to say we still aren't corrupt as fuck.

We most definitely are.

Today, my problem is Jack Jethro, a bookie we banned from the Lucky Kings weeks ago. He's a piece of shit who frequents casinos in search of desperate people who gambled all their money away. For years, we allowed him to find clients here for a fee. But then another bookie offered us a higher price. So we ended our agreement with Jack, but the fuckers like a gnat that won't go away.

When I enter the room, Jack sits in a chair, thrumming three fingers against the table in front of him. His thumb and pointer finger don't reach the table because they're now stubs. I cut them off a year ago when he failed to pay us our full percentage. Now, he's about to lose more.

I slam my palms on the table. "Did you think if you came during the day, I wouldn't find out?"

He stares at me, gritting his teeth, but fails to answer.

"What did I tell you about coming here, Jack?"

The motherfucker struggles for words, so I help by backhanding him in the face. Knock some sense into his dumbass.

This is his second strike.

I give single warnings to people and expect them to listen.

I consider myself kind for giving them that.

There's no third chance with me.

"If you don't reply, I'll cut your tongue out instead of a finger." I get into his face and hear his teeth rattle.

"I need the money," Jack cries out. "I depended on the income, and you … you just cut me off!"

I can't help but chuckle at the mention of *cutting him* off.

He rubs his sunken eyes, drawing my attention to the track marks on his arm.

I reach across the table, snatch his arm, and dig my fingers into his skin. "I cut you off because you weren't paying what we demanded."

Jack grimaces, attempting to jerk his arm away, but I press down harder. "Your sixty percent cut was making it hard to live, Antonio."

"Which is why we terminated our agreement with you." I release his arm, and it falls slack on the table. "And what was it you said? You'd find better work elsewhere?" I cross my arms and smirk. "How's that going for you, considering you're back here?"

"No one else will do business with me." Jack gets a brave hair up his ass and spits on the table. "Thanks to your family."

I sigh, debating how much time I want to spend with him. I have a long-ass to-do list for today, and there isn't a large enough time slot to torture a man who only has a year max before he pisses off someone else and they murder him.

I withdraw my pistol. Jack's eyes widen, and he pulls a gun from his jeans pocket. I smirk again as he awkwardly handles the gun, nearly fumbling it from his hold. He releases a long groan while focusing on how to work it. Fucker should've practiced handling a gun with three fingers to at least pretend he isn't a total moron.

"Let's see who has the better shot then, shall we?" I wait for him to point his gun at me before pulling the trigger.

We're so close that it doesn't take long for the bullet to strike him. It travels underneath his skin, into his muscle, and makes its final contact through his skull in only seconds.

Some men don't pay attention when they take a man's life.

Not me.

I enjoy watching.

The sound of a bullet shattering through a skull always provides me peace.

Gives me a moment of solace from my fucked-up world.

Jack's pathetic body collides with a steel chair before crumpling to the floor. A crimson red pools around his body.

I stroll toward him, sweep my Oxford through his blood, and kick him in the face, leaving a blood smear on his cheek. "I always warned you to be faster with everything—counting money, answering questions, and apparently pulling the trigger. I'll collect any additional money you owe me when we meet in hell."

Two of my men, Leo and Rafael, assist me in disposing of Jack's body. We don't invest too much time into it, given Jack has pissed off a roster of people enough to want him dead. So we toss him into a dumpster in a remote alley, knowing it's scheduled for pickup this evening.

After I finish, I visit my father in his office. He, Sonny, Vinny, and I have offices within the casino. It serves as our central hub to conduct business.

My father sits behind his desk while Sonny looms in the corner, wearing his usual disgruntled, constipated expression. Both hold a drink in their hands.

"You take care of Jack?" my father asks, resting his glass on the desk.

I tuck my hands into my pockets. "Yeah."

Sonny exaggeratedly checks behind me. "Where's Vinny?"

"Something came up," I lie.

Vinny's job is to deal with fuckheads like Jack, but I'm always left to pick up his slack. When I talked to him this morning, he confirmed he'd meet me at the casino in an hour. Five hours later, and he's still a no-show.

"Something came up, or did he pull another disappearing act?" Sonny nudges his thick-rimmed glasses up his nose.

Sonny is a royal pain in my ass, right up there with Vinny on the list of people who provide me constant headaches. What aggravates me the most with him is his harbored resentment over my father being boss, not him. Thank God the impulsive hothead isn't. And since he isn't boss, I have no obligation to answer him, so I ignore his question.

"I need to get home," I tell my father, checking my watch.

"It's a little early to call it quits," Sonny grunts before downing his drink and setting it down.

I glare at him. "Of course someone with no one waiting at home for them would say something like that."

Sonny grunts again, shoving his gray hair from his eyes with both hands. "I was too busy working my ass off for this family to find a new wife."

"Hmm." I click my tongue against the roof of my mouth. "That sucks."

Sonny has no children because he can't find a woman willing to tolerate him long enough to have a family. His first wife went missing in Canada during their honeymoon. The second walked in front of a bus in traffic. He hasn't had a third.

I leave his office and drive home. When I turn on the private road that leads to my house, my mind drifts to Gigi and the gala. A few days before the gala, Benny came to the casino to see me. We shared a drink, and when he asked what happened at L'ultima Cena, I told him it was nothing but simple conversation. He accepted my answer but made it clear I was on their radar.

Not that I gave a shit.

Radar or not, if I see his sister, I won't keep my hands to myself.

I hit the button on my car dashboard to open the gate and garage door. My secluded home, nestled in the outskirts of New York suburbia, has miles between me and any neighbors. Before her death, I gave Sienna, my wife, free rein to choose our home; my only request was privacy. She went with some medieval Tudor home once owned by a former president.

At first, I hated it, but it's grown on me. As I've raised my daughter here, it's become more than just a place to lay my head at night; it's become our home.

We moved in right after we found out she was pregnant with Amara seven years ago. This is the only home my daughter has known. It holds so many memories with us. It'd almost feel like losing a part of my soul if we moved.

My body is sore as I unlock the wrought-iron door, enter the passcode, and press my finger against the scanner. When I walk inside, I pass the monitor that provides live feeds from the cameras inside the house and around the property.

"Good evening, Antonio," Clara greets, emerging from the corner while wiping her hands on her apron.

"Hi, Clara," I say in exhaustion while entering the living room to find Damien, my *caporegime*, sitting in a chair.

Damien motions toward my shirt. "You look like you had a good day."

I pull at my shirt collar, noticing the red stain—residue of Jack the sleazeball. "Typical day at the office."

"Daddy!" Amara bursts into the living room, clutching a doll in one hand and a stuffed pig in the other.

I kneel, lifting her into my arms, and all the tension that's taken permanent residence in my body loosens some. Amara never fails to help give me pause from the problems on my mind.

"Can we have pizza tonight?" she asks, pouting her lip. "I had veggies for lunch, so I'm all healthy!"

I kiss the top of her head before settling her onto her fluffy, sock-covered feet. "I'll think about it."

"She had two carrots," Clara says from behind me before joining us in the living room. "I don't know if that qualifies as *veggies*."

Amara frowns at being ratted out.

"Yo, Amara!" Damien says. "You'll never grow as tall as a unicorn if you don't eat your veggies."

"See!" Clara squeals. "Didn't you just say you wanted to grow a glitter horn from your forehead? That takes eating *lots and lots* of vegetables, sweet girl."

Clara is my biggest help with Amara. She's her nanny, tutor, and grandmother. She's my mother-in-law. I can protect my daughter, but there's a long list of shit I can't do. My French braids are pathetic. I pick out the wrong pink outfits. Clara's my savior, helping me not feel like a complete failure as a father.

Amara holds up her tiny finger with pink glitter polish. "I'll put veggies *on my pizza* then."

"If she wants pizza, give her pizza," I say in fake annoyance before tickling Amara's side.

These three are the only people who witness this side of me —the one not absorbed in viciousness.

In public, I'm a killer.

A corrupt man who preys on desperation.

Someone you never want to cross.

But with my daughter, I'm the proud father who attends her

dance recitals and hangs up painted unicorn pictures on the fridge.

Turning to Clara, I mouth, "*Cauliflower pizza.*"

Clara laughs and turns into the kitchen. I walk across the marble flooring and through the arched hallway to my bedroom. After showering, I change into fresh clothes without blood on them.

The smell of Clara's sweet pizza sauce fills the air when I leave my bedroom and return to the living room. Amara is sitting cross-legged on the carpet, watching TV, with stuffed animals circling her. I plop down next to her.

"This might be my favorite episode," Damien says, stretching his legs and pointing at the TV.

I peer back at him. "You can head out if you want."

"And miss out on Clara's infamous pizza?" He shakes his head. "No way."

Damien crashes here so much that he has his own bedroom. We've known each other nearly our entire lives. His father was one of my father's capos. A rival casino family bombed his family's home, killing his grandparents, parents, and younger sister. In one night, he and his brother, Julian, lost their entire family.

"Yeah, Daddy!" Amara says, resting her head on my shoulder. "Damien loves Grammy's pizza … and watching cartoons with me!"

"That's right," Damien says. "Amara always knows best."

Amara grins from ear to ear.

I kiss the top of her head and sit there with her as she watches cartoons. I try to pay attention to Tweety Bird, but it's a struggle. My thoughts are on Vinny, the family, Gigi.

I'm so fucked … and dead if Cristian finds out I've grown an obsession with his daughter.

5

GIGI

"How's work at the gallery?" I ask Natalia before shoving a bite of mango gelato in my mouth.

"Good," she replies. "I wish we were busier so I could make more commission. It's a small business, though, so hopefully, Bonnie can find more artists to buy from."

"Sounds like I'll need to come in and purchase new artwork."

She smiles. "I think you've bought more than enough there."

"I'll tell my dad and Benny to get their asses there then."

Other than my family, I have a total of one friend. Natalia.

She has no affiliation with any Mafia families. We met in high school, where we were the social outcasts at Fenimore Preparatory School. She was the underprivileged principal's daughter on scholarship, and I was the dangerous Mafia king's daughter who trusted no one.

Some kids wanted to be my friend because I was considered cool, while other parents didn't want their child associated with me. On top of that, as someone who deeply distrusts people, I second-guessed everyone.

She was my chemistry partner for a semester, and we clicked.

Even after graduating and her attending college, we've remained close.

Our focus moves to the entrance when it chimes. Vinny enters the shop with another man as if he owns the place. Since my father protects the business for a fee, I'm aware that isn't true, but that's Vinny's nature. It's why I've always kept my distance from him. He's too reckless for my liking.

I frown, wishing it were the other Lombardi, and stare at the door to see if that wish comes true. It doesn't. Bruno slides his chair closer to our table when Vinny approaches us.

Vinny flashes him a harmless smirk, assuring Bruno he's not feeling like a total sociopath today.

Bruno crosses his arms defensively and glares at Vinny. He never messes around when it comes to my safety. My father assigned Bruno as my bodyguard when I turned ten. His father was my mother's bodyguard, and I love that shared connection. At times, I know he's bored with the babysitting job, but he never complains about it.

"Gigi Marchetti," Vinny greets before moving his gaze to Natalia. "And who is this?"

A sour taste seeps up my throat as Vinny stares at her in desire.

"No one," I instantly say, narrowing my eyes at Vinny's predatory gaze.

He offers his hand to Natalia. "Vinny Lombardi."

"Natalia." She tucks a loose strand of her black hair behind her ear and shakes his hand.

There's an impulse to slap it away when I notice the interest on her face. I shoot Vinny a hostile look when he releases Natalia's hand, pulls a card from his pocket, and offers it to her.

"Call me," he says as she takes the card and plays with it in her hand.

"Absolutely *do not* call him," I stress, not caring if I piss Vinny off.

Bruno snorts.

Vinny returns my glare and ignores my disrespect.

I'm Cristian Marchetti's daughter. He won't dare lay a hand on me.

Natalia, unfortunately, is beaming.

I don't blame her. Vinny is attractive with jet-black hair, a strong jawline, a body built like a defensive linebacker, and a manipulative face. He carries himself well, flashing his Rolex and gold necklace, and is a pro at sweet talking. If I didn't know how mentally unstable he was, I might've fallen victim to his charm too. My father would've killed him for that. Maybe I need to pretend to like him so he stays away from Natalia.

"In fact, I'll throw it in the trash for you." When I attempt to swipe the card from Natalia's hand, she stops me.

"Don't toss it, and I look forward to talking to you soon, *Natalia*." Vinny winks before walking away and placing his order to the woman behind the counter.

My chair makes a scuffing noise on the linoleum floor as I scoot closer to Natalia.

"Don't call him," I say in my best warning tone. "I'm serious."

Natalia twirls the card between her fingers and stares down to read it. "Why? He seems nice."

"Saying Vinny Lombardi is *nice* is like saying swimming in an alligator-infested swamp sounds fun. Anyone who knows him knows he's far from nice."

Bruno, my favorite wingman, nods in agreement.

She slips the card into her purse while staring dreamily at Vinny.

Noooo.

Natalia is foreign to my world.

Even though we're friends, my father still forces me to keep her at a distance. He investigated what little family she has. Like me, her mother died when she was young.

As I watch my best friend, I know my warnings are falling on deaf ears. Vinny will lead her to heartbreak or worse—death. I know what just happened at the gelato shop will change all our lives.

6

ANTONIO

"Are you aware Vinny is dating Gigi Marchetti's best friend?" Damien asks me while we're in my home office.

I pause mid-sip of my Macallan. "Excuse me?"

"Natalia Carprio. They studied at Fenimore Prep together." He shifts in his chair and taps his finger along the side of his glass. "I'm not surprised Vinny took an interest in her, but how the hell did she get caught up in his web?"

Damien has never been a Vinny fan. They didn't get along growing up, and I lost count of the number of times they fought each other in my parents' backyard. He's never feared Vinny's *I'm next in line* threats.

I grit my teeth. Of course Vinny would hide that from me.

My free time has been limited, so I haven't kept tabs on Gigi as much as I'd prefer. Lucky Kings is the busiest it's ever been, and Vinny is a regular no-show. My father suffered a stroke two months ago, so I'm picking up both of their slacks now. All while balancing my own duties and trying to be a decent parent.

"I can look into it, if you want?" Damien asks.

"Are they going out in public together?"

"Yes."

I press my fingers to my temples. "Fuck."

My brother is contracted to wed Serena, the granddaughter of Jacob Silverman, a casino tycoon who owns a chain spanning the Florida coast. Before putting a pen to paper, Jacob insisted Vinny maintain a low profile with women, stick to brothels, and not embarrass her.

His dating Natalia will void their agreement. Vinny is also possessive over women and sees them as property. The ones who've tried to leave him disappeared. We don't need Jacob terminating the contract or Gigi asking Cristian to get involved because Vinny killed her best friend.

I knock back my drink, the taste of malted barley sweeping down my throat. "I'll talk to him at dinner tonight at my parents."

Damien scratches his head. "Those are always fun."

"They're a fucking nightmare."

Twice a month, my father requires us to have dinner at his home. As much as I hate it, Amara enjoys spending time with them and getting out of the house.

"You're late," I tell Vinny when he enters the parlor room.

"Too much pussy, too little time." He shrugs.

Glaring at him, I motion toward Amara on the floor, practicing spelling in her workbook.

He plops down on the suede leather couch and inches closer until we're out of earshot from her.

"When did you plan on telling me you're hanging out with Gigi Marchetti's best friend, a woman *not* involved in this life and who isn't your future wife?" I sneer.

"I didn't think you'd care. She's just another cunt on my list." He cracks a smile. "You're only concerned because you have a thing for Gigi. I can set something up for us, if you want?"

I scrub a hand over my face. I've had no contact with Gigi since the Mayor's Ball, and as risky as it is, I can use my brother's stupidity to my advantage at least once. He owes me for covering all his problems.

"Next time you meet with Natalia, tell her to bring Gigi," I say.

"Look at this." He rubs his hands together in excitement. "My younger brother *finally* wants to have a double date."

My jaw tightens at how high school he sounds.

"I'll talk to Natalia," he continues. "I'm *very* persuasive with her." The ridiculous expression on his face looks just as fucking high school too.

Our mother walks into the living room, interrupting us. "Dinner is ready." Her tone is sweet, but the problem is that even her sweetest tone is laced with animosity.

She turns without bothering to wait for a response, and the click of her heels fades in the distance.

I help Amara to her feet and carry her school supplies to the foyer as she trails behind me. I drop her stuff by our jackets so we don't forget them. Clara takes her homeschooling very seriously.

"Your father should arrive at any second." My mother takes a seat at the dining room table. She glances at Vinny while delicately draping a napkin over her lap. "I'm glad *everyone* showed up this week."

Marsha Lombardi is your stereotypical Mafia wife. She went into her marriage hoping for true love but received nothing but malice.

Nothing was good enough for my father.

At first, she tried everything to get his approval. She threw parties, hid criminal evidence, and convinced women to blow their husband's money at the casino. When it didn't work, she became bitter and selfish. He also expressed his unhappiness with her for failing to birth a third child—a daughter—for him. Out of spite, he impregnated one of his mistresses, only to birth another boy.

I'll never forget the day my mother found out because the doctor's nurse called the wrong number to confirm the OB-GYN appointment. In a fit of rage, she burned all his suits and the valuable artwork inherited from his grandfather. My father kicked her out of the house for a week in retaliation, forcing her to sleep at my aunt's.

Sometimes I feel sorry for her. But then I remember she's also a shitty person. She never stepped in during my father's violent *training* sessions. Instead, she spent her time vacationing, shopping, and brunching.

I've now accepted who they are. That doesn't mean I allow Amara to be around them without me though.

"I'm a busy man," Vinny grumbles as we sit.

The crystal chandelier above us illuminates the dining room table, which is large enough to sit twenty-four, yet only five places are set. The Lombardi operation is immense, but our immediate family isn't.

I hear the sound of my father's cane hitting the floor before I see him. He's been using the cane more since his stroke.

"My Amara, the sweetest granddaughter in the world," he says as soon as he sees her. He doesn't greet anyone else.

Amara slides off her chair and runs toward him. "Nonno!"

He props his cane against the table to pull her into a tight hug. "I missed you, sweetheart."

She bursts into giggles while he attempts to spin her, nearly losing his balance, and then he carefully helps her back in her seat.

My father was a shit dad to Vinny and me growing up. He was a drill sergeant, a don preparing for his sons to take the reins. Instead of fatherly insight, we received punches in the face for acting out and kicks to the stomach if we incorrectly disposed of a body.

He's a great grandfather though. It's surprising to see this callous man treat her with such a caring manner.

My mother, on the other hand, lacks that warmth with Amara. I'm sure she loves her, but Amara reminds her of how she failed to birth a daughter.

The chef and servers start delivering the first course after my father sits beside my mother. We make small talk—never discussing business in front of my mother and Amara.

"Vinny, we need to start planning your wedding," she tells him.

He snarls, "Hard pass on that topic right now."

She cradles her wineglass while shifting her focus to me. "We should find you another wife as well, Antonio."

"I've already paid my dues," I reply, shaking my head.

Eight years ago, I married a woman I didn't love for the sake of the family. That won't happen again.

"It's been forever since Sienna's death," she argues, and I clench my jaw.

"If Daddy gets a new wife, will she be my mommy?" Amara asks with a gap-toothed smile, sounding so fucking innocent.

She's been on a *why don't I have a mommy* kick recently.

I can give my daughter anything she wants but that. Getting married again solely to give Amara a stepmother is delusional. My marriage to Sienna was a nightmare, and although Amara is the only blessing to come out of it, I still hold a grudge against my father for sticking me with her.

I shoot my mother a disapproving look. She doesn't need to fuck with my daughter's head. She's already done enough damage with her sons.

"Amara, why don't you see what sweets Chef Kathy made for us?" my father suggests, always one to read the room. "I think she baked your favorite snickerdoodle cookies."

She peers at me for permission.

"Go ahead," I say.

She jumps out of her chair and runs to the kitchen.

I clear my throat and stare at my mother. "I'd appreciate you not speaking like that in front of Amara. Or better yet, speaking of me remarrying, period."

"It was only a simple question, Antonio," she replies, clutching her pearl necklace in one hand and her wineglass in the other. "I can ask around, see who's available—"

"What did I just say?" I snap.

"Focus on Vinny's nuptials," my father says before gulping down his Jack and Coke.

"I'd rather we revisit the conversation of Antonio marrying," Vinny argues.

"I'd rather you do as I say unless you want to live on the streets and marry one of your cunt whores you spend too much time with." My father uses his glass to point at Vinny. "Don't think there isn't word of where you spend your free time … or better yet, *not* your free time since you're slacking on your casino responsibilities."

"Everyone has a mistress." Vinny chugs his wine.

My father glares at him. "Hide them better then."

"You sure didn't do a good job of that, did you?" My mother scoffs at him. "You knocked up your whore and have a bastard son somewhere."

"Shut your mouth, Marsha," he warns, shoving his chair out and standing. "Vinny, wear a condom so you don't get your mistress pregnant"—he pauses to snarl at my mother—"until *after* you marry your bitch wife." He snatches his cane, calls Vinny a fucking idiot, and leaves the room.

My mother waits until he's out of the room before speaking. "I can't believe my father chose *him* as a husband for me."

I rub my temples, a headache forming in my skull.

"Daddy!" Amara dashes into the room, holding a plate. "There are so many cookies!"

I rise from my chair. "You get *one* for now, and we'll save the others for later."

My sweet daughter, who's too good for this world, holds up a finger. "One *now* and then another before bed?"

"We'll see." I kiss the top of her head.

"You're a better father than yours," my mother remarks, grabbing hold of the wine bottle and filling her glass to the brim. "Let's pray it stays that way."

"Thankfully, Clara is a wonderful grandmother and role model to her," I say, curling my lip at her before ushering Amara out of the room without waiting to hear her reply.

"Bye, sweetie," she yells to our backs. "Grandma loves you."

"Love you too!" Amara shouts, cookie crumbs falling from her lips.

Vinny follows us outside, and before we leave, he says, "Tomorrow night. My place. Natalia and Gigi will be there."

Vinny's condo is in the heart of the city—somewhere you'll never find my ass living. The level of security is limited, and the fewer eyes on my family, the better.

When I walk in, Natalia is on the couch with a wineglass in her hand. I can't blame Vinny for wanting her. She's beautiful and his type with sleek black hair, tawny skin, and red lips. It's a shame she lacks the brain capacity to understand how vicious my brother is and will find out the hard way when she finally decides to escape the nightmare of him.

There's no sign of Gigi.

Natalia reaches inside her purse, rummages through it, and extends an old-school flip phone in my direction. "Gigi told me to give you this." Her stare is filled with apology and a touch of fear.

I take the phone from her, my expression neutral. "I take it she's not coming?"

She shakes her head.

I don't say *thank you* or another word before leaving Vinny's condo. When I walk outside, a downpour surrounds me. A flash of lightning tears through the sky.

I toy with the burner in my hand, sharing the same apprehension Gigi did with the one I'd given her. Burners, or any device, holds its dangers. I won't dare bring one inside my home and put my daughter's life in jeopardy.

When I open the phone, I find two numbers in the Contacts.

Saved as Princess and the local insanity facility.

I click on Princess and listen to it ring.

"Hello?" Her voice carries a soft, tired tone, as if she's half asleep but forcing herself to stay awake to wait for my call.

Ignoring the rain, I step off Vinny's porch and wander down the sidewalk. "Got your gift."

"Considering you called, I figured."

"What does this mean?"

"You tried giving me a phone first. What did you intend I do with it?"

"It was my ticket to see you again. Any way you can sneak out and meet with me?"

She scoffs. "Do you remember where I live?"

The Marchetti Mansion's security outdoes Guantanamo Bay. No one has been able to breach their walls. Even though I've never been to the mansion, I've driven by the gates. They're always under constant supervision by armed guards.

I lick raindrops off my lips. "What do I need to do? Hunt you down?"

"I'm attending the charity masquerade ball tomorrow. Maybe I'll see you there." She ends the call.

I shake my head and shove the burner into my pocket before driving home. I don't park inside the garage. Instead, I keep my car just outside the gate, which is two acres from the house. In the morning, I'll instruct my security team to check the phone for anything suspicious.

Gigi doesn't seem like the malicious type, but just like she doesn't completely trust me, I feel the same. Especially when I have more than myself to worry about.

All the lights are off inside the house, and I key in the security protocols. After changing my clothes, I sneak into Amara's bedroom. She's sleeping, and I shake my head when I hear the hint of a snore.

I didn't want a daughter. Sure, that sounds harsh.

Daughters in this world are seen as bargaining chips.

Sons are born for succession and daughters for marriage alliances.

I won't do that to Amara.

Sitting on the edge of her bed, I check she's tucked in tight before my gaze lands on the framed photo collage on her nightstand. Clara made it for her.

In one photo, Sienna cradles Amara in her arms on the day she was born.

Another displays Sienna, Amara, and me standing together in front of a Christmas tree.

The last one captures Sienna staring straight at the camera, laughing.

I grab the frame and run my thumb over Sienna's face. Amara carries traits from us both. Her hair, as black as mine, flows past her shoulders while her ivory complexion resembles Sienna's, complete with the freckles that grace her nose.

I hate she shares those similarities with Sienna because I fucking hate Sienna. She was selfish, and that selfishness got her killed and left my daughter without a mother.

I return the frame to Amara's nightstand, press a light peck to her forehead, and leave the room. The door clicks as I gently shut it and trek down the hallway to my bedroom.

My home spans ten thousand square feet and features three wings. Clara stays in one, Damien in another, and Amara and I share one.

The bathroom tiles are cold against my feet when I swing the glass shower door open and turn on the water. Tomorrow's to-do list creeps into my thoughts like a bad memory as I undress and step under the showerhead. As water pours down my body—dripping down bruises—thoughts of Gigi hijack that list of responsibilities.

My brain lingers on all the things I want to do to her. As I think about her sweet body and how I want to see more of it, my cock hardens. I wrap my hand around it, stroking myself, while imagining her naked, on her knees, sucking my dick in that smart mouth of hers. When I come, I moan her name through my lips. As the cum washes down the drain, I wish it were sliding down her throat instead.

After I shower and dry off, I call my mother.

"Hello?" she answers with a slight slur that causes me to roll my eyes.

Balancing my phone between my shoulder and cheek, I lock my gun in my nightstand drawer. "I need an invitation to whatever masquerade ball is tomorrow."

"I thought you didn't like things like that."

"I do now."

"All right, I'll make a call."

"Also, what the fuck is a masquerade ball?"

7

GIGI

"Gigi, my beautiful girl," Aunt Helena says, her voice hitching with emotion as she stares at me through the reflection in my closet's full-length mirror. "So much like your mother."

All my life, I've had compliments thrown at me—gorgeous, smart, breathtaking. None of them ever warms my soul like comparisons to my mother.

People don't only speak about Benita Marchetti's beauty. They also sing of her kind soul.

"Your first masquerade ball," Aunt Celine adds while joining us.

I run my fingers down the crimson lace gown. Aunt Helena hands me my burgundy suede heels, and I sit on the ottoman to fasten the straps around my ankles.

When we're finished, my father and Benny stand at the base of the stairs, waiting for us. Tonight will be my first event without Benny, and there's no veiling the concern on their faces. At first, my father said no to my attendance. My aunts saved the day and promised to watch over me. Bruno and Luca will also escort us.

"Enjoy your night," my father says with reluctance, his

Adam's apple bobbing. "You'll be the most breathtaking woman there."

"Thank you." I grin, lifting my mask to reveal my face. I chose a black cat-eye-shaped one with cascading opals hanging from the bottom.

"Bruno stays with you at all times." And just like that, his attitude went from a sweet father to an overbearing one. His attention cuts to Luca. "And you watch every inch of that place."

Luca furrows his brows. "I can't believe you're forcing me to go to this shit."

"Well, believe it," my father snaps.

Aunt Helena shakes her head at Luca's attitude.

Luca might be her son, but everyone knows you respect the boss at all times.

My father and Benny kiss my cheek before I climb into the back seat of Luca's Suburban. When we leave, I pull my phone from my clutch after it beeps with a text.

Natalia: Have fun! Your dress is gorgeous!

I frown, wishing she were with me.

Me: What are you doing tonight?

Natalia: Dinner with Vinny.

I gulp in distaste. As much as I love Natalia, she's pissing me off. I've warned her against Vinny so many times that it's probably coming off as controlling.

Me: Be careful with him.

Vinny has her wrapped around his finger, whispering lie after lie into her ear. He swears he'll marry her, which will never happen. Natalia will be his mistress, not his wife. And eventually, when she opens her eyes and realizes what a monster he is, I'll have to run to my father to protect her from Vinny's fury.

I dread that day.

The masquerade ball is unlike any event I've ever attended.

It's like being whisked into a fairy tale.

Masked guests congregate in the ritzy room. I adjust mine to make sure it's level against my face.

"This is the perfect storm for someone to do something stupid," Luca comments, straightening the lapels of his black Armani suit. "We don't know who any of these incognito motherfuckers are."

I side-eye him. "You could also be one of those incognito motherfuckers if you wore your mask."

I bought him and Bruno matching ones. Unsurprisingly, both declined to wear them.

"I'm not putting shit on my face," Luca said. "Be grateful I'm going."

Even though Bruno has attended plenty of these events with me, he still stands out among people. He's nearly seven feet, with a buzzed haircut and a mustache that stretches along his entire upper lip.

Luca, on the other hand, would fit in if he didn't glare at every person as if they wanted to mug him. He's tall, approaching thirty, and while I'm not into cousin-cest, there's no denying he's handsome.

Luca checks his phone like he's waiting for my father to change his mind and instruct him to bring me home. "I'll give you a thousand dollars to leave."

"Do you really think I'd find that bribe impressive?" I extend my leg to show off my heel. "My shoes cost more than that."

He scratches his temple. "Five grand. Final offer."

"My clutch was more expensive." A clutch I conveniently forgot in the car. My phone, which tracks my every move, is also conveniently there.

There are pros and cons of being tracked.

The pro: if I'm kidnapped, my father will find me.

The con: if Antonio shows and shoves me into another closet, my father will also find me.

"What's your price, then?" Luca asks while Bruno mutters, "You're wasting your time."

"Tell my father you're chaperoning me one night, drop me off wherever I want, and wait until I tell you to pick me up," I answer.

"Why do I feel like you've had that on the tip of your tongue for the perfect opportunity?"

"Because I have." I run my hand through my necklace, fingering the layers that start with a choker and end at the curve of my breasts. A large opal hangs in the center.

"Oh, how I don't miss being your age," Aunt Helena says. "The tracking, the wishing you could sneak around, the curiosity." She sighs and shuts her brown eyes as if reliving the memories.

Luca directs his gaze to her. "Mom, you're still tracked everywhere."

Her grin stretches from ear to ear. "Yes, but by my husband, the man I love."

"It's different when it's ordered by the man you love. It makes you feel"—Aunt Celine pauses to search for the right word—"protected."

A blue masked man approaches us, interrupting our conversation, and removes his mask.

Tommaso Cavallaro.

The son of Severino Cavallaro, don of the Cavallaro family. Severino is one of my father's closest allies. He helped my father get retribution for my mother's death. In exchange, they signed a contract for Benny to marry Severino's oldest daughter, Neomi.

A union neither Benny nor Neomi wants.

Tommaso is dressed in a black pinstripe suit.

Poor guy.

I'm sure he thought he looked smooth when he left the house. Someone should've told him his suit resembles one of those cheap mobster costumes people wear on Halloween.

"Gigi, you look gorgeous," he says with an arrogant smirk.

His compliment is bold, and no way would he have said it if Benny were beside me.

I hate that Tommaso recognizes me. My mask isn't doing as great of a job as I hoped. Although I can also blame that on standing between two Marchetti men.

"She'll pass, Cavallaro," Luca replies before I can.

I glare at my cousin. "Oh, come on. He's harmless."

Technically, Tommaso isn't harmless.

He's still the son of a don, but everyone knows he fucks up a lot.

"Let her dance," Aunt Helena scolds. "You can easily watch them." She fixes a stern stare on Tommaso. "He isn't dumb enough to try anything slick."

Luca crosses his arms.

Bruno shakes his head.

"You know what? I'll give her permission then." She nudges me toward Tommaso, and he catches me in his arms. "Go dance the night away, bella."

"Fine." Luca rubs the back of his neck. "Cristian will know this was your idea. I'd rather not get my ass chewed out."

"Stay close," Bruno warns, edging closer to Tommaso.

Even though Tommaso isn't my ideal dance partner, it beats spending the night with Luca and Bruno stuck up my ass. They've made it clear their goal is to bore me to death until I decide to leave.

Tommaso tucks his mask into his pocket. His hand is sweaty when he takes mine. He leads me to the dance floor—not directly in front of my family, but within eyesight.

The orchestra at the front of the room starts a new melody. Tommaso keeps a tight grasp on me as we dance, yet there's still a subtle gap between us. I hoped dancing with him would distract me from thoughts of Antonio, wondering if he'd show tonight. It does the opposite.

I wrinkle my nose at Tommaso's strong cologne and focus on not stepping on his shoes. We've never shared a conversation before, and I don't know where to start. I peer past his shoulder and study the covered faces around us.

Is Antonio one of them?

I hope not.

If he is, that means he's dancing with someone else.

I don't want him dancing with anyone but me.

Tommaso breaks our silence. "We could ask our parents to marry us."

I wince. His idea reminds me of why I always avoid him.

When I fail to reply, Tommaso reverses his course, colliding with another man's shoulder, who looks at him in annoyance.

While Tommaso is attractive, that doesn't compensate for his lack of intelligence. You can extreme-home-makeover a man's appearance, but you can't fix stupid.

I clear my throat. "Benny and Neomi already have a contractual marriage between our families. As I'm sure you've heard, I'm not available for marital arrangements."

I look at Luca and Bruno, who are now in deep conversation with the new sheriff. My aunts are nowhere in sight, most likely making their way through the crowd and socializing.

Tommaso smiles charismatically while preparing his argument. "But—"

A masked man interrupts us. "I'd like to cut in." He wedges himself between us without waiting for Tommaso's response.

I immediately recognize the deep, assertive voice, and warmth floods my body.

My blood, my heart, every inch of me feels alive when he's near.

Tommaso's lips flatten. "Whoa. Who the fuck do you think you are?"

Antonio faces Tommaso and lowers his mask. "Go find another dance partner because she's no longer available."

Tommaso turns his head in the direction of Bruno and Luca.

Antonio laughs harshly. "Don't you even think of running to the Marchettis." He nudges Tommaso away. "If you do, I'll drag you out back, call every bookie you owe, and offer to pay double your debt for each organ they remove from your body."

Tommaso winces, all confidence dissipating from him. "Whatever, man." He tips his chin up and walks away.

I hold my breath when Antonio turns to me. A black velvet mask covers half his face. When I attempt to remove it, he snatches my wrist, stopping me.

"Oh, come on. Let me see my Romeo's face," I tease, shuddering as he smooths his hand over my skin.

"Romeo?" He drops my wrist to circle his arm around my waist and tug me closer. "Our families aren't at war, princess."

"Never say never." I lift my arm, offering him my hand, and we start dancing.

"Does your family plan to go to war?" He uses his finger to trace the rhythm of the orchestra's instrumental rendition of Johnny Cash's "Hurt." "Or do you call me Romeo because I'm off-limits, yet you desire me?"

"The only man I'll ever desire is the one I marry, who I'll give my heart to one day."

"Give your heart to one day?" he asks mockingly. "What if I rip your heart from your chest and take it? What will you do then?" Not an ounce of humor is in his tone. He tightens his grip on my hand, lowers it, and forcefully plants it against my chest.

I open my mouth, but no words come.

He bows his head and rests his forehead against mine. The movement isn't gentle.

"I'm not the type to ask for something or wait until it's given to me, princess. If I want it, I take it."

I catch my breath when he spins me and then tugs me closer.

"If you even think about giving your heart to another man, I'll dig my filthy hands into your chest and rip yours out, artery by artery, to stop you." He smirks. "And I'll never give it back."

Why do his murderous words send chills up my spine?

Make me want to hand him my heart, no questions asked, no matter how dangerous he is?

Maybe I'm as deranged as him.

My eyes meet his—at least what the tiny slits in his mask allow. My heart begs for mercy, as I'm terrified of his words, and batters against my chest beneath our hands.

All my life, vicious men have surrounded me.

But at this moment, I swear I'm staring straight into the devil's soul.

This man will drag me into his purgatory.

"I'd rather keep my heart in my chest, thank you," I finally whisper.

"Then we'll go with plan B."

"What's plan B?"

"You trust me enough not to let anyone else own it, and I'll make sure it never stops beating."

"You shouldn't promise that to a person you hardly know. You can't want someone's heart, *love them*, after just a few inter-actions. I'm not someone who believes in love at first sight."

"Oh, princess, I'm not confessing my love for you. Love and trust aren't parallel."

"Love is trust."

"Love is a bullshit excuse to sell heart-shaped candies." He pauses and skillfully leans me backward in a dip, my head hovering so close to the floor that it nearly hits it.

I gasp, ignoring the stray hairs that break free from my crystal clip, and wait until I'm upright before replying, "You say that about love because you've never experienced it … never felt heartbreak like so many others have."

"Heartbreak is a fraud." His expression darkens. "Trust me, Giana, I've held another man's heart in my hands. It doesn't easily break."

My hands rest on his shoulders. "You're so romantic."

"Which of our few interactions gave you the idea I was romantic?"

"The part where you asked me not to give my heart to anyone else or—I don't know—when you forced my dance partner to switch places with you."

"Is it not clear I want you?"

I shiver, goose bumps spreading along my skin.

"I want to *own* you," he adds. "I want to touch you. *Fuck you.*"

"No one will ever *own* me. And the only man who will ever *fuck me* will be my husband."

I need to pull away from him.

But I can't.

As fucked up as it is, I want every second I can get with Antonio. Maybe I'm as messed up in the head as everyone else in our world.

Maybe the ugliness, the recklessness, the sins have seeped into my being.

What is it they say? You become your environment.

Maybe Antonio is waking it up, showing me who I truly am.

Even wearing the mask, I know my desire is clear on my face.

"Come on. Let's go," he says in the same *I want to fuck you* tone.

"Go where?"

"Wherever I take us."

"There are eyes everywhere I go."

"Then maybe I should gouge those eyes out."

A wave of dizziness hits me as he unfastens my clip, releasing my hair to drape across my exposed shoulders.

He separates from me and stretches out his hand, withdrawing little by little, testing me. "How brave are you, princess?"

When I take his hand, I blame it on a lapse of judgment.

Or maybe it's my obsession with him.

The drug of Antonio Lombardi I've formed an addiction to.

We keep our heads low while he leads me off the dance floor to the exit. I silently pray no one is watching, and with each step, my heart races faster.

The veil of a moonless night surrounds us as he guides me to the courtyard that, like the inside of the ball, looks like it was plucked straight from a fairy tale. If I ever marry, this is where I want my wedding.

Antonio doesn't give me time to admire the beauty of the greenery, hydrangea bushes, or cherry trees. The low lighting of the courtyard is on our side as he guides us through its paths. Thankfully, it's surrounded by high walls that offer seclusion.

We cross a bridge over a koi pond and a bubbling fountain. He stops in an isolated corner of the courtyard, away from the noise and commotion, and whips me around. Then his lips crash into mine.

He curls his hands around my waist, holding me, and we kiss as if our lives depend on it. Even though I can hardly breathe, I don't pull back for air, out of fear he'll stop. Every inch of me trembles, making me weak in the knees. Antonio lifts me and sits me on the stone wall while keeping our mouths locked.

I'm panting, my need for him growing stronger.

I should've chosen a shorter gown.

It'd have made it easier for him to touch me and relieve the ache between my legs.

But lucky for me, Antonio is a great problem solver. I moan when he breaks our kiss, grips my hips, and settles on both knees. For a lucky second, I discover a gentle Antonio as he hikes up my dress and arranges himself between my thighs.

My heart burns with need, beating so intensely that I'm positive he can hear it.

Boom.

Boom.

Boom.

Antonio said he'd rip my heart out if I gave it to anyone else. Right now, I want to hand it over to him myself and allow him to take everything from me.

He mutters something beneath his breath, but I can't make out his words.

My blood sets on fire when he feathers his hand over my thigh before sweeping kisses along it until he reaches my center. He sucks over my lace panties, and I'm ready to die in the euphoric feeling of his lips on me. His movements are slow and deliberate, as if we had all the time in the world. I've never experienced something so erotic in my life.

"I'd bet everything I own that you taste as good as you smell," he says roughly.

I sink my nails into my palms when he rips my panties down my legs. He curls his hand around my thigh, and I shamelessly hold him in place when he licks up my folds.

He flicks my clit once.

Twice.

Three fucking times.

All so dreadfully slow.

Then he places a single kiss on it and ends all that gentleness.

My brutal monster returns.

He eats me out like he's starving.

A man who's never been fed a decent meal in his life and I'm a delicacy made perfectly for him.

My body shakes, and he doesn't come up for air. Not even when I clutch his shoulders and gyrate my hips against his face.

I've never had a man touch me like this, taste me like this.

Hell, I've never had a man do anything.

Then five words ruin everything.

"I'm looking for Gigi Marchetti."

I tense at Luca's voice.

You've got to be kidding me.

There's only one thing I want more than Antonio's mouth between my legs pleasuring me: Antonio alive.

If anyone catches us, he won't have a tongue to eat me out with.

"Antonio." I tap his head.

He ignores me, and my legs tremble. This man gives no fucks about risking his life to keep his tongue between my legs. I'm so close, and the sensation of his tongue overtakes me. He restrains me, licking and sucking, and his fingers join his tongue.

I buck my hips against his face as he relentlessly tongue- and finger-fucks me until I fall apart. My entire body shakes as he slides out from underneath my dress. He stands tall and straightens out his suit. His eyes never leave mine as he licks his lips. I've never seen his face so intense.

"Gigi!" Aunt Celine yells.

"Have you seen a woman, burgundy dress?" Aunt Helena calls out.

I push at Antonio's chest. "You need to go."

"When can I see you again?" he asks, completely indifferent that there's a damn search party coming for me.

"I leave for Italy in three days."

He helps me down from the wall. "Where in Italy?"

"Gigi!"

I tense at Bruno's voice, and as I clumsily attempt to smooth out the wrinkles in my dress, the realization of what we did hits me. My stomach sinks. I feel easy, cheap, like I fell into his trap, knowing his only interest is to *touch me, fuck me, own me.*

"I'm sure your sources can figure that out."

"Your father keeps your whereabouts very sealed." He runs

his hand through his thick hair. "Trust me, it's hard keeping track."

"A prince always finds his princess." I won't make it so easy for him next time.

"This isn't a fairy tale. There's only one way this story will end. In tragedy."

"A tragedy can be beautiful though."

"A tragedy isn't beautiful, princess. It's death."

"Am I worth death to you, Antonio Lombardi?"

"I'll answer that when I know."

8

GIGI

Oh, Italy, how I love thee.

The destination for mouthwatering food, lovers, and decreased Marchetti security.

Yesterday, my father chartered a private jet for me. I spent the ten-hour flight binge-watching reality TV while Bruno slept. We arrived late, and I passed out as soon as I slipped into bed.

I regularly visit my aunt Aida, my mother's half-sister in Tuscany.

Before my grandfather married my grandmother, he had a fling with a woman here and got her pregnant. Even though they never married and he returned to New York, he still provided for them. He also took frequent trips to visit Aida, and my mother would accompany him. After his death, she started taking me with her.

Aunt Aida lives in a charming cottage tucked away in the countryside, where she and her husband, Felice, manage an olive grove.

Even though the mansion in New York resides on a large property, it doesn't match Tuscany's lush hills and sprawling valleys.

The cottage is a century old, and Aunt Aida renovated it

while still maintaining its rich history. It's also very small, so my father paid for two more cottages to be built on the property—one for us and the other for a bodyguard. He always sends me here when he's having trouble in New York and worried for my safety.

I start my day on the cottage's terrace, sipping espresso while enjoying the fresh air. My thoughts drift to Antonio, and I shake my head, remembering I basically told him to do a Where's Waldo of my location in Italy.

He sent me a single text after the ball.

> Villain: I will find you, princess.

That's what I saved his name under in case anyone ever finds it. Everyone knows not to put real names in burner phones.

Antonio's *I will find you*—that I, for some reason, keep reading in Liam Neeson's voice—is a loose threat. Men in his world hardly have time to see their families, let alone travel across the world to find someone they want to fuck.

I never replied to his text, deciding not to make it easy on him. I already turned into Easy McGee that night when I allowed him to go down on me in freaking public.

Who even does that?

A woman desperately infatuated with the wrong man—that's who.

I'm starting to understand Natalia's reasoning for not walking away from Vinny. She knows he's dangerous, but there's a pull to him, shackling her, and she can't break herself free.

That's me with Antonio.

A girl obsessed with the villain.

Even though my family is cordial with the Lombardis, my father isn't a fan. He once told me they were referred to as scum before Vincent succeeded his father. He cleaned up their name —the best he could. The Marchettis and Cavallaros are still the most respected families in the city though.

"Knock, knock," Aunt Aida says, her Italian accent heavy. She makes a knocking motion while joining me on the terrace, where I'm lounging on an ottoman. Her linen pants blow in the breeze as she sits across from me.

"Good morning." I smile.

"I made baked eggs and sausage."

My stomach grumbles at the mention of food, especially hers. She's a goddess in the kitchen.

Her olive complexion is free of makeup, and not one wrinkle materializes when she grins. "What would you like to do today?"

"Breakfast, then shopping."

"Sounds like a plan." She fusses with her black hair flying in every direction of her ponytail. "Felice is staying behind. He's short-staffed on the field and has to put in extra time."

My bed is calling my name after our long day of shopping.

Bruno and I tell Aunt Aida and Felice good night before strolling to our adjacent cottages. With matching stone and terra-cotta exteriors, they look nearly identical, but while mine has two bedrooms, Bruno's only has one.

"See you in the morning," he says before we go our separate ways. "Call if you need anything."

"Good night," I sing out.

When I enter the cottage, I shut the door and rest my back against it, taking in the space.

Every detail—from the exposed natural beams to the vaulted ceiling—was chosen by my mother. It's cozy, understated, and so unlike the mansion. Both designed by her, both holding a special piece of her.

I shower and change into a silky nightie, and as I nestle into bed, the burner vibrates in my nightstand. I brought it to Italy, just in case, but had no expectations.

I collect the phone from the drawer and play with it in my hand. It feels so light in my palm. Nothing like my iPhone.

When I flip it open, there's a text.

Villain: Come outside.

No freaking way.

He's messing with me.

I grip the phone as if it held my future, waiting for it to vibrate again.

Nothing.

Sighing, I toss it next to me. It bounces off the mattress and vibrates again simultaneously.

I leap across the bed to catch it.

Villain: Don't ignore me.

I hit the Reply button.

Me: Don't play games with me.

Villain: Come outside and make sure no one sees you.

"I will find you, princess."

Aunt Aida's village is private and nowhere near a city. No one has ever hunted me down here. Antonio has better odds of finding a leprechaun at the end of a rainbow.

That still doesn't stop me from jumping out of bed and walking to the double French doors. I peel back the curtain, peeking outside before cautiously stepping onto the terrace. I clutch a hand to my chest, searching the area, and someone steps into my view.

My calmness surprises me, and I don't scream for Bruno. I stand there, frozen, as the person comes closer. It's dark, but I'll always know his stature.

Antonio stands in front of me, in the flesh, confirming he most definitely found me.

I launch forward to grab his elbow. "Are you fucking crazy? Bruno will kill you."

The man has ears like a hawk.

"Do you think I care?" Antonio asks indifferently.

"Not only will he kill you, but my father will also figure out a way to resurrect you so he can kill you again."

"I waited until everyone's lights were off."

"How long were you waiting out there?"

He checks his watch. "A few hours."

"Stalker." I raise my hand on his elbow to smack his shoulder.

"It seems if I want to see you, I must resort to stalking." He tips his chin toward the doors—a silent demand for us to move our conversation inside.

I bite my tongue.

Inviting him in is a big deal.

In horror movies, they always say, don't invite a vampire inside your home. This is for sure the equivalent.

Even though I somewhat trust Antonio, I still question his motives. His family can use him as the perfect pawn to destroy mine.

Charm the Mafia king's daughter.

If my father knew I was even contemplating this, he'd ban me from ever leaving the mansion again.

Antonio captures my hand, reading the distrust on my face. No longer waiting for an invite, he leads me inside. He releases me, slams the door shut, and locks it behind us.

I bump his shoulder while closing the curtains to show my disdain of his rudeness. He takes three long strides across the room to the bed, sitting and spreading his legs wide, hanging his hands between them.

Our gazes instantly collide.

His eyes are a wicked storm.

Laser-sharp.

Pitch-dark.

Piercing me.

Antonio is a hurricane.

And I'm the victim, ignoring every warning.

I abandon our eye contact to drink him in.

He's swapped his normal business suit for a crisp black shirt and relaxed black trousers. The epitome of an Italian heart-stopper.

I finally break our silence. "Where are you staying?"

"I have family about an hour from here."

"Did you travel alone?"

"To your aunt's?"

"To Italy."

"I brought my daughter, her nanny, and one of my men."

I backtrack a step, blindsided. "You have a daughter?"

It takes him a moment before he nods, and regret floods his face. His expression mirrors my father's when someone mentions me. The fewer details others know about their daughters, the better.

I lower my eyes to his hand. No ring. But that doesn't mean he isn't married. Plenty of men have no problem slipping off their rings when away from their wives.

Because, we all know, seven out of ten single men are married.

"I'm not married, if that's what you're thinking," Antonio assures.

"That's what they all say."

I allowed a married man to go downtown on me.

Let's just add home-wrecker to my résumé.

My mouth turns dry, making it hard to speak. "If there're children, there's always a wife."

Divorce is practically illegal in this world. A woman leaving her husband is frowned upon. She's shunned and considered a wife unable to please her husband. Some even choose suicide over divorce, fearing public scorn more than death. It's sad, honestly.

Antonio rubs his temples with his knuckles. "I was married."

I rack my brain for recollection of hearing about his marriage, but nothing. "Where is your wife now?"

"Dead." There's no sadness in his answer. No grief.

That should be red flag number five hundred.

"I can't stay late," he says, changing the subject. "I suggest you go to bed earlier tomorrow."

"Who said I want to see you tomorrow?" I cross my arms. "I didn't exactly invite you over tonight."

"Wrong." He thrums his fingers over his jawline. "You instructed me to find you in Italy." He stands, grabbing my arm, and tugs me closer. "Did you think I wouldn't?"

I gasp when he presses his thumb under my chin to raise my eyes to his.

He tips his head, running his lips along my messy hair. "I follow through when challenged. I always win."

I shiver when his lips drift from my ear to my neck. He sucks along my jawbone, soft, then hard, then soft again, the sensation causing my body to heat in all the right places.

"Who ..." I catch my breath. "Who said I want you to come back?"

"You can either let me in willingly, or I'll find my own way in."

"FYI, my bodyguard is here."

"FYI, I don't give a fuck." He laughs callously, pausing his assault on my skin. "And don't think I'm not aware of his separate cottage." A tsk leaves him.

"He'll sleep in here then."

His mouth moves to my ear, and he bites into the cartilage. "You allow any other man to sleep here, bodyguard or not, I'll slit his throat, tie you to the bed, and force his blood down your throat."

I nudge his shoulder, but he doesn't move an inch. "One

rule, if I even consider allowing you to come back: you never touch Bruno, my aunt, or her husband."

"I never said I'd kill him for shits and giggles. I said I'd kill him if he was in your bed. You'd be the reason for his death."

"Isn't that a bit extreme?" I ask when his wicked lips return to my neck. "I mean, we've hardly …"

"Hardly what?"

"Spent time together."

"What does that have to do with anything?" He runs a single finger along my bottom lip. "You didn't care about how much time we'd spent together when you were letting me taste your sweet pussy in the courtyard."

My cheeks heat.

He lowers his hand, easing an object from his pocket, and just as I catch the flash of a knife, he cuts down the middle of my nightie. The nightie falls to the floor after he slides it off my shoulders.

I suck in a breath when he dips his cold hand inside my panties. He smirks arrogantly when he finds me drenched in need for him.

"Why did you come here, Antonio?" The question comes out in three labored breaths.

"For you."

I curl my toes when his finger brushes my clit. "Why?"

He doesn't answer.

At least not vocally.

He shows me.

He rips my panties down my legs and smashes his mouth to mine. I wrap my arms around his shoulders when his tongue slides inside my mouth.

Antonio tastes like brandy and dinner mints.

Like an addiction.

I allow him to turn and push me onto the bed. He remains fully clothed, his face unreadable, while coasting his gaze down my body. An insecurity I've never experienced follows.

"Antonio—" I start but slam my mouth shut when he clasps his hands around my ankles, spreads my legs, and drags me to the edge of the bed until my ass halfway hangs off.

Without warning, he releases an ankle to slide one finger inside me.

Two fingers.

Three fucking fingers, as if I were as easy to stretch as cheap Lycra.

I wince, and a pain shoots through my body, forcing me to shut my legs on reflex.

"Nuh-uh," he scolds, digging his bony elbow into my free leg and pinning me to the bed. "This is day one of me stretching this pussy out, getting you ready for me." His gaze clashes with mine as he *stretches* me, his thumb making small, torturous circles on my clit.

He's gentle with my clit while his fingers move savagely inside me.

When I stop fighting, he briefly removes his fingers to reposition my body, tossing my thighs over his shoulders to give himself a better angle.

My fingers find his hair, tearing at the roots, and I drive my hips forward, meeting each thrust of his talented fingers while rotating my hips.

I attempt to rise on my elbows, to watch him, but can't gain the strength. All my energy is taken by fucking his fingers back. Dropping my shaky hand, I cup it over his on my clit and use my palm to force him to rub me faster. Tingles rush up my spine as I arch my back, and my heart clatters against my chest.

Sure, I've orgasmed before.

They were nothing like this though.

It isn't rushed in the courtyard or given by yours truly.

This is different.

Antonio is in control, but I'm collecting the benefits.

"Oh-my-fucking-God," I moan, my legs trembling.

I lose Antonio's hand as an orgasm shatters through me. The

sound of him unbuckling his pants joins my frantic pants. He wastes no time before shoving them down. His erection springs forward, only inches from my opening. I lick my lips. He's thick and large and beautiful.

It takes all my strength to prop myself on my elbows and watch the show of him jerking himself. Swear to God, if I was in charge, he'd win an Academy Award for best performance in an action movie.

I'm entranced as I watch him.

The sight of this gorgeous man pleasuring himself in front of me.

Embarrassingly, I want to lick the sweat glistening along his hairline.

Lick the pre-cum at the tip of his dick.

My mouth waters at the thought.

Antonio has dragged this fiend out of me.

Someone who wants to try all the dirty things with him and only him.

There's a sense of trust and power when he slams his eyes shut. There's never been a time Antonio didn't give me his full attention. He's always in control, anticipating someone to do something, trusting no one.

He thrusts his hips, mirroring how I was only minutes ago. My fingers turn numb as I hold back from reaching forward and running them along his cock.

I'm too chickenshit.

He hasn't fully dragged me from my cocoon.

I lick my lips again and rotate my hips forward, ready for round two.

But I freeze when his body shudders.

A deep groan leaves him, and he opens his ravenous eyes to drown in mine.

I glance down, fascinated, when the first drop of cum drips from his tip. He inches closer until his cock meets my entrance. When I attempt to clamp my legs shut, his body stops them.

He strokes himself faster and faster, his elbow hitting my thigh. On his final thrust, he gasps my name. His entire body shakes, his orgasm an earthquake inside him, as he releases every drop of his cum between my legs.

Before I can take another breath, he collects as much cum as he can on his fingers and sinks them inside me, ravenously pumping them.

"When I leave here, I want you to play with yourself again," he demands, forcing his cum deeper and making small circles. "I want you to slip your fingers in and out of your pussy."

While there's no way I can complete a sentence, his words are articulated.

"My cum stays in here," he adds, slowly withdrawing his fingers. "Don't you dare shower or clean it. When I return tomorrow night, I'd better smell me inside you—do you hear me?"

I stay quiet, pressing my palm to my stomach to control my breathing.

He wants me to go to bed and, like ... incubate his cum inside me?

That's how pregnancies happen, and Antonio will one hundred percent die if he impregnates me.

He buckles his pants, drapes his body over mine, and grabs my jaw. "If you don't, I won't let you come next time, nor will I be nice about it. Do you want that, princess?"

I shake my head the best I can in his constraint.

He pats my cheek. "That's my good girl."

Then I watch as he leaves without saying another word. Lying here, I process what happened and press my hand between my legs. I play with his cum between my fingers, focusing, and bring my finger to my mouth, sucking on it.

It tastes salty.

Foreign.

"Not too bad," I mutter, my eyes on the French doors.

My knees are weak when I roll out of bed and change into a not-ripped nightie. I glare at the ripped one.

Antonio will get a bill for that.

When I return to bed, I squeeze my thighs together, not wanting to lose a drop of him.

My thoughts are everywhere as I lower my hand between my legs.

When I glide a finger inside myself, I say it's for me. That I need another orgasm. Not because Antonio ordered me to do so.

I moan his name when my body hits the brink again.

We're playing a dangerous game.

Sleep shunned me last night, but the tiredness is worth it.

Antonio is my first text of the day.

> Me: I really need to shower.

Rubbing my thighs together, I strangely enjoy his cum inside me.

My phone immediately beeps with his reply.

> Villain: If I come there tonight and my cum
> isn't still inside you, we'll have problems,
> princess.

> Me: What will you do, huh?

Unfortunately, there isn't an eye-roll emoji on this generic-ass flip phone.

> Villain: Test me, princess. Shower, and I'll
> shove you on your knees and come down
> your throat until you can no longer breathe.

Jesus, does this man think he has golden cum or something?

Sorry, Antonio, but unlike water and common sense, there is no shortage of cum in this world.

Me: You are seriously a psycho.

Villain: I'm also the only psycho you'll ever allow to touch you.

Another text comes through before I reply.

Villain: And let's not forget, your body enjoys this psycho's touch—fucking craves it actually. So don't act so innocent.

His certifiable response shouldn't make me as giddy as it does.

There's a pep in my step as I slide out of bed and get ready for the day—sans shower. I do change my panties though. He'll have to get over that.

Sunlight bathes my skin as I stroll to Aunt Aida's cottage. My Hermès sandals brush along the cobblestone with every step I take. Aunt Aida, Bruno, and Felice are at the table when I walk into the small kitchen.

"Good morning," I sing out.

The mouthwatering smell of Aunt Aida's fresh croissants hangs in the air, escaping through the open window. My stomach growls.

"You sure are chipper this morning," she says when I sit beside her.

Bruno narrows his beady eyes in my direction. "It should be illegal for someone to act that chipper in the morning."

"It's just so relaxing here." I spread a napkin across my lap, collect a croissant from the basket, and drop it onto my plate. "A stress reliever."

So are the orgasms Antonio gave me.

Aunt Aida reaches for my hand and squeezes it. "The offer to move here is always open, dear. You could meet a nice man and live a normal life without ... all the violence." She peers at Bruno in apology. "No offense."

"None taken." Bruno shoots her what little smile he can. "I'd consider that a boring life though, so please, for the love of God, don't move here, Gigi."

Aunt Aida has made it clear she isn't a fan of the brutality in our lives, but she always welcomes Bruno with open arms. She bakes his favorite sweets during every visit and sends him Christmas gifts. Like me, she sees the men behind the carnage and knows there's a soul beneath there.

She's offered me permanent residence in Italy countless times. As much as I love it here, it'll never be home. I'm a New York girlie through and through.

A *Marchetti.*

And no matter how much I hate the brutality that comes with my life, I'll never leave my family. The chaos is the only home I've ever known.

I smother honey on my croissant, my mind drifting to Antonio as I eat.

"What would you like to do today?" Aunt Aida asks.

I chew the bite of my croissant. "You know, I was thinking we could just relax. Read a book, lounge, and eat all the sweets we bought yesterday."

She grins. "I love that idea."

"I don't mind helping in the field then," Bruno tells Felice.

The olive groves are their primary source of income. Whenever we visit and Bruno has free time, he always offers to help Felice. My vacations in Italy bore him. When I told him it was a self-care opportunity for him, he told me his self-care was homicide.

The men leave after breakfast. Aunt Aida and I chat while cleaning up. We spend the rest of the day lounging on the terrace, catching up with life, and binging baked goods.

Antonio is in my thoughts all day, a brain-eating infection I can't get rid of. When the breeze hits the patio at a certain angle, I *smell* him.

Not his cologne.

His cum.

The way he marked me.

And I grin, anticipation settling inside me as I wait for his next visit.

Wearing my sexiest lingerie, I sit in bed and wait for Antonio.

As the night grows later and despite my attempts to stay awake, I doze off.

The first time I wake, I check the time.

Two in the morning.

No Antonio.

So I shut off the lamp and snuggle into my pillow.

The next time is abrupt.

An intruder rips my blanket off me, smothers his hand over my nose and mouth, and roughly squeezes my cheeks. The mattress dips when he crawls into my bed.

His body lingers over mine, a haunting ghost, while his free hand delves underneath my lingerie. He forces my legs apart, yanks down my panties, and sinks to his knees between my parted ones.

I suck in deep breaths when he withdraws his hand and don't scream for help or panic. Instead, I maintain my composure and inhale the intoxicating smell of my newest obsession while awaiting his next move.

Goose bumps spread along my skin when he pushes my knees forward, causing them to nearly hit my chest, and traces his tongue up my center.

"Good girl," Antonio praises from between my legs, taking

another swipe with his tongue before shoving a finger inside me. "The taste of us is fucking delectable."

I grin at his appreciative groan as he eases up my body.

He grips my jaw, forcing it downward, and jams his finger inside my mouth. "Tell me how good we taste together," he orders, his lips almost touching mine.

Since his finger is lodged halfway down my throat, responding isn't easy, so I choose not to.

He forces another finger inside to prove he doesn't appreciate my disobedience, thrusting them past my tonsils, causing me to gag. "I asked you a question."

With his fingers still in my mouth, he repositions himself. It's too hard to keep track of his movements. Somehow, he's shifted to straddle one of my legs, pressing a knee against my core.

I nearly choke on his fingers when he rubs his knee against my clit in circles.

It isn't gentle but feels so damn good.

Antonio is teaching me I enjoy roughness.

His fingers stay in my throat while he pleasures me with his knee. I dig my nails into the sheets, unable to stop myself from gyrating my hips against him.

He doesn't flinch when I bite into his fingers, only forces them deeper. So I sink my teeth into his knuckles while frantically thrusting against him. My movements become wilder when his erection caresses my thigh. It's so erotic how we slide against each other.

When he nuzzles his face against my neck, I feel his labored breathing on my skin. He eases his fingers from my mouth, only a few inches, to provide me a twinge of breathing room. Not that it lasts long. Each time he rotates his hips, he thrusts his fingers farther down my throat.

He moves us up.

I move us down.

He straightens his back, allowing himself a better angle. I do my best to anchor my free ankle around his for the same reason.

My stomach tightens. Every limb in my body tenses as I reach my brink.

My pace grows faster.

Faster.

Faster.

So does his.

Until we can't take it any longer.

I'm the first to break.

I moan before biting into his knuckles so hard that I'm positive I broke skin. My body shakes as he pulls back. I control my breathing as Antonio unbuckles his pants and furiously strokes himself.

"Fuck," he drawls.

Just as he did last night, he releases himself between my legs and presses his cum deeper inside me, filling me up with him.

He releases his fingers from my mouth, only the tips brushing along my lips, and lowers down my body. I inhale sharply, my heels sliding against the bed when he flicks his tongue against my clit.

Those heels then press into the sheets when he plunges his tongue inside me.

He dips it in once.

Twice.

Three times.

Then licks me a final time.

My heart races as he moves up my body. He drops his hand from my lips to my throat and wraps his fingers around it. I open my mouth wider at him, once again, restricting my air. I'm gulping for breaths when he lowers his head above mine. His teeth tug at my lips before he plunges his tongue inside. Just as I'm about to return the kiss, he rears back and spits in my mouth.

My attempt to jerk away from him is useless since my head

is pinned against the pillow and he's holding me down. His spit pools at the base of my throat, gagging me as his fingers did. I stare at him, wide-eyed, as he works his jaw above me.

"My hand doesn't move until you swallow," he says roughly.

Since I don't want my obituary to say, *Gigi was a sweet woman, taken too soon after choking on a cocktail of her and Antonio's cum. Rest in peace*, I gulp.

His spit trickles down my throat, leaving a taste both sweet and salty.

Antonio gives my throat a tiny squeeze before releasing me.

"Good girl." He pats my cheek. "Now that I've given you a better sample, you can do as I said." His mouth hovers over mine, licking my lips. "Tell me how much you fucking love the taste of us."

I hesitate.

Should I be honest or lie?

I smirk against his lips. "While I enjoyed the sample, I don't think that's enough to say *I love anything*."

I *love* that I feel his small smile against my mouth. That gentle side of him is short-lived before he bites into my lip and inches backward.

"It appears we both need more then." He delves his fingers into my hair, raising me forward, and stands tall on his knees, his grip tight on my scalp. "I'll fill your mouth with my cum, *giving you more*, and you'll give *me* more by working on your subpar gag reflex."

He situates me, kneeling so my face is level with his waist. I make out the silhouette of his dick, already hard again, and can't stop myself from licking my lips. His hand stays in my hair when I open my mouth, and he guides his cock inside.

My cheeks hollow, and he doesn't stop until my forehead hits his stomach. I choke, my eyes watering, and he pulls out a few inches, giving me some relief.

I hate that he's right.

That my gag reflex is subpar.

I need to prove him wrong.

This is a new experience, but I've watched enough porn to give a semi-decent performance.

I drag my tongue down his length and love how he shudders. His cock jerks when I start stroking him. It isn't enough for my villain.

"You don't work on your gag reflex with your hand." He rocks his hips forward. "Quit playing and suck."

His cock feels almost thicker when he fills my mouth the second time.

"Relax your jaw," he instructs, digging his fingers into my scalp.

I do as he said, moving my mouth up and down his erection.

He hisses, his grasp on my hair loosening. "That's it, princess. Show me how well you take my cock in that pretty mouth of yours."

I wish I'd kept the light on to see his face.

The pleasure in his voice, mixed with his groans, becomes my new favorite song. He throws his head back. His cock pulsates on my tongue. There's no warning before his warm cum spills inside my mouth.

He grips the back of my neck, his fingers digging into the skin. "Don't you dare swallow yet."

I hold my breath as more cum comes.

"It's unfortunate I can't see my cum on your tongue tonight." He jerks me closer until his entire cock is back in my mouth. "We'll save that for another time."

I gasp for air when he releases me.

"Now, stick out your tongue."

My jaw is sore as I do.

His hand moves from my neck to face, cupping it. A chill shoots up my spine when he runs his thumb along my tongue, playing with his cum. The restraint not to swallow melts away when he collects enough to coat my lips with it.

His tone is low when he says, "You're about to learn a lot in Italy, princess, and it won't be its history."

"Hey, babe. How's it going in New York?" I ask when I answer Natalia's call. "You miss me yet?"

Her response isn't as laid-back as mine. "Good … but, uh …"

My shoulders stiffen. "What?"

"Vinny killed a man in front of me."

Even though I'm not shocked, I pretend to be. "Why?"

"Over a parking spot, Gigi, at *a fucking ice cream shop*. It was fucking crazy."

"This is what I warned you about." I try not to sound like a parent scolding their child. "Vinny is irrational and stupid."

"I'm beginning to see that," she mutters.

"What are you going to do?"

"I don't know."

"Break up with him."

"I need to just think about everything."

"He's dangerous, Natalia. I'm sure you knew that before, but murdering someone in front of you proves it."

She's quiet for a moment.

"Whatever you decide, you know I have your back, right?"

"I know." She blows out a long breath as voices form in the background. "I need to get back to work. Talk later?"

"Of course. Stay in touch. Promise?"

"I promise."

I frown when we end the call.

Before I allow Antonio between my legs again, I need him to agree that he'll convince his dimwit brother to leave Natalia and *not* kill her after.

Speaking of my villain.

He left seconds after making me swallow his cum last night, not giving me the opportunity to see him in the light. My pride is too strong to text and ask if he's coming tonight.

If he does, my work is cut out for me.

Asking him to control his brother will be a challenge.

But I have something to use as leverage.

Me.

Antonio arrives late again, but I'm better prepared this time. I left the lamp on and downed an espresso an hour ago, so I'm fully alert.

"She's awake this time."

My attention sweeps from the TV to him standing in the doorway. Him not making a sound when sneaking in here isn't surprising. He's notorious for his ability to easily creep on his prey.

Neither of us speaks as he enters my bedroom. I fidget with my blanket, remembering what we did last night.

He runs his hand along the edge of my bed before tearing my blanket from the bed. "Take off your clothes."

I gasp, my arms wrapping around myself, but don't move.

No, I'm a woman on a mission.

"Before I do, I want you to promise me something," I say.

He freezes and raises a brow.

"Make Vinny break up with Natalia, and please don't let him hurt her."

"I don't take orders from you." His voice drips with smugness.

"That wasn't an *order*. I obviously said *please*." I scoot down the bed to face him when he approaches me.

He kneels so we're at eye level. "Men say *please* to me all the time and beg for their lives when I tie them to chairs. That doesn't mean I'll listen."

"Do you also stick your cock in those men's mouths?" I smile, proud of my response.

"My cock taking residence in your mouth doesn't mean I make promises to you. It simply means I want my cock sucked." His smile isn't sarcastic like mine. It's fueled with callousness.

"He'll kill her."

"I'm sure you warned her against him, and she failed to listen."

"I was warned about you, yet here I am, failing to listen."

"Maybe you should've."

"She made a mistake, Antonio."

"That's unfortunate for her." His tone is all business, as if he'd loaned me money and I was in default. He picks up the picture frame on my nightstand, studying the photo of my mother and me, and then returns it.

"He's your brother." My throat burns at how difficult he's making this. "Talk to him."

"I don't control another man's actions or give two fucks about their relationship." He reaches out, stroking my chin with his long fingers, as he has nearly every night he's visited, soothing me when I wish it didn't. "As long as it's not another man touching you, I couldn't care less."

"Why just me?"

"I don't share," he states matter-of-factly. "When someone is mine, they're *mine* and *mine only*."

"I never agreed to be yours."

"Your body confirmed it was mine last night."

"Do me *one* favor. *Please*."

He sweeps his hand over my cheek, his face mellowing. "I'll give you plenty of favors, but not that."

"If something happens to her, it'll *hurt me*. *You'll* hurt me by not stopping it."

He glowers. "I never promised I wouldn't hurt you."

"You asked me to trust you."

"Having trust in someone doesn't mean they won't hurt you."

I touch his face, running my palm along his hot cheek. I feel the thick tension underneath his skin as if it embedded itself there years ago. "I know you well enough to know you won't hurt me, Antonio."

"Me not *physically* hurting you doesn't mean I won't emotionally." He works his jaw, my hand on his cheek following the movement. "I won't kill you, Gigi—I promise you that. But that's *all* you have my word on." He collects my hand in his free one and presses a kiss into my palm. "You needed to trust me to give me your body. So I earned your trust. Trust doesn't mean I owe you any favors."

I wince, escaping him, his touch like poison now. He slides closer, attempting to stop me from doing the same with his hand, but doesn't fight me when I swat it away.

Shame and embarrassment possess me.

I push him so hard that he nearly fumbles backward. "So this was only sex to you?" My words are said through clenched teeth. "Fuck the Marchetti princess and earn cool points with your third-rate family?"

He slaps his palms on the bed on each side of me. "I traveled all the way to Italy to see you."

"No, you came to Italy to *fuck me.*" Spit follows the last two words, hitting his cheek.

He turns quiet.

All my life, I've watched my brother use women.

I've seen other men do the same and heard the stories.

I stupidly believed it was different with Antonio.

Believed I wouldn't fall victim to the same trap.

"Leave." I point at the door. "Right now."

He inches so close that our chests touch. "What if I don't want to?"

"I don't give a fuck what you want anymore. Get out."

"You think you can force me out?"

"I'll scream bloody murder until Bruno comes in here." I pause to jab two fingers into his forehead. "He'll put a bullet through that ugly, manipulative brain of yours." When I go to push his forehead again, he grabs my wrist. "One less Lombardi in this world, the better."

"You scream, and I'll thrust my cock down your throat so hard that you won't speak for a week."

I wet my lips before brushing them against his. "Do it then."

"Don't test me, princess."

He bites into my lip, his sharp canine breaking skin, and I struggle not to flinch.

"Don't test me, Lombardi." As soon as he releases my lip, I sink my teeth into his as hard as I can. "You'd better kill me now because if you don't, I'll tell every man in my family what you've done with me the past few nights."

While my bite didn't cause him to flinch, my threat does.

He rears back to glare at me. "Don't act like you didn't fucking want it."

"Consent or not, if I tell my father you even touched me, he'll kill you." I pat his shoulder and make my voice as mocking as possible. "You might think you know me since all you've seen is the sweet Gigi, but if you try me, I'll show you my claws." I dig my nails into his shirt. "There's Marchetti blood inside me. I'm the one woman you don't want to piss off because I come with a death sentence. No judge. No jury. Straight to the grave."

He bruised my heart, so I want to annihilate his—if he even has one to do that to.

"Leave, Antonio," I say, gritting my teeth. "I'll give you sixty seconds before I scream."

His face darkens. "You make me leave tonight, I won't be back, Gigi."

"Good." I shove him away, grab my alarm clock, set it for sixty seconds, and hold it up on display. "Your time starts now. Fifty-nine. Fifty-eight. Fifty-seven …"

9

ANTONIO

"This is so yummy, Daddy." Amara takes the last bite of her gelato. "Can I order another?"

I squeeze her shoulder as I stand. "Another round for everyone?"

Amara holds up two fingers. "Two scoops, please!"

"I'll try pistachio this time," Clara adds from the chair beside her.

"Ask if there's a vodka flavor," Damien says. "For you and me both."

When my father questioned why I was taking Amara to Italy, I told him she deserves a vacation for once in her life. So I've tried to have fun here as much as I can.

We rode the gondolas, visited a medieval castle, dined in the best restaurants, and I bought her everything she picked out while shopping.

I spend my days with her.

My nights with Gigi.

Damien watches Amara and Clara when I visit her.

Standing in line, I think of how I accidentally mentioned Amara to Gigi. It's public knowledge I have a daughter, but few know what she looks like or where to find her. I hardly trust anyone with something so precious, which is why I lied about staying with my family. While I do have family here, I wanted us to stay safe and private. So I rented a luxury villa for the four of us here.

Amara never meets women I become involved with. Not that I have relationships. There were a few women I fucked on occasion, but I've never had anything serious. And nothing in nearly a year.

Besides not having the time to put into a relationship, my daughter questions me about every single fucking thing in the world.

"Daddy, why do people wear glasses?"

"Daddy, why don't you have a girlfriend?"

"Daddy, is my heart supposed to beat, or am I dying?"

I don't need to give her more topics for questions, nor do I want someone else to answer to.

"Prossimo!" the clerk behind the counter yells out.

"Due gelati," I say. *"Banana e pistacchio."*

The clerk yells my order to the kid scooping the gelato.

I tap my foot, waiting for the gelato, and bring them to the table after they serve me.

"Thank you, Daddy!" Amara shimmies in her chair when I set the bowl in front of her.

As soon as I take a seat, Damien leans toward me. "We need to talk tonight."

I practice Italian with Amara, read her two bedtime stories, and tell her doll good night three times before tucking her in. The moon is full when I walk onto the terrace where Damien is nursing a vodka soda.

He slides a full glass across the table to me when I sit. "You're gambling with death, Antonio."

I play with the glass in my hand. "The fuck are you talking about?"

"You know exactly *who* I'm talking about." He runs his hand through his short hair.

"No, I fucking don't."

"Where are you going at night then?"

"To fuck hookers."

"Bullshit." Damien is the only man who dares to speak to me like this. "You've never been a hooker fan." His voice drops. "You're sneaking around with Marchetti's daughter."

"You don't know what you're talking about."

"I didn't know you had me track Gigi here so you could see her yourself for pleasure. I thought it was to have something over Cristian's head."

I stay quiet, running my finger along the rim of the glass. "It's over now. Too complicated." I knock back my drink.

He furiously shakes his head. "It's not over."

Silence takes over the air.

"She'll be your weakness."

"Amara is my only weakness."

"You're right. Gigi isn't your weakness. She's your death wish."

I wasn't as sly as I'd hoped on my mission to hunt down Gigi. Unbeknownst to Damien, in the beginning, he helped me. I'd told him to find the pilot who flew to Italy that day. He did.

Cristian might've paid a hefty sum for the pilot to keep his mouth shut, but blackmail always trumps money. All we had to do was show him a picture of him ass-fucking the nanny, and he provided every detail we wanted. Then it took me another twenty grand to bribe people to find where Gigi was staying and where her aunt lives.

I set my glass down. "I'm going for a drive."

"Any woman," he mutters. "You could have any woman you want, *but one*. And you chose her."

I fucked up with Gigi.

Last night, I spent the drive to her cottage arguing with my father over his frustration about my *little field trip*, then Vinny, then a deal gone wrong. I eventually hung up on him. When I walked into Gigi's, I anticipated reprieve from the chaos. Instead, she wanted to talk about the source of it. Frustrated, I treated her like one of the lowlifes I deal with on a daily basis.

I hide outside her cottage while waiting for everyone to go to bed.

For two hours.

Fucking stalker-style, just as she said.

Giana Marchetti is a habit I can't shake.

Is it because she's forbidden?

I told her I wouldn't come back if she kicked me out. As the Lombardi most known for keeping his word, I failed.

Last night, I saw a different side of Gigi.

Like me, this woman I've grown obsessed with has a ruthless side.

I can't wait to bring out more darkness inside her. Anyone with Marchetti blood inside them can't survive without the wickedness of it. She's witnessed her father, her brother, and I'm sure every man in her life do horrific shit. It was bound to rub off on her.

As soon as Bruno's light shuts off, I walk to Gigi's door.

I'm choosing her over death.

My Grim Reaper has black hair, an ass to die for, and a heart I want to rip apart.

Her door is locked.

Too bad my little pain in the ass doesn't know locks never stop me.

Bank vaults. Security alarms. Cryptocurrency mines.

All simple to break into if you know what you're doing.

I can pick a locked door in my sleep.

I grin when the door clicks open.

Surprise, princess.

10

GIGI

"I knew you'd come back." I flip on the nightstand lamp while in bed when Antonio appears in my bedroom doorway.

Okay, I was eighty percent sure he'd return tonight.

He casually slips his hands inside his pockets and leans against the doorframe, unfazed by me calling him out.

"Now, get out." I point toward the hallway.

He dismisses what I said with a scoff.

"News flash, Lombardi: I'm not a girl you can use for fun."

"How exactly did I use you, princess?"

I mock his scoff. "Uh, I don't know; maybe the blow job or vagina licking."

He stares at me, amused. "I can't believe I ate the pussy of a woman who refers to it as vagina licking."

"And I can't believe I let a man like you near my vagina."

"You can't honestly think I traveled all this way for a blow job or to eat your pussy, which, I'd like to point out, I already had a taste of before coming here." He strolls into my room as if it belongs to him and I'm the unwanted visitor. "I could've done any of those things in the comfort of New York, saving myself time and all the damn headaches you continue to give me."

"Men do plenty for sex."

"I want to fuck you, princess. You're correct about that. I rarely waste my time pursuing women, yet here I am, visiting your cottage every night." He lowers his head to mine. "You see, Giana, it's so much more than that."

My voice shakes. "If you're not here to fuck me, then what are you here for?"

"I'll answer that when I know."

He said those same words at the masquerade ball.

He brushes his lips against mine. It's gentle, so unlike him. I open my mouth, accepting his unclear answer because it's so Antonio.

A man whose actions speak more than words.

With our mouths still connected, he moves to the edge of my bed, unbuttons his shirt, and lets it slip off, revealing his toned six-pack.

Antonio is a killer, a man who tortures others.

However, he's also the most beautiful man I've ever seen.

My villain gives me butterflies.

Butterflies I know he'll destroy later, but, hey, butterflies are pretty in the beginning, right?

He lifts the blanket, exposing me in my nightie. The cool breeze sweeps over my skin and leaves goose bumps in its path.

"Like you said, you knew I'd be back, yet you didn't sleep anywhere else or ask Bruno to sleep here for protection from me." He straddles me, his weight heavy on my body. "Because you, Gigi Marchetti, like it when I touch you, use you, whether or not you want to admit it." His sinful eyes sharpen on mine. "If your mouth won't admit it, how about we let your body speak for itself, then?"

"I can't sleep with you, Antonio. I'm saving myself for my husband when that day comes."

"It's funny you still believe another will ever have you." He runs his thumb along my chin. "I've come between your legs, pushed my cum inside you, so I own you."

I moan when he slips his hand beneath my nightie, drags my

panties down my legs, and tosses them across the room. He freezes when I slam my legs shut and pays me a curious glance.

"Tell me a secret."

"Excuse me?"

I chew on my lower lip. "Tell me a secret."

He digs his fingers into my thigh. "I'm not one for pillow talk."

"You want me? Tell me a secret."

"You don't think I could force your legs apart right now and fuck you?"

"You could, but you're not a rapist." I've heard plenty of rumors about him, yet not one of sexual assault. "Now, tell me something no one knows." I drop my hand to his, which is underneath my nightie, wrap my fingers around his wrist, and hold it still.

He can overpower me, like he said. It's a risk I'll take.

His face clouds with frustration as he peers down at our hands. "I don't respond well to ultimatums."

I ease my legs open a few inches and guide our hands between them along my folds. Even though I try, I can't choke back my groans.

Antonio's jaw clenches, making it clear he wants to rip me apart. "If I tell you something, I get to hold you down, tie you up, do whatever the fuck I want to do with you."

"One secret. One touch."

"Fuck off," he snarls, shoving my hand off as if it suddenly bit him. "If I entertain your game, I want more than a simple touch."

"Fine." I'm testing him, but I still desperately want him. "One secret. You can do whatever you want for five seconds." I hold up a finger and stare at him seriously. "No sex. I won't give you that."

"My secret is that I'm seriously considering sticking my cock inside you, consent or not. To see how well you can take it." He roughly presses my legs farther apart.

I squeeze my legs together again. "Nice try, but that doesn't qualify."

His face is untrusting as his Adam's apple bobs.

A hush falls over the room.

Antonio doesn't possess that type of relationship with me.

He doesn't with anyone.

Sharing secrets is seen as a weakness and stigmatized in our world.

He rears back, and I'm positive he's leaving. But he doesn't.

"I dread the day my brother succeeds the family." His voice is low—so low—and controlled. He speaks precisely, with every word carefully chosen.

Then he immediately parts my legs and jams two fingers inside me.

I close my eyes as he strokes me. "Is that because you want to take over?"

He works his fingers in and out of me, and even with my eyes closed, I can feel his gaze on my face. "No, but the day he does, our entire family is fucked."

"Everyone says you'd make a better boss anyway."

"No need to stroke my ego, princess. I already plan to eat your pussy."

He's surpassed his five-seconds limit.

Not that I'm complaining.

I squirm beneath him. "I'm not stroking anything of yours again."

"Lies, Giana. *Fucking lies.*"

I tremble, hating how he's right.

It's only because I want experience.

Not because I want every part of him he'll offer.

Not because I want him to want me like he's never wanted anyone.

"Now, my turn." He rotates his fingers, stretching me, and I scrunch my face as pain shoots through me.

I inhale a deep breath and exhale when he adds another finger.

I grew up in a world of pain. It's only natural that I enjoy it too.

"On a scale from one to ten, how much are you lying about not wanting me to fuck you?"

I'm surprised I can speak as his fingers move faster. "You decided the subject of your secret. It's only fair that I do the same."

"It'd better be a good one if you don't want me half-ass eating your pussy."

I highly doubt Antonio has ever half-assed eating pussy.

He doesn't half-ass anything.

My eyes shoot open when he rams a fourth fucking finger inside me.

I gulp. "I'm scared I'll always be alone—a Mafia princess forever stuck in her castle, who will never find true love."

He smirks, as if my secret invigorates him, and slides my legs over the sheets to position himself between them while skillfully keeping his fingers inside me.

I shamelessly widen them to provide him more room.

He lowers his head to where I want but then lifts to lock gazes with me. "I don't want you to ever find true love, princess, because any other man who tries to rescue you from your castle will die at my hands."

He doesn't wait for a response. Instead, he slides his tongue down my slit, bites a fold, and jerks his head to the side like he wants to rip me open. Then he pleasures me. Even though he's only touched me a few nights, it's like he knows exactly what turns me on and how to meet my needs.

I make him stop periodically to tell me secrets. It's not every five seconds though. He does the same, but his timing is always right before my orgasm.

"I dreamed about killing a man for holding the door open

for you and staring at your ass," he tells me through gritted teeth.

"I've never shared a bed with anyone."

"My favorite drink is cognac in the winter and whiskey in the summer."

"I've thought of you while touching myself."

"I forced Vinny to ask Natalia about your favorite body wash so I could smell it as I jerked off in the shower."

"I shouldn't want you like this." My body is on fire, feeling higher and higher, and I never want to come down.

Minutes pass before he comes up for air, still fingering me, and says, "I fucking hate you for making me want you like this. You deserve for me to torture you just for that."

He plays with me until I fall apart. As my body trembles, he pins it to the bed while working his way up my body until his waist is above my face. I gulp right before he feeds me his cock.

"This mouth is mine." He slides his cock inside it again. "For the rest of our fucking lives. You'll never pleasure another man with it."

He viciously fucks my mouth.

"Don't you dare swallow," he says as he comes in my mouth. With his hand still around my throat, he jerks me up. "Show me."

I hold out my tongue, and he groans.

"Now, swallow it little by little."

I gag a few times while obeying.

Antonio isn't gentle with me.

He treats me like a rag doll in bed rather than a princess.

It finally makes sense why princesses in the stories run away for normal lives.

Okay, not to be face-fucked, but for the freedom to choose their husbands.

To have a lover who isn't afraid to break them or taint them.

But unlike the fairy tales, my story with Antonio won't end happily ever after.

He'll never love me.

He damn sure will never be my husband.

His world is filled with pure chaos, where evil produces evil, and love is a term they merely mock.

Love doesn't exist for a mobster.

All that exists for him is tragedy.

11

ANTONIO

"How was Italy with Gigi Marchetti?" Vinny asks me.

I glance around and clench my fist, contemplating smashing it through his ugly-ass face. We just ended a family meeting at the casino. Men with listening ears are everywhere.

I don't bother looking back as I turn and speed-walk down the hall with Vinny trailing me. "What the fuck are you talking about?"

"Oh, come on." He laughs. "Natalia said Gigi was in Italy. You randomly went there, your first vacation ever. It was easy to put two and two together."

I ignore the rain while leaving the building. "Did Gigi tell Natalia something?"

"Hell no." Vinny brushes away the raindrops pelting him in the face. "When I asked, she claimed she had no idea. Gigi usually keeps her in the dark." He ups his pace to slap me on the back. "Don't worry. I'm the only one who knows, and I'd never throw you under the bus."

I huff and slip into my car.

Vinny jumps into the passenger seat.

I start the engine and turn on the windshield wipers.

"Speaking of Natalia, you need to end shit with her before Father finds out. It's a bad idea."

"You're the last person to decide what's a bad idea." He coughs into his bruised hand. "Marchetti." He coughs again, more dramatically this time, like the little bitch he is.

I ignore him and slam my foot on the gas.

"Hey, man, I get it." He leans back and buckles his seat belt before lowering his voice, as if someone were hiding in the car. "On a serious note, we need to do something about Sonny."

"Please clarify what you mean by do something."

"I was made aware that he's talking to men privately, doubting my ability to lead the family once Father dies."

"No one should have one conversation about Father dying. He's perfectly healthy." I tighten my grip on the steering wheel.

I don't trust Sonny either and can see him scheming, thinking the throne belongs to him after my father's death. I've even considered using my knowledge of his shellfish allergy to my advantage and slipping seafood into his favorite lasagna to kill the motherfucker. We can't accuse him of shit without evidence, and we damn sure can't kill him without my father's permission.

"Come on, Antonio," Vinny groans. "Everyone knows Father is getting too old."

"He's of sound mind."

Fuck Vinny for even questioning him.

I want to punch him in the face just for that.

"For how long? What are we on now? Stroke number two?" He holds up three fingers. "Or is it three?"

"Sonny won't do shit," I assure him. "He's not stupid."

At least while our father is still alive.

If worse comes to worst, I'll kill him myself if I have to and deal with the consequences.

We might share blood, but blood is easy to drain from someone.

TWO MONTHS LATER

The next time I see Gigi again is at a local festival.

I'm sitting at a picnic table when I spot her walking with Natalia and Bruno. As I watch her, the temptation to follow them is strong. Amara is with me, so I can't. I'll have to wait until later to drag Gigi away.

Amara swings her legs back and forth while shoving a snow cone in my direction. "You want some, Daddy?" Blue juice drips down her chin.

"All yours, sweetheart." I pull a napkin from the holder and lean across the table to wipe her chin, only for more to drop moments later.

When she finishes her snow cone, I clean off her face again. Then Clara, Damien, and I hang around the festival for another hour before heading toward the exit. People step to the other side of the pathway when they see me. A few nod their heads respectfully while others avoid eye contact.

"I just love our friendship bracelets," Amara says, proudly holding up her arm to show off the new bracelet hanging from her wrist.

Earlier, we stopped at a small vendor's tent selling beaded bracelets, and Amara chose one for all of us.

Her beads spell out *Best Daughter Ever*.

Mine says *Girl Dad*.

Clara's is *Pretty Grandma*.

And she giggled up a storm while handing Damien his, which spelled out *Coolest Dude Ever*.

I lift our clasped hands to show mine off. "I think it's my favorite piece of jewelry."

She stares innocently from my bracelet to the Rolex above it. "More favorite than your watch?"

"Ten times more favorite."

She nearly loses her footing when stopping beside a trash can. "How about you throw away your watch? That way, the bracelet will be the only thing on your wrist."

Damien snorts behind me while carrying the goldfish Amara won in a game.

Leave it to my daughter to call my fucking bluff. As much as I love her, she just requested I toss a fifty-thousand-dollar watch in the grimy-ass trash can.

Amara stares at me in expectation.

I kneel to her level and switch my watch from one wrist to the other. "There. That better?"

"I want it to be your favorite bracelet, Daddy." She frowns, then grins moments later, showing off her missing front tooth. "Just like you're my favorite person ever, ever, ever."

"Amara," I say softly, "no matter what, you're always my favorite. There will never be anyone, any bracelet or watch, more my favorite than you." I kiss the top of her head and stand.

"Always, always?" she chirps.

I squeeze her hand. "Always, always."

Glancing back at Clara, I see her hands clasped to her chest as she offers me a heartfelt smile. Her new bracelet is also on her wrist, and her T-shirt says, *I'm a grandmother. What's your superpower?*

Thankfully, Amara's focus shifts from the watch to requesting I let her get a deep-fried Twinkie next time we come. Not fucking happening.

Her energy and questions are short-lived, and by the time we arrive at Damien's SUV in the parking lot, she's sleeping in my arms, her face buried in my shoulder. I'm careful not to wake her while buckling her in the backseat of Damien's GL 550.

"Drive them home and stay at the house," I instruct him while Clara climbs into the backseat next to Amara. "I'll find a ride home later."

"A problem I should know about?" He raises a brow.

"No, I just saw someone I need to speak with."

He stares at me skeptically but doesn't ask any more questions.

After they drive off, I return to the festival in search of Gigi. She's sipping a frozen lemonade when I find her. I maintain a safe distance while following them, waiting for the perfect opportunity. It comes when Natalia and she walk into the women's restroom, and Bruno enters the men's.

All eyes turn to me when I step into the restroom. I stand at the door, trying not to appear creepy or intimidating, but honestly, any man in the women's restroom looks like a fucking creep. Thank fuck it only takes Gigi a second to realize I'm there for her.

She beelines toward me with Natalia on her heels. I grab her hand and drag her outside to behind the building.

"Tell Bruno that Gigi needs a tampon and to walk you to the car," I direct Natalia, not bothering to release Gigi.

"He'll want me to go with them," Gigi argues, fighting my hold.

I shoot her an annoyed look. "Not if she tells him you're bleeding every-goddamn-where."

Natalia shifts from one foot to the other in unease. "Will she, uh … be bleeding if I leave?"

"No, I won't make her bleed." I clench my jaw.

"It's fine," Gigi tells Natalia. "Just give us a minute. There are tampons in the backseat of Bruno's SUV. Grab them, and I'll meet you back inside the restroom."

"Scream if you need help," Natalia nervously says.

The fact that she's scared of me but fucks my brother is laughable. If the roles were reversed and it was Vinny pulling her from the bathroom, he'd be less gentle about it. The poor girl will find that out sooner or later.

Gigi frees herself as soon as Natalia disappears around the building. "Antonio, what the fuck—"

I clamp my hand over her mouth, muzzling her words, and drag her into my chest. "Shut the fuck up."

The brat bites my fucking finger, so I roughly plant my fingers into her cheeks so deep that I feel her teeth through them.

"Keep your head down, or you'll regret it," I say, guiding her away from the restroom.

"That won't look suspicious or anything," she mutters beneath my hand.

I release her but don't say a word while leading her to the mirror maze house near the back of the festival. Earlier, Amara tried to go inside it. The attendant stopped her and said it was down.

My daughter wasn't happy about that.

I sure as fuck was because it helped create my plan to get Gigi alone.

So while Clara directed a disappointed Amara to another ride, I paid the attendant two hundred dollars not to allow anyone else entry. He told me okay and slipped the cash in his shirt pocket.

The attendant is still at the entrance when Gigi and I arrive. "All yours, man." As he lowers his phone, his attention slips to Gigi when he opens the door and ushers us inside.

I ignore Gigi's questions while navigating us through the maze until we reach what I consider the middle.

She gasps when I turn her around.

"Why the fuck haven't you called or texted?" I ask.

She glares at me, twisting her wrist as if it pains her. "Why haven't *you* called or texted?"

I snarl, but since we're on limited time that I don't want to waste arguing, I spin her around and press her against the mirrored wall. She doesn't put up a fight when I collect her wrists and pin them to each side of her.

Crowding behind her body, I press my chest against her. She

arches her back, whispering my name, and it's my favorite sound in the world.

Inching back, I bow my head to admire the view of her plump, perfect ass. My cock twitches when my gaze drifts to the mirror beside us, showcasing her from a different angle.

I could stare at this beautiful woman for the next eternity and never tire of the view.

She stares back at me, waiting for my next move.

My princess, letting her villain take control.

My hand nearly feels on fire when I palm her bare ass, gripping it tight, as if it's my most-prized possession. She moans as I play with her thong string stuck between her ass cheeks. I twist it around two fingers, and it snaps when I jerk her backward.

Fuck, I've missed her.

I can't wait to touch her pussy.

Slapping her ass, I relish the sound of the impact and watch it bounce. She gasps, so I do it again, harder this time. My goal is to make her feel the sting of my hand all night. The cheap fluorescent lights above us are so bright that it's easy to make out my handprint on her skin.

Yes, bruise for me, baby.

Let me mark you in ownership.

I flex my fingers before slipping them between her legs. They tremble as I caress her clit. I wickedly grin when I find her pussy soaked.

Resting my chin on her shoulder, I suck on her earlobe and whisper, "You're always so drenched for me, princess."

She grinds her ass against my erection and moans.

"I bet your pussy gets wet just thinking about me, doesn't it?"

She peers back at me. "We need to hurry, Antonio. Bruno will get suspicious the longer I take *in the restroom.*"

Ah, yes. Thanks for the reminder of our little bodyguard problem.

It's her fault we can't take long, so she needs to suffer for not finding a better way to ditch Bruno. I lick down her neck, separating her legs with my knee to provide a better angle to pleasure her. I don't waste a second before shoving nearly my entire hand inside her.

She groans at my lack of gentleness, and her knees weaken. As I finger-fuck her, I work on unbuckling my belt with my free hand. I'm so worked up that my hands slightly shake.

I consider myself a very skilled man, but this is a challenge.

To fix that, I kneel, bury my face between Gigi's legs, and eat her pussy while unfastening my belt.

Her pussy smells like heaven.

Tastes so damn sweet.

I want to fill it with my cock so she tastes like me.

Like us.

My depravity mixed with her pureness.

I'm a starved man, a fiend for her.

She shudders, nearly falling to her knees, and I steady her while placing a single kiss on her pussy before standing. Shoving my pants and briefs to my ankles, I free my cock. It's hard and throbbing.

She's panting when she turns and stares down at me. There's a nervousness on her face when she lowers her eyes to watch me stroke myself. All the other times we've been together, it's either been dark outside or in the dim cottage. Neither of us has been on display like this before.

My insides tighten. I want to fuck her.

God, how I want to fuck this woman.

She isn't ready though.

I'll respect her saving herself for her husband since that man will eventually be me. I'm also not fucking her for the first time here and when we're in a hurry. When I fuck Gigi for the first time, I don't want it rushed, so I can relish every second I'm inside her.

But right now, I'll take everything I can get from her.

I remove my blazer, spread it along the floor, and roll my

sleeves to my elbows. "Get on your hands and knees and feed me your pussy."

She scrunches her face. "You know that floor is filthy, right?"

I lie across the blazer, knowing she's right, but at this point, I don't care. "I dare you to get a little filthy with me, princess."

I love that she doesn't second-guess herself before walking toward me.

My good girl.

Always listening when it comes to me pleasuring her.

I lie on my back, drop my pants further, and prop myself on my elbows. "Your pussy over my face."

Her steps are slow as she comes closer. I help guide her to her knees as she settles herself and then push up her skirt. When she doesn't stick her pussy close enough to my face, I drag her down more.

Her pussy is wet, glistening, begging for me to pleasure it.

"Stick my dick in your mouth while I eat this pussy, princess," I instruct her.

When she hesitates, I thrust my hips forward. I feel her breath on my cock, her lips brushing along the tip, but no longer care if she sucks me or not.

I grip her ass cheeks, digging my fingers into them as I level her thighs with my face and eat her pussy like a man who doesn't know when he'll get his favorite meal again.

Because that's our reality. I never know when we'll see each other again—or *if* we'll see each other. It's always a game of sneaking around, and I fucking hate it.

She's so wrapped up in my mouth between her legs that she doesn't even attempt to suck my cock.

Her gasps set me on fire. Every nerve in my body tingles.

It's always like this with Gigi.

I can't even imagine the high I'll get when I finally fuck her.

… and I will fuck her.

My cock aches with need, and I want to shove it down her

throat. With the way she's falling apart above me, no way can I stop though. It'd be a fucking crime to.

Her breathing is frantic, and every muscle in her body tightens at once. I rearrange us, raising her hips, and thrust my fingers inside her pussy—adding to her ecstasy while still feasting on her.

As she comes, I suck on the sensitive skin of her thigh before burying myself in her pussy and licking up her wetness. She collapses on my face and catches her breath.

I smack her ass before grabbing her hair in my fist. "Suck me, princess, and then I want you to swallow every drop of my cum."

Her pace starts slow. I fall on my back and enjoy her mouth. It's wet and hot and perfect.

My blood pressure rises. I hold her ass down, and she struggles to breathe as I fuck her face, feeding her every inch of my cock. Her jaw is more relaxed than it was in Italy. She's getting comfortable with me.

"Look up, princess," I say. "Eyes on the mirror, so you can watch yourself suck this cock."

She moans and holds herself up with her palms, and I love that she can see herself deep-throating my dick.

"I'm so close," I pant.

My stomach muscles clench when I release in her mouth.

"Take it all, princess," I say. "I can't hold your mouth open, so you'd better make sure that a drop of cum doesn't go anywhere but that sweet mouth that sucks me so good."

She shivers at my praise.

When I'm certain she's sucked every drop from my cock, she slides her knees along my blazer. I hold her wrist to help her up before bringing myself to my feet. I lick my lips, savoring the taste of her, and adjust her skirt back into place.

"Leave with me." My request shocks us both.

I see the temptation on her face, but she shakes her head.

"I wish," she says in a low tone before biting her lip and

smoothing a hand over her shirt. "We've already been gone long enough. Bruno will for sure know something is up when he sees me like this."

She's right.

Gigi looks like she's been thoroughly fucked—albeit face-fucked, but still.

Her hair is messy, her face hot, her skin red, and her makeup smudged.

I pull up my pants, and while buckling them, I press my lips to hers, hoping it'll help put her at ease. If Bruno catches us, then he catches us. If Cristian finds out, then he does. Even though it'd be bad timing since I'm dealing with Vinny's shit, I'd never make her face the repercussions of being with me alone.

"If he gives you trouble, call me," I tell her.

She runs her hand along my arm and kisses me and pulls back when her Apple watch beeps.

"A text from Natalia. She said I'd better get my ass back to the restroom before Bruno calls my father."

Her watch beeps again.

"I have to go," she rushes out.

"I'll call you tonight. Keep your burner close." I kiss the top of her head.

We hold hands as I walk her out of the mirror maze, and when we go our separate ways, I hate the harsh truth that hits me. Gigi is taking me over, and it'll be the fight of my life making her mine.

12

GIGI

"Leave with me."

I replay Antonio's words in my mind on my walk back to the restroom. Bruno asks me what the fuck I was up to, and I refuse to answer him. Natalia shoots me a nervous look.

I feel bad putting her in that position.

Well, technically, it was Antonio who did, but I could've stopped him.

I just didn't want to.

His words stay with me for the rest of the night.

What would've happened if I had left with him?

If we ran off for the day, a week, the rest of our lives?

I scoff at how unrealistic that is.

My father would tear the entire continent apart to find me.

I hate that my relationship with Antonio, or whatever the hell it is, is cloaked in secrecy. I fear it always will be.

Billie Eilish's "Everything I Wanted" plays in the background, and over a dozen lit candles surround me while I take a bath.

I grab the burner perched on the tub's edge when it beeps with a text.

> Villain: How are you feeling?

I can't help but smile as I reply.
He's checking up on me.
I feel like a giddy girl whose crush spoke to her for the first time.
Ew. So not fitting in with your Mafia princess reputation, Gigi.
The phone beeps again.

> Villain: Thank you for getting dirty for me, princess.

I hit the Reply button.

> Me: You're very welcome for sitting on your face.

> Villain: I'm open to you doing that anytime you want.

> Me: I might have to take you up on that offer.

My eyes widen as I hit Send.
Are we ... sexting?

> Villain: You'd fucking better.

My blood hums in my veins, excitement flooding me.
This is kind of fun.
So I up the ante. I hold up the phone and snap a picture of me naked in the tub—my face not in view, of course. I've heard enough horror stories of revenge porn.
The phone rings not even ten seconds later.
My cheeks warm, and I nearly drop the phone in the water.
I clear my voice before answering, "Hello?"
"Princess," he groans. "I'm making you pay for that picture."
"Why?" I whisper.

"Because I want to drive my car to the mansion and drag you out of the bathtub to take you home with me."

I rub my thighs together. "What would you do once you had me?"

"I'd put you in my bed and fuck you until our bodies could no longer move."

"Antonio." I sigh.

"Gigi." His voice is gentler this time. "You have no idea how bad I want to make you mine."

I've rarely had gentle Antonio. Even though I enjoy the lunatic side of him, I also find comfort in his softness too. It's like receiving a tight hug after a nightmare from the very monster who haunts you.

"Even saying that is crazy," I say.

"You already know I'm fucking crazy, princess."

I gulp in nervousness. "What do you want from me, Antonio?" I shut my eyes, already fearing the answer. He's made it clear he wants me, but does wanting someone also mean loving them?

I want Antonio, and I know he wants me. I just don't know if he's capable of giving me everything I want.

Love. Affection. A man who wants me and only me.

I want the fucking fairy tale, dammit.

"I want to own you," he says.

"What if I want to own you?" I whisper.

"Princess—" He stops, and I hear voices interrupting him from continuing. His voice trails off, as if he's moved the phone to prevent me from hearing their conversation.

His voice is irritated when he returns to our call. "I need to go."

"Okay," I say softly.

"Plan another trip to Italy."

"Okay."

"And, Gigi?"

"Yeah?"

"You're already starting to own me."

"We need to talk," my father says as I sit beside him at the dining room table for breakfast. The sharpness in his tone tells me that Bruno was a little snitch.

I'll return the favor and tell side-chick number two that he has a live-in girlfriend.

"About what?" I arrange my napkin in my lap to distract myself from glancing at him or Benny across from me.

"Bruno said you ran off somewhere at the festival." He holds up his hand. "And don't try to feed me a story that you were hanging out in the restroom for nearly *a fucking hour*."

"I started my period and needed a tampon." I reach across the table and select a blueberry muffin from the bowl.

"We're not fucking stupid, Gigi," Benny scolds. "You're randomly disappearing. Spending time in public restrooms like they're holding a fucking yoga class. You're up to something."

"I'm not up to anything." I roll a muffin crumb between my fingers. "Sorry for attempting to have some privacy. I'm tired of always having a bodyguard up my ass."

Usually, my father will never tolerate someone speaking to him as I just did.

Not even Benny is allowed that level of disrespect toward him.

"You want to know what I'm tired of?" My father seethes, slamming his fist on the table. "You sneaking around like there isn't a permanent target on your goddamn back."

"I'm not sneaking around." I push a muffin bite into my mouth to swallow down my dishonesty.

"Don't look at me and lie. It's insulting." He turns his head to the side, and I gulp at the sound of his neck popping. Leaning in, he plants his elbows on the table and laces his fingers together. "Now, tell me a name. The longer you take, the longer I'll torture him."

"There is no one." I stupidly gesture toward Benny. "Why does he get to sleep with whoever he wants, but Lord forbid I do anything." I slap a hand over my mouth, appearing guiltier than I intended.

"Does that fucking mean you're sleeping with—" Benny starts.

My father raises his hand, cutting him off the same way he did me.

He stares at me with hostility. "Tell me what you're up to, Gigi, and I mean, *now*."

"Nothing." I throw my muffin at Benny, and he catches it before it whacks him in the face. It's a juvenile move, but I'm pissed. "I'm just … frustrated."

"Frustrated with what?"

"Do you expect me to sit here and never have a life? A boyfriend? A husband? A family of my own?"

"I don't expect that from you, no."

"What if I'm ready to explore my options then?"

His serious demeanor turns into amusement. He's about to mindfuck me, like he does everyone else. "Do you have someone in mind?"

"Why would I tell you? You'll kill him."

His failure to answer confirms my statement.

"Do you want me to stay miserable forever?" I take a sip of orange juice to soothe my burning throat.

"I didn't know you were miserable."

"I have no friends—"

"You have Natalia," he interrupts.

"Sure, but you limit my time with her."

"That's because her boyfriend is a fucking moron," Benny says.

My father isn't concerned with Natalia's love life, so he doesn't acknowledge Benny's comment, which is a plus for me. If he finds out she's dating Vinny, he'll for sure forbid me from spending time with her.

He relaxes in his chair, his elbows leaving the table. "As much as I want you to have your freedom, I care about you staying alive more. If there's someone you'd consider marrying, provide a name for me."

My father must really think I lack intelligence.

Whoever's name I provide will be dead by the end of the day.

"What if I want to date around before choosing a husband?" I ask.

Benny scoffs and runs his hand over his scruffy cheek.

"Dating around is ridiculous," my father argues. "No one does that."

I frown. "Literally everyone does."

"You're not *literally everyone*," Benny says. "You're Cristian Marchetti's daughter. That changes shit."

Before my father has a chance to add his input, his phone rings.

He pulls it from his pocket, stands from his chair, and checks the caller. "I need to take this." He points his phone in my direction. "Be smart, Gigi. Or you'll have ten bodyguards *up your ass.*"

I shift in my chair to look at him. "What about me going back to Italy?"

"Done." He peers at the ringing phone. "Pack your bags."

"You suck," I whine to Natalia over the phone. "We need one last shopping trip before I leave."

"Trust me, I'd love to shop, but I have to work," she replies. "My boss is already pissed and on the verge of firing me because Vinny won't stop coming to the gallery, causing problems."

"You know what my answer to that problem always is."

She sighs. "I plan to break things off. I just need to figure out how."

As much as I want to talk to Antonio about it again, the last time didn't go too well. If Natalia's life is at stake, I won't hesitate to involve Benny or my father though.

"I have to go," she says with a groan. "Have fun in Italy, and make sure to text, call, and FaceTime."

"You know I will."

After showering, I towel-dry my hair while moving from my en suite bathroom to my bedroom.

Soft, warm light spills from my nightstand lamp, casting a gentle glow in the room. I climb into bed and lounge with my back against the headboard.

The ambiance of my bedroom always relaxes me. The shag rug, pillow-soft bedding, and dark purple color scheme provide comfort while the hand-crafted Italian furniture and sparkling chandelier above me add a touch of luxury.

I turn my TV on to drown out my voice from my bedroom before calling Antonio.

"I'm leaving for Italy tomorrow," I tell him when he answers.

"For how long?"

"I haven't booked a return flight yet." I prop the phone between my ear and shoulder while freeing my hair from the towel. "It depends on how long it takes you to get there."

The line falls quiet for a moment.

"It might take me a few weeks."

I frown, and this time, it's my silence.

"My situation is more complicated," he says, as if reading my mind. "Traveling across the world is harder for me."

I nod and twirl a strand of wet hair between my fingers. As

someone unemployed with no responsibilities, it's easy for me to leave anytime I want. It isn't the same for Cosa Nostra men. My father and Benny only travel when it's business-related. Vacations aren't in the cards for them.

"I know." I blow out a breath and comb my fingers through my hair. "It just sucks."

He grows quiet again, and there's an audible commotion in the background.

"Where are you?" I ask.

He seems taken aback by my sudden question. "Sitting in my car."

Antonio always talks to me at night, in his car, so that isn't unusual.

"Where at?"

"The casino parking lot."

"How was your day?"

"Shitty."

"What happened?"

He chuckles. "Trust me, you don't want that story time."

"I hate that you can't tell me things," I grumble.

"How about you tell me about your day instead?"

"I'm sure mine will sound terribly boring compared to yours."

"Amuse me, princess."

"I went shopping."

After Natalia said she couldn't shop, I invited Aunt Helena and Aunt Celine. They're always up for a shopping trip.

"What'd you buy?"

"Lingerie." I brush my legs against the soft sheets. "I'll show you when you get to Italy."

He chuckles again.

Two chuckles in one conversation is a record for him.

His chuckles are never upbeat though.

They're tired and rigid. I'm learning that's who Antonio is.

"Call me later and describe it to me," he says. "I want to know what it looks like on you."

"I need to call you later to tell you this?" I switch the phone from one ear to the other.

"Yes, because I want to be home so I can jerk off to the image of it and your voice." His response sends goose bumps prickling along my skin.

"You'll see it in Italy." I lower my voice while sinking my toes into the sheets. "It'll give you more incentive to come."

"If you're going to Italy, that's the only incentive I need." His voice turns darker. "Prepare yourself."

I gulp. "Prepare myself for what?"

"For me to pleasure you so good that I ruin you for any other man."

"What if I want to ruin you for all other women?" I whisper.

"Ruin me away, princess."

13

ANTONIO

Vinny never comes to my home, so that's the first sign I know he fucked up.

The sweat on his face and shirt and his puffy and bloodshot eyes are the second. I've pepper-sprayed enough men to know that's what happened to him.

"I fucked up, Antonio." He paces in front of my desk in short steps.

I drop my pen, pick it back up, and clutch it between my fingers. I picture it's Vinny's neck since I know whatever he's about to say will make me want to wring it.

My gaze sharpens on him. "What did you do?"

He stops to pinch the bridge of his throat as if guiding the words out. "I killed one of Marchetti's men."

I wait—I fucking pray—for him to tell me he's kidding.

That he isn't that fucking stupid.

He doesn't.

He lifts his chin and lingers, waiting for me to offer a solution.

I throw my pen on the desk. "Did he try to kill you first?"

Vinny flares his nostrils. "*Technically,* you could say he threatened me."

I clench my fist, wishing I could knock him the fuck out.

"Natalia broke up with me, and I lost my shit. You know how bad my temper is."

When he rubs his eyes with fisted hands, I smile in satisfaction, knowing he's only worsening the irritation. I want the pepper spray to burn into his pupils, eat them away, and blind him—a punishment for his stupidity.

"She ran to Cristian," he yells when I fail to reply.

"Does that surprise you?" I stand while struggling to keep my voice low since Amara is here. "I'm sure that's the first place she went." I massage my temples. "Were there any witnesses?"

He scrubs a hand over his face.

"Does anyone know you killed him?" I grit out each word.

"Natalia," he says lowly.

"I could fucking kill you," I roar, unable to stop my fury from breaking free. My heartbeat is so erratic that I'm certain I'll suffer a heart attack. "You just declared war on the Marchettis."

I shove him, and he stumbles back into the bar cart. Liquor bottles shatter.

The motherfucker just broke the pact we share with the other families, granting us a death wish against the city's deadliest family.

He grabs an unbroken bottle of whiskey from the bar cart and twists off the cap. "Cristian took Natalia to dinner *publicly* to fuck with me." He rebuilds his defiance, and his loser attitude returns after he takes a swig of the whiskey. "I guarantee they're fucking and she's telling him all our secrets."

"Did you tell her our secrets?"

He shrugs, not answering like a petulant fucking child.

I guarantee the idiot doesn't remember what he shared with

her because he thought she'd never leave him, or if she attempted to, he planned to kill her before she had the opportunity to run her mouth.

Vinny's recklessness has gotten worse in the past few months. The more our father's health declines, the more he gloats about taking over the family. Being boss isn't all he wants. He wants to be king of New York, to beat out Cristian, and that's asking for nothing but trouble. And now, he's carried that problem straight to me.

"You can fix this, right?" he asks before taking another swig of whiskey. "Talk to Gigi since you two are close."

I wince at him saying Gigi's name. "Don't act like this isn't what you wanted all along. Your intentions have always been to take on Cristian with your *I want to be king* bullshit. You don't think word of that wouldn't get back to him? He's been waiting for you to fuck up." I snatch my blazer from the back of my chair and throw it on. "Congratulations. You started that war. Prepare for it. Now, come on."

He runs his hand down his wrinkled slacks. "Come on, where?"

"We need to tell our father what you did."

I instruct Vinny to follow me to the casino. Unsurprisingly, he bails. When we hit a main street, the coward speeds off, runs a red light, and makes a U-turn to drive in the opposite direction.

Unlike him, I won't sit around and wait for Cristian's retaliation.

I'll bail him out *again*.

"This stays between us," my father says, indicating the space between us with his finger after I tell him. "If your uncle or others find out about this, they'll further push the narrative that your brother is unfit to lead."

I stand, facing him at his desk, and tighten my jaw before gritting out, "Have you considered that maybe he is unfit to lead?"

His back straightens in his chair. He pretends to be more offended than he truly is. "He's my firstborn son."

"Firstborn doesn't mean fit to lead."

I'm so tired of the *firstborn* bullshit.

They should choose bosses based on merit, skill, and responsibility.

Not bloodline.

"Do you want to lead this family, Antonio?"

"No." I crack my knuckles. "But I also don't want to pay the price for his recklessness. Vinny's actions carry consequences not just for himself. They affect every person in our family, your men's families, and the Lombardi legacy."

My father busted his ass to restore our family's name, and Vinny will sabotage all his hard work.

He sweeps a hand over his wrinkled face. "My goal since I took over after my father was for this family to remain safe, respected, and not to lose nearly everything again. You're all my responsibility until the day I die."

"It's also your responsibility to leave the family in capable hands when you're gone."

"Find your brother," he says. "I need time to think alone."

I turn and storm out of his office. If my father doesn't start cutting Vinny out, there's a chance I'm close to being done with the family. There's too much at stake for me to lose.

My daughter. Clara. All the people I protect daily.

If Vinny takes over, I'll always choose them over a criminal enterprise destined for ruin.

Hell, destined for ruin now after what he just did.

I hold back my anger to punch every wall while leaving the casino. As I drive away, I keep a watchful eye on my rearview mirror. That'll become a new habit. I'll also put extra security on

Amara, and unfortunately for her, leaving the house will be limited.

Before returning home, I stop at a park to call Gigi. Her voice never fails to release the tension in my body. I'm also desperate for any information on the Vinny situation. I doubt Cristian has provided her with any details about Vinny's fuckup, but Natalia might have confided in her.

If Vinny is smart, he'll shoot Natalia in the head to silence her from telling Cristian anything.

Cristian doesn't provide security for anyone he doesn't care for or find as an asset. He also doesn't give two fucks that Natalia is Gigi's friend. All he cares about is that she has information on Vinny.

"Hey," Gigi answers with obvious wariness in her voice.

"Hey."

She doesn't waste a second before saying, "You need to control your crazy-ass brother."

"What do you mean?" It's a fucking insult to her to play stupid.

She scoffs as I step out of my car. "Don't act like he didn't come to you."

"Vinny keeps plenty of shit from me, Giana." I stroll through the park, ignoring a group of teenagers arguing over who did the most speed tonight, and drop a hundred in a home-less man's cup.

"He's harassing Natalia—"

"Your friend should've known that'd happen. You fucking warned her." I blow out a desperate breath. "Can you tell me anything?"

"No," she says sharply, almost offended I asked. "You know I can't."

I frown yet understand.

"You know my father always gets vengeance for his men. He wouldn't be the man he is if he didn't."

My throat goes tight, and I pull my phone away from my ear

when it vibrates to find my father calling through. "I have to go."

She ends the call.

Nothing else needs to be said.

We know Italy will never happen.

We also know our families are headed for war.

I send my father's call to voicemail and head toward my car. We need to swallow our pride and find a solution with Cristian. We can pay him or offer a percentage of the casino. Anything to avoid a war.

I wait to call my father back until I return to my car.

"Get to the casino," he demands.

When I get to the casino, Vinny's Mercedes is parked in the rear parking lot. He flashes his lights in my direction and waits until I step out before doing the same.

"Why'd you tell him without me?" He slams his car door shut.

"I told you, we were going to tell him. Did you think I wouldn't just because you pussied out?" I don't bother glancing back at him as he follows me or when I key in the casino's passcode to the back door and jerk it open. "You created this mess. Now, you need to fix it."

He trails me as I return to our father's office. I knock on the door with my knuckle and wait for him to yell, "You can enter," before stepping inside.

My father is still behind his desk. The only difference between then and now is that his Glock is positioned between his daily pill organizer and a half-empty glass of Jack and Coke. When he notices Vinny behind me, he picks up the Glock. I move out of the way when he lifts it and aims at Vinny.

"You have no idea how badly I want to shoot you right now."

My father shuts one eye to focus on him like a target. "To kill you, throw you in a ditch, and allow the maggots to eat your futile brain."

Too bad he won't pull the trigger.

My father is a menace who doesn't have enough guts to shoot his son … unfortunately.

Vinny raises his hands. "It was a mistake. A man pointed his gun at me, so on instinct, I shot first." He drops his arms when my father lowers the gun and returns it to his desk.

There's an urge to grab it and shoot Vinny myself.

"Cristian called me." My father glares at Vinny. "He knows you killed Dario."

"Dario," I repeat. "At least you didn't kill a high-ranking soldier."

"High ranking or not, he killed one of Marchetti's soldiers over a whore." He stares Vinny down and curls his lip. "I'm disgusted to call you a Lombardi."

I nod.

Vinny lifts his chin—a laughable tough-guy attempt. "Men kill for their women all the time."

"The bitch wasn't yours, Vinny," my father huffs.

Another nod in agreement. I feel like a fucking bobblehead.

"Now, I convinced Cristian to hand over the cunt for a *hefty price*, of course." My father jabs his meaty finger in Vinny's direction. "Which you'll reimburse me for. You can have the whore and do as you please."

"Wait." I draw in closer, finally speaking. "Cristian is giving you Natalia?"

If Gigi finds out Cristian handed her best friend over to Vinny, she'll never speak to him again. With Cristian's cunningness, I'm sure he'll cover his tracks and convince Gigi that all guilty fingers point to Vinny.

"We're meeting Cristian tonight." My father checks his watch. "Before then, you need to select a man for us to give to him in exchange for the one you killed."

"Wait," I repeat, clenching my jaw as I step closer. "One of our men has to die because of his mistake?"

"Yes." My father's face lines with displeasure. "I just ask you to select someone we don't find valuable."

I jerk my head toward Vinny. "Can I nominate him?"

"Funny, Antonio." Vinny forces a harsh laugh. "You know, you're beginning to sound like a traitor."

I refuse to take his deflection bait. "And you're beginning to sound like a fucking degenerate."

"Enough," my father yells, his voice slicing through our tension. "Make your decision, Vinny."

"Sacrificing one of our innocent men is reckless." Disputing his command is another sign of disrespect and puts me on slippery ground. I no longer care.

"None of our men are innocent," he fires back.

"They don't deserve to die for Vinny's carelessness."

We expect our men's loyalty. And now, my father wants us to betray that loyalty and hand over one for slaughter.

"Yeah." Vinny steps forward, his confidence building by the second. "I say we meet up with Marchetti and kill *him*."

Fuck. He is delusional.

The disgust is clear on my father's face. "This is the only"—he pounds his fist on the desk—"the *only* time I step in for you, Vinny. Don't fuck this up or do anything stupid moving forward. Make your selection."

Vinny nods in false understanding before sliding his attention to me. "Come on. I guess we have a decision to make."

I shake my head. "This is on you."

I'm not a good person.

It's not an attribute I wear as a badge of honor, but I have no problem acknowledging it. I murder, bribe, and engage in criminal activities like they're my salvation.

That doesn't mean there isn't guilt when we invite Paul to join us on a *special errand*. His face lights up like the fucking Fourth of July. He thinks he's receiving a promotion when we're sending him to his death.

At least Vinny chose well. Paul has fucked up twice, and he's bound to fuck up again and end up dead anyway. The difference is that it would've been for *his* fuckup. Not Vinny's.

Vinny squirms in the passenger seat as we drive. I ball up my fist, fighting the temptation to deliver a blow to the back of his head and tell him to calm the fuck down.

My jaw tenses so tight that I'm sure it'll fracture while my father parks his Lincoln in the back alley where he arranged to meet Cristian. We silently wait in the car until a black Escalade joins us.

We step outside, and Cristian and his *consigliere*, Rocky, emerge from the SUV. A burst of screams erupts from the backseat, and Rocky drags Natalia from it. She struggles to escape Rocky's hold as we walk toward Cristian.

Rocky being Cristian's right-hand man isn't surprising. The scarred fucker is a torture fan and as sadistic as they come. While we all do our fair share of torture, Rocky practically comes in his pants from it.

I watch Cristian's every move while Vinny focuses on Rocky restraining Natalia. The overhead light shining down the alley displays the strain on Vinny's face and the pronounced veins standing out on his neck.

My idiot brother loves Natalia.

That, or he can't stand seeing someone touch what he considers his property.

Rocky slaps his hand over Natalia's mouth to muffle her screaming.

Thank fuck.

It was grating on my nerves.

Like a loyal dog on a leash, Paul sticks by my side until Vinny pushes him toward Cristian.

"This the one?" Cristian stares at Paul cold and emotionless—as if Paul were just a face in the crowd, not someone he plans to murder.

"What does he mean?" Paul looks at each of us, seeking answers. "The one what?"

If he can't put two and two together, he deserves to die early anyway. Cristian removes a silenced pistol from his blazer and shoots Paul in the head. Paul recoils from the impact and collapses on the concrete beside a discarded McDonald's wrapper and a pile of cigarette butts.

Cristian played no mind games with Paul. Gave no small talk—just straight execution.

Natalia screams louder and fights harder against Rocky.

Like she'd ever stand a chance against him.

"Your son sure loves to run his mouth to the women he fucks," Cristian informs my father, now fully entertained. "Business with the Corobras—drug smugglers all of us agreed not to associate with since they lace their drugs with shit that is killing people in our city." He tsks. "The other families won't be happy about that."

My father flinches at Cristian's words.

I flex my fingers. Even though I say it frequently, I've never wanted to kill Vinny more. Cristian's accusations are worse than Vinny murdering Dario. Vinny has tarnished our family's loyalty.

We aren't doing shit with the Corobras—no business, no small talk, no fucking breathing in the same room. In our pact with the other families, it's forbidden. Not that I'd ever do business with them anyway. No thank you to fuckers who lace their drugs with fentanyl. Four of our men have overdosed within the past month.

My father grips his cane stronger. He won't publicly rip

Vinny's ass. No way will he show an ounce of emotion in front of Cristian.

Sometimes, the firstborn is also the first to die.

Hopefully, that's Vinny's fate because I'm sick of his shit—*especially* for doing business behind the family's back.

I creep closer to Vinny and nudge his elbow. "What the fuck?" Anger ripples up my spine like an added ligament.

Vinny doesn't reply. Natalia is his main concern.

Cristian continues his show. He snaps his fingers, and Rocky hands Natalia off to him as though she were a gift.

"The code to Vinny's safe is Natalia's birthday," Cristian says before rambling off all the other shit Vinny told Natalia that he shouldn't have.

Natalia is a snitch.

The little sympathy I had for her is gone.

I don't care if Vinny takes her, if Cristian shoots her, or if we throw her off a fucking roof.

Cristian turns to Vinny. "At your home in Brooklyn … Thirteenth Avenue, am I right?"

Unsurprisingly, Cristian has outmatched Vinny.

This meetup isn't to make a deal or hand over a rat.

It's to prove a point.

His plan to provoke Vinny is working perfectly.

We're fucked, and if Vinny doesn't keep his cool, we're fucked and dead.

"All this information has come from this one here." Cristian taps the gun against Natalia's temple. "Burly's Cleaners … through the back."

It's time I step in.

"You said fifty thousand dollars, Marchetti." I force myself to remain calm. "Hand over the girl, and this business is over."

Cristian shakes his head and presses the gun against Natalia's head. "I've changed my price."

"To what?" my father asks.

Cristian moves his gun from Natalia's head to aim it at Vinny. "Him."

"The fuck?" Vinny squares his shoulders and beelines toward Cristian.

I block Vinny's path, and to my relief, he doesn't put up a fight.

I point my gun at Cristian. "Cut the shit before I blow your head off, Marchetti."

"Do it." Cristian smirks when he sees my gun trained on him. "There are things I need to argue with my father about in the afterlife. Plus, my son would become a monster, avenging my death. My guess is, you'd lose at least half your men."

Cristian raises the stakes as four figures, each armed with an AK-47, step into our view—four of *Cristian's* men. Even if I take a shot at Cristian, we'll die.

"Marchetti, this is out of line," my father warns. "This isn't the way we conduct business."

"It is when your son kills one of my men," Cristian replies before wagging his finger at him. "That changes the rules." He keeps his gun aimed at Vinny while maintaining eye contact with my father. "I know it's extreme to tell another boss to sacrifice their son—"

"I'd die before I gave up my son." My father stabs his cane into the concrete. "If you came here thinking that would happen, you're crazy."

"Oh, what I just said is a sliver of what he told Natalia. He gave her so many secrets. I know where the guns … the cash is. Sweet Natalia, she told me so much, and I'll fuck more information out of her." Cristian slips his gun underneath Natalia's dress to between her legs, causing her entire body to shake.

"Vinny, Natalia will be in my bed night after night," Cristian continues because the antagonizing fucker doesn't know how to shut up. "And each time I spill my cum inside her, she'll tell me more about your small dick and moan out all your secrets."

"You motherfucker!" Vinny charges toward Cristian.

I stop him again, but this time, it takes my father's help.

Cristian stands there, gloating, loving every minute of Vinny's tantrum.

My brother and Natalia are the only ones who aren't controlling their emotions. We have to restrain Vinny tighter when Cristian dips his head and kisses Natalia's neck.

"Cristian, you called me, and we made an agreement," my father says. He's speaking clearly, but there are signs of him physically weakening. This situation, particularly Vinny, is taking a toll on him.

My father signals to Paul's lifeless body, his blood seeping on the concrete. "I delivered my end of the agreement. Don't you dare disrespect me with this juvenile game. You're wasting everyone's time. I'll see the girl on the streets eventually."

"Yeah, bitch," Vinny snarls to a struggling Natalia. "You wait until I get my hands on you. We'll have some real fun."

I release Vinny and run my hands through my hair. "Jesus."

My father raises his voice. "You can't protect her forever. It'd be in your best interest to hand her over. She means nothing to you."

Cristian eases the gun from under Natalia's dress. "Oh, she means everything to me." His eyes never leave Vinny's while he traces the gun along Natalia's quivering cheek. "I will marry her."

"The fuck you will!" Vinny screams, attempting to run toward Cristian again.

Cristian stops his men when they advance closer and draw their weapons again. I clutch the back of Vinny's shirt and yank him backward.

"You have something else to say, Vinny?" Cristian yells. "Feel free to attempt to murder me. Until then, Natalia will become my wife. The longer I have her, the more info I'll drag out, detail by detail." He jabs the tip of his gun against Natalia's cheek, withdraws it, and then plays with the gun in his hand. "Until next time, gentlemen."

We are so fucked.

14

GIGI

My trip to Italy is the opposite of what I imagined. I haven't spoken to Antonio since our call after Vinny killed Dario.

Someone needs to put a bullet through Vinny's head, pronto.

To add to my stress, Benny told me Natalia is marrying my father. When Natalia first broke up with Vinny and I learned he wanted to kill her, I suggested Benny marry her. My father dismissed that idea.

So on a whim, I told him to marry her. I didn't believe he'd go through with it. My hope was for Benny to talk his way out of the Cavallaro contract since he doesn't want to marry Neomi anyway. He calls her a fucking maniac, and while I always appreciate madness in women and know Neomi would give my brother a run for his money, my best friend is more important.

I also know my father isn't marrying Natalia out of the kindness of his heart. He always has ulterior motives, and I'm nervous about his motives with her. It's not like he'll love her and they'll have a real marriage.

When Natalia calls me, I fake excitement.

"Hello?"

"Hi," she replies slowly.

"It's about damn time you called."

"Your father stomped on my phone and threw it into orange juice."

"Ugh, that sounds like him."

"Did he tell you that …" Her voice trails off.

"That you're marrying him?"

"Yeah … that."

"He didn't. Benny did."

"Are you okay with that? Do you think it's weird?"

"You're marrying him so you don't die. I'm plenty okay with that. It's not like you two will actually date and be intimate." I squeal, almost sounding like Aunt Helena. "I'm trying to clear my schedule here to come home for the wedding."

Not like I have a schedule here.

I just need time to process everything.

"Let me know," she says. "We'll pick you up from the airport."

She changes the subject and asks me about Italy. I tell her about the weather and shopping. I don't mention Antonio.

There's no point.

After what happened, I'll never have a future with him.

It's been years since I've suffered a sleep-paralysis episode, but tonight, it came back with a vengeance. Clutching my chest, I sit in bed and fight for every breath. The dark bedroom only amplifies my terror.

It's not only the sleep-paralysis episodes that torment me. The aftermath is just as torturous. It's even harder to figure out how to explain it to people.

There isn't an easy way to describe the experience of waking up with no muscle control. You feel suffocated, like you're dying, and then come the vivid hallucinations.

So I haven't told anyone.

All my life, my father has protected me from killers, but he can't do the same with the monsters inside my head.

My sleep paralysis made its debut right after my mother's death and returns during stressful times.

It's the same situation with each episode.

A shadowed man appears in my doorway.

Sometimes, he enters the bedroom.

Sometimes, he stands at my bedside.

Other times, he stays in place, just fucking terrifying me.

I switch on the light and ease out of bed. There's no going back to sleep.

My body shakes as I stare at the doorway while restlessly pacing the room.

It's not real, Gigi.

Not fucking real.

Without thinking, I pick up the burner and call Antonio.

This isn't your typical cliché drunk call.

No, it's an *I'm half asleep, and I need to hear a voice that puts me at ease* call.

It's four a.m. in Italy, which makes it eleven p.m. in New York, fitting our usual call schedule anyway.

I hold my breath while listening to the ringing.

"Hello?" he answers. His voice is restrained, and he doesn't attempt to hide the tension.

If I wasn't freaking out about my paralysis, I'd shut my eyes to mourn the days he always added princess to his greetings.

"My father is marrying Natalia." I slap a hand over my mouth.

That wasn't supposed to be our conversation starter, but honestly, I never had one. And no way am I telling him I can't sleep because I see evil shadows in my bedroom.

A moment of silence passes before he says, "Yeah, I know."

He sounds so numb and callous.

So this is what it feels like to fall in love with someone and then become complete strangers.

"How?" I ask.

"He told my father."

"Of course he did." I keep staring at the doorway while slumping against the edge of the bed.

I'm proud of myself for maintaining my composure. I've never broken down and told my family about my sleep paralysis. No way am I opening up to a man who's becoming nothing more than a short chapter in my tale.

"I'll miss you, Antonio," I say so softly that I'm unsure if he'll hear me.

"Stay safe, Giana." He sighs. "This isn't our end."

I end the call when a tear slips down my cheek and lower myself to the floor. Hugging my knees to my chest, I stare at the doorway.

Monsters don't only disturb my sleep.

They're in my everyday life.

15

ANTONIO

I haven't slept in thirty-six hours. Even if I try, there's no way I can shut my eyes. Guilt keeps creeping up my throat like painful heartburn.

I let my daughter down.

Let Gigi down.

Sacrificed one of my men for the error of another.

Then Gigi's call amplified the chaotic mess in my head.

"Daddy! Watch this!" Amara squeals when I enter the dance studio I had built in our home last year.

I watch her perform her new routine in her sparkly pink tutu. If anything provides me a brief reprieve from the shit show that's my life, it's seeing my daughter happy—witnessing her, for even a moment, experiencing somewhat of a normal life.

Unfortunately, Amara also suffers from Vinny's actions. I pulled her out of dance classes and will only allow privates in our home. Her teacher, Pippa, comes to our house three times a week to rehearse with her.

Pippa is next to me, snapping and counting out the steps for Amara. When Amara nails a move she's been struggling with for the past few weeks, Pippa nudges my shoulder with hers.

I like Pippa, and she's one of the few people I'd allow to

bump my shoulder without being elbowed in the face. Not only is she Amara's dance teacher but she's also Damien's ex. They broke up after Pippa told him the life was too much to handle. Despite her ending their relationship, I trust Pippa. It's the only reason I agreed to dance lessons to begin with.

Amara shyly bows before hugging me and then Pippa. "Do you want to see the new dress I got yesterday, Ms. Pippa?"

Pippa grins down at her. "You don't have to ask me twice to see a new dress."

Amara dashes out of the room.

Pippa turns to me once Amara is out of earshot. "She misses classes. It's nice for her to get out of the house and hang out with other girls her age, Antonio."

I massage the space between my brows with my thumb. "That's not an option."

She sighs, and her voice softens. "You have to let her live."

"*Letting her live* is exactly why she can't attend classes. Hopefully, she can rejoin them soon. Until then, we stick to privates."

She squeezes my shoulder. "Got it."

Her curly hair creates a curtain between us as I follow her to the living room. Amara is already waiting for us, wearing her new Burberry dress. I had Clara buy her something to apologize for her lack of dance classes. I'm not ashamed to admit I'm one of those parents who compensate for their subpar parenting by buying their child material items.

"So cute," Pippa says animatedly. "Do they have that in my size?"

Amara twirls in her dress like a ballerina before repeating half her dance number. We give her another round of applause. Pippa stays for another half hour, answering endless dance questions for Amara and catching up with Clara. She hugs them goodbye, and I escort her to the front door.

"See you Thursday," I say. It's a demand, not a question.

Pippa turns to look at me. "Thursday."

I hold the door open for her. Just as she slips past me, she collides with Damien and stumbles backward.

"Shit, sorry, Pippa." Damien reaches out and grabs Pippa's elbow to stop her from falling. He moves away and gestures for her to go ahead once she's stable.

"Damien," Pippa breathes out, her green eyes avoiding his gaze.

Their uncomfortableness screams through the air louder than some men I've killed.

Damien nods, understanding their silence as if it's their form of communication.

Just as I'm about to kick them out since I don't have time for relationship drama, Damien says, "Let me walk you out."

Pippa inhales a deep breath and silently walks with Damien to her silver Audi.

Damien helps her into the car and then joins me in the doorway.

"You good?" I ask.

He shakes his head. "I want someone keeping an eye on her when she comes and goes from here."

"Done."

When Pippa reaches the gate, he dashes to his Mercedes, jumps inside, and follows her.

I walk inside at the same time my phone rings. "Yeah?"

"We have a Vinny problem," Sonny says on the other end. "Meet me at the casino immediately."

One day.

I want just one day when I don't have to deal with Vinny's bullshit.

Hell, I'll settle for an hour at this point.

The stress of this life will have me in my grave before forty.

Only thirteen years to go.

A headache presses into my skull as I enter the back entrance of Lucky Kings. I want to kick everyone out at the sound of slot machines firing off and people cheering.

"Your brother is out of fucking control," Sonny yells as soon as I walk into my father's office. "Out of fucking control!" He swings his arms up, nearly knocking down a photo of my father with New York's governor.

Did the fucker drag me here to waste my time and tell me the obvious?

I ignore Sonny and look at my father. He has one hand on his desk and the other on his cane. His face is void of emotion.

"There was a failed hit on the Marchettis," he explains.

"A failed hit *by your brother*," Sonny adds like I can't put two and fucking two together.

There's a certain irony in how closely Vinny's and my situation mirrors my father's and Sonny's. He isn't as impulsive as Vinny, but Sonny prioritizes his personal interest over the family's welfare.

"Tell me what happened," I say.

"Vinny got word that Cristian, Natalia, and other Marchetti members were at L'ultima Cena," my father starts. "When they left, your brother and his minions drove by and greeted them with gunfire."

"Where is he now?" My body pulses with anger.

"We're unsure," my father replies. "He isn't answering his phone."

"He knows he failed." Sonny thrusts his chest forward.

"Was anyone hurt?" I rub my forehead.

"Only Dino." My father tightens his hold on the cane before lowering himself into the leather chair. "But that motherfucker will probably brush it off."

Dino isn't only one of Cristian's highest capos. He's also his brother-in-law. Which means if his wife likes him, she'll push Cristian for revenge further.

Uncle Sonny draws closer to us. "According to our

sources—"

I speak over him. "You mean, the *sources* who accompanied him on this failed drive-by?"

My brother is already surrounding himself with rats—scums of the earth.

"I should be next in line," Sonny huffs out. "Vinny isn't responsible enough for the job. Too hotheaded."

"We've already had this discussion," my father warns him.

Sonny holds up a finger. "Look, I wouldn't mind the Marchettis out of the picture either, but we need to act smarter—"

I talk over him again. "Whoa, you're as nuts as Vinny for saying that." I whip my focus to Sonny. "The Marchettis will *never* be out of New York."

Many men have tried.

All those men died.

I'm not putting my daughter's life on the line because these dumb fucks have a hard-on about *running the city.*

"We need to kill the girl," my father comments, dragging me away from my thoughts of strangling my uncle. "Vinny will stop creating problems if she's no longer alive."

Sonny violently shakes his head. "No matter what, Cristian wants to kill Vinny. So we either allow him to kill Vinny or we kill Cristian. If we kill Cristian, we need a fail-proof plan to get it done."

"We're not killing anyone," I say. "We need to speak to Vinny first."

"Sonny, I need to speak with my son." My father jerks his head toward the doorway.

Sonny opens his mouth to argue, shuts it, and refuses to look at us as he leaves the room.

"Find your brother," my father demands. "*Now.*"

My father's demand is easier said than done.

Vinny has gone MIA after his fuckup.

I've had a man watching his house for a week and nothing.

My brother attempted to murder Cristian Marchetti and left us to deal with the aftermath.

Every day, I witness my father's stress growing. Sonny and the others are on his ass, pressuring him to find Vinny and punish him. There's even talk of banishing Vinny from the family.

The problem is, banishment doesn't mean taking away his work badge and kicking him out. It means death.

"Antonio," my gate guard, Vito, says through the phone, "the dance teacher is here, asking to speak with you."

"Let her through."

I hang up and check my calendar. Amara isn't scheduled for a dance lesson today.

I leave my office and wait for Pippa at the front door. Her body is stiff as she walks toward me.

"Antonio"—her voice is shaky—"I need to talk to you."

Fuck me.

I know what someone looks like when they're about to ask for protection.

"Come on." I motion for her to come inside.

She follows me into my office, and I shut the door behind us. I don't bother to sit. Neither does she.

She also, thankfully, gets straight to the point. "This might not be my place to tell you this, but I feel like you should know."

I raise a brow, waiting for her to continue. She struggles to spit it out. So I stroll to my bar cart, pour her a glass of whiskey, and offer it to her.

She downs it in a single gulp and sets the glass on my desk. "Your brother is sneaking around with Carmela's father, Rocky."

I remain silent while replaying her words in my head. "Rocky ... as in Marchetti's Rocky?"

"Yes." She absentmindedly pokes my rug with her sneaker. "Carmela and I live in the same building, and I've seen them together a few times. People are talking about Vinny attempting to kill Cristian, so it didn't make sense for them to associate with each other." She holds up her hand. "And if you know this already, please don't kill me. I promise, you're the only person I've told."

If I ever touched Pippa, Damien would lose his shit. He'd lay down his life for her.

"Thank you, Pippa. Please keep this between us."

Pippa is silent as I walk her out, and Damien arrives right before she leaves like last time. I'm smart enough to figure out he planted a GPS somewhere—on her phone, her car, wherever—and plans their run-ins here, making it appear as if they're random.

He catches her by the elbow as she passes him. "Everything okay?"

"Of course." She brushes loose strands of hair away from her eyes and gently pulls from his grasp. "I have a dance class in twenty minutes." Without waiting for a response, she hurries to her car.

"You can't follow her," I say sternly as Damien stares at Pippa. "I'll have Vito do it."

"I need to—"

I hold up my finger and talk over him. "We have serious business to discuss right now."

Damien waits until we're in my office before asking, "What was that about?" His attempt to hide the accusation in his voice fails.

"I'm not fucking Pippa," I say point-blank. "She was here to inform me Vinny is sneaking around with Rocky and Carmela."

Like me, it takes him a moment to digest the news.

"Rocky is flipping on Cristian?"

"Rocky is flipping on Cristian," I confirm.

For decades, Rocky has held an unwavering loyalty to Cristian, doing his bidding and carrying out brutal murders on his behalf. His daughter, Carmela, has also been Cristian's steady fuck for years. My guess is that he's replaced Carmela with Natalia, and neither of them is happy about that.

What I would give to see the expression on Cristian's face when he discovers his right-hand man and ex are betraying him.

If Vinny wasn't involved, I'd love the news. Something is morbidly fascinating about watching a family collapse from within.

I snatch Pippa's glass from my desk, refill it with the same whiskey, and pass it to Damien. Then I fill mine.

"Damn." Damien lowers himself into a chair. "You can't trust anyone anymore."

I shoot him a look because my thoughts are the same. It's always those closest who fuck you over because it blindsides you.

He flinches before waving his glass toward me. "Except me because, you know, I'll always have your back."

I circle my desk, settle in my chair, and knock back my drink before setting it down. Pressing my palms against my forehead, I rub them into my skull.

"What do we do?" Damien asks.

I lower my hand. "It seems my brother needs to die."

Damien leans forward and rests his glass down on the desk. "Hopefully, Rocky is the one who kills Cristian, so we don't have to clean up Vinny's involvement."

I scoff. "Have you met Benny Marchetti? He's just as much of a psychopath as Cristian. He will slaughter everyone involved in his father's murder."

He nods in agreement.

"If anything happens to me, you remember where to take Amara?"

"Don't say shit like that, Antonio."

"Promise me, Damien."

He looks me in the eye. "I'd give my life for that little girl. I'll always get her to safety."

He and Clara are the only ones who know my evacuation plan if anything happens to me. There's only one place they'll remain safe, one person who can easily hide them.

I'm worried I'll have to use that plan soon. Vinny shared information with Natalia he shouldn't have, and now, Cristian is using that against us.

All actions Vinny should've died for, yet my father failed to reprimand him.

Because of that, he believes he can get away with anything.

But not this. No, he signed his death certificate.

And I no longer care to help him out of it.

He's on his own.

Now, we have to wait for everything to implode.

THREE WEEKS LATER

I'm shocked when the burner rings.

Today, for some reason, I slid it into my pocket before leaving for the casino.

Juggling paperwork, I balance the phone between my car and shoulder to answer. "The princess has called."

"Where is she, Antonio?" Gigi yells. Her voice trembles before sobs break free.

I stop, losing my place in the papers. "Who?"

"Don't bullshit me."

"I'm not bullshitting you."

"Your piece-of-shit brother teamed up with Rocky and kidnapped Natalia." Her tone hardens, the sobs turning into anger. "I'll never forgive you for this."

"Gigi, I promise you, I don't know where she is."

"Start arranging your brother's funeral, Antonio. And that's *if* my father is even generous enough to give you his body."

16

GIGI

All I can do is sit and pray Natalia doesn't die. I'm in Aunt Aida's kitchen with her and Bruno, drinking latte after latte while anxiously awaiting updates.

My father and his men are skilled in finding people, but time is of the essence here.

Vinny and Rocky are a deadly, psychopathic duo. Rocky also knows the inside of my family operations.

"Poor girl." Aunt Aida reaches across the table and gently squeezes my hand. "The offer to stay here still stands, honey."

I sniffle.

Vinny is a little bitch. He isn't some lovesick man who took the woman he loves. No, he did it because he'd lost control over her. Since my father taught me to trust few, I'm not sure if I believe Antonio when he said he doesn't know where Natalia is.

Would he actually turn on his brother?

A wave of nausea washes through me when my phone rings.

My father's name flashes on the screen.

He said he'd call when he had another update, so this call is either bad or good.

Please be good. Please be good.

Bruno stops his pacing.

Aunt Aida slides closer to me.

"Tell me you found her," is how I answer.

"Natalia is home safe," he replies.

"And Vinny?"

"I know nothing regarding Vinny."

Vinny is dead.

Good riddance.

Four nights later, I'm jolted awake by a sound on the terrace.

I throw off my duvet cover, slide out of bed, and grab the gun Bruno gave me earlier, *just in case*. Everyone is on edge now. Bruno no longer helps Felice in the fields. My father banned me from leaving the cottage. Even though I'm not in New York, I'm still on lockdown.

I should call Bruno about the noise and have him come over to investigate. But I don't because, quite simply, I'm stupid. I hope it's Antonio, sneaking to see me—not *kill me*, obviously.

Stepping out, I meet the coolness of the night while clutching the gun.

A silhouette occupies the spot where Antonio stood during his first visit. I aim the gun in that direction, trying to recognize the person stepping forward.

A whiff of cigarettes hits me.

He doesn't smell like Antonio.

And as he comes closer, it's clear he isn't.

A scrawny man raises his hands above his head in innocence while holding a box between them. "My cousin Antonio asked me to give you this," he says slowly in an Italian accent.

I retreat a step and raise my gun as he offers me the box. "Open it."

"What?" he stutters.

I gesture toward it with my gun. "Open it."

An endless number of potential threats exists inside that box.

A bomb.

Anthrax.

Or really, anything Antonio-related at this point.

Either way, I'm not about to be stupid *and* a bombing victim.

The man sets the box on the table and wiggles the lid off.

"Take everything out," I instruct, my tone sounding a little too much like my father's.

He extracts a small sheet of paper and a single black rose. He stares at me in question.

"Go ahead."

He turns away and leaves, looking over his shoulder numerous times, anxious I'll shoot him.

When I finally pick up the paper, a small message is written on it.

> GIGI,
>
> YOUR FATHER MURDERED THE HEIR TO OUR FAMILY, WHICH MEANS WAR.
>
> TO YOU, I'M NOW THE VILLAIN, AN ENEMY OF YOUR FAMILY.
>
> STAY IN ITALY AND BE SAFE.
>
> I'M NOT DONE WITH YOU YET.
>
> —ANTONIO

What the fuck does *I'm not done with you yet* mean?

Is it a threat?

I crumple the note in my hand until it becomes a wad the size of a tennis ball and then grab a candle lighter from my nightstand. My heart feels as on fire as the paper when I light it and watch it burn to nothing but ash. Then as much as I want and need to do the same with the rose, I can't. Instead, I set it on my nightstand.

All night and the day after and the day after, the reality of Antonio's note hits me harder.

Antonio is my family's enemy, making him *my* enemy.

It's always family over everything.

He is loyal to the Lombardis.

Me to the Marchettis.

That'll never change.

And now, there's no time for sadness.

No time to play the victim, or I'll become one.

Each day, I watch the rose continue to die.

When the last petal of the black rose falls, I return to New York.

17

ANTONIO

Vinny is dead.

I predicted his death as soon as I learned he had taken Natalia. We discovered his bullet-ridden body in our family's Cape home and are attempting to fit all the pieces of his death into the fucked-up puzzle it is.

All we know is that with the help of Rocky and Carmela, he abducted Natalia. Everything is blank after that—no fucking pieces. Someone wiped clean all the house's security footage and fingerprints.

It's obvious Cristian was involved since Natalia is back at the Marchetti Mansion.

We also found Rocky and Carmela dead in her apartment— my guess, also by the hands of Cristian.

My father is manic, fueled by the grief of losing Vinny, and wants Cristian to know *we know* he's responsible for my brother's death. I already talked him out of killing one of Cristian's men this morning to send a message. We need a plan before starting a Marchetti murder spree. So I tell him I'll call Cristian and talk with him myself.

With Cristian, it's better we speak with words, not violence. *For now.*

"Marchetti, we have a problem," I say as soon as Cristian answers my call.

"And what would that be?" His response is edged with sarcasm.

"Cut the shit. You murdered my brother."

"Are you sure about that?"

"Yes." I don't expect him to admit anything.

"You have the wrong man."

"Christ," I hiss. "This is why people hate talking to you. We know you wanted him dead, and we also found out about his little kidnapping plan with Carmela and Rocky. We found his body, and all the cameras have been wiped clean. We're not stupid."

A moment of silence passes.

"My father wants you to hand over Natalia."

"No," he replies sharply.

"Cristian, you don't want a war."

"I will kill every man, including you, who tries to hurt her. Do you understand me?"

"He was my brother."

"And she is my wife. I care about her more than you did him."

I shake my head to shake away the truth of his statement. "That makes you weak."

He scoffs. "No, Antonio. That makes me crueler. Something to make sure I live for, and I'll kill every motherfucker who threatens that."

"Look at it from my father's point of view. What if someone killed Benny?"

"Vinny would've ruined your family's legacy. Be happy, Antonio. You're next in line now and better suited for the job. Now, are you done wasting my time?"

"I'm done." I grit my teeth. "Watch your back, Marchetti."

I end the call and toss the phone on the passenger seat.

The truth of his words strikes me. I've been so busy that I didn't realize it.

I'm now the successor to the Lombardi throne.

Fuck me.

That isn't the only truth.

Cristian could've gotten rid of Natalia after killing Vinny.

He cares about Natalia more than we thought.

Fuck me again.

"Cristian won't hand her over." I flick a penny on the table and watch it spin. "He cares about her."

Snubbing out his cigarette in a full ashtray, Sonny huffs in the chair beside me. "Does that bitch have a golden cunt?"

"She's his weakness. His vulnerability." My father smirks across from me. "We use that against him."

"We use the bitch and Cristian's daughter." Sonny lights another cigarette. "That's how we hit Cristian where it hurts. He needs to suffer the pain of losing them before we end his life."

I down a shot of gin and pour another one.

My father shakes his head. "No. We need to kill Benny first."

Using my glass, I gesture toward him. "We go for Benny and Natalia."

Sonny shoots me a suspicious look. "Not the daughter?"

"We kill Natalia first since she's the reason Vinny is dead. Benny is the next to go. We finish with Cristian. Let the Marchetti empire fall to the useless daughter. She'll let it crumble, and then we'll take everything she has and kill her."

I told Gigi to stay in Italy to protect her. No one knows where her aunt lives, and I intend to keep it that way. If it comes down to Natalia and Gigi, sorry, Natalia. The girl has become quite the fucking headache anyway.

"Welcome to war, gentlemen," my father announces to the men in the room, rubbing his palms together in excitement.

He's ready for his revenge.

Everyone nods.

Myself included.

18

GIGI

Loneliness.

Confusion.

Heartache.

Those emotions reside in my stomach when I return to New York. The usual excitement I feel from being home isn't there.

When Natalia and Luca pick Bruno and me up from the airport, I hug her tight, grateful she's safe.

We go to lunch and then the bridal shop, where I find the perfect bridesmaid dress. I help Natalia with hers—an A-line gown with a scoop neckline. It's simple, how Natalia prefers, and she looks beautiful in it.

My mind is flooded with countless questions about her and my father.

Him marrying her because Vinny wanted to slice and dice her is understandable, but why not end the engagement now that he's dead?

It's because the Lombardis still want her dead, right?

Because Vincent wants to kill Natalia in revenge for Vinny's death.

I try to tell myself those are the reasons they're still marrying. Not that they actually like each other. No way is my best friend in love with my father. And it's not like my father is capable of loving anyone not blood-related.

Natalia and I hang out for the day, and I don't see my father until dinner. That's when I learn their relationship isn't just a facade to spare her life. In their engagement role-playing, they fell for each other. My best friend will be my stepmother.

I mean, I can't blame two people who shouldn't fall in love for falling in love.

I'm over here falling for a Lombardi, for Christ's sake.

As weird as I think it is—because come on, no one will believe me if I said it isn't—I'm okay with it. I haven't seen my callous father show tenderness since my mother. And even with her, he wasn't a great husband. He expressed his regret to me for that after her funeral.

But as I sit with them at the dining room table, I can see Natalia thaw the coldness in his heart, softening some of his wickedness.

I'm also relieved my father isn't marrying that traitorous bitch Carmela. Pre-betrayal, Rocky attempted to persuade my father to marry Carmela for years. I'm sure his engagement to Natalia played a large part in them double-crossing us, but neither my father nor Benny has given me many details on what happened.

I wait until after dinner, when the mansion has descended into stillness, before visiting my father in his office.

"Hiya, Dad," I greet, walking into his office after hardly knocking.

My father shifts his paperwork out of the way and settles back in his massive executive chair while I take the one across from him. Being a man of few words, he waits for me to speak first.

"So …" I pause, my mouth dry. "You and Natalia?"

This might be the most awkward conversation we've ever shared.

"Are getting married, yes." He runs a hand over his jaw. "Don't give her a hard time on that."

I hold up a finger. "(A) She's my best friend. I'd never." I raise another finger. "(B) It's better than having a stepmother I can't stand ... or one who tells me to eat more vegetables."

He tilts his head to the side. "No one has ever told you that."

"Nor do I want it to start." I smirk.

"Get out of here." He shakes his head and waves toward the door.

"That was me saying, I approve." I cross my legs and blow out a breath. "I also appreciate that it gives me a free pass."

"Excuse me?" There's a rise in his voice.

"A free pass to date whoever I want because all I'll need to say is, *Well, you married my best friend.*" My comment is risky, but I got a somewhat-chill version of my father earlier.

"Sometimes, I hate that you're such a Marchetti." He grabs a pen and plays with it between his fingers. "Anything else I need to hear you talk shit about?"

"Don't go to war with the Lombardis."

"If they try to fuck with me, I will." He stares at me skeptically. "Is there a reason you don't want me to?"

I pretend to examine my manicure. "Of course not."

"Gigi, secrets don't stay secrets for long." His brows wrinkle.

I'm a big dummy.

I just made it obvious there's a reason I don't want him touching them.

This was a mistake.

"Good night, Daddy." I stand. "I'll give you your fiancée back when I'm done hanging out with her."

It was pointless to ask my father not to go to war with them. If he killed Vinny, they'll want revenge, and my father is more of a *kill before being killed* man.

I know I can't save Antonio from my father's wrath.

And I'm not sure if he can save me from his family.

I'm a Marchetti, and if they declare war on my family, it's war on *all of us*.

And who is the best pawn for war?

The princess of the family.

Me.

I go back to my bedroom where Natalia is and pretend everything is okay. When she leaves, I call Antonio's burner.

It goes straight to voicemail.

I throw the phone across the room.

If anything helps with a depressive episode, it's shopping.

A new pair of heels for when you're lonely and you need to brighten your day.

A new handbag to help you forget the man you were falling for completely ghosted you. Oh, and he might also want to kill you, *literally* making *you* a ghost.

My sleep paralysis has worsened, and I have an episode nearly every night now. I still refuse to talk to anyone about them. That's between me and the sleep gods. And apparently, that god is mad at me for something.

I'm in the dressing room, mid-change of a little black dress, when the door opens. I turn, clutching the dress to my chest as a figure wearing all black joins me. His heavy frame takes up nearly half the space.

"I told you to keep your ass in Italy," Antonio sneers, shutting the door and locking it behind him.

His tone is as cool as ice, yet sexy as hell. It reminds me of all the times he used that same voice to praise me for sucking his cock so good. Goose bumps rise on my skin like warning signs.

How the hell did he track me down here?

I'm alone, but Bruno is just outside the dressing room.

Antonio creeps closer, and I inch back a step.

I don't yell for help because, God, I've missed him.

The villain I invited to my bed and into my life still makes me weak in the knees.

"You're not supposed to be here," he scolds, removing his blazer and draping it along the chair.

"Pretty sure *you're* not supposed to be here."

"As soon as we're finished, pack your shit and return to Italy."

"I forgot the part where you have any say in what I do."

He chuckles deviously. "I have *all* the say in your life."

"You're mistaken. A man who has *all the say* in my life doesn't resort to sneaking into dressing rooms to see me."

Antonio brings his hand to my neck and cups it—not applying as much pressure as he's capable of. He sweeps his thumb along my throat. It's slow, soft, and intimate. His thumb rests on my jugular vein, feeling my erratic pulse.

I swallow when he squeezes it once before gripping my chin and forcing me to look at him. His gaze is piercing as our eyes meet.

He jerks me closer and sinks his teeth into my bottom lip. When I open my mouth to gasp in pain, he kisses me and pushes my back against the wall.

He holds my face tight, starving my breaths but giving me his.

When he finally pulls away, his lips linger on mine as he says, "It's been a little complicated trying to see you, princess."

I shiver when he caresses my cheek.

"Too complicated to call me?" I rasp. "I call bullshit."

He snatches the dress from my hand and tosses it to the side. He retreats a step, and his eyes roam down my body while he takes in the image of me wearing only a lace bra and thong.

His face is haunting, like he's wondering what to do with me next. I shiver from the intensity of his stare, and he smashes his mouth against mine again. Lowering his hands, he curls them around my ass cheeks, gripping them tight before hoisting me up against the wall. I wrap my legs around his waist, but he doesn't allow me to stay there long.

I wiggle in his hold, unsure where he's going with this, and allow him to make every move.

When we're together, my body always becomes his.

To play with. To pleasure. To provide pain. I'm his favorite toy.

"There's my good girl," he says under a whispered breath. He folds his arms under my thighs, as if performing a bicep curl, situating my pussy at his face. Then he slides my panties to the side. "Mmm, always so wet for me."

I shudder.

"I've missed you, princess." He lowers his head and licks up my slit.

"I've missed you too," I say with a low groan. If there's ever a way for Antonio to get a sweet side of me, it's when he's pleasuring me. I'm at his mercy.

I nearly buck off the wall when he nestles his entire face between my legs and eats me out so, so, so good.

Fuuuck.

I never want him to stop.

To leave me again.

Antonio is the only man who's ever touched me like this, and I don't know if any other could drag out this side of me. He makes me comfortable with him, with my body, with my sexuality.

He said he wanted to ruin me for any other man, and that's exactly what he's done.

My pussy clenches. All he's using is his mouth, and I'm already so close. My body pulses with pleasure, and I'm there … there … *so fucking there.*

Then he stops, and I nearly fall forward since I was embarrassingly humping his face.

"Who killed my brother, Giana?"

Talk about a total orgasm kill.

Instead of answering his badly timed question, I grind my hips forward. He tsks and anchors me in place.

Son of a bitch.

"Was it Natalia?"

I remain quiet, squirming in his hold.

Who wants to talk about murder mid-orgasm?

Especially the murder of a sleazeball like Vinny.

"Your father?"

I give him silence, wavering to the side when he releases an arm from under my thigh.

He gathers my hair in his fist and tugs me forward. "Benny?"

I smirk at him and shrug.

"Fucking tell me." He rolls his tongue along my inner thigh, just inches from my pussy.

"I don't know anything about your piece-of-shit brother," I hiss, pulling at his strands the same way he did with mine. "Why don't you visit him in hell and find out for yourself if you're so concerned?"

How dare he!

Months have passed without a word from him—until now, because he wants information. And he thought I'd easily fall into his trap by using a little tongue work.

"Now that we've established I'm not telling you shit, either leave or finish what you started," I snarl.

"Look at my princess," he says in a pleased tone. "It seems the more I shove my cock into your pretty little mouth, the filthier I make it."

"Your cock will never be in my mouth again unless I'm biting it off. I'll mail it to your father so he can bury it next to your brother's worthless body."

When he releases me, I lose a breath and catch myself before collapsing on my knees. I glance up at him, and a sinister smile forms on his perfect face.

He scrubs a hand over his jaw. "Since it seems you're not

telling me anything of value and forgetting your fucking manners, I'll fix that problem."

I snort as he starts unbuttoning his pants. "Your warnings don't scare me."

"They should." He lowers his pants, snatches the back of my head, and drags my face to his erection. His cock is hard and throbbing.

He holds me in place, using his free hand to grip the base of his dick, and presses it against my closed lips. "Open, Giana."

I glare up at him.

He sighs. "If you don't open your mouth right fucking now, I will never play with your sweet pussy again." His voice turns taunting. "Now, my sweet princess, you don't want that, do you?"

I hate his manipulation tactics, but, damn him, does it work.

The moment I lower my mouth *just a little*, he juts his cock forward, opening it further. He holds me in place as he starts fucking my mouth. His dick grows fuller and fuller with cum with each thrust. Spit slips down my throat, and my jaw turns sore. I get more turned on by the second.

And since my villain knows me so well, he loosens his hold on my head and says, "Lower your hand and play with your clit," in a heavy breath.

I drop my hand between my legs and circle my clit with the pad of my finger. His hand moves from my head to my throat when I moan loudly.

"Keep quiet as you slurp on my cock," he demands.

My body quivers, and I grow lightheaded as I try to focus on playing with myself while sucking him off.

Reaching down, he grabs the dress I was trying on earlier, spits on it, and pushes it into my hand between my legs. "Ride that, princess. Press your pussy against it and pretend it's my fat cock."

The silk is soft against my pussy as I rub against it.

Antonio is dirtying me up again.

Making me his filthy girl.

"That's it," he groans, watching me grind it up and down my folds.

His body shudders moments later, and he doesn't give me a warning before letting his cum spill into my throat. When he's finished, he releases my head, snatches the dress, and collects the few drops of cum on the tip of his dick along his finger before spreading them along the dress.

"Fuck that with my cum on it," he orders. "Spread my cum all over your addictive pussy."

That's exactly what I do.

I get lost in the moment, and he kneels in front of me, watching me in awe. My knees are sore against the rough carpet, but I don't care.

Antonio snatches the fabric from me and holds it in place while I thrust against it, panting and moaning. When he knows I'm close, he moves the dress, leans forward, and works three fingers inside me. I rotate my hips, and he easily finds my G-spot like it's a route he takes daily. I ride his fingers, fucking them hard, until all the blood rushes between my legs.

He smirks, as if he feels that sudden heat, and crushes his mouth against mine, swallowing the cries of my orgasm. He holds me as I fall apart, and I nuzzle my face into his shoulder as he continues fingering me.

When he's finished, he falls back, running the dress through my folds to collect my cum with his, and then licks the spot. Even though we haven't had sex yet, I feel like I've already given this man every piece of me.

We're both sweaty and sticky as we catch our breaths.

"Get your ass to Italy before I shove you in a box and ship you there myself," he says harshly before standing and helping me to my feet.

"Why do you care if I'm in Italy?"

"You're smart." He pulls his pants up and buckles them. "You fucking know why."

"I'm not leaving New York just because your crazy family wants to hurt mine."

"Are you that fucking dense, Gigi? Do you know what will happen if one of my men dares to touch you, *to hurt you?*"

I silently stare at him, unsure how to answer.

"I'll have to slaughter them."

"My father will protect me."

He raises his brows. "Like he protected Natalia from Vinny? Natalia should be happy he got to her before Vinny did something crueler, like rape, cutting off a limb, or blowing her head off. And since you have Marchetti blood, they'll want to do worse to you. I'll have to kill my own men if that happens, so get the fuck out of New York. Do you understand?"

I cross my arms.

"Giana, this isn't a game. Promise me you'll go to Italy."

"I can't. Benny is getting married. I have to be there for the wedding."

"You've got to be fucking kidding me," he mutters. "As soon as the wedding is over, you leave. Do you hear me?"

When I don't answer, he steps forward and crowds me against the wall. "Promise me." His voice breaks at the end.

For the first time, Antonio shows that he fears something.

"I promise," I whisper.

He kisses my lips slowly and leaves, taking the dress with him.

As I get dressed, I feel guilty because I know I won't keep my promise.

19

ANTONIO

I've kept tabs on Gigi as if she were a stock I'd invested every penny I had in.

This woman is my obsession, but it's more than purely physical.

Gigi isn't just a woman I'm attracted to and want to fuck.

I'm willing to die for her, and if anyone tries to harm her, they'll unleash the darkest demon living inside me. Which means, as bad as I want to make her mine, I can't yet. She's safer being just Cristian Marchetti's daughter right now than she is his daughter *and* mine.

"If Cristian knows we're watching her, he'll kill us," Damien tells me. "He'll automatically think it's for the opposite reason of why we are."

When I can't watch Gigi, Damien or Julian, does it for me. If someone were to find out, I'd easily twist the truth and tell them I was using Gigi as a weapon against Cristian. I was honest when I told Gigi I'd kill anyone—Lombardi or not—if they laid a hand on her.

Amara, Clara, and she are my top priorities to keep safe. Cristian might consider children off-limits, but that doesn't mean Amara is safe from the violent crosshairs. Too many deaths happen as a result of *wrong place, wrong time* circum-stances.

"You'd better go unnoticed then," I say. "You and Julian are the best at surveillance."

That isn't a lie to stroke Damien's ego. His dad was the best at intelligence gathering and passed that trait down to his sons. He also has great connections, which is how I easily snuck into Gigi's dressing room unnoticed.

My cock twitches as I think of her. I haven't fucked another woman since the first time I laid hands on her. Even if I tried, guilt would consume me.

I'm not Gigi's enemy.

I'm her stalker.

A man who has it bad.

And one who doesn't easily give up.

I crack my neck from side to side and walk into my father's basement. I'm already dreading the family meeting tonight. We used to hold them a few times a week. Since Vinny's death, they've been less frequent.

My father—at the head—Sonny, and other high-ranking members are seated at the large table. A table made of pure gold with an *L* carved in the middle. My father loves it, and it cost a pretty penny. I find it gaudy as fuck.

Men greet me with head nods when I take the seat next to my father—Vinny's old chair. There were no questions asked the first time I sat there, and I've done it every time since.

"Antonio," my father greets, "we need something from you."

All attention is on me, and from their expectant expressions, I know they were discussing whatever *they need* before my arrival.

I scrub a hand over my mouth in dread. "Let me hear it."

"As you know, we made an arrangement with the Silvermans for Vinny to marry Serena."

Fuck. I should've known this was coming.

"Find someone else," I quickly say, only looking at my father.

My father draws in a breath and slowly releases it. "We signed a contract, Antonio."

"And the person in that contract is dead," I argue. "Which makes the contract also dead."

If he's so concerned about the contract, he can dig up Vinny's body and marry it to Serena.

"It's important we keep our word," my father continues.

"Keep your word and have someone else do it then." I tug my phone from my pocket, Google Serena's full name, and display her photo to the table. "She's cute. Now, which one of you lucky men wants to marry her?"

Granted, there aren't many single men in the room.

"Why are you so opposed to marrying her?" Sonny asks, eyeing me suspiciously while leaning back in the chair and crossing his arms. "Word is, you've been keeping company you shouldn't—"

Baring my teeth, I slam my hand on the table and cut him right the fuck off. "I'll slit your fucking throat if you sit there and try to throw false accusations around."

Sonny's insinuation implies he knows about Gigi, which means he's either having me or my men followed. And my reaction to that further proved him right.

"Accusations?" My father's gaze bounces from Sonny to me. "What does that mean?"

Sonny stares at me mockingly, self-satisfied with his little game.

"He doesn't mean shit," I reply, curling my lip while leaning closer toward Sonny. "He thinks he's slick, trying to manipulate me into marrying Serena. Do I have women I fuck? Yes. Do I want a wife? Fuck no. Now, like I said, pick someone else." I jerk my jaw toward Sonny. "He seems committed to having a marriage with the Silvermans." I mimic the mocking smirk he gave me. "Congrats. You get another wife. Let's hope this one doesn't walk in front of a bus."

"Oh, come on, Antonio—"

I talk over Sonny. "I could kill you right now for even disrespecting me. Now that Vinny is gone, *I'm* next in line. Not you."

We're putting on a show for other men. Another one of my father's capos, Nuncio, sits next to Sonny, his mouth pinched into a thin line of disapproval. He and I have never seen eye to eye. He was closer with Vinny.

Next to him is Emilio, Nuncio's son and Sonny's godson, and I notice him wince.

My father loosens his collar. "They want you, Antonio."

I shake my head. "No."

His tone deepens. "Do it for the family. As you just told Sonny, you're now my successor."

All eyes are on me.

If I disrespect the boss, then when I take on that role, they'll think they can do the same with me. I need to put on an obedient show for the sake of that.

"You're right. I'm sorry," I lie. "We'll speak about the details later."

Sonny grunts, as if not believing me.

"Yes, we will work out the details and share once we know the plan," my father says while staring at me, stone-faced.

Our conversation shifts from marrying me off to the next move in our conflict with the Marchettis and then to casino business. Throughout that time, I brainstorm ways to get out of this marriage with Serena.

When the meeting is finished, I linger as the men leave until it's only my father and me.

He stares at me grimly. "The marriage with Serena will happen, Antonio. I'll see how much time I can spare you before it does."

"The marriage with her won't happen." I furrow my brow. "If you want me to succeed you, you'll find a way to break that contract." Standing, I lower my fingers, flex them, and set them on the table. "Otherwise, I'll let Sonny take that position and live a peaceful fucking life."

"Now's not the time to play games."

"Which is why I'm being completely up front with you." I stop talking when my phone rings, and I find a text from Clara. "I need to get home to my daughter, who *won't* have a new step-mother named Serena."

Now, I'd love for her to have a stepmother with the surname Marchetti, but that's an entirely different conversation.

I exit the house through the back door to prevent a run-in with my mother and find Sonny standing next to my car, waiting for me.

"Step away from my car before I bash your skull into the window," I warn.

He moves closer as I circle my car. "We need to speak privately."

"No, we don't."

"Why are you keeping tabs on Gigi Marchetti?"

I ignore him and unlock my car.

"Either use her as a pawn to get back at Cristian or leave her the fuck alone, Antonio."

I open my car door and wait for him to go on. Sonny plays dirty, so as much as I don't want to entertain him, I need to know what he knows.

He comes closer, and we're face-to-face, staring each other down.

Getting out of the marriage with Serena won't be my biggest problem.

It'll be dealing with Sonny's ass.

He puffs up his chest, and I can't stop myself from chuckling harshly.

"Your father might be oblivious to what you're doing, given

his health is in the shitter and he lost his son, but I'm more keen to my surroundings."

"I don't take well to threats, Sonny."

"I don't take well to men in bed with our enemy."

"News flash: I couldn't give two fucks what you take well with unless it's staying the fuck out of my business." I punch him in the face, shake out my fist, and leave.

"It'll happen again," Dr. Dante Wright says, stepping away from my father. "His health is declining significantly." His passive tone lacks empathy. "And his line of work only makes it worse."

My father suffered a mini stroke. Luckily, it was at a family dinner, so Amara, my mother, and I are the only people who witnessed it. I intend to keep it a secret from everyone else.

Like him, the aftermath of Vinny's death has taken a toll on me. My burden is different. My father has become withdrawn, resulting in me picking up his responsibilities, along with mine. That limits my time with my daughter, my sleep, my fucking sanity—the little amount I have to begin with.

I nod toward Dante. "Thank you."

"Thank you, *son*." My father attempts to rise from the couch in Dante's office. His face is pale and saggy.

Dante stands tall in the doorway, not providing any bedside manners or assisting to help him to his feet. He also refuses to meet my father's eyes.

Our father's eyes.

Dante is my father's secret child. Some know his name but never anything more. And Dante wants to keep it that way.

Lithica, Dante's mother, decided she wanted nothing to do with my father after my mother snuck into her house and attempted to slit her throat. Lithica remarried, and that man raised Dante as if he were his.

Every so often, against the will of Dante, my father would visit him during his early years. As Dante grew older, he refused to see my father until he got sick. Dante only agreed to become his doctor after I cashed in a favor with him.

My father grunts as I assist him to his feet.

Dante stares at us in a *time to leave* expression. When my father moves too slowly, he opens the door.

I shake Dante's hand after my father walks past him. "Thanks."

He glares at me. "Get out, Antonio."

His *get out* has two meanings.

He wants my father to get out of his office.

He also wants me to get out of this life.

My father's hand trembles on his cane, and I steady him on the walk to my car. He groans when I help him into the passenger seat.

"People are turning on me," he says as I drive. "I'm making a statement tonight to tell them you're stepping up as boss."

I slam on the brakes, causing the truck behind me to blare its horn and swerve to the right. My nostrils flare as I parallel park in front of a row of business buildings.

"Sonny is planning something. I'm sure of it." He presses his knuckles against his lip to mask his anguish or anger ... I'm not quite sure ... and then pulls them away. "He wants to be boss. You can't let that happen. Do you understand?"

My father knows he's a boss on the brink of losing his empire. Sonny wants my father to promote him. Now that he knows that won't happen, I'm positive he's plotting behind our backs. He wants to turn my father's men against him.

Or me.

"There are two things I want to happen before I die." My father holds up two fingers. "You take over the family." He drops one finger. "Cristian Marchetti to suffer and lose his son, as I did mine." He lowers the other one.

I turn quiet.

"You don't want those things as well?"

"I'd rather kill Sonny."

Not wanting to avenge Vinny's death is a bad look.

I'm relieved he's gone. Call me a heartless bastard all you want.

Just because he was my brother doesn't mean I had an allegiance toward him once he started being dumb.

Blood is thicker than water, but it's also harder to clean up.

20

GIGI

After my father and Natalia's wedding, the spotlight moved to Benny and Neomi's nuptials. Neither wants to marry each other, and they made that clear the night of their engagement party. Benny took Gretchen, a housekeeper he regularly slept with, into the mansion's billiards room. Neomi saw them, and in revenge, she joined them … with another man.

Even though I wasn't in the room when said murdering happened and I didn't ask for details, I heard them all. Neomi had dropped to her knees in front of the man, claiming an eye for an eye while appearing to prepare to suck the man off in front of Benny. So my brother blew the guy's brains out. Hopefully, they had gotten all their hostility out of their systems because after today, they're bound to each other until death.

Sitting in the cathedral pew, I watch Neomi walk down the aisle as the bridal chorus plays. I look away from her to Benny.

A very pregnant Natalia leans toward me and whispers, "Benny isn't Benny-ing the way I thought he would."

I smirk.

While we expected a miserable Benny today, that's not what we're getting. He isn't staring at Neomi with disdain. He's staring at her like a loving husband would look at his wife. It isn't dramatic, like those crying grooms people rave about on social media, since I doubt he even has the emotional capacity to shed a tear, but there's a look in his eyes I never imagined seeing.

I smile wide as they recite their vows and kiss.

Their union makes our family stronger. The Cavallaros are a resourceful family.

We're all in the high of the romance around us … and then all hell breaks loose.

Two men enter the cathedral and start shooting.

I should've known we couldn't get away with *two* peaceful weddings.

People scramble, duck behind pews, or reach for their own guns.

Benny tackles Neomi to the ground. My father shields Natalia and me before pushing us in the direction the priest is running while he stays behind. Surely, he knows the best hiding spot. Natalia blocks her stomach as we follow him. Unfortunately, the priest doesn't care about our lives. As soon as he enters a room, he slams the door shut and locks us out.

Okay, rude.

God had better retract his ticket to heaven.

I check three doors before finding one unlocked. We run inside, lock it, and stare at each other in shock until the gunfire dies down. Crawling on the floor, I inch the door open, peek around the corner, and make sure the coast is clear before we return to the nave.

People are standing, readjusting themselves, and children are crying.

My father rushes over to us. "You two okay?" He stands back to scan our bodies and inspect us for wounds.

"Yeah," I croak out.

Natalia flings her arms around him, and I walk toward a dead body in the middle of the aisle.

Poor Neomi.

Whoever the dead asshole on the floor is, he ruined her big

day. I want to snatch my father's gun and shoot him again just for that.

Inching closer, I spot another dead man slumped against the floor. Blood drips down the side of his head. Even though I don't recognize any of the men as Lombardi doesn't mean they aren't. I only know a few of their men. At least none of them are Antonio. That's all that matters to me.

"Has anyone seen my daughters?" Concetta, Neomi's mother, yells.

We hear a sharp scream from a back hallway before anyone can answer her.

My stomach twists as the crowd rushes toward it. Benny is in the lead. I grab Natalia's hand, and we follow them.

When we reach the emergency exit, Neomi's younger sister, Isabella, is blocking the door. My gaze follows hers to Neomi's older sister, Bria, and I gasp when it lands on Neomi. A man is restraining her, holding a gun to her head, and she struggles to free herself.

Benny stops Severino when he attempts to go to her.

Severino snarls at him, "That is my goddamn daughter."

"Who is now my wife. I'll handle this," Benny argues while watching the man. "Lower your gun and release her before I blow your head off."

The man jams the gun harder into Neomi's head. "And I'll do the same with hers. You pull the trigger, I pull mine."

Neomi grimaces before shutting her eyes, as if preparing herself to die. A tear slides down her cheek.

"I have a clear shot," my father says to Benny, only loud enough for us to hear.

"If someone hurts my wife, they die at my hands," Benny replies. "No one else's."

This is why I'll always feel safe with Benny. Unlike Antonio was with Vinny, I'm not scared for the day he takes over the family.

"You do know crazy men with guns surround you," Isabella

says to the gunman, sneering out each word. "You won't leave here alive, so let my sister go."

"If I don't bring this bitch where she needs to go and finish the job, I'll die," the man fires back. "Either way, I'm a dead man." He pulls back and curses when Neomi bites his hand.

The movement gives Benny an opening, and he shoots the gunman in the head. The man's body slumps backward. His blood and brain matter shower Neomi.

"Forgive me, Father, for I have sinned," Benny says.

Neomi runs straight to him, wraps her arms around his neck, and burrows her face into his chest. Benny smooths his hand along her back, telling her she's safe.

"Do you think the Lombardis are behind this?" Natalia whispers to me.

I blow out a long breath. "I'm praying they aren't."

"If they are, all of them will die." She's telling me something I already know. "Your father already wants to kill them, and now, Severino will want revenge and answers for what just happened to Neomi."

"I know." A tightness forms in my gut.

She wraps her arm around me as we leave. "Remember all the times you told me to stay away from Vinny, how you were only doing it for my own good, and how frustrating it was when I didn't listen?"

I nod.

"I'm asking you to do the same thing with Antonio." She squeezes me. "He's a Lombardi. They can't be trusted."

21

ANTONIO

I burst into my father's office to find him and Sonny smoking cigars. "Did you call a hit on Benny Marchetti's wedding?"

Last night, I made it clear to him that if he wants me to take over the family, he must include me in all decision-making.

Nothing happens without my approval, especially anything Marchetti-related.

I give no fucks if we kill a man who owes us money.

Hits on other families during weddings? Yeah, I'd better approve that shit.

My father tokes out a circle of smoke. "What are you talking about?"

"Someone shot up his wedding." I shut the door. "They attempted to kidnap his wife, Severino's fucking daughter, and Benny killed them."

"They weren't our men," Sonny says with certainty.

I walk toward him. "How do you know?"

Sonny settles his cigar on an ashtray on the edge of my father's desk. "We did a head count this morning. Not to mention, none of our men would do that without your father's okay."

"Did Vinny get an *okay* from him before abducting Natalia?"

I stare at Sonny with distrust. "And how long have you sat there, knowing this information, and not said anything about it to *your boss?*"

"Since we weren't involved, I didn't find it important." Sonny takes a hit from his cigar.

My father stiffens in his chair, and I wait for him to throw something at Sonny, reprimand him, punch him. He doesn't.

"*Not important?*" I fume. "For all we know, the Marchettis assume we're responsible."

"The dead bodies aren't our men." Sonny shrugs again. "So it's not our problem."

I raise my voice. "You don't think they'd consider we hired outside help?"

Sonny shuts his mouth, and it takes him a moment before he says, "I couldn't personally care less if they think it's us."

"Do you want to die, you imbecile?" I clench my fists. "We need to reach out to the Marchettis, let them know it wasn't us."

"Since when are you pussy of the year, Antonio?" Sonny huffs out.

I storm across the room, snatch him by the collar, and lift him to the wall, clutching his throat. "A pussy?" I laugh cruelly in his face, spit flying from my mouth and landing on his cheek. "This is why you're not next in line, you stupid son of a bitch. If I kill or shoot up a wedding, I'll make it clear it was me. If I don't, I'll also make it clear it wasn't me." I release him with a shove. "Not to mention, they killed every man in that church. That'd make us look weak, you dumb motherfucker."

Sonny heaves out breaths while straightening his suit.

"He's right," my father says.

Sonny shakes his head. "Maybe the family would've been better under Vinny's control."

"I can let you join Vinny if you'd like?" I raise a brow.

"You two are only hurting the family." He waggles his finger between my father and me before storming out of the office.

"Look into this," my father tells me. "I want every fucking detail."

ONE WEEK LATER

"Tommaso Cavallaro is dead," my father informs me when I walk into his basement, where Sonny, Nuncio, and he are seated around the poker table with cards in their hands.

"Good fucking riddance." I sit down next to him, flip my Zippo lighter open, and watch the flame burn.

Tommaso was a fucking idiot, and he touched what's mine when he danced with Gigi at the masquerade ball. He deserved to die.

Lately, it's been a shit show within our family. It didn't take long for me to gather *every fucking detail* of the Marchetti-Cavallaro wedding. Tommaso owed money to Sammie Karpenko, the city's cruelest loan shark. I'm sure he's the one who shot up Benny's wedding and killed Tommaso after he didn't pay up.

On top of that, I've been dealing with Sonny using my father's failing health against him. The other day, he made a move against the Marchettis. He instructed two of our men to follow Benny home from the club and kill him. Both of our men died. Benny didn't.

When I found out, Sonny insisted my father okayed it. And since we were surrounded by other men, my father agreed with him, not wanting to appear incompetent. He either didn't remember or knew admitting that Sonny went behind his back would make him look weak.

Later, Emilio told me in confidence that my father had told Sonny no, yet Sonny did it anyway. When I brought it to the attention of my father, he brushed it off. So I have to sit back while knowing Sonny is playing games with my father's head. I'm close to snapping.

"That's great news for us," Sonny says, rubbing his palms together. "His death makes the Cavallaros weaker. No son to take over the family."

I cringe, hating the sound of his congested-ass voice.

"His death also makes the Marchettis vulnerable," he continues, grinning in delight. "Benny will be busy consoling his *poor wife*. Every single one of them is in a moment of weakness. The perfect time to strike."

This stupid motherfucker.

"Easier said than done, huh?" I ask him. "We recently tried to *strike* them, and two of our men are dead." I slam my Zippo on the table, and their glasses rattle. "If anything, their guards will be up more than ever."

Sonny pinches his lips. "Where does your loyalty lie, Antonio? Do you want the Lombardi name running the streets of New York?"

My blood turns hot.

The Lombardi name will never run New York. It'll only fill the obituaries if we aren't careful. It's time I step up, and later tonight, I'll tell my father I'm ready. I failed to set Vinny straight and look at what happened. Sonny needs to learn I'll make the rules going forward.

"You want to talk about loyalty, Sonny?" I slam the Zippo on the table, stand, and kick my chair toward him, causing him to wince slightly, but he quickly regains his composure. "Loyalty means thinking about the entire family, not only your selfish interests. Soon, I'll be don, and I don't want it to be a mess when I do." I step closer to get in his face. "If you keep playing with me, I'll not only cut you out of the family tree, but I'll cut your tongue out, too, so I never have to hear you speak again. It's not as if you have anything of value to say anyway." I smash his cup against the table, grab a sliver of glass, and hold it to his throat. "Maybe I should go ahead and do it."

Sonny's Adam's apple bobs, and he licks his front teeth while smiling at me. "Do it. Show me you're my don and slit your uncle's throat."

"Antonio," my father warns.

I ignore him and inch the glass into Sonny's pudgy neck.

"Antonio!" My father bangs his fist on the table, and poker chips go flying. "I'm still head of this family, and I'm ordering you to fall back."

I ease the glass sliver away from Sonny's throat and toss it on the table but maintain my glare on him. "Soon, I'll make every decision. Every. Single. Fucking. One."

Sonny juts out his jaw and crosses his arms. "And here I thought, the power was getting to Vinny's head."

"I have to go." I point at Sonny. "Don't do anything stupid."

Unfortunately, Sonny isn't the only person I should've said that to.

22

GIGI

I swear, we've lived in constant chaos since Benny's wedding.

Today is Tommaso's funeral. A heavy veil of rain assaults us as we stand in the cemetery. My heart hurts as I watch Neomi and her sisters grieve while they lower his casket into the ground. Deep down, I know his death will provide him more peace than this life ever did.

Benny tracked down the men responsible for his death. It wasn't the bookie, surprisingly. Tommaso's friends were the ones responsible for Neomi's attempted kidnapping and his murder. It served as another reminder that you can't trust anyone.

The Cavallaro sisters are holding themselves together better than their parents. Neomi's mother, Concetta, is completely consumed with her grief. When the girls and Severino attempt to comfort her, she fights them off.

Benny holds Neomi's hand as the priest says his last words, and I softly squeeze her shoulders while standing behind her. He separates from her when my father calls him over. Neomi continues playing referee with her parents. When her mother starts stomping through the graveyard, Neomi kicks off her heels and follows her.

"I don't know if we should help Neomi or just let them handle it within the family," I say to Natalia.

"I asked your father for his advice this morning," she replies. "He said to be there for Neomi. Neither of us can understand what it feels like, losing a child, you know?" She slumps her shoulders and rubs her belly.

"Hopefully, we never have to either."

A lightning bolt crackles through the sky, and thunder angrily rolls through the storm clouds. I look at Neomi in curiosity when she stops and stares in the distance, almost in a daze.

I inch closer in her direction at the same time she screams, "Benny!"

She changes course and sprints toward Benny but doesn't make it far. Her body jerks, and she collapses to the ground. At the squeal of tires, my attention flies from her to a car driving away. People scatter—either chasing the car, running from bullets, or dashing toward Neomi.

My breath catches in my throat, and I swipe rain off my face as I run to her. When I reach her, Benny is crouched at her side.

I cover my mouth with my hand, vomit threatening to surface. Benny searches her for more wounds, and tears fall down my cheeks as he begs her to open her eyes. He scoops her up in his arms and carries her to my father's SUV. He and my father don't wait for anyone as they speed out of the cemetery.

My head spins as I follow Neomi's sisters, and we run to Bria's car. I jump into the passenger seat, and she guns the gas so hard that we all go flying forward.

"God, please let her be okay," Isabella says next to me, swiping away tears.

I grab her hand and squeeze it.

The urge to vomit resurfaces.

I've never seen my brother so frantic.

So fearful.

He's scared of losing his wife the same way we lost our mother.

We're directed to a private waiting room at the hospital, and no one speaks as we wait for news about Neomi. She fought for her life during the drive to the hospital, and unlike my mother, she was alive when they arrived.

When Dr. Jansky enters the room, Natalia grabs my hand and clasps it inside hers. He's the doctor who broke the news of my mother's death so many years ago. The first man who broke my heart without even knowing.

"Neomi is stable," he tells us.

Relief washes over the room.

"Oh, thank God," Concetta cries out.

I glance at Benny, and his face reveals more than just relief. Vengeance is written all over it, as if it's become a part of his skin. He's ready to make whoever hurt Neomi pay.

"She got lucky," Dr. Jansky adds. "Thankfully, the bullet didn't cause internal damage. She lost a significant amount of blood, so we had to perform a transfusion." He straightens his glasses. "I want to keep her here for a few days to watch her recovery." His eyes meet Benny's. "They are transferring her to the second floor. A nurse will come and let you know when she's able to have visitors."

After Dr. Jansky leaves, Concetta, Bria, and Isabella go outside for fresh air. Severino remains in the room, his hand cradling his face. When he finally lowers it, I see the same thirst for revenge as Benny's.

Benny and my father leave the room.

Natalia and I do the same seconds later and walk toward the vending machines with Bruno behind us.

"Do you think Antonio shot Neomi?" Natalia asks, her voice hushed as I enter the numbers for my selections.

I cast a glance at Bruno, who's checking the hallways, and whisper, "Antonio would never harm Neomi."

At least, I hope he wouldn't.

But at this point, I don't know what to think anymore.

Natalia stares at me skeptically.

"Let's just wait for details. Okay?"

"Wait for the details that the Lombardis did it," Natalia says in total certainty.

I glare at her.

"This thing between you and Antonio needs to end. I'm scared he'll harm you, Gigi. Emotionally … and physically."

"Antonio would never."

"Can you say the same about the rest of the Lombardis? If it comes down to you or his family, who do you think he'll choose?"

I gulp and snatch my snacks from the vending machine. "Please … just don't mention anything about Antonio to my father."

"Your secrets are always safe with me." She stops abruptly to correct herself. "Unless your life is in danger. Then all bets are off. Your father will know everything, so he can kill whoever hurts you."

Antonio was worried about war before, but he has no idea the storm they've unleashed. They'd better pray Neomi lives because the Marchetti wrath is sheer terror.

"It was a Lombardi," Benny tells my father in the hospital hallway. "One of Cavallaro's men took a picture of the license plate and ran it through the system."

I stay around the corner, my back plastered against the wall, and silently beg for invisibility while straining to hear their conversation.

"Stupid fuckers didn't even use an unmarked car," my father says tensely. "It's like they want us to know it was them."

"Word is, it was Lombardi's last wish to kill me. A son for a son."

"Last wish? What does that mean?"

"I have no idea, but I'll ask him that question right before I kill him." Benny releases a stressed breath. "But first, I need to make sure my wife is okay."

"I'm proud of you, Benny. I don't know if I say that enough, but I'm honored to be your father. What happened to Neomi wasn't your fault. It was Vincent's. Don't let your mind go there."

"Is that how you felt when Vinny took Natalia?"

"At first, no. I almost let it eat me alive. But then I realized it was more important to help my wife deal with the trauma of what had happened than feel sorry for myself."

"I'm going to kill them for creating that trauma."

"Take care of your wife. Then we'll kill them."

Bruno calls my name, and I back away from the wall. He drives me home, and I wait to cry until I'm in my bedroom.

It's time for me to fulfill my duty to protect my family.

For me to abandon my innocence and become a ruthless Marchetti.

I need to speak with my father.

My life is about to change.

23

ANTONIO

There's nothing better than seeing my daughter happy.

After weeks of Amara's persistent pleas, I relented, allowing her to return to dance classes on the condition that Damien or I was in attendance.

Sitting in the packed theater's aisle, I watch Amara's show, and when it ends, I stand, giving them a standing ovation. The dancers take their final bows, and Pippa leads them offstage.

I rub my temple with one hand and withdraw my phone from my pocket with the other. During the show, I kept it on silent. My daughter deserves an hour of my undivided attention. A list of missed calls and text notifications crowd the screen.

"Fuck," I hiss, and that gains me a dirty look from the yuppie parents beside me.

I glare at the high-powered stockbroker who turns to glare, and his wife shakes her head in distaste.

Little does the asshole's wife know, I'm not the only one who has blood on his hands. A decade ago, her husband paid us a hundred grand to murder his competition for a job promotion.

I stand, elbowing the side of the asshole's head, and walk into the lobby. The first call I return is Damien's.

"Neomi Cavallaro was shot at Tommaso's funeral," he immediately says with no greeting. "The target was Benny. Neomi was hit by accident."

"Fuck!" I roar, gaining disapproving looks again. "Did Sonny call it?"

"Your father."

I tighten my grip on the phone. "Come to the theater now."

"Already on my way. ETA: five minutes."

"Meet me in the lobby." I end the call and hit my father's name.

Voicemail.

I try again.

Voicemail.

I'm on call number fifteen when Damien enters the lobby.

"Take Amara and Clara straight home," I instruct. "Lock the place up. Have every man we can trust there. No one comes and goes from there unless I say so."

I find my father alone in his basement. The only light comes from a solitary lamp, and he isn't paying attention to *Jeopardy* on the TV. He's staring into space, as if someone turned off a switch in his brain.

My father, once a strong and vicious man, feared by many, now looks so helpless. Not one man is by his side.

It's a reality check really.

People will respect you one day and discard you the next.

Once you become weak, you're useless.

"I'm sorry, Antonio," he says, sinking further into the leather recliner. "It was … a lapse in judgment."

"Why?" I scream. "Why would you do something so reckless?"

"Cristian murdered my son." He slams his trembling finger into his chest. "It was only fair that I caused him the same pain.

A son for a son." He squeezes his eyes shut. "My mistake was choosing an unskilled shooter. I never intended for the bullet to hit Severino's daughter."

"Unskilled shooter? Who the fuck shot her?"

"Ricky."

"Your babysitter?"

He winces at my response.

I've been careful not to refer to Ricky as his babysitter before.

Sonny brought Ricky into the family even though he's incompetent as fuck. So I gave him the job of hanging out with my father. He helps him with his medication and takes him to physical therapy every day. I never mentioned *shoot someone for him* in the fucking job description.

"Were you with Ricky when he shot her?" I kneel in front of him and get in his face. "Answer me!"

He nods, and his voice is hoarse when he says, "Yes."

I curl my hands into fists. "We agreed not to do anything stupid."

"Not doing anything stupid makes us weak!"

Sonny got in his head. I'm sure of it.

"Congratulations." I inch back and stand tall. "You just fucked us. The Marchettis and Cavallaros won't sleep until every man in our family is dead after this. And I'll be the first person on their list. *A son for a son*, right?"

The reality of his mistake finally dawns on him.

His hand shakes as he reaches out toward me. "Antonio—"

"Fucking save it." I stare at him in repulsion. "I need to get my daughter to safety before a Marchetti bombs my house or kills her for"—I stop and raise my voice—"your fucking lapse in judgment!"

"Antonio." He struggles to get my entire name out.

I blink, stopping to pay close attention to him.

"Anton—" This time, his voice is slurred. "Anto—" He

attempts to reach for his cane and sways forward before losing his balance.

I rush toward him when he collapses out of the recliner. "Dad!"

He grabs my wrist as I help him to his feet, and I realize he can't stand on his own. As I hold him up, one side of his face droops. He opens his mouth, attempting to tell me something, but all that comes out are muffled sounds.

My forehead lines with sweat as I frantically pull my phone from my pocket. In my gut, I know this is different from any of his other strokes.

I clutch him tight, as if I know this is the one that will take him from me, while calling 911.

"Everything is okay," I say. "You'll be okay, Dad. I promise."

He grips my arms tight, staring at me in apology, as I help him outside to the ambulance. The EMTs transport him to the same hospital where Neomi is recovering from the bullet wound he caused.

24

GIGI

The sound of my knock on my father's office door echoes through the dark stillness of the mansion. Before coming downstairs, I downed a glass of wine and meditated for forty-five minutes. It's what a girl should do before deciding to change her entire life.

"Yes, Gigi." My father briefly glances up at me, not in the mood for meaningless conversation.

I wander into his office and anxiously run a hand down my silk pajamas before taking a seat across from him. "I think it's time I get married."

His dark brows draw together, and he sighs. "Now isn't the time for games."

"The Lombardis declared war on us, Daddy. Other families will choose sides, and we need everyone to choose ours."

He stares at me, and for *his* first time ever, he's speechless.

I inhale a soft breath. "They are responsible for kidnapping Natalia, for shooting Neomi, for trying to kill my brother—"

"How do you know that?" he interrupts.

I chew into my lip. "I sort of … eavesdropped."

He shakes his head yet allows me to continue. It makes me

proud that he's willing to hear me out. I feel like he's giving me a seat at the table.

"They want us dead."

He nods in agreement yet continues to give me my moment.

"And if there's anything I've learned, it's that marriages forge alliances among families. Stronger connections increase the likelihood of winning. I'm open to marrying someone who will help us."

The room falls silent for a moment until he violently shakes his head and says, "Gigi, I promised your mother you'd select your husband."

"And I will choose him. You'll provide me with a list of options, and I'll choose one." I stand and fight for my voice not to tremble. "I'm ready to do this. It's time I contribute to this family."

25

ANTONIO

I sit in the hospital room, listening to the machine's persistent beepings, while my father fights for his life. Today's stroke was the worst he's ever suffered.

I'm the only person at his bedside. My mother claimed she was too distraught to drive to the hospital. None of his men have called or come to check on him. Their silence speaks volumes of their loyalty—or lack thereof.

Earlier, I paid a nurse to provide me with information on Neomi's condition. My headache lessened some when she informed me Neomi was awake and in better condition than my father. She also informed me Benny had the look of a man driven with a desire for revenge.

I have to be smart about my next move, but I'm also limited. As much as I need to leave the hospital and make calls without possible listening ears, I can't. He isn't safe alone here. Anyone can come in and kill him. I won't risk it.

Damien told me Sonny called a meeting and suggested he step up as boss until my father heals. I have no idea what's transpiring behind my back.

Sonny is getting what he wants.

War.

Not only with the Marchettis, but with me as well.

A civil war.

A war between rivals.

I need to be ready.

It was only a matter of time before someone leaked my father's room number. The Marchettis have better connections than us. They also have the Severinos, who are just as resourceful as them.

We're so fucked, and I'm on my own.

While sitting in the dark room, I feel so fucking lost and hardly notice the movie playing in the background. My attention shifts to the door when it creeps open.

I crack my neck.

Do motherfuckers think I'm as stupid as my brother?

I flip on the lamp next to me, shift in my seat, and find Benny standing in the doorway. He doesn't look guilty or taken aback by my catching him.

"I figured you'd come roaming in here like the vermin you are," I snarl.

This is exactly why I refused to leave my father's bedside. Our brains think too much alike because I'd do the same thing if I were in Benny's shoes.

"My guess is, you're not here for a welfare check," I continue. "What was your plan? Come in here and kill him?" I scoff, shaking my head. "Did you not consider that they'd check the cameras and see you?"

"My men are good at erasing camera footage," Benny replies.

I scoff again.

"But since I don't like witnesses, I'll have to also kill you. What was it I heard he said?" He drums his finger against his chin. "A son for a son? Me for Vinny."

Of course he heard what my father had said. The only

person who would've leaked that is Sonny's traitorous ass. He wants the Marchettis to kill me, so he doesn't look like he has my blood on his hands and can easily become don.

"My father is dying, Benny," I tell him, nearly out of patience with this conversation.

With this life.

With this bullshit.

"Do me a favor and allow him to pass in peace," I add.

"No." He pauses for a moment before adding, "Men who call hits on other men don't deserve favors."

"I didn't know about the hit." I rise to my feet, too tired for this bullshit yet knowing this is just the start of the war I'll soon be facing. "Had I known about it, I'd have advised him against it, as I've done several times since your father killed Vinny. Whenever he wanted to strike, I talked sense into him."

He levels his stare on me. "What happened this time, then?"

"My father has struggled with health issues for the past two months, and his decision-making has been limited. Yesterday wasn't his first stroke, but it'll be his last. We will place him in hospice until he goes."

Telling Benny this is risky.

What do I have to lose at this point though?

"Good." Benny smirks. "It's time he rots."

I wince, my muscles tensing, as we stand only a few feet away from each other. "I don't believe my father would've okayed the hit if he had been in his right state of mind."

"But he did. Right frame of mind or not, he needs to pay for his mistake. Unless you'd like to?" He raises a brow. "Make the prince pay for the king's wrongs?"

"I don't want you dead or to go to war with your family."

"Bullshit. My father killed your brother."

"Because my brother was stupid enough to kidnap your father's fiancée." I interlock my fingers together and rest them on my forehead. "My uncle Sonny has called my legitimacy to become boss into question within the family. He and Vinny were close. He's made it clear to the family that I am a traitor for not wanting to ruthlessly murder your family." I lower my hand to jerk a finger toward my father while staring at Benny in confliction. "As soon as he dies, everything will change. Whether that's good or bad depends on who takes over. Sonny wants to be king and wants you dead. He's the one who sent men to follow you to the club the night your car was shot up."

Benny smiles while inching toward my father. "Let him try."

The tension in my body grows when he reaches forward and snatches his breathing mask off his face.

"Rot in hell," Benny says, pulling the mask back and quickly spitting in my father's mouth.

He backs up, and I immediately punch him in the face. As bad as I want to blow his brains out, I can't do that in the hospital.

The motherfucker laughs and rubs where I hit him. "If your dad makes it out of the hospital alive, my wrath will be ten times worse than that." He leaves the room.

I believe Benny.

Which is why my wrath needs to exceed his.

Exceed Sonny's.

I want to strangle my father for what he did, but I still have a loyalty to him.

It's time I find out if anyone has any fucking loyalty to me.

"Here we fucking go," I grumble toward my father.

26

ANTONIO

"Vincent Lombardi, the notorious Mafia boss of the Lombardi crime family, was pronounced dead this morning."

With the flick of my thumb, I change the TV channel.

"The streets of New York City are safer now that Vincent Lombardi, feared crime boss—"

Next channel.

"If you or a loved one has been affected by—"

I turn off the TV.

Unsurprisingly, my father never recovered from his stroke. He was put in hospice in his home after leaving the hospital and died without anyone by his side. You wouldn't have believed that from his funeral though. Everyone in the Lombardi organization showed and faked cordialness, but the unspoken tension was like a tightly wound coil that would unravel soon. Men who were loyal to my father for years are now against me. Every inch of them reeked with betrayal as they stood next to Sonny.

Sonny enters my father's office while I'm clearing it out, and I refuse to acknowledge his presence. Nuncio stands behind him, looking torn between guilt and smugness. I'd bet my share of the casino that Sonny promised him something in exchange for turning against me. Probably moving up in rank.

"Look, Antonio," Sonny says, clasping his hands together. "We can do this the hard way or the easy way."

I play with a bookend in my hand, moving it from one to the other, and click my tongue against the roof of my mouth. "You should know I don't deal well with threats, *Uncle*, nor do I enjoy doing shit the easy way."

He stands taller but can't quite hide the hunch in his back. "Agree to me stepping up as boss. Tell our men today."

I sharply laugh. "Fuck off."

"You can be my capo."

"Fuck you and your little traitor behind you." I waggle the bookend toward Nuncio.

Nuncio puffs up his chest.

Sonny levels his voice. "I've done this longer than you."

"Correct, which means your brain is fucking dead." I stare at him, stone-faced. "You'll be the next man to suffer from bad health and bite the dust. With your health and that figure, I'll give you two years before you're annoying the fuck out of Satan in hell."

"You're a smart man—I'll give you that—but I'll make this family stronger." His face reddens. "We'll run this city. I don't think you can lead us into that."

Nuncio nods behind him as two other men join him.

I clear my throat and look Sonny straight in his cataract-ridden eyes. "Go fuck yourself."

He throws a manila folder across the room, and it lands on the desk with a weighted thud. "Until next time then, nephew."

I rub a hand over my jaw, watching them exit the room, and wait to open the folder until they're gone.

I flip through the photos of Amara and me.

Clara and Amara.

And Gigi.

"Motherfucker." I hurl the folder across the room.

Visiting Seven Seconds is risky.

I'm doing it for Amara.

For the men who remain loyal to me, refusing to switch to Sonny's side and risking their lives for it.

Benny agreeing to meet with me was a surprise. It could be a setup, and maybe I'm walking straight into a death trap. Although, in the years I've known Benny, he's given me better respect than any other Lombardi. But given all the bullshit that's happened, there's a possibility he'll shoot me as soon as he sees me. Never put anything past the Marchettis.

People stare as I walk through the hallway in the back of the club, and one of Benny's men stops at a door before opening it and gesturing for me to go inside.

My hands are sweaty, yet I keep my cool as I walk inside.

"Antonio Lombardi," Benny greets dryly, sitting behind his desk and not bothering to stand. "Shouldn't you be out somewhere, mourning your father's admission into hell?"

I grit my teeth, shut the door, and walk to him.

Benny reclines in his leather chair, propping his feet up on the desk while drinking. "To what do I owe the pleasure of this unwanted visit?"

"I told you there'd be problems with my uncle upon my father's death," I tell him straight up, no time for bullshit.

"You did, but I don't understand what that has to do with me. I'm not in your family—thank God." He directs his glass toward me. "Sucks for you, though. Good luck in your fighting."

"I need your connections." I pinch the bridge of my nose, hoping to ease the stress. "Out of respect for your father, Severino has cut off all relations with my family. That includes selling us firearms. I need you to convince Severino to change his mind and help me out."

Severino is the top supplier of illegal weapons in the country.

His connections led to Neomi and Benny's contractual marriage. In the past year, he's limited his business with us, but after Vinny's behavior and the wedding incident, he terminated all association.

Benny drops his feet, leans forward, and settles his elbows on the desk. "Even if they didn't cut you off then, do you think they'd sell anything to a Lombardi after one shot their daughter, you fucking morons?"

I hold back the impulse to shoot the pompous asshole in the head. "I'm here to make a deal. We have great connections overseas. I have multiple reps with banks the United States hasn't even heard of. Any connection I have is all yours. Talk to your father and Severino. Help me out here."

"But will those connections overseas be on your side or your uncle's?" He downs his drink.

"My uncle wants your family to pay for Vinny's death. He will go after Natalia, Gigi, and Neomi if he has to. You will also go to war with my family if my uncle takes charge."

"I'd better keep all those weapons connections for myself then, huh?"

"I have a daughter, Benny. She's six, and she already doesn't have a mother. I can't leave her alone in this world."

"I have no heartstrings for you to tug, Antonio. If that's your plan B, it won't work." Shaking his head, he places his glass on a coaster. "I suggest finding her somewhere to go because you'll die if you don't win."

My jaw tightens, the muscles rigid. "I guess we'll all get ready for a game of bloodshed."

"Can't wait. Save me a seat." He stares down at his phone when it vibrates. "I have another meeting to attend. You can see yourself out."

"Don't say I didn't warn you," I say before leaving his office.

Plan one fucking hundred failed.

Now, onto the next.

27

GIGI

I flip through the folder of prospective husbands my father handed me three weeks ago. I've read each paper so many times that I've practically memorized every man's bio.

It's not exactly easy to select a husband from a résumé. None of them have social media, which isn't surprising. There are plenty of news articles about them, referring to their influence, criminal history—or lack thereof—as well as their net worth.

My mouth is as dry as a desert when I pull the top paper from the stack, shut the folder, and place it on top.

"There he is," I whisper to myself, tracing my red-nailed finger along his name. "My future husband."

I asked my father to keep the news of my potential marriage a secret until I reached a final decision. I want no outside influence on my decision. It's for me and me only.

There's also so much happening in the family that I don't want to stress anyone. Natalia's due date is quickly approaching. Benny and Neomi just finished building a new home on the property, only a few acres from the mansion. They deserve that excitement without me interfering with husband-picking.

"I still don't understand why you're going to Chicago solo," Natalia says, making herself comfortable on my bed while I pack my overnight bag.

I shove three pairs of black lace panties inside. "Shopping."

"And I can't go?" She scrunches her nose.

Since she found out that Antonio went to Benny's office, Natalia has been keeping a closer eye on me. I've even caught her checking my phone a few times, most likely looking for traces of Antonio.

Speaking of Antonio …

There's been nothing but radio silence from him.

Whatever we had between us is over now.

"I'm buying my baby brother gifts you can't see." I hate lying to her. "Plus, you need to stay in New York in case your water breaks. My father would lose his shit if you were in a different state so close to your due date."

"True." She snatches a pillow and levels her elbows on it. "I'm surprised he's even letting you leave."

"Bruno will be with me."

She furrows her brows. "Are you keeping something from me?"

"Oh, shush." I flick my hand through the air. "You know every move I make."

"At least bring Neomi or Benny with you. Neomi never turns down a shopping trip."

"They're busy." I zip up my bag.

"I don't like you traveling solo."

"Again, *Bruno will be with me.*"

Two of the men on my potential husband list live in the city. I didn't choose them because my father already has strong connections here. New York is covered. The Cavallaros and O'Connors promised to have his back and refuse any business dealings with the Lombardis.

I chose a man who lives in Chicago, but I need to meet him before committing to marriage. A man can easily manipulate his reputation on paper and online.

I hug Natalia goodbye, kiss her belly, and Bruno and I drive off toward Chicago. He rolls his eyes when I turn on Taylor Swift, and when he takes a phone call, my mind drifts to Antonio. Sadness rips through me, and I gulp at the realization he'll never be my husband.

That thought was only wishful thinking by a naive me.

The dark princess foolishly believed she'd get a sparkly fairy tale.

Maybe Antonio isn't my destiny.

Maybe the love of my life is waiting for me in Chicago.

When I meet Elijah Becker in the lobby of the Waldorf Astoria, my stomach is a roller coaster.

"Gigi Marchetti." Elijah says my name like a well-rehearsed poem written on his lips, like I already mean everything to him.

As if he's already decided I'm his future.

Bruno stands a few feet away from me, giving us some privacy. As a show of respect, Elijah nods toward him.

Bruno watching us feels strange.

Like an overprotective brother chaperoning my first date.

Elijah grabs my hand and brushes his lips against it. His hand has the perfect balance of tenderness yet roughness.

I should be blushing.

Swooning at the romantic gesture.

But I can't stop comparing his lips on my skin to Antonio's.

The first time Antonio touched me, it wasn't gentle.

It was menacing.

With one touch, Antonio burned my skin, branding himself on me. Sometimes, I still feel the heat on every inch where he put his hands and mouth on me. Antonio will always be an invisible mark on my skin. A secret flame that only I'll ever feel and see.

Elijah's touch barely ignites a spark inside me.

Give it time, Gigi.

Get to know him.

Not all loves are instant. Some gradually unfold.

Elijah clasps our hands and leads me outside while Bruno follows us. The wind brushes my cheeks as he guides me toward a black Rolls-Royce Phantom. Bruno takes the front passenger seat, and Elijah joins me in the back. He slides close, his thigh brushing mine, and I inhale the strong scent of his cologne. He smells expensive, manly, meh.

Antonio's cologne smells sexier.

Dammit.

Will I always compare any man to the first one who broke my heart?

"You look beautiful," Elijah says, interrupting my thoughts.

I feel his intense stare on me even through the dimness of the car.

"I've seen pictures of you, of course," he continues. "Yet they do you no justice. You are absolutely breathtaking."

"Thank you." A hint of shyness washes over me.

Maybe Elijah can break the chains of my obsession with Antonio.

His driver drives us to Obelix, my favorite restaurant in the city. Either Elijah chose it out of sheer luck, or my father provided him with that detail.

Bruno sits at the bar, drinking water, while our server escorts us to a secluded table away from the other diners.

Elijah is a gentleman.

A charmer.

But not Antonio charm.

More crooked-politician charming.

He's handsome with a perfectly shaped nose, dimpled

cheeks, and a tan, heart-shaped face. He speaks well, like a natural-born congressman who fell on the wrong side of the law.

And he's wealthy with powerful connections. According to the info sheet my father provided, Elijah has great weapons connections and affiliations with three senators, a Supreme Court justice, and the head of the ATF.

The perfect package.

We order our food and talk for hours, like two old friends reconnecting. There isn't one awkward silence between us. Time passes, and we finish two bottles of red wine.

I've made the right choice.

Elijah will make a great husband.

"I want to marry you, Gigi," he says bluntly before we leave.

His statement makes my head dizzy.

Or maybe it's the wine.

Probably both.

He runs his napkin along his lips. "I know you live in New York, and I'm not a fan of long-distance relationships, so I'll purchase a home in New York. We can fly back and forth on my jet. Whatever you want in this life, Gigi, I will give you."

I smile at him.

He grins. "A smile is good."

My smile grows.

He pushes his hand into his black blazer and withdraws a black velvet box before sliding it toward me.

I wince.

Whoa. This is moving fast.

Please don't drop down on one knee here.

He chuckles, as if reading my mind. "Don't worry, this isn't your wedding ring." He opens the box, revealing a sparkling solitaire diamond on a band adorned with smaller diamonds. "It's a promise ring."

It isn't promise-ring material.

It's straight engagement-ring material.

"If you say yes, I'll schedule a meeting with my jeweler, so we can create the ring of your dreams. Be my wife, and I will make you happy every day of your life. I will protect you. Protect your family. And spoil the fuck out of you."

My smile grows times two.

"Yes," I whisper.

28

ANTONIO

ONE MONTH LATER

"Your mom is getting sketchier and sketchier," Damien tells me over the phone as I exit the casino. "So I'll reiterate again, don't tell her shit."

Sonny pretty much abandoned the casino and all his responsibilities associated with it after my father's death. Smart on his part since it would've made it incredibly easy for me to kill a man who showed up to his nine-to-fucking-five every day.

Me? I'm here, day after day, taking care of business while waiting for him to show his hideous-ass face.

He's done nothing but make threats while not following through. He's waiting for the perfect time to strike, so I need to be ready.

Not every man joined him. Some kept their loyalty to the Lombardi name.

Twelve men who once served under my father left with Sonny, and ten stayed with me. The others fled the state, not wanting to choose a side.

I've already killed three of Sonny's men, which drops him down to nine. I shot two others and instructed them to deliver messages to Sonny. There have been rumors he's recruiting men off the street to join him, providing them with a false hope of being involved with a Mafia crime family. Sure, the job sounds enticing in the beginning. What he fails to inform them is untrained men end up dead within the first month. That's why every man of mine was brought into the family through merit and affiliation.

I grit my teeth while approaching my car. "Don't worry. I've kept her in the dark, where she belongs."

Men have been watching my mother. I tested her loyalty and learned we couldn't trust her. I told her I'd be at certain locations at exact times, and Sonny's men would conveniently arrive there. She's a fucking traitor.

"She's been to the hair salon twice and nail salon four times," Damien continues. "When Pippa and I were dating, I always paid for that shit. And let me tell you, that isn't fucking normal."

The fact that I can't trust the woman who brought me into the world is unfortunate. She's either using the salons as a way to meet Sonny or deliver messages to him.

"Tell Julian to continue following every move she makes," I tell him. "She's bound to slip up."

"On it," Damien replies, and we end the call as I slide into my car.

Then I call my rat of a mother.

"Hi, honey," she coos on the other end as if I were a small child. The pep in her voice makes me sick to my stomach.

"What did you do today?" I'm not one for small talk with people I don't trust.

"Oh, nothing." She drags out the last word. "Just brunch and stuff."

I'm fighting for my family's life, and she's *brunching. What a joke.*

I scratch my cheek. "Do you think it's a good idea to *brunch,* given our circumstances?"

Her laughter grates on my nerves. "Brunch is always a good

idea, honey. Maybe we should have brunch sometime this week."

I tighten my grip on my phone. "What about dinner tonight?"

"Of course." That pep in her voice explodes with excitement. "You tell me when and where, and I'll be there."

"What about your house? A good ole-fashioned family dinner."

"Oh, terrific! I've missed those. Will Amara be there? I miss my granddaughter so much."

"Yes," I lie, my fingers digging into the phone.

My daughter isn't going anywhere near her shady ass.

"Five o'clock," I say. "We'll be there."

I'm potentially walking into a death trap, but fuck it.

When I walk into my mother's house, she's waiting for me in the foyer.

Looking past me, she frowns. "Where's Amara? I wanted to show her your father's favorite places in the garden. It'd be a great reminder of him."

I raise a brow. "In the dark?"

She stumbles for words to mask her bullshit lie. "I mean, we have lights out there."

"Clara is bringing her."

"Oh." The word pops out of her mouth. "Clara is coming as well?"

"I figured they'd like to get out of the house and enjoy a nice meal with the *family* we have left. Father would've liked that."

"Yes ... he would've." She slides her hands down her designer dress.

I walk farther into the home, and she gasps when she notices Damien behind me. Good thing my father never used her for help on luring people in because she fucking sucks at it.

"Oh, I didn't know Damien would also be joining us." She's so disappointed that you'd think I told her that brunch was now illegal.

Damien closes the door and then smiles mockingly at her. "I just had to have one of your home-cooked meals, Marsha."

She appears frazzled and carefully walks in her heels like she's never worn a pair before. The usual dinner staff is nowhere to be found. What's even more surprising is she scurries into the kitchen—somewhere she never goes during family dinners because she refuses to mess up her nails while cooking.

I draw my gun and trail her to find Sonny in the kitchen. His chest puffs up when he sees me, and we raise our guns at the same time. Damien is behind me seconds later, his gun also pointing at Sonny.

"You stupid motherfucker," I yell, charging toward him.

He snatches my mother and plants his gun against her skull. "Sorry, Marsha, baby. I'm only doing this to make sure I'm still alive to protect you."

My mother trembles in his hold. "My son would never hurt me." Her gaze lands on me, and her voice is stern. "Just let him take over, Antonio. He'll do right by the family. I promise."

"You're really over there, protecting a man holding a gun to your head?"

"Just shoot Sonny. Who cares if he shoots Marsha in the process?" Damien says mercilessly yet also sounding bored. "It's clear she can't be trusted."

"I never liked you," my mother snarls at him.

Damien makes eye contact with her. "And I don't give two fucks."

I pull the trigger. The bullet smacks into his shoulder since that's the only clear shot I have without possibly hitting my mother.

Sonny cries out, his body falling back and smacking into a

cabinet. He drops his gun, and my mother immediately snatches it. She stands tall in front of Sonny, as if his bodyguard, and raises the gun toward Damien and me.

"I'm only doing this for your own good," she says, her voice shaking as she holds the gun as steady as she can.

Sonny snatches a dish towel and presses it against his wound, applying as much pressure as he can.

"Step down, *please*," my mother begs.

"This was your plan tonight, wasn't it?" My arm flexes as I tighten my grip on my gun. "Get me here alone and then let him kill me?"

She gasps. "Of course not. Sonny only wanted to talk with you."

I scoff.

Damien snorts.

She scrambles for words while glancing at the door. "His men—"

"Don't you dare say a word, Marsha," Sonny grunts, grabbing her waist with one arm and tugging her back. He captures the gun from her hand while groaning at his shoulder wound.

If only I could've shot him in the head. I'd find his brain matter in the kitchen more appetizing than anything my mother could've prepared.

She continues standing in front of Sonny, and I hear a rush of voices.

Sonny cackles. "Your death warrant is here, Antonio. Have fun trying to outpower ten of my men versus you two."

I glance back at Damien, and right before I can shoot Sonny again, Nuncio appears in the doorway. Since I didn't put this past my mother, I have an escape plan for Damien and me.

I jump over the island while we exit through the kitchen staff's entrance. Nuncio chases us, and Damien shoots at him while I key in a passcode to enter the underground passages my father secretly constructed before he and my mother moved in.

The door beeps, the keypad turns green, and I open the steel door. Damien slips inside and slams the door only seconds before Nuncio reaches us. Nuncio bangs on the other side and tells us we're dead men.

My adrenaline is wild as we run through the tunnel, and I direct him toward one of the three exits. We jog the mile run to the hidden exit, and Julian awaits us. I dig the remote from my pocket and press my thumb against the button.

I grin at the sound of a loud boom.

Damien laughs.

Julian shakes his head and calls me fucking crazy.

Before we walked into my mother's house, we dropped bombs into the bushes beside the front door. I'm always prepared for violence.

"This isn't fucking over," Damien says, adjusting his collar as we duck into Julian's SUV.

"It's just started." I wipe the side of my mouth as Julian speeds off in the opposite direction of my mother's house. "If Sonny survives that bomb, I'll gut him alive and record him screaming in pain, so I can listen to it anytime I'm having a bad day."

"Uh …" Julian pays me a quick glance. "I don't know if this is a bad time to tell you this, but …" He hesitates.

"Spit it out, Julian."

"Gigi is engaged to Elijah Becker."

I sit in my car, chewing on a toothpick, while parked in front of the Chicago high-rise. People pass by as I slip on black leather gloves and exit my car. Lucky for me, Julian has great connections in Illinois. I hand the employee a folded hundred, and he waves me in through the back door.

There's a long list of reasons I dislike Elijah Becker.

First, I hate his piece-of-shit family. I killed a few members years ago, including his brother. Well deserved, of course. Elijah never sought revenge for his brother's death. Instead, he sent me a bottle of Dom Perignon. He's now his father's successor to their crime empire.

Second, whenever I was around him in the past, he annoyed the ever-loving fuck out of me. The man laughs at his own jokes, flexes his money like it makes his dick bigger, and has the shiny face of a family full of criminals. Pot calling the kettle black on that last reason, but I don't give a fuck.

Third and most important is his newfound interest in Gigi. According to my sources, she visited Chicago, had dinner with Elijah, and then returned to New York. That isn't some mere coincidence. It doesn't take many brain cells to figure out their game.

Elijah would be a great ally to Cristian because he does a great job of hiding how crooked he is. No way am I letting him get his hands on Gigi.

It'll be fun to take my frustrations out on him.

I take the stairs to his penthouse, key gripped in my hand, and let myself in. The place is silent and empty, and I pour a drink before making myself comfortable at the dining room table while waiting on Elijah.

Two hours later, the door opens, and Elijah comes into view with a woman behind him. I watch as she giggles annoyingly while following him into the living room.

"Suck this dick," Elijah tells her, slumping on the couch as the blonde kneels between his legs.

I down my drink, stand, and stroll toward them. "Well, well, well, what do we have here?"

Their attention snaps toward me as I join them.

Elijah narrows his eyes at me. "What the fuck do you want, Lombardi?" His voice has an irritating slur.

He nudges the girl with his knee, and she starts unbuckling his belt.

I work my jaw. "Stay away from Gigi Marchetti."

He scoffs. "Not happening. She's my fiancée."

"What?" The woman jerks away from him. "You're getting married?"

He grabs her long hair and pushes her head down. "Shut the fuck up and put your lips on my cock."

She winces in pain.

I withdraw my gun from my pocket.

Elijah relaxes against the couch cushion, unfazed. "You kill me, you'll piss Cristian Marchetti off."

I shrug. "In case you didn't hear, I'm already on his kill list."

His shoulders stiffen some. "What do you want, then?"

"I told you."

He smirks. "Too bad. Gigi is mine."

Gigi is mine.

I swallow back the urge to slit his throat and throw him out the window for uttering those words.

But I can't kill him yet.

I need to use him first.

29

GIGI

Meet my baby brother.

Spend all day at the hospital with Natalia, my father, and the newest member of the Marchetti family.

We haven't had many days that were just … positive.

That's all today will be. A positive party.

I drive to the hospital alone. Since Bruno is sick, I instructed him to stay home and rest. The trip to the hospital is short, and my father went to great lengths to ensure they provided privacy for them during Natalia's stay.

My first mistake is paying more attention to my playlist than my surroundings. No way will that make my father proud. My second mistake is assuming daylight offers me safety. I should've known better.

I park in the hospital's lot, step out of my car, and stop when I notice a black car brake behind mine, blocking me in. Antonio appears in front of me, the gun in his hand pointed in my direction, sending shivers down my spine.

So much for that to-do list and a positive party, dammit.

"Really?" I stare at him in disbelief. "I could easily scream right now."

I should scream right now.

"Your *fiancé* is tied up in my trunk," he says, his voice devoid of emotion. "You scream, I'll kill him. I also put a bomb in your brother's car that will go off if you don't get in mine in the next five seconds. Do you want them to die?" He jerks his chin toward his car. "Your choice, princess."

Oh, this manipulative motherfucker has finally resorted to manipulating me.

I've become one of his many puppets.

"Now," he yells. "And leave all your shit in the car."

I hold my palms toward him in surrender and walk to his car. He trails me so close that his chest grazes my back before opening the passenger door and motioning for me to get in. I huff while dropping in the seat, and he slams the door behind me.

I've officially become the easiest kidnapping victim in history.

Hell, I made it so simple for him.

But he knows my weaknesses.

Knows how to make me surrender to him.

Like a starved person lured into a trap by a warm meal.

"You'd better not be fucking lying," I sneer, yanking the seat belt across my body when he joins me in the car.

He slams his foot on the gas, and we speed out of the parking lot.

"When have I ever lied to you?" he finally asks when we're out of sight from the hospital.

I scoff. "I don't know if you've *ever* been honest with me." Crossing my arms, I glare at him and slap my leg. "Kidnapped by my ex-boyfriend. What a way to ruin a good day."

What a fucking lunatic.

Typical Lombardi.

I should've listened to the gossip to never trust one.

And to kidnap Elijah?

What the actual fuck?

He interrupts my thoughts. "I love that you refer to me as your ex-boyfriend."

"I hate you," I hiss.

"No, you don't."

"Just wait until my father finds out about this. You won't make it past a day of having me."

He clicks the turn signal and cuts a right.

At least my kidnapper follows traffic laws.

"I'm serious, Antonio. He'll kill you." I twist in my seat, looking in the back, as if I have X-ray vision to see if Elijah is in the trunk. "And in case you didn't know, Elijah's family is also dangerous."

"You don't want to marry Elijah."

I roll my eyes. "And why is that?"

"He's weak."

"You have no idea that he's weak."

"Gigi, he's currently in my trunk. That should make it obvious he's weak."

"And what about you? You had to kidnap me, and now, we're what … on the run? It seems like you, my villain, are the weak one."

"If that were true, *I'd* be the one in the trunk."

"Show me the proof he's even in there. I don't believe you."

"Patience, princess." He tsks. "As soon as we reach our desti-nation, your fiancé will make his appearance."

"Speaking of appearance, what the hell happened to you?"

The man who's abducted me isn't *my Antonio.*

No, he kind of looks like hell—probably because he's been through hell. His cheeks, which I've felt between my legs so many times, have more scruff than I've ever seen on him. Even the stubble can't mask the exhaustion there.

The depth of his eyes holds nothing but darkness.

Hollowness.

A man who's already lost so much and refuses to lose any more.

My poor, violent villain in black armor.

In this world of chaos, violence is how he survives.

His lifeline.

And he's proving it.

He doesn't answer my question. Instead, he turns on a desolate road, driving us farther away from the city. So I stay quiet, denying my kidnapping Romeo the satisfaction of hearing a single word slip from my lips.

A loud thud comes from the trunk when Antonio makes a sharp right. I peer at him, and any doubt he has *someone* in the trunk is gone.

But how the hell did he know about Elijah?

My father made every husband prospect sign NDAs.

I'm so in my zone that I stupidly don't pay attention to his direction. If I were smart and not in love with my abductor, I'd pay attention to every detail to plot an escape.

We're in the middle of nowhere when he turns down a long drive to a cabin and parks. My heart races, the reality of what's happening finally settling into my stomach. Antonio steps out of the car, opens my door, and jerks me from my seat.

I dig my heels into the ground, resisting him from dragging me inside the cabin, and curse when one breaks.

Damn you, Prada.

He throws me over his heavy shoulder in annoyance.

I bite into his shoulder over his white button-up. He doesn't flinch while stomping up the steps and into the cabin. I'm cursing and punching my fists against his back, and he tosses me on a sectional couch. I land on it with a similar thud as whatever —or *whoever*—in his trunk.

When I attempt to spring forward, he places his hands on my chest and launches me backward. My head slams into the back of the couch, and I scowl as he towers over me.

"Don't you dare fucking move from this couch," he demands.

"Why are you doing this?" My throat feels scratchy and raw.

"So you don't die," he says, exasperated with me.

I wince. "Why would I die?"

The pain in my ass leaves the cabin without answering me.

This is my time to run.

Just as I start to jump up, a man I didn't notice in the corner takes two swift strides forward and stops me. He crosses his arms, his face full of threats as he silently tells me to sit my ass back down. I cross my arms, mirroring him, and he nudges my shoulder back. His push isn't as hard as Antonio's, but I still end up with my ass back on the cushions.

I could attempt to crawl over the couch and run.

Where would I run to though?

I have no idea where I am, no phone, and Antonio would probably catch me outside.

I just need to wait it out until my father finds me.

He found Natalia, another victim of Lombardi's sticky fingers with people, within a day. No doubt he'll do the same with me.

My attention snaps to the doorway when Antonio returns. As he drags him inside, Elijah grunts, his ankles and wrists bound. He wobbles while Antonio leads him around the couch. Antonio pushes Elijah to his knees in front of me before releasing him.

I throw my arm out toward Elijah, who's staring at me in desperation. "How does kidnapping him protect me?"

It's fucking nonsense. I might've fallen for Antonio's games enough to allow his manipulative fingers inside my vagina, but that easy Gigi is gone. No more will I believe in his scheming ways.

Antonio doesn't reply, like the little snake he is. No wonder that's his pet of choice.

Elijah's head snaps in Antonio's direction, and he snarls, "I'm going to kill you, Lombardi."

Antonio chuckles at the threat.

He and Elijah are both killers.

I have a feeling Antonio is better at it though.

"Here's your *fiancé*, princess." Antonio's lip curls in disgust at the last word, as if he swallowed poison.

He withdraws his gun from his blazer and presses it against Elijah's head. The satisfaction on his face is seriously demented. I move forward, but Corner Man appears behind me and does the same to my head. The barrel of the gun is so cold that I feel it through my hair. Antonio casts him an unreadable look, and the man nods since they apparently have their own language.

The man retreats a step and switches spots with Antonio.

Now, Antonio's gun is against my head.

Corner Man crams the gun barrel into Elijah's skull like it's a cork he's unscrewing. Elijah clenches his hands and attempts to pull away, but can't.

"Now, Elijah," Antonio says calmly, "let's play a game."

I turn my head, causing the gun to slightly slip away from my head. "Who do you think you are now? Jigsaw?"

Antonio plunges his free hand into my hair, grabbing a fistful, and jerks my head to the side. He presses the gun to my neck, placing pressure on my vocal cords as if he wants to crush them so I'll shut the fuck up.

"Quit playing games, Lombardi," Elijah spits.

Antonio smiles cruelly. "You want me to let you go?"

Elijah's face is red and sweaty. "Don't waste my time asking stupid questions."

"If I let you go, then I kill Gigi."

I fight against Antonio to glare back at him, panic setting through my blood. "What—"

Antonio speaks over me. "*Or* I release Gigi and kill you."

"I'm not a man who plays games, Antonio."

"No games. A simple question." He slides the gun along the crook of my neck. "You have three seconds, or I kill you both."

Elijah cowardly glances at me. "Sorry, Gigi," he says without a second thought. "I—"

Antonio releases his gun from my neck and shoots Elijah in the head before he can finish his sentence.

"What the hell?" I shriek as Elijah drops to the floor, blood gushing from his head on the black-and-white patterned rug.

Antonio steps away from me. "Looks like you're back on the market, princess."

"First, I'm not fucking stock," I shout. "Second, that doesn't mean I'm open for anyone else. And last-fucking-ly, I was perfectly content with marrying Elijah, and then you had to ruin it."

Antonio circles the couch and kicks Elijah's body while keeping his unsettling gaze on me. "Word of advice, princess: don't ever marry a man who won't die for you."

"You pretty much forced me into not marrying him."

"If someone held a gun to my head and asked the same question—save me or you—it'll always be you."

I release a noisy breath. "Not everyone is as batshit crazy as you."

"Which is why no one else can have you. Why I'm the only man for you." He snaps his fingers toward the man, motioning for him to leave, and then steps over Elijah's lifeless body as if it were a curb before kneeling in front of me.

He catches me by the throat and restrains me when I attempt to scoot away from him. My heart races, and I inhale his scent as he gets in my face. I shiver when he nuzzles his face over my cheek.

"The only person who deserves you, your pussy, your heart is someone who'd bleed for it." He licks up my neck while squeezing my throat. "Don't you ever fucking settle for less."

I attempt to gulp, but his hand on my neck prevents it. "Oh, so settle for someone crazy, like you?"

"Settle?" He pulls back. "Settling is a contractual marriage to make Daddy happy. Us? We're different. Our hearts burn for each other. We're a fire that can't be tamed." His hand around my neck loosens yet still lingers on my skin.

My heart aches at the truth of his words.

But it also aches at what I know.

My father will kill Antonio for this.

I'll be his downfall.

"Take me back, Antonio." I shut my eyes. "You can drop me off within walking distance of the hospital, and I'll return to my car. I won't tell my father anything about this."

"I don't think you understand, Gigi."

"Understand this is some sick game all you men play?"

He releases his hand from my neck. "No, that if I don't protect you, Sonny will gut you like a pig."

I scrunch my nose at that visual.

"That's his preferred way of killing. And since he knows killing you will hurt both your family and me, he'll torture you and most likely tape it so we can see every detail of how he brutally murders you."

My head spins at the mental image. "My father will protect me."

"I'd rather protect what's mine." He rests his forehead against mine.

"I'm … I'm not yours."

"You've been mine since that day at the warehouse." He presses a kiss on my forehead. "Quit pretending you think otherwise."

I hold my hand to my chest when he pulls back and stands.

"Let's take care of this body," he tells the other man when he returns and peers at me. "I'll call your brother, let him know you're okay, and then you can tell me what color bow we should put on Elijah's body after I package him up as a present."

30

ANTONIO

"Protect her with your life," I tell Leo after we pack Elijah's useless body in my trunk.

Gigi refused to pick his bow color, so I went with red. It matches the blood matted in his hair, and I'm always up for color coordination.

"You know I will," Leo tells me.

Leo is my cousin and has been just as involved in this life as I have. I trust him, and he hasn't turned his back on me for Sonny.

I didn't kidnap Gigi to keep her in some dark cellar and torture her. I took her because I'm fucking obsessed with her, and if anyone attempts to take that obsession away, I'll slit open every vein in their body and watch them slowly bleed to death.

Since I have dozens of missed calls from Benny and unknown numbers, I'm sure the Marchettis know I have her. I wait until I'm back in my car before returning Benny's call. They need to know I have no intention of hurting Gigi … and I also have no intention of releasing her until Sonny is dead.

"Hello, Benny," I say when he answers my call. "It's Antonio."

"Where the fuck is my sister?" he screams. "Every minute you fail to tell me is another minute I'll spend torturing you."

I work my jaw and start the car. "I'm not letting her go."

"What do you want? Guns from Severino? Done. Now, let her go."

Done, my ass.

Even if I agreed to this deal—which I won't because it means I'd lose Gigi—he's full of shit anyway. As soon as I showed up for this *deal*, they'd kill my ass.

I crack my neck. "I didn't take Gigi to blackmail you. I took her to protect her."

Benny scoffs. "We protect her just fine."

"Natalia was kidnapped. Neomi shot. Both of those done by the hands of Lombardis." I curl my palms into fists, just thinking about something like that happening to Gigi.

"Thank you for reminding me," Benny interrupts. "I'll make sure you suffer extra now."

"My uncle wants to kill Gigi to get to me. I can't let that happen."

"Why would he kill my sister to get back at you?"

"Because I love her."

There's a moment of silence. My confession was never supposed to slip from my mouth. *My truth* was supposed to stay hidden.

"She will stay with me until I kill my uncle," I continue. "No one will know where she is. Including you."

I end the call.

Now, I have a priest to kidnap.

The smell of incense is heavy, and the cathedral is quiet when I enter. I scan my surroundings without seeing anyone.

Desperate times call for desperate measures.

I head straight to the confessional, open the door, and tug the priest out.

"Please, I beg of you," he pleads as I position him in front of me. He looks around nervously as if searching for an escape. "I stopped dealing with your kind after the last wedding, where I was almost killed."

"Sorry," I say with no apology in my tone. "One more wedding." I glance up at the ornate ceiling. "Forgive me, Father. I just need to borrow him for a few hours."

31

GIGI

"What's your name?" I ask, glaring at the dark-haired man.

He stands in the corner while I'm on the couch, and instead of answering me, he just stares at his phone.

I'm unsure how much time has passed since they dumped Elijah's dead body in the trunk like he was used furniture headed to the donation center, and Antonio left.

Now, I'm stuck with a man who has yet to utter a word in my direction. I hold one eye open, as if sizing him up, contemplating whether I could take him and make a run for it.

My conclusion? No way in hell.

He might be on the younger side, but he's solidly built and would outrun me in a minute. There's no innocence on his face —a sign he's been involved in this life for a while. And given how he didn't flinch while disposing of Elijah's body, murder doesn't bother him.

I shrug. "I guess I shall call you my babysitter, then."

He continues to ignore me.

"Oh, come on." I throw my head back. "I like calling people by their names. I'm a woman with manners, thank you very much."

He slides his phone into his pocket. "Leo."

I make myself comfortable on the couch because, hey, I might as well. "Well, *Leo*, if you let me go, I'll tell my father of your good deed. He'll reward you for it—monetarily or possibly give you a chance to join the Marchetti family—which, from the way it seems, will give you much higher odds of living than with the Lombardis."

He crosses his arms. "I'm good."

"Think of all the things you could do with the cash." I tap the side of my temple. "Leave the country. Buy a Lambo. My father has plenty of connections."

"How about you keep your mouth shut, and I won't send one of your pretty little fingers to your father in a box?"

"Asshole," I mutter.

"Don't try to bribe me with your bullshit, and I won't act like one."

"At least you admit you're an asshole."

"Consider yourself lucky Antonio likes you. All I see you as is a pain-in-the-ass woman I'm risking my life for because I'll always have Antonio's back. That doesn't mean I won't point out that you're a liability."

"How do you know Antonio likes me?"

"You're still alive." He jerks his head toward the bloodstained rug.

I slam my mouth shut. *Fair point.*

Leo fishes his phone from his pocket and starts texting.

I take in the cabin and search for clues about where I am. It's most likely a hideout.

The view from the window is nothing but trees.

What's Antonio's plan for me?

Fingers crossed it's not murder.

A nagging memory reminds me of Lombardi's reputation of untrustworthiness.

Antonio can easily see me as collateral.

I rush to the window overlooking the driveway when I hear movement outside the house. Antonio steps from his car and jerks someone from the backseat. I clutch my stomach as I watch him shove his gun against the back of a priest's head while pushing him toward the porch.

It's the same priest from Neomi and Benny's wedding.

The one who ditched our asses and left us for dead.

I turn to look at Leo. "He kidnapped a fucking priest?"

Leo shrugs, not answering.

"What the hell?" I scream when Antonio enters the cabin with the priest.

Antonio nudges the priest forward into Leo's waiting arms. "Watch him."

Leo directs the priest toward a chair.

He trembles from head to toe while sitting down and then rubs the spot on his head where Antonio's gun was.

Without saying a word, Antonio walks out of the cabin. I stand there, shuffling from one foot to the other, not knowing what to do. I glance at the priest apologetically when he whimpers. Leo rolls his eyes in annoyance.

Everyone's attention shoots to Antonio when he returns, holding a shopping bag. He charges across the room, clamps his hand around mine, and jerks me down the hallway. I jump when he pushes me into a room and slams the door shut behind us.

He thrusts the bag into my arms. "Here."

"Please don't be an Elijah body part," I whisper, gripping the side of the bag as if it holds a bomb. "Please don't be an Elijah body part." I hold in a breath while sinking my hand inside.

The first item I pull out is a lacy bone-colored veil.

Weird.

The second … a long white dress.

"What the …" I run my fingers over the silk before raising my gaze to Antonio's.

He clutches his hand over mine on the dress and squeezes it. His touch shouldn't be as comforting as it is.

"Don't worry, princess," he says in an unapologetic tone. "You can choose your dress at our next wedding."

Reality crashes through me.

The wedding dress.

Veil.

Priest.

Oh my fucking God.

This bastard just keeps getting crazier.

"Are you nuts?" I drop the dress and veil on the bed. "I'm not marrying you."

When I attempt to rush past him and leave the room, he snatches my elbow. I try to remove his hand while he spins me around to face him.

"You *are* marrying me." He squeezes my elbow. "Now, put on the dress."

I narrow my eyes at him, and when I jerk out of his hold this time, he lets me. "Piss off."

He grinds his teeth. "Now's not the time to test me, princess."

"*Test you?* Why would I ever marry a psychopath who not only kidnapped me but also a priest? Not fucking happening."

"Put on the dress," he snarls.

I stand tall. "No."

He inches so close that we're standing toe-to-toe, and his lips brush my nose as he speaks. "Do you remember what I said at the hospital? I put a bomb in Benny's car. He's at the mansion now, which is great timing for me because when I blow up his car, it'll also take out the mansion."

I shudder at his evil smirk.

"And let's not forget, princess. I know where your sweet aunt in Italy lives."

"You wouldn't dare," I sneer.

"I will do that *and more* if you don't change into that dress, put a smile on your face, and marry me."

I glare at him.

"Change." He retreats a step, snatches the dress from the

bed, and shoves it back into my hands. "Or do I need to dress you myself?"

My heart feels almost ill.

This is the man I thought I loved.

"Can you at least give me some privacy?" I gesture toward the door.

He shakes his head. "Change *now*."

I stubbornly don't move.

He grits his teeth. "If you don't put that dress on in the next thirty seconds, I'll kill the priest." His stare levels on me—the most intense I've ever seen from him. "His blood will be on your hands, princess." His touch is cold as he taps his fingers along my bare arm. "Surely, that'll send us both to hell, you allowing me to murder a priest for your stubbornness."

Arguing is a waste of time.

He's forcing me to marry him—whether I like it or not.

I can either do it wearing a white dress or a bloodstained one.

I'm spewing every curse word I can while stripping out of my shirt.

Antonio scoffs when I attempt to cover myself while lowering my shorts. "I've seen, touched, and tasted every inch of your body. No need for discretion."

"None of those will ever happen again," I huff out. "And where did you even get this stuff?" I slip on the dress without bothering to look at it.

"The dress store."

"Smart-ass." I sigh, straighten my shoulders, and motion down my body. "Are you happy now? Is this good enough not to become a corpse bride?"

He licks his lips while creeping his gaze down my body. When he appears satisfied, he tips his head toward the veil. "Don't forget that."

"You're joking?"

He stares at me, deadpan.

"Fine." I snatch the veil and struggle to put it on.

Antonio grabs it and spins me around. My breathing hitches when he stands behind me. He runs his fingers through my hair before gently clipping the veil in. Goose bumps form on my arms.

This is out of fear, Gigi.

Not lust.

"My princess," he whispers before shifting me to face him. "My bride."

"Your forced bride." I refuse to meet his eyes. My blood pressure spikes when he reaches out and brushes his callous fingers over my cheek.

"Either way, *my bride.*"

He lowers his hand to grasp mine, interlocking our fingers, and guides me out of the bedroom.

"I swear on every shoe I own, if you play the *here comes the bride* song, I'm jumping out of that window and making a run for it. I don't care if an animal ends up eating me alive or not."

He keeps a firm grip on me while I attempt to break out of our hand holding.

Leo and the priest are in the living room waiting for us.

The poor priest's panicked gaze bounces from Antonio to me. "Are you … forcing her to marry you?" he asks in alarm.

"I'm forcing *you* to marry us," Antonio counters.

Leo drags the priest to his feet and holds him by his arm until he's perfectly balanced.

The priest straightens his collar. "I don't feel comfortable doing this."

Antonio shifts me so I'm facing him, his eyes on me while he still speaks to the priest. "I'll make a generous contribution to the church for your services, Father." His lips twist into a smirk. "Now, time to say our *I do*s," princess."

"No." The priest shakes his head violently. "This goes against my ethics."

Leo steps forward, and the priest jumps when he holds a gun to his head.

"Start," Antonio orders him.

The priest stares at us, bug-eyed.

"I said, *start*," Antonio roars.

The priest jumps, which only causes his head to bump against the gun. I offer him a reassuring smile as he begins. His voice grows shakier with every word he says.

My mouth turns dry. I do my best to maintain my composure as Antonio slips his hand into his pocket and retrieves a ring. He plays with it in his free hand, between his fingers. Even though I'm not seeing it up close, it sparkles in the light, and I stare at it in awe.

Elijah's ring was impressive, but it didn't make my insides tingle like Antonio's.

Antonio tenderly slides the ring onto my trembling finger with ease. I peer down at it, moving my hand, and watch the diamond shimmer. Even though he didn't give me the perfect wedding, he is providing a perfect ring.

My villain.

So many sides to him.

He doesn't give me much time to admire it before connecting our hands, gripping mine tightly, and the priest begins the … *ceremony*?

I'm not sure what else to call it.

Forced matrimony?

I recite my vows faintly, a mere whisper.

Antonio's tone is controlled and flows like liquid.

His eyes aren't predatory when they meet mine.

They're possessive.

Though this is a forced marriage, I won't lie and say there's no intimacy here.

Antonio brushes his thumb along the side of my hand, relaxing me.

"You may"—the priest rubs his eyebrow—"kiss the bride."

Antonio curls his hand around the back of my neck and pulls me toward him. His lips creep closer, and right before they reach mine, I smack a hand over my mouth.

"Move your hand, or I'll bite it off," he demands.

I clasp it tighter and shake my head.

His hand around my neck inches up, and he tugs my hair, causing my head to fall back. I'm proud of how well I keep my hand on my face. He chuckles at my defiance before shoving me backward. I gasp when my back hits the wall, and he rips my hand away from my mouth, slapping it against the wall. While keeping my hand trapped underneath his, he smashes his lips against mine.

I can't stop myself from opening my mouth and surrendering to our kiss. He presses his tongue into my mouth, and everyone around us fades away as we kiss for the first time as *husband and wife*.

Gone are thoughts of a forced marriage.

He forced my hand, though never forced my feelings for him.

My breaths are shallow when he pulls away.

He caresses my cheek, and his eyes gleam. "Time for pictures, *wife*."

"Not happening." I roll against the wall, away from him, while coming to my senses. "There shall be no proof of this"—I flick my hand through the air—"fraud of a marriage."

"Call it a fraud marriage again, and I'll keep the priest here to marry us every fucking hour," he says, snatching me before handing Leo his phone.

Antonio holds me, and I glare at Leo as he takes a photo.

When he hands the phone back to Antonio for his approval, Antonio shakes his head and gives it back.

"Smile like you're happy, princess," Antonio says.

I don't.

So we do it again.

Over and over.

I finally give in after photo attempt twenty-two.

"Good girl." He pets my head and then leads me into the kitchen.

A document is on the table.

"Sign." Antonio holds out a pen.

I inch closer to the table and read it.

A marriage certificate.

I shake my head, refusing to accept the pen.

He clicks the pen open, steps closer, and sticks the ballpoint against my neck. "Sign your name, *Gigi Lombardi*, or I'll sign it with your fucking blood."

I swallow as he presses the pen deeper against the vein and can almost feel it ready to pop.

"Fine," I snarl, grasping his wrist to remove the pen.

This time, when he offers it, I take it.

My signature is messy, I misspell *Lombardi*, and I spit on the paperwork when finished.

He smirks deviously before holding out his phone to show me one of the pictures we took. "What a happy couple we are."

"You asshole."

"You mean your husband."

32

ANTONIO

I toss a duffel bag of cash into the backseat with the priest and unlock the car. "You're free to go."

The priest hurriedly opens the door, hitches the bag over his shoulder, and nearly falls out of the car. He grunts before sprinting toward the cathedral without looking back once.

Sure, I kidnapped him.

At least I compensated him generously for his services.

I drive off.

My next task is preparing my package for Cristian.

A full moon hangs in the sky as I unload Elijah's body from my trunk, snap a picture, and then text it to Cristian.

> Me: I told you I'd keep Gigi safe, and that includes preventing her from marrying unworthy men.

Next, I send him one of the wedding pictures I forced Gigi to take with me.

After hitting Send, I slip the phone into my pocket.

Damien meets me in the warehouse and laughs as he unties the bow around Elijah's neck. He then helps me load the body into a plastic barrel filled with acid.

Now, it's time I find Sonny.

"How is she?" I ask Eden over FaceTime.

Eden is Dante's fiancée. Their home on the outskirts of the city is Amara's safe house. Damien took her and Clara there after my father's death. Shortly after, Clara's sister, Kicia, started having health complications.

As much as Clara didn't want to leave Amara, Kicia needed her help. So I had one of my men escort Clara to Chicago, and Eden has been watching Amara.

Years ago, Dante and I made an agreement. I killed a man for him, and in return, they'd hide Amara if I ever needed the help.

"Good," Eden replies. "We watched a movie and just finished a bowl of ice cream." She brushes her bangs away from her eyes and glances away. "Amara! Daddy is on the phone. You want to tell him good night?"

"Yes!" Amara yells from a distance.

Eden passes her the phone, and Amara appears, holding it too close to her face.

"Hi, Daddy!" she chirps, chocolate remnants on her cheek.

My chest feels hollow because I can't be there with her. Even though I'm doing this to protect her, something makes me feel like not being with her is wrong.

I smile at her gently. "Hey, sweetie. Are you having fun with Aunt Eden?"

"Yes!" She innocently grins. "She watches movies with me and my stuffed animals." Holding up her hand, she wiggles her fingers. "She painted my nails too!"

"Pink sparkles. They look pretty on you, sweetie."

We chat for another thirty minutes. She tells me about her day and all the fun she's having with Eden. I've tried visiting

Amara every other day, but it's a process. Two men follow me, and then I change cars three times and stop for twenty-minute intervals throughout the drive. I assume every possible risk when it comes to her safety.

"Sleep tight," I say after her fifth yawn. "Sweet dreams."

She frowns. "I wish you were here to tuck me in and give me good-night forehead kisses."

My chest twists. "I'll be there soon, okay?"

"You promise?"

"I promise." I press two fingers to my lips, kiss them, and touch the screen.

She mimics me. "Night, Daddy."

Eden takes the phone from her. "She's in good hands, Antonio. I promise."

"Thank you, Eden."

We end the call, and I spend the next four hours following Nuncio in hopes of finding Sonny. So far, the pathetic bastard hasn't proven himself valuable. Time is conspiring against me. The longer I wait, the weaker and unprepared I'll be.

When Nuncio leaves the strip club and goes home, I drive toward the cabin to get a few hours of sleep and check on Gigi.

I purchased the cabin five years ago for no reason other than to use it as a hideout if needed. No one except a few of my men know about it. Since I used the name of a deceased man from Missouri, it can't be traced back to me either. It's amazing how easy it is to steal dead people's identities online.

Leo drops the book in his hand when I walk inside. "Hey, boss."

"You can go home for the night." I loosen my tie.

"You sure?" He rubs his eyes tiredly. "I can stay in the guest room … or in my car if you want privacy. Keep an eye on things."

"Your choice."

He forces a yawn. "I'll hang out in my car and keep an eye out for you."

I nod and slip into the bedroom to find Gigi snuggled under the comforter, sleeping with half her face smashed against the pillow. I tiptoe toward the bed, strip down to my boxers, and carefully lie beside her.

Next to my wife.

I've envisioned Gigi as my wife countless times.

It sucks I had to strong-arm her into it.

She'll forgive me in the end.

If not, I'll fuck her until she gives me my pardon.

I'm woken up an hour later.

It isn't by Sonny finally coming for his war.

Or a Marchetti.

It's by my wife, freaking out next to me.

Trembling and gasping for air.

What the fuck?

33

GIGI

"Gigi."

The familiar voice pulls me from my panic.

"Gigi."

I gasp for desperate breaths, my fingers clawing at my throat like the grip of my sleep paralysis continues to restrain me.

"Are you okay?" The voice almost sounds like background static.

Calm down, Gigi.

Calm the fuck down.

"Gigi," Antonio repeats, deeper this time.

I'm not sure how long it takes me to settle myself. I don't open my eyes, but I sense him watching me. He's running circles with his thumb over my hand, slowly easing my anxiety.

"Just a nightmare, is all," I finally whisper while lying on my back.

"That wasn't *just a nightmare.*"

While his tone is soothing, I know he won't let this go.

"Just go back to sleep," I croak. "It doesn't matter."

I blink, the only light source from a crack underneath the door. My muscles tense as I remember where I am and how I got here.

I went to sleep alone.

When did Antonio join me?

"Come here." Without giving me the chance to argue, he drags me into his arms.

I rest my cheek on his warm chest.

It's a comfort I didn't know I needed.

While it's not exactly morning, this is our first time technically waking up together. In Italy, he always stayed just long enough for me to orgasm and then left.

"What was the nightmare about?" he asks.

"It wasn't a nightmare." I squeeze my eyes shut. "It was sleep paralysis."

He's officially the first person I've disclosed this to.

"Can you explain what that is to me?" He massages the bare skin of my shoulder.

"It's more than a nightmare. I'm awake and conscious, but I have no power over my body. My mind plays tricks on me. I'm unable to move, speak, anything really. It feels so real and fucking terrifies me."

It's ironic.

Antonio's hands have killed so many men that I'm surprised the metallic stench of blood isn't on his skin. He took me against my will, yet I've never felt so comfortable with someone.

"I get them when I'm stressed and mentally struggling," I continue.

"Stressed?" He runs his hand over my hair. "Why are you stressed?"

Even though he can't see my face, I glare at him.

"You know I'd never hurt you."

"You already have," I say.

"I brought you here for your safety."

"And the forced marriage?"

"To *protect you.*"

I lift my head to smack his shoulder. "Don't bullshit me, Antonio. You did it to have leverage over my father, so he'll help you with the war *your family* started. Our nuptials were born from your desperation, not your love or desire to *protect* me." The reality is bitter as it leaves my tongue, and I fall onto my back.

He props himself on his elbow, staring down at me. "Don't fucking act like you mean nothing to me, Giana."

"I am *nothing* but your prisoner. Your *forced* wife." My voice turns spiteful. "The exact thing I was never supposed to become."

"The first time you allowed me to taste you was the day you became *mine*. Just like I became yours."

"How convenient you did nothing about it until it benefited you."

"Sonny wants to kill you."

"My father will keep me safe."

"How did that go for Natalia and Neomi? I won't risk something happening to you—kidnapping, rape, murder. I'll make sure a man dies before even getting close to you. Like I told you last night, I will always keep you safe and lay down my life for yours."

"Oh, yes, thank you for the reminder that you killed my fiancé."

"Like you'd have ever actually married Elijah." He says his name with disdain.

"He would've given me a *peaceful* marriage."

"Our marriage will be peaceful."

I slap the mattress. "You're literally holding me hostage in the middle of who the fuck knows where. That's far from peaceful. As soon as I get out of here, I'll annul this sham of a marriage."

I gasp when he rolls over, shifting his weight to his knees, and straddles me.

His fingers clasp around my throat, constricting my airflow. "One thing that'll never leave this sweet mouth is that you'll *annul* our marriage or divorce me." His grip tightens. "I'll be your husband today, tomorrow, until you draw your last breath. If you ever think of marrying another man, I'll drop his corpse at the mansion's doorstep."

"Then I'll find another husband." My answer comes out strained in his hold.

"And he'll pay for that with his life." He lowers his head until his lips hover above mine as I suck in air. "Every single one will die."

He's so deranged.

And it's hot as hell.

He inhales sharply as if drawing in those short breaths I'm managing.

I grab his wrist, my nails digging into his skin, and he allows me to pull his hand away. "You wouldn't dare."

"Oh, princess." His laugh is demented. "I'll serve their dismembered limbs to you on a platter at your favorite restaurant. Don't fucking test me on that."

He kisses me, and there's a sting when he bites into my lower lip.

This man and I are a toxic cocktail that's both terrifying and thrilling.

I squirm beneath him. "You might kill them, but I'll fuck them before you do."

He captures my hands, slamming them against the mattress, and grinds his body into mine. Unable to hold back, I raise my waist and arch my back. He groans, rotating his hips against mine. Shivers travel through my body when his erection glides against my thigh.

I lick my lips.

God, I missed this.

Missed him.

It's been so long since he's touched me.

"No other man can get your body going like I can … *like this,*" he hisses in my ear, his stubble brushing against my cheek.

I moan, hating the truth of his words, and drift my hand up

his bare back. His skin is hot, on fire, my villain raised straight from the depths of hell. He wastes no time before tearing my panties down my legs.

We rush every move we take.

Racing against the clock.

Folding my legs to my stomach, he lowers himself between my thighs. He spares me no mercy while thrusting his fingers inside and ravishing me with his tongue. I writhe beneath him, offering myself and inviting him to consume me however he wants. My thighs shake, my body crumpling underneath his weight, but he doesn't stop until I come undone. He creeps back and sinks to his knees. I feel the intensity of his eyes on me.

"Princess." He smooths his hands up my legs and releases them flat on the bed. "You always said you'd save yourself for your husband. Well, here I am."

My heart flutters in my chest as anticipation consumes me. Husband or not, if Antonio had met me in Italy the last time I was there, I'd have given him myself. I've always wanted him to be my first.

"Then what are you waiting for, *husband?*" I sound more confident than I feel.

He shifts, removing his briefs, and settles between my thighs. I can't stop myself from tensing up. I so desperately want him, yet I'm also a ball of nerves.

What girl isn't her first time?

He brushes his callous hand over my stomach, over my breasts, and caresses my chin.

My villain.

Murderous one minute.

Comforting the next.

"Relax for me, baby," he says, raining kisses up my neck. "I can't promise this won't hurt, but sometimes, there's beauty in pain. Do you want me to gently ease into you, gradually stretching you, or quickly thrust into your sweet pussy, then stop so you can adjust to my cock?"

I didn't expect this much decision-making during sex.

He presses his lips against mine, sliding his tongue along the seam, and pushes his tongue inside my mouth. I curl mine around his, sucking on it, and he moans.

"Ease," I say into his mouth. "Stretch me slowly, Antonio."

"Easing into your pussy it is," he says.

A giddiness fills me when I detect a trace of a smile on his lips.

He drops soft kisses down my chest. I gasp when he teasingly sucks the space around my nipple, licking across it before taking it in his mouth. My nervousness lessens when he does the same with the other. His teasing helps my anxiety.

He showers kisses down my stomach before sucking on my clit. I'm so wet that I'm dripping on the sheets and seriously reconsidering the slow option. I didn't know it'd take this fucking long.

He falls back between my legs and grunts while stroking himself. My body feels on fire when he lowers his head and spits on my pussy. He rubs it against my clit before pushing it inside me.

I lick my lips, proud of myself for not freaking out as he moves up my body and then presses the head of his cock against my opening. If this were anyone else, even Elijah—RIP—there's no way I'd feel so calm.

Antonio does what he said he would. He gradually slides inside me. I can tell from his breathing that it's taking all his restraint not to fully plunge his cock in deep.

I don't care about a condom. If this is our only chance to give ourselves to each other, I don't want a barrier.

Only him and me, skin to skin.

Lover to lover.

Husband to wife.

The more he's inside me, the more comfortable it gets.

"Go deeper," I murmur. "I need to feel all of you, Antonio."

As if my words are a kick to his back, he drives his dick all the way inside. I inhale a breath at the sudden sting. Antonio wraps my legs around his waist and allows me to adjust to his size before moving.

His first stroke is agony.

The pain lessens with the next.

By the third, the discomfort becomes pleasure.

My breathing is wild as I rotate my hips and meet his thrusts.

The sheets become a tangled mess as he fucks me softly. With every stroke, he becomes wilder. Our shadows dance on the wall while the bed slams against it, drowning out our moans and bodies slapping into each other's.

I fuck him back while never wanting this to end. Our movements are so frantic that I know there will be bruises tomorrow.

"Only me," he says roughly. "You are mine, Giana Marchetti."

I shiver, goose bumps covering my skin like a tattoo.

"Only me," he repeats, withdrawing and gliding back in. "Fucking say it, princess."

I cry out in pleasure.

It's not like I can form words at the moment.

He runs his fingers up my body and back to my throat. "Fucking say it, or you won't say another man's name in your life."

"Tell me you're mine first," I dare, my voice strained from his restraint.

"Princess, I've been yours since you saw me execute a man." His thrusts grow faster, and his words are said through rushed breaths. "And even in death, when I pay for my sins, you will own me."

My heart is on overdrive as I scrape my fingers down his arm and grab his free hand. He gives me a last squeeze before releasing my throat and allowing me to guide our attached hands between my legs.

Together, we massage my clit before lowering our touch to

where his cock meets my opening. He spreads our fingers apart, scissoring them around his cock, and he drives in and out of me.

"I'm yours, Antonio. Will only ever be yours."

My declaration is our undoing.

He possesses me, pounding into me and claiming me.

I unravel first.

"Oh my God, I'm there," I whimper.

My body trembles, my jaw quivers, and I sink my nails into his thigh.

I want to break skin, dig them in so deep that he'll bleed for me.

He rises to his knees and fucks me faster.

Harder.

Until he's taken everything and it's his turn to fall apart.

His weight collapses onto mine as he fills me with his cum.

And for the first time post-sleep-paralysis episode, I drift back into a peaceful sleep.

Antonio, my captor, has provided me refuge from my fears as he lies beside me. He pulls me into his darkness, freeing me from my own.

"Where's my captor?" I ask Leo. My legs are sore as I walk into the living room.

After waking up to an empty bed, I searched the closet for something to wear and showered. With limited options, I changed into a man's button-up in the closet and yesterday's skirt.

Antonio could've at least given me a heads-up to pack a bag for my abduction.

"Out," Leo replies from the couch.

"You're my keeper, then?" I open the fridge and pour a glass of orange juice.

Since the cabin has an open layout design, Leo watches every move I make. I join him and lounge on a chair. My gaze lowers, and I notice they've replaced the rug stained with Elijah's blood. Maybe this maroon will blur out their next victim's.

Fingers crossed it isn't mine.

But Antonio is right. I trust him not to hurt me.

The problem is that other Lombardis want to.

Luckily, Antonio has given my prisoner ass somewhere nice to stay. The cabin has an aroma of cinnamon and is tastefully decorated with plush furniture and expensive appliances. The cinnamon is most likely to mask the smell of homicide.

"I suppose, Marchetti." He scratches his neck. "Or I guess it's *Lombardi* now. Welcome to the family, new cousin."

"*Cousin*? You're Antonio's *cousin*?"

"Yeah." He tugs on the collar of his black V-neck.

I blink, searching for any similarities between them. He has the signature dark Lombardi hair, but his face is squarer and more boyish.

"Is Sonny your dad?" I take a sip of orange juice.

"Fuck no, thank God. My mother was Uncle Vincent's sister."

"*Was?*"

"She died when I was twelve."

I soften my voice. "I'm sorry. I hate that part of this life."

"It was breast cancer. Unfortunately, I can't get revenge against that."

"Either way, I'm sorry, Leo."

He side-eyes me as if doubting I have that kind of empathy in my heart.

Geesh, he's been around heartless men for too long.

He rubs his forehead, clearly not wanting to chat about his family. Well, *anything* really.

"So ..." I tap my nails against my glass. "What made you choose Antonio's side instead of Sonny's?"

He shrugs stoically. "Antonio is rightfully next in line. My mother raised me to have loyalty. Antonio is my cousin and the rightful boss of our family." He scowls at me. "You're an awfully chatty prisoner."

"So I am a prisoner?" I raise a brow.

"You're Antonio's obsession." He clears his throat. "His *wife* now."

My lips part at that reality.

I still haven't fully processed it.

"When can I talk to my family?" I hold up my hand, showing off my ring. "I need to tell them I'm a married woman."

"Oh, they already know." For the first time, Leo smirks.

"*How?*"

"Antonio sent your father a message."

"Did that message include a dead body?"

He doesn't answer.

I throw my head back. "Oh, come on. I'm Antonio's wife now. Shouldn't that mean you should have loyalty to me too?"

"My loyalty to you is keeping you alive. That's all."

I chug my orange juice, stand, and stomp to the kitchen for a refill.

If Antonio doesn't want me to play the pain-in-the-ass hostage, he needs to answer some questions.

34

GIGI

I've always said there's no way I can survive without my phone, but here I am, surviving.

Surviving yet bored out of my mind.

Leo isn't exactly the president of great conversation and has the worst response to my questions.

"What's your favorite show?" I ask.

He glares at me. "I don't watch TV."

"Can we go out for mimosas and brunch?"

"There's food in the kitchen."

"Can you DoorDash me sushi?"

He completely ignores me.

Defeated, I retreat to the kitchen to tragically make something myself … and hopefully not burn the cabin down with me stuck inside.

However, it won't be the worst situation if the place keeping me hostage catches on fire. Given I can escape, obviously.

An hour later, I'm stacking pizza on two plates and returning to the living room. Because I'm so generous, I hand Leo one. He stares at it suspiciously for five minutes before eating it, as if wondering if I sprinkled poison on his pepperoni.

I grab the remote and flip through the movie options.

"I should've attended law school," I say while we watch *Legally Blonde*. "I'd make an amazing attorney." I straighten my shoulders and gesture in his direction with my pizza. "*Your Honor, I have receipts and screenshots.*"

Leo snorts. "Any judge and jury would rule in your favor in fear of your father slaughtering them."

I scowl. "My dad isn't that terrible."

"He's known as Monster Marchetti for a reason."

Yet Antonio went against him to protect me.

After we finish the sequel, I'm about to tell him he's responsible for dinner when Antonio walks in, holding a plastic bag tied at the top.

"There's my captor," I announce, pointing in his direction with the remote.

He glares at me and whispers something to Leo. Leo rises from the couch and offers Antonio a head nod before leaving the cabin. Clearly, he hasn't accepted our friendship card yet since he doesn't glance in my direction.

Rude.

"How was your day?" Antonio drops the bag on the kitchen table.

"How one would expect while held captive." I join him in the kitchen. "And in case you've never been held hostage, spoiler alert: it's boring as shit."

"Don't act like you didn't enjoy being held captive last night when I fucked your nightmares out of you and gave you the best sleep of your life." He unties the bag, revealing to-go containers.

"I was in a post-sleep-paralysis coma." I press my finger against my skull. "My brain doesn't fully function during those."

Turning, he wraps his arm around my waist and pushes me against the counter. "Oh, princess. Sleep paralysis or not, you know I have the power to fuck every demon out of you—anytime, anywhere."

I close my eyes and fail to suppress a moan when he rotates his hips, pressing his pants-covered erection against my core.

"Now, let's eat before I spread you across the table and enjoy you for dinner instead." He squeezes my hips and lifts a brow.

Even though I'd have no problem with that, I decide to play difficult hostage. I rip away from him and sit at the table. He passes me a plate and sets one on the table for himself. I dump chow mein and an egg roll on it. Instead of eating, I watch him.

This man has touched every inch of me, fucked me, killed for me, but this is the first time we're sharing a meal together. It feels so domesticated.

If being held against your will can be domesticated.

"So …" I finally wrap a noodle around my fork. "What's your endgame here?"

He waits until he's done chewing before answering, "Keeping the people I care about alive."

"And I'm one of those people?"

"You're here and not dead like Elijah, aren't you?"

I drop my fork. "You're not going to hurt my father, are you?"

"I'll kill anyone for you." His tone is devoid of sarcasm.

Antonio isn't a man of many words, but when he promises violence, there will be violence.

"Why me, though?"

"I've asked myself that question plenty of times."

"And have you come up with an answer yet?"

"I've come up with plenty."

"Like?"

He reaches out and cups my chin with two fingers. "Because you drive me fucking crazy—in both good and bad ways. Because when I touch you, it's as though these violent hands of mine find peace, solace for a moment. There's a deep sense of dread that if something happens to you, I'll become the sinister man people see me as to avenge your death. I'm a man who loves few, and I have yet to figure out why you fucking consume me."

I gulp, unsure of how to reply to his words. They weren't what I had expected. I'd assumed he'd say something along the lines of, *Because I like fucking you*, or his simple answer of, *You're mine*.

Antonio had captured my soul in his dirty hands. Neither of us had planned for this to happen.

And now, we can't stop it. It's not like you can tell your heart to just stop loving someone. Our hearts beat for each other. We need the other to survive in this insufferable world we were born into.

"Does that answer your question well enough?" he asks.

I nod, his words seeping into my brain and embedding themselves there.

This is what I've always dreamed of.

I wasn't made for a Prince Charming who sits on a shiny throne with the envisioning of creating world peace. Mine has vendettas, bloody hands, and a black heart only I possess the power to tame.

I'm not destined for a happily ever after.

I wasn't put on this earth to be a princess.

I'm here to control my villain's darkness.

"One more question," I say, my voice hoarse.

He tilts his head to the side.

"You said you'd kill *for me*. But would you ever kill me?"

He stares at me intently. "Do you plan to do something that'd make me want to kill you?"

My eyes widen, and I refuse to answer.

"Would *you* ever kill me?" he pushes.

"I mean, you are holding me hostage."

He lifts his hips to drag something from his pocket and slides it on the table toward me.

I gulp, staring down at the wood-handled box cutter. The initials *AL* are carved into it. He motions toward the cutter, a silent demand, and I take it, playing with it in my hand. I click it open and slide my finger along the edge.

Antonio rises from the chair, snatches my wrist of the hand holding the box cutter, and hoists me up. He doesn't release me when I'm on two feet. I huff when he pins me against the table, keeping his grip on me, and uses my hand to push the blade against his neck.

"Slit my throat, princess," he tells me, his windpipe moving under the blade with each word. "Kill your family's enemy. The man who took you against your will. The one who clearly stated he'll kill everyone you love if he has to."

My hand shakes, and when I try to pull it free from his throat, he doesn't allow it.

I could never harm Antonio, much less kill him.

Even if it's the smart thing to do.

In an instant, he snatches the cutter from my hand and tosses it on the floor. It lands against the wood with a loud *thack*. He cups his hands around my waist and settles me on the edge of the table. I bite into my tongue when he flips my skirt up and positions himself between my legs.

My breathing turns ragged when he slips my panties to the side and drives three thick fingers deep inside me. I attempt to wiggle backward when it becomes too much, but he doesn't allow it.

"Would you rather kill me or fuck me, princess?" he asks, working his fingers in and out of me before smirking. "With how wet you are, we both know the answer. Unless, similar to me, killing gives you a thrill." He hurriedly shoves down his pants and replaces his fingers with his cock.

My careful Antonio from last night is gone.

My villain is back.

His hips pump up and down, and he fucks me so hard that the table slides against the floor. Our plates fall off. I hold on to his shoulder as my ass starts slipping off the table. I moan, throwing my head back, and it bumps into the table. I wince at the pain but don't stop him. My desire for my husband overtakes any other emotion.

"Fuck," he groans, scrunching his face while focused on his

cock inside me. "I'll let you drain all the blood from my body if it means I can keep fucking you like this."

I tighten my legs around him and whimper.

He chuckles wickedly. "That turns you on, doesn't it, princess?" His pace grows faster. "I love that I'm the only man who knows how dark you are. You, baby, are far from the sensitive princess others see you as. There's sin in your heart, just like me, and that's why we're destined for each other."

I cry out when he spins me around, slaps my hands on the table, and enters me from behind.

"And that's why I'll kill anyone for you." He smacks my ass hard.

My body is on fire as I brace myself against the table while he viciously pounds into me.

"Oh my fucking God," I scream between pants while slamming my hips backward to meet his every thrust.

He gives my ass another whack. "That's right. Fuck me back, my dark princess."

35

ANTONIO

"I'm only doing this because I detest your son-of-a-bitch uncle," Cernach Koglin tells me before opening a bag of firearms. "And before I give you these, I want to make a deal."

Cernach is the boss of the Koglin Irish mob based out of Boston. Now that we no longer have Severino for weapons, I had to seek them elsewhere. It took a shit ton of cash and twenty calls to convince Cernach to meet with me.

He was hesitant about involving himself with a family against the Marchettis. He and Sonny have also never seen eye to eye, and I really think that's why he's helping me out.

I raise a brow, unloading three AK-47s while we stand in the warehouse in the middle of nowhere. "What kind of deal are you looking for?"

"After you kill Sonny and his men, you marry my daughter, Riona."

I hold up my hand, showing off my wedding band. "I can't do that. I'm already married."

"To who?" he grunts.

"Giana Marchetti."

"Giana Marchetti …" He pauses as if not believing it's who he thinks it is. "As in Cristian Marchetti's daughter?"

"The one and only."

He barks out a laugh. "You're married to the daughter of the man who wants to murder you? How'd you manage that?" He runs his hand through his beard. "You hold a gun to her head?"

"I'd never do anything like that." I smirk.

He snorts before rubbing his hands together and scanning my men behind me. "If you can't marry my daughter, then I want one of them to." He drums his finger along his chin. "I want a capo … someone high in rank. Not some schmuck."

I exchange glances with Damien, Julian, and Emilio.

Emilio surprisingly chose my side over Nuncio's. It probably helped that he can't stand his father either.

A moment of silence passes.

None of them steps up.

Understandable.

Cernach is a mean bastard, and I wouldn't want him as a father-in-law.

When Cernach realizes no one is jumping to marry his daughter, he points at each of them, one by one. Damien is last, and his face clouds with annoyance when Cernach's attention lingers on him longer.

"Damien," Cernach says with full confidence. "You're the type of man I desire my Riona to marry."

Oh fuck.

Damien is the most controversial selection of them, and Cernach knows that.

In fact, it's likely why he chose him. Cernach loves starting shit.

It's also a smart choice for Cernach. Damien holds high rank and is smart as hell. People fear him.

Unfortunately for Damien, committing to marrying Riona is serious. He can't bail on that decision later.

Cernach's bulgy eyes are full of enticement as he waits for Damien to answer. "No contract, no guns."

I shake my head.

Unlike my father, I won't force this on my men.

"Sorry, Cernach—" I start but am interrupted by Damien stepping to my side.

His gaze is cold as he stares at Cernach. "I'll do it."

I hold up my hand. "Damien—"

"I'll do it," Damien grits out.

"Excellent." Cernach snaps his fingers in the air.

One of his men hands him a document, and Cernach drops it next to the guns.

He draws a pen from his coat and taps it against the papers. "I need both of your signatures here, and the deal is done. You can take your weapons and leave."

"You'll also continue providing us with firearms." Damien jerks his head toward the paper. "I want that in writing."

"And going forward, you only charge us half," I add. "Damien is a capo. He's worth it."

Damien's forehead is sweaty when he grabs the pen, reads over the papers, and scribbles his name. He holds it out to me.

"You sure?" I ask under my breath while taking it from him.

"If this is what it takes to get rid of Sonny, then that's what I have to do."

I lower my voice. "You know who Riona is, right?"

He straightens his collar and fails to meet my eyes. "I know exactly who Riona Koglin is."

Damien signing the agreement will save the Lombardi throne.

Pippa will never forgive him for marrying her cousin though.

No one has said a word since we got in the car after our meeting with Cernach. Julian and Emilio are both aware how big of a deal Damien marrying Riona is.

Damien tightens his jaw and flexes his fingers around the steering wheel as he drives.

I dig my phone from my pocket when it vibrates and check the screen.

Unknown caller.

"Yeah?" I answer.

Anytime Sonny or one of his men calls, it's from a private number. After they discovered we put trackers on two of their phones, they ditched them. Sonny has three numbers, and there isn't a single record of his name with any network. It's a wise move on his part since he's aware of how good we are at hacking into systems and finding people.

"Nephew," Sonny says on the other line.

"Sonny," I bite out, and Damien veers to the side of the road. "Please provide your location, motherfucker."

His unhealthy ass coughs on the other end. "Oh, so funny." He hacks again. "Your mother would like to speak with you."

I swallow down the sour taste suddenly forming in my mouth. "I'll pass on talking to that rat."

"Antonio, honey," my mother says, "listen to Sonny. He knows what's best for this family. You were never intended to be boss."

"I *am* the boss of this family," I snarl.

"Vinny was next in line, but he's gone. Sonny is fit to be don, and you need to let him have it. He should've stepped up a long time ago when we realized Vincent was becoming useless—"

"Don't say another fucking word," I hiss.

"Antonio, listen."

"No, *you listen*. This proves you're as heartless as everyone says."

"Stop pretending any of us have hearts. I'm doing what's necessary for us to stay alive."

"Bullshit. You know Sonny doesn't want me alive or to run the family *side by side*. You're clueless, and he will kill you."

She sighs. "You're so much like Vincent."

"That isn't the insult you think it is. He dedicated his life to protect our family. Now, tell me where Sonny is or stop wasting my fucking time."

The line turns quiet.

"Find me, *nephew*," Sonny says.

The call ends.

"That's exactly what I plan to do," I mutter as Damien swerves back onto the street.

36

GIGI

"We need to call my father," I tell Antonio when he returns to the cabin and walks into the bedroom.

"No," he says sharply, stripping out of his blazer and undoing the top button of his shirt.

"Let me at least tell him I'm okay," I beg and press my palms together in a praying gesture. "Please."

While Antonio was gone, I fell asleep on the couch and dreamed that my father found us at the cabin. He held a gun to Antonio's head and told him he would have granted Antonio mercy if he'd allowed me to call him.

I woke up in a panic as intense as when I do after a sleep-paralysis episode. That nightmare is all I've thought about since.

"I enjoy hearing you beg," he says, sitting on the edge of the bed. "If I wasn't pressed for time, I'd have you begging with my cock down your throat."

"I'll do that later *if* you let me call my dad." I grin.

"I don't play well with extortion."

"Do you play well with your dick in my mouth?" My cheeks pinken at my response.

My question is asking for trouble, and the intensity in Antonio's eyes confirms it. As tempting as that sounds, I need to stop talking about dick sucking because the phone call holds a higher priority.

"Just a quick call, Antonio. That's all I'm asking for."

He stares at me in deep contemplation on whether he can trust me.

I pout my lower lip.

"Don't try anything sneaky." He pulls a flip phone from his pocket. "Otherwise, I'll confine you in this room and never let you leave."

"Who, me?" I innocently press my palm flat on my chest.

He doesn't appreciate my humor as he hits a name on the phone and puts the call on speaker.

My father answers after two rings.

"Marchetti," Antonio says nonchalantly, as if they were about to hold a simple convo about the weather. Not my hostage situation.

"The bastard I'll kill soon," my father unsurprisingly snarls.

I shut my eyes, hating the reality of his statement. Eventually, Antonio will face his wrath, and no one has survived that fury. It's not a question of *if*. It's *when*.

"You mean your son-in-law?" Antonio corrects, all businesslike.

I wince and glare at him.

First, he needs to play nice.

Second, *son-in-law*? What the fuck?

Then I remember Leo told me my father knew about my marriage. At the time, I wasn't sure whether to believe him. I mean, you can't trust someone who says they don't have a favorite TV show.

"You signed your death wish when you took my daughter," my father replies.

I gulp, appearing more stressed about the threat than Antonio does.

"Did you like the picture I sent?" Antonio asks. "Consider it a present. I even wrapped it in a bow for you."

Present? I mouth to Antonio. *What present?*

"I'd have preferred it was your dead body," my father fires back.

"Body?" I hiss, launching forward to smack Antonio's arm.

He ignores me while keeping his attention on the phone.

"But no worries, Lombardi," my father continues. "I informed Elijah's family you murdered him, so now, you have another family wanting to kill you. The more, the merrier for me." He tsks. "Now, if you bring Gigi to me right fucking now, I'll call them off."

He's such a liar.

Antonio shakes his head. "That's off the table."

"Lombardi—"

"But I am generous enough to allow you to speak with her." Antonio positions the phone near my mouth but refuses to let me hold it.

"Hi, Daddy," I say loudly in the speaker.

"Gigi, are you okay?" His voice is frantic.

I fiddle with my hands in my lap. "Yes, I'm fine."

"Where are you?"

Antonio shoots me a sharp look. If I tell my father even one clue, I'll be signing his death certificate.

"I have no idea." Technically, it's the truth. I don't know where the cabin is.

"Has he hurt you?"

"No," I quickly reply. If anything will put him somewhat at ease, it's that.

Antonio lowers his head and speaks clearly. "I told you, I'm protecting her. Now, you've learned she's safe." He abruptly ends the call.

The ringtone is annoying as it blares through the room. Antonio ignores it.

"Hey!" I make a grab for the phone, but he yanks it away. "I wasn't finished talking to him."

He tucks the phone into his pocket. "I don't care."

I cross my arms. "Was the *present* Elijah's body?"

"Why does it matter?" He scratches his cheek.

"Uh, because he was my fiancé."

His eyes narrow at my last word. "He was just as much as your fiancé as I am a good man."

"Killing him only created more problems for you. Like my father said, there's another family who wants you dead."

"Also like your father said, the more, the merrier."

"You're seriously fucked up in the head."

"And you love it, so what's that say about you?" He raises a brow.

"Elijah didn't deserve to die for agreeing to marry me."

He flicks his hand through the air. "Spare me the trying-to-make-me-feel-bad bit. It won't work."

"His family at least deserves his body."

"I owe them nothing."

"Antonio—"

"Elijah was a coward willing to trade your life to save his," he seethes, as if vividly remembering every detail of what happened in the living room. "He was also a coward when I murdered his brother."

"Wait." I grimace, holding up a hand, and scoot a few inches away from him. "You murdered his brother *too*?"

"Years ago." He stretches out his arms, curls his hands around my ankles, and jerks me back to where I was.

I shudder when he runs his thumb along my heel and massages it. His hands are chillingly cold, but the way he's kneading my skin feels amazing.

"Look at you," he says with almost a mock in his tone. "Ready to commit to someone without even knowing their past."

"My father provided me with details on my options, and I chose Elijah."

"Your father needs to do better research, then."

"Don't insult my father." I scowl at him. "And you never

gave me time to uncover your murderous past before marrying you. At least with Elijah, I had a choice."

His gentle massaging dissipates when he digs his finger into the top of my foot. "Elijah would've seen you as nothing more than property … a transaction."

"And you view me as the same—an alliance with my family or some deal, I'm sure. You're no better."

"That's where you're so wrong." His jaw tics. "If your father offered me an alliance in exchange for divorcing you, I'd choose our marriage. If he said divorce you or die, you'd be a widow. If Sonny said it's you or me, I'd die. I'll always sacrifice myself for you."

Why does his reply set my blood on fire?

Since I'm not sure how to answer that and death talk isn't exactly a fun time, I change the subject. "Why did you murder Elijah's brother?"

"He was responsible for Sienna, my ex-wife's, death."

"How?"

"Sienna was an addict—well, a former addict, depending on the day you talked to her. I tried every option to get her help—expensive rehab facilities, medicines, every holistic approach, whatever she wanted— but she always relapsed. It was hard on our marriage—a marriage neither of us wanted." His face turns rigid.

"Her family was from Chicago and friends with Elijah's. On her last visit there, she bought drugs from Elijah's brother, Grant. Even though the Beckers hid it well, Grant was running the largest narcotics operation in Chicago. Grant sold her drugs laced with fentanyl, and she died. When I learned Grant was responsible for her death, I killed him. Elijah knew it was me but did nothing about it because he was happy to be next in line in taking over his family."

I violently shake my head. "No. My father would've never set me up with a man in the drug trade." He despises them and tries to get rid of them in the city.

"Elijah kept his hands clean of the drugs, but that doesn't mean he wasn't profiting or clueless about where the money came from. He stayed as squeaky clean as he could to maintain his government contracts." His hand leaves my foot, and he massages the skin between his eyes.

"I'm sorry for your loss," I whisper sorrowfully. "Sienna didn't deserve to die like that."

"It wasn't my loss. It was Amara's."

"Did you love Sienna?"

"No. Nor did she love me."

I play with my wedding ring, circling it around my finger.

"If you don't like it, I'll buy you a new one."

"No." I raise my hand. "It's perfect."

Every detail of the ring is distinctive with its gold band, handcrafted with willow-like vines and clusters of dark rubies around them, giving it a Gothic look. A giant triangle-shaped diamond lies in the middle.

For the first time, I peek at Antonio's hand. I never thought to check if he was wearing a wedding band, and I can't help but smile when I see one.

He's letting me mark him as he is with me.

And now, there's a huge chance I'll lose him.

My stomach drops, and I hate what I'm about to say. "This won't end well, Antonio. My father will never make a deal. He'll pretend to negotiate with you and kill you in the end."

He grabs my hand and presses it to his lips. "Then I'll die."

"Antonio—"

A different phone rings, interrupting us. He digs it out from the other pocket and answers after checking the caller ID.

"Give me five minutes," he tells the caller and hangs up. "I have to go, but first, I want you to promise me something."

I blink away tears. "What?"

"If you have sleep paralysis, you wake me up, or if I'm not here, you call me."

I dip my chin toward his phone. "Give me a phone to call you, then."

"You ask Leo to call me."

I sigh. "That doesn't sound nearly as romantic."

"I'm serious, Giana."

"Oh, like you'd drop everything and come save me from my imagination?"

"I'd drop everything for you for any reason. I'd kill for you, steal for you. Anything you need, I'm there, princess."

He stands, opens the closet, and pulls out items. I watch as he shrugs on a thick black coat and slips black leather gloves into his pockets.

"Be good," he says before kissing my forehead.

My heart breaks as he leaves.

From my dream to the tone in my father's voice, I know it's too late.

Antonio won't stay alive long, and I don't know if I'll be able to survive a life without him.

37

ANTONIO

We enter the strip club from the back to avoid drawing attention. The loud music blasting through the place is grating. I can't wait to kill these motherfuckers so I can return to my silence.

All the patrons' attention is on the women dancing onstage. I scan the crowd and immediately spot Nuncio in the corner, mid-lap dance. The idiot believes he's discreet and separated from the crowd.

A few more of Sonny's men are spread throughout the room, either watching the dancers or getting their own form of lap dance. All of them are in their own little worlds.

Example nine hundred fucking thousand why my father was a superior don than Sonny would ever be.

Also why I'm a better fit.

During turf wars, you never allow your guys to act so stupid, especially in public with their guard down.

I slip my gloves on and grip my pocketknife while easing toward Nuncio. He's so entranced by the dancer grinding on his dick that he doesn't notice me. Her back is to him, and he's gripping her pigtail. With every move she makes, he grunts so loud that neither of them senses my presence. In one swift motion, I cup the back of his neck, drag his head down, and slit his throat. I smirk when the first drop of crimson red drips onto his chest.

He gags, as if preparing to vomit, and more blood sputters from his fat throat. It grows heavier and starts splashing the dancer's back.

She stops. "Swear to God, if you come on me again—" Her words stop when she turns around and realizes it's not his jizz, but his blood. She slides off his lap and screams as more blood gushes out.

I yank his head to face me, and his eyes are panicked.

"Fucking traitor."

Nuncio weakly reaches out, as if asking me for help.

"This is for my father." I kick his chair, and he tumbles off it.

He holds his hands up in a begging gesture as I withdraw my pistol and point it at him.

A thrill sets in when I pull the trigger, shooting him in the head.

There's no better satisfaction than revenge.

And the motherfucker made it so easy for me.

The gunshot diverts all attention away from the women as people search for the source. Jersey, one of Sonny's guys and a twat who once pledged his undying allegiance to my father, hurls a woman off his lap. Dancers disregard their money and clothes to run into the dressing room.

Jersey hops onstage and grins as if ready for fun. Disco lights sparkle around him, and he aims his gun at me. I stand tall and smirk at him.

"It's about damn time we killed you," he shouts, and the music stops.

Out of the corner of my eye, I see the DJ hightailing it toward the dressing room. Two doormen remain off to the side, watching the shit show, but not stopping us. I wouldn't risk my life for the sake of the job either. I'm sure the owner, Sammie, is hiding in his office, waiting until the bloodshed ends to leave.

More men on both sides join us. A few of Sonny's men run out of the club. I raise my pistol, and when Jersey squeezes the trigger, I duck and dodge the bullet.

I flash a smile when I return fire on Jersey, and the bullet lands smack dab in his forehead. His head hits the pole when he stumbles back, and another man sprints to him. While he attempts to help Jersey, I kill him next.

A two-for-one discount.

I take in my surroundings.

Damien has the barrel of his Glock underneath a man's chin and squeezes the trigger. His brain matter splatters all over the liquor bottles and glasses.

"Motherfucker!" Declan screams when he's punched in the face before killing the man.

I whip around when gunfire comes my way and shoot back.

We don't stop fighting and shooting until all of Sonny's men are dead.

Correction: *all but one.*

We find one cowered behind a speaker. He drags his knees to his stomach when we approach him.

"Please," he begs, his lower lip trembling. "Don't kill me."

"Jesus." Damien stops next to me and wipes blood off his forehead. "What's he? Fourteen years old?"

"Fift—" The boy trembles. "Fifteen."

"It seems the rumors about Sonny just accepting guys off the street with no experience are true," Damien says while Rafael wraps his tie around his bullet wound.

This kid, along with the others, means nothing to Sonny.

That's another difference between him and me. I'd never ask my men to do something for me that I'd never do for them. It's fucking leadership and how my father and I built loyalty. You don't win by letting your men take your downfalls while you sit boastfully on your throne.

I stare at him, contemplating what to do. Before coming in here, I made it clear any man loyal to Sonny needed to die. I remember how Cristian let Eddie live, and he came for revenge years afterward. Survivors are never good. They either rat you out or seek vengeance later.

The boy slams his eyes shut, and a tear falls down his cheek.

Sighing, I drop my gun to my side.

"Get off the streets and stop working for Sonny," I tell the kid. "Or next time, you'll end up dead."

Either by me or someone else.

He hesitantly nods. Damien snatches him by the collar to bring him to his feet and walks him out. I roll my neck and cut my gaze across the room to ensure we didn't miss anyone.

"This is going to cost you, Antonio." Sammie strolls toward me, scrunching his weathered face while observing his club.

I toss four thousand dollars on the stage. "Here, and you can have whatever is in these dead fucks' pockets." I retrieve another stack of cash. "This is for the dancers. Let me know if they need more. As for the damage, send Sonny the bill."

I'm grasping what it takes to be king, and it has a shit ton of killing.

Good thing it's what I've done all my life.

"Do you want to talk about Cernach?" I ask Damien when we get into the unmarked car we drove to the club.

He shakes his head. "It's a sacrifice I'm willing to make. Marrying Riona will keep us alive."

"Do you plan to tell Pippa?"

He winces at her name and shoves his bloody gloves into a plastic bag to dispose of later. "She ended what we had a long time ago."

"If you don't want to do this, I'll find another way."

His jaw flexes. "There's no other way, Antonio. We already have the firearms."

Just as we're about to pull away, the boy from the club pounds on my window.

I hit the button to lower it.

He sticks his head through. "Sonny knows where your secret cabin is."

38

GIGI

The bedroom door swings open, and a silhouette appears in the darkened doorway.

I scream because it's all too familiar.

So much like my sleep paralysis.

Is it paralysis … or is this reality?

It always takes my brain forever to figure that out.

Only this time, I can scream.

So that's exactly what I do.

The figure takes a few steps toward me.

"Come on, Gigi." The masculine voice is harsh yet gentle at the same time.

Weird. My sleep paralysis entity never speaks.

"Gigi!" He shakes me.

I blink, coming to my senses, and realize it's not a hallucination.

It's reality.

"We need to go."

Leo.

I pull back when he grabs me. "What—"

"We need to leave *now.*" He snatches my hand and tugs me out of bed. "Yeah, I'm getting her in the car now, Antonio."

"What's …" I rub my tired eyes. "What's going on?"

"Sonny knows you're here," he says, rushing me out of the room.

I hurriedly snatch my heels and the blazer Antonio switched out his jacket for earlier and nearly trip as Leo drags me out of the cabin.

I'm putting a lot of trust into Leo when I climb into his black sedan. He can very well be kidnapping me from my kidnapper.

I can't help but snort at the irony.

Antonio clearly trusts Leo enough to watch me, but traitors always strike when you least expect it. After Rocky betrayed my father, I learned anyone can flip at any time.

Leo speeds off and leaves the cabin behind. He tosses his phone toward me, and it lands on my lap with a thud. Antonio's name is on the screen.

"We're leaving now," Leo says while driving down a shadowy road. "Are we meeting at location one or two?"

"Two," Antonio replies.

"What's one and two?" I ask, but no one answers.

"Shit, I'm getting a call," Antonio says. "Hurry and call me if you have any problems."

He hangs up, and I play with the phone in my hand. I can easily sneak and call my father. Even if I called his number, set the phone to the side, and allowed him to hear Leo while tracing the call.

"Don't even think about it," Leo says, grabbing the phone. "I think you'd rather be with me than dumped on the side of the road as Sonny searches for you."

"Rude," I grumble.

We're quiet, and he focuses on navigating the roads. When we spot another set of headlights, my breathing hitches. Leo veers to the shoulder of the road, and the other car does the same.

Clasping my palm to my heart, I take deep breaths. As soon

as Leo puts the car in park, Antonio steps out of the other car. He opens my door, helps me out, and directs me to his.

A minute later, I'm in his car, and we're driving away.

"Where are we going?" I ask him.

He ignores me and continues driving.

"Antonio!" I yell. "Where are we going?"

He concentrates on the road, his shoulders hunched forward. "You'll see when we get there."

I accept his answer and allow him to focus on the road.

As he drives, I watch the clock on the console. Thirty-seven minutes pass before we arrive at our destination. Somehow, he took a backward detour in the suburbs of the city, and we're back in a wooded area. I recognize the location where the wealthy reside if they desire privacy. Wherever this is, it's an upgrade from the cabin.

The driveway has pathway lights, but it's still difficult to take in my surroundings in the dark when he parks in front of a home.

Antonio unsnaps his seat belt, and I do the same before stepping out of the car. He rests his hand on the base of my back and guides me toward the front door. A light above the porch provides some illumination, and I notice bright flowers and a small bench on the porch.

Antonio knocks once.

Twice.

Three times.

A light flicks on in the house, and someone peeks out a window before answering the door. Antonio ushers me inside and gently shuts it behind us.

We're in a foyer, and the man appears in front of us.

"What the hell, Antonio?" He shakes his head while staring me down. "You know I have no problem with Amara staying here, but no way in hell am I taking the Mafia princess you kidnapped into my home."

I stare at him, silent and speechless.

This is Antonio's fight.

He's the one who brought me here, knowing this man would have a problem with it.

"A few days is all I'm asking," Antonio says. His tone isn't demanding, nor is he threatening him. He's not one of his men.

"No," the man replies sharply.

"She's my wife, Dante, which means she's family."

Ahh, another clue.

He's somehow on Antonio's family tree.

"*Wife?*" The man runs his hand through his curly brown hair and pulls at it. "What did you do, Antonio?"

"You got married?"

That question doesn't come from the man.

The feminine voice flows from down the hallway. Dante pulls at his hair again, and a redheaded woman steps to his side. She rests her hand on his chest and releases a long yawn.

Her gaze flashes to me, and she smiles.

"She's his damn hostage, Eden," Dante informs her. "*And Cristian Marchetti's daughter.*"

"Oh," she draws out in understanding.

I'm just a giant liability around here, apparently.

"Antonio hasn't hurt me," I rush out. "It's … complicated. We have history."

This place feels safer than the cabin, and if Amara is here, it definitely is. Antonio wouldn't hide her just anywhere. Whoever Dante is, Antonio trusts him. And since I don't recognize him or the woman, they're more likely not involved in our world.

Dante works his jaw while glaring at Antonio.

She steps forward and holds out her hand toward me. "I'm Eden."

I swear I hear a breath of relief leave Antonio.

"Gigi." I shake her hand and smile.

Dante doesn't introduce himself or shake my hand.

I sure as hell don't get a smile from him.

"Dante, her life is in danger," Eden says in sincerity, running her hand over his chest.

"And your life will be more in danger if we're hiding Cristian's daughter," Dante argues.

"One night." Antonio holds up a finger. "I'll take her somewhere else tomorrow."

Dante pushes his rimless glasses up his face. "We're not risking our lives with her here, Antonio. We're risking Amara's."

"My father would never harm a child," I input with absolute certainty.

Dante finally takes a good look at me. "Your father isn't the only one we're worried about."

"One night," Antonio pleads. "I need her safe so I can track Sonny. I'm close, Dante."

"This is cute." Eden wiggles her fingers between Antonio and me. "Very *Romeo and Juliet.*"

"They both die at the end," Dante points out. "That's not a very enticing argument to let her stay here."

"*Romeo and Juliet* remix," Eden corrects before waving me forward. "Come on, Gigi. It's too late for you to travel anyway. You can sleep in the guest room."

"One night," Dante says with disapproval. "That's it."

"Thank you," I softly say.

Antonio lowers his head and kisses me. "I'll be back. You're safe here." He moves his gaze to Dante. "Thank you, brother."

Brother?

Whoa.

Is this … the mystery Lombardi brother?

I should've connected the dots, but I was a little consumed with them arguing over whether I'd be sleeping on the side of the road or not.

I slip off my shoes and have to squeeze between Dante and a cabinet before following Eden down a hallway.

"Don't worry about Dante." Eden saunters through the

house, wearing striped pajamas, and her hair is clipped back in a bun. "He likes to stay out of that life as much as he can."

"People have always wondered who he is," I say. "Some even swear he isn't real, just some hoax Vincent put out."

"He's very real, but he tries not to be—at least with the Lombardis." She turns the corner and walks into a bedroom. "That's why he changed his last name, but he knew, sooner or later, he wouldn't be able to escape it." She sighs, turning to face me. "It seems that day has come."

A sense of guilt creeps in.

I'm putting these people in danger.

Eden taps the bed. "Make yourself comfortable. There's an en suite bathroom if you want to shower, and it's stocked with anything you'll need. Get some rest, Gigi." She kindly smiles before leaving the bedroom and gently shutting the door behind her.

I run my hand along the navy-striped comforter. It's a standard guest room with nightstands and limited decor. On the nightstand is a sign that lists the Wi-Fi name and password. I pick it up, repeating it mentally, in case there's a time when I can use it.

Crawling into bed, I snuggle my face into the pillow. I try to stay awake until Antonio comes home, but can't stop myself from softly dozing back to sleep.

I'm woken by a click of the door, and from the faint light on the nightstand, I see Antonio enter the bedroom. He strips off his coat, tosses it onto a chair, and then sits down to remove his shoes.

He carefully walks to the bathroom, as if not wanting to wake me. I hear the shower turn on and count to thirty, giving the water time to warm up, before slipping out of bed. I crack the bathroom door open to find Antonio already in the shower. Water splashes down his long, robust body. I squeeze my thighs together while watching him.

God, he's sexy.

Perfection.

And now, mine.

He holds out his hands, and I notice a flash of red drip from his knuckles. The red fades with the water and washes down the drain. I strip out of my pajamas and wander toward the shower.

His muscles flex when he shifts in my direction. He pauses and opens the shower door—like a *pass go* signal. Goose bumps layer my skin as I step inside the shower. He shuffles back, allowing me most of the water, and I hiss at the heat.

As soon as I shut the door, he captures my waist and draws me closer to him. His large hand sweeps over my face, and he tightly cups it.

"You okay?" he asks in a low tone.

I inch back to allow him more water and reach out to run my finger along a cut on his face that wasn't there earlier. "Yeah."

"You're safe here."

"It seems that my being safe here doesn't make everyone else safe though."

He rubs his thumb over my bottom lip. "Don't think like that."

I blink away water from my eyelashes. "It's hard not to."

"Hmm," he hums. "How about I give you something else to think about, then?" He scrapes his thumb along my lip before slipping it inside my mouth.

I wrap my lips around it as he spreads my legs with his knee. He enters two fingers inside me and then makes a V with them to stretch me. My legs shake. Even though he hasn't moved his fingers, I'm already anticipating the pleasure. Antonio never fails to make me feel on top of the world.

I dig my fingers into his shoulder to hold myself up when he lowers his hand from my mouth while sliding his fingers out of me. He cups my breast, brushing his thumb over my nipple, while dipping his finger back inside me.

He continues slowly stroking me while moving to the other breast.

It's torturous.

But the good kind of torture.

My typical villain.

Never letting me get anything easily.

When he adds a finger, my knees start wobbling, and he palms my ass to further keep me in place. I buck against his hand, and even though the shower is massive, it's hard to get the perfect angle in here. To better help me, he raises my leg and rests my foot against the edge.

I grind against his hand. Our bodies are slippery while gliding against each other, both of us needing as much friction as possible. I moan when he backs me up against the shower wall. The cold tiles bite into my skin, but I'm so close to coming apart that I ignore it.

My body is falling …

Falling …

Falling …

Antonio keeps me pinned against the wall as my orgasm shatters through me. He doesn't give me a second to recover before shoving me to my knees, fisting his hard cock, and stroking himself. He's hard, throbbing, and only inches from my face.

Water drips off the tip.

I blink.

No, water and *pre-cum* are at his tip.

I lick my lips.

"I remember you saying something about putting my cock in your mouth in exchange for a phone call?" he rasps.

Pain shoots through my head when he drives his hand into my knotted hair, grabbing a handful to yank me closer to his cock.

"Open wide, and I want every fucking inch of my cock inside that sweet mouth," he instructs. "Or I'll cause more pain than that."

I gulp in air, and he groans when I take the tip of his cock between my lips and suck.

Maybe I won't listen this time.

Maybe I'll tease him a little.

Almost as if he can read my mind, he tightens his hold on my hair and shoves his entire cock inside my mouth until my forehead is pressed against his abs.

"Deep-throat this cock, or don't waste my fucking time," he groans.

I hollow my cheeks and suck in what breaths I can through my nose as he fucks my face. He shakes his head in disappointment the few times I gag. My jaw aches as he furiously thrusts in and out of my mouth, hardly letting me up for air.

He shifts himself, and when I glance up, I find him collecting water in his free hand. When he dumps it over my head, I attempt to pull away, but his hold on my hair doesn't allow it.

And he does it again.

And again.

The water creates more difficulty to focus, and he plants my head so tight against his stomach that my hair sticks to his skin.

Antonio never takes it easy on me.

He likes to test me in the bedroom—well, the shower in this case.

"Play with your clit, princess," he demands. "Get yourself off as you suck my cock."

I slightly raise my knees, allowing my finger enough room to slip between my legs and run over my clit.

"Your clit doesn't like it gentle, baby," he says through rushed breaths. "Touch it like I do. Merciless. Rough."

I listen to him because he knows what my body likes better than anyone.

Better than even me.

His touch is magical. Skilled. Like it was tailored perfectly for me.

I play with myself but am unsatisfied because I need *him* to do it.

He pumps his hips, smacking them against my face so hard that I'm nervous he'll break my damn nose. I lose the ability to even find my clit. His hand descends my neck, and he tips his hips to gain a better angle.

"Gigi," he groans as his cock twitches, and he comes inside my mouth.

As soon as I swallow, he scoops me up and drops me on the shower footrest, where bottles of shampoo and body washes are lined up. He kneels and shoves his mouth between my legs, eating and playing with my pussy exactly how he instructed me.

I nearly wrap my legs around his neck like a snake as I fall apart again. His name leaves my mouth in stuttered groans. When I throw my arm out to grasp the wall, it knocks over every bottle in my way.

But my villain isn't finished with me yet.

He helps me to my feet, and as soon as I'm fully stable, he whips me around and places my hands against the wall. I moan when he tips up my hips and enters me from behind.

Then he fucks me as hard as he fucked my mouth.

My eyes water.

My head moves up and down, and I have to hold myself back to stop it from smacking against the wall.

Thank God the water drowns out our sounds, but being quiet is still a struggle. I do my best though because I don't know how close the other bedrooms are.

He pulls all the way out of me. "Am I fucking my wife or the woman I abducted?"

I push my ass back, silently begging for him to return his cock inside me.

Instead of doing that, he cups the back of my neck, turns my head, and presses his lips against mine. "Answer me."

"Your wife," I sigh.

He slaps my ass. "That's fucking right, princess."

For a girl held captive, I sure had a good night's sleep.

I can credit that to Antonio fucking me into exhaustion and then snuggling with me after.

Fun fact: Antonio Lombardi is the big spoon.

Hell, am I even considered a captive anymore?

I'm sure if I asked Eden to borrow her phone, she'd probably let me. But that'd create problems between her and Antonio. I need to figure out a plan to contact my father without anyone else knowing.

The bed is empty when I wake up. I didn't hear Antonio leave this morning. Yawning, I crawl out of bed and find a stack of clothes on the chair.

Apparently, I didn't hear whoever delivered the clothes either.

I change into a pair of joggers and a sweater that hangs off one shoulder. When I leave the bedroom, I follow voices into the kitchen. Eden is loading the dishwasher and talking to someone. As I step around the corner, I see a young girl sitting across from her.

"These marshmallows are my favorite," she chirps and then shoves a bite of cereal into her mouth.

I gulp and run my hands down my sweater before entering the kitchen and making my presence known. Their attention whips to me.

"Good morning," Eden greets with a grin.

I return the smile. "Morning."

"Who are you?" the girl asks.

"She's my friend," Eden tells her.

"You're pretty." The girl, whose dark hair is a wild mess on top of her head, perks up in her seat. "I'm Amara. What's your name?"

I shyly wave at her. "Gigi."

Meeting your boyfriend's—er, *husband's*—daughter might be more nerve-racking than meeting the parents. And that's saying something, considering his father attempted to kill my brother.

"Gigi," Amara says, tilting her head and pausing as if thinking. "My daddy likes that name. Whenever I ask him what his favorite name is, he always says Amara. But when I ask what his *second* favorite is, he always says Gigi." She doesn't understand how big of a deal her words are. "I like your name too. That might be my second favorite." She turns her head to look at Eden. "Well, you and Gigi are a tie!"

Swear to God, my heart lights up in my chest.

"Are you hungry?" Eden asks.

"Have Lucky Charms with me!" Amara bursts out, patting the stool next to her. "Auntie Eden lets me eat them all the time!" She holds up her spoon and cheekily grins.

"I'd love to have Lucky Charms with you." I shuffle into the kitchen, pour a bowl, and sit beside her.

I hate whenever Antonio leaves without saying goodbye or telling me where he's going. Hell, I hate when he leaves, *period*, because there's always a chance he won't come back. Each day we spend together, the anxiety of him being taken away from me heightens. Sure, he never leaves with the intent of dying, but his life is so reckless and volatile.

I love Antonio.

There's no better word to describe my feelings for him.

I've always known he was the man for me, but I tried convincing myself it was purely physical since I was too chicken-shit to admit it.

He's the Romeo to my Juliet—minus the dying part, hopefully.

"Oh, your ring is so pretty!" Amara says, breaking me away from my thoughts. "Did you get that from Daddy?" She rotates in her chair and is practically on her knees to get a better look at my finger. "He bought one just like it before and said it was for someone special!" She's beaming over the fact she knows this.

I blush.

Amara also provides an element Antonio needs in this life.

Kindness.

I hold up my finger to allow her a better view and smile.

How long has Antonio had this?

I want to ask Amara more questions, but I'm not about to interrogate a child.

I'll wait to do that with her father.

On my way back to the guest room, I stop mid-step when I spot a home office … and a computer. I glance side to side to make sure no one is around before easing the office door open and gently shutting it behind me.

Dante's medical degrees hang along the walls.

A doctor … *hmm.*

I circle the desk and stoop down in front of the desktop computer, wishing it were a laptop that I could easily drag with me on the floor. I pull the keyboard off the desk and set it on my lap, and as soon as I hit a key, the screen comes alive.

And it's password-protected.

Shit!

I type in my first guess: DrDante

Wrong.

ImnotaLombardithankGod

Wrong.

Just as I flex my fingers to try another, someone says, "What the hell do you think you're doing?"

39

ANTONIO

Right when I start trusting Gigi, I catch her sneaking behind Dante's desk, trying to use his computer. And knowing her, she's not trying to shop online or check the weather.

At the sound of my voice, she scrambles to her feet. I draw my pistol from my waistband while circling the desk and back her into the wall. My expression is stone-faced while she peers at me, and I raise the gun to her neck.

"I asked you a question," I say as she nervously gulps.

"I was just, uh …" Her eyes are fixated on the gun. "Trying to Google something."

"Google what?"

"The population of New York?"

"You expect me to believe that?"

"No, but can you please get that damn gun away from my neck? We both know you won't shoot me."

I trace the gun barrel along her neck with a featherlight touch. "Don't mistake my past kindness for weakness, princess."

"You won't kill me with your daughter in the same home."

"I have no problem killing someone, *even in the same room*, if you're a risk to her." I move closer until our lips touch. "And you using that computer, up to something sketchy, is a risk to her."

"You know I'd never risk your daughter's safety, Antonio." She playfully licks my lower lip before sucking on it. "And if you don't believe me, pull the trigger." *Another lick.* "Shoot me."

My testy wife.

Sometimes, I let her get away with too much.

Maybe I should remind her who's boss.

I tilt my head and run my tongue along the area where I placed the gun on her neck. A wave of satisfaction washes over me when she shivers, and goose bumps pop up on her skin as I lower the gun between her breasts.

She's right. I can't kill her.

Just like she proved the other day that she can't kill me either.

Our deaths might be because of the other, but our hands will never be dirty.

That doesn't mean I can't frighten her a bit.

"I wanted to email my father, let him know that I'm okay, to protect you," she whispers. She trembles beneath my touch when I guide the gun along her nipple and slowly trace a circle around it.

"How exactly does that protect me?"

"It'll ease his anger toward you."

"Nothing will ever ease your father's anger." We both live in the Always Angry as Fuck Club.

"It'll help if I remind him I'm safe." She shudders when I drag the gun back along her chest to the other nipple and do the same.

"He'll never believe you're safe with me."

"The more I tell him, the more believable it becomes."

"Wrong. Keep your hands away from the computer. Do you hear me?"

"Fine, I'll send him a raven or something."

"Then I also need to keep you out of the yard." I lower my

hand and slip it under her pants, running my finger along the hem of her panties.

"I'm only trying to help, Antonio," she says, her breathing growing ragged.

"Help me by behaving," I rasp into her ear before shoving my hand into her panties and cupping her mound.

She groans, shifting her weight along the wall, and pushes her hips forward.

"It seems I need to fuck you into obedience," I tell her. "Punish you with my cock until you learn to be a good little hostage for me, huh?"

"I thought I was your wife, not a hostage."

"That's right." I tsk. "It'll give me much better satisfaction, knowing the woman I'm punishing with my cock wears my ring on her finger."

I reposition us for a better angle and slide a finger through her opening. She's so soaked for me that I could drown in her pussy.

"You think, as a Mafia princess, you get to make rules," I say. "But when my hand is in your panties, when my cock is down your throat, or when I'm worshipping your perfect body"—I stop to grind my hips against hers while dipping one finger inside her—"I make"—I drag my finger out before shoving it in roughly, then do the same between words—"Every. Single. Fucking. Rule."

My cock jerks in my pants. I need to get her out of this office and back into the shower, where I can drown out our moans with water. Or, fuck, maybe I'll toss her into my car, take her somewhere secluded, and fuck her in every position with only nature as our witness.

"I want to hear you remind yourself that," I tell her as I continue finger fucking her. "Who makes the rules?"

She swivels her hips forward. "I have the pussy, dear husband. So in case you weren't aware, I make—" she then says the rest of her words like I did when I shoved my fingers inside her—"Every. Single. Fucking. Rule." She lowers her hand between us and clasps it over mine in her panties. "As your princess, I am your equal. And if you want me to be yours, you need to learn that."

Fuuuck.

If my obsession with her wasn't enough before, now, it burns hotter than my thirst for revenge against my enemies. I lower my head, press my tongue between her lips, and devour her mouth as our bodies slide against each other's.

We have to stop.

We need to fucking stop.

Unfortunately, I can't fuck her right here, right now.

"Take me somewhere," she whispers into my mouth. "I need you inside me."

I continue playing with her pussy while fighting with myself to pull away.

"Daddy! Are you here?"

If any words have the power to separate us, it's those.

Gigi jumps, and I step away from her. She drops to her knees, hiding behind the desk as I wipe my fingers down my pants.

Amara appears in the office doorway. "Hi, Daddy! I'm so happy you're back." She glances around the room and scrunches her nose. "What are you doing in Uncle Dante's office?"

"I just needed to grab something for him," I say, straightening myself.

"Like what?"

Jesus, her curiosity.

I quickly snatch a pen from the desk. "This?"

"A pen?" Her face scrunches more.

"It's his favorite, and he forgot it." I slip the pen into my pocket. "I need to run to the bathroom real quick, okay?"

"I'm trying to find my new friend, Gigi! We're going to watch a movie."

"I think I saw her somewhere around the kitchen when I walked in. I'd look there, sweetie."

"Okay!" She takes off, running back down the hallway.

Gigi crawls out from behind the desk and runs her hand down her pants to compose herself. "That was a close one." She glances at the computer. "But seriously, Antonio, it'll help if I can send my father a simple *I'm alive* email."

"We already called your father, remember? He knows you're alive." I take a step closer to her. "Now, stay out of here unless you want me to lock you in the guest bedroom or take you somewhere that doesn't have windows, let alone electronics."

"Ugh, you're such a lame abductor."

"Oh, yes, you thought I was so lame when I was playing with your wet-as-fuck pussy."

She flips me off. "You've never heard of people faking attraction to their kidnappers as a means to escape?"

"Even the best porn star couldn't fake the sound you make when we're together." I suck on the tips of my fingers, tasting her. "I could dip you into fucking water, and your pussy still wouldn't be as wet as when I touch it." I remove each finger, one by one. "Now, be a good little hostage, and I'll let you come on my tongue tonight."

There hasn't been a time when I haven't found Gigi to be the sexiest woman I've ever laid eyes on, but as I stare at her right now, there's so much more to her than her beauty.

I don't only see the woman I'm crazy about.

I see the woman I want a family with.

Standing in the corner, unnoticed, I silently watch her with Amara. They're sitting on the floor, and Amara's legs are stretched out toward Gigi. While Gigi paints Amara's toenails, she giggles and tells her how ticklish she is. She then starts babbling about loving and missing her dance classes. Gigi focuses solely on Amara, absorbing her every word.

The two people most important to me look like a family. I'll do anything to make it stay that way.

I move closer to better eavesdrop on their conversation.

"Have you ever taken dance classes?" Amara asks Gigi.

"I did." Gigi screws on the polish cap, sets the bottle aside, and then blows on Gigi's toes. "When I was in high school, my father let me take them for two years."

"Did you love it?" Amara chirps.

Gigi grins at her. "I loved it."

"Can I show you my dances after my toes dry?"

"Of course." Gigi nods and then gasps, placing her hand to her chest. "*Or* I have a better idea."

Amara perks up while still careful not to mess up her toes. "What's that?"

"You teach me your dances because I bet you're a great teacher."

"I'd love that!" Amara squeals, wiggling her toes while squirming her shoulders in a dance-like movement.

My happiness fades, my shoulders slumping, when I remember I can't savor this moment for as long as I'd like.

Amara's smile stretches from ear to ear when I fully enter the room. "Daddy! Look! Gigi is here!" Just as she's about to stand, she remembers her toenails and gives a cute glance at Gigi, as if asking for approval.

Gigi carefully runs a finger over her big toe. "All good."

Amara jumps to her feet with a burst of energy and rushes toward me. She wraps her arms around my legs and turns to look at Gigi. "Gigi is painting my toes." She holds up her foot to show me the purple polish. "She's also wearing that really pretty ring you bought!"

I wrap my arm around her shoulders and hold her tight. "Gigi is my friend."

Gigi cringes at my calling her *friend*, but I'm not sure what to tell Amara yet. Lord knows if I say *wife,* there's no way in hell she'll let me leave for another day with the endless questions she'll have.

"She's my friend too!" Amara dashes toward a flustered Gigi, but when she stumbles on the rug, Gigi immediately catches and steadies her. "Gigi told me I'd make a good dance teacher, so I'm going to teach her all the things Ms. Pippa taught me."

Gigi stands tall next to Amara.

"I'm sure Pippa would be proud," I say. "You're the best dancer in her class."

Amara beams at the compliment, swivels on her toes, and starts her training. Gigi shyly grins at me before turning her attention to Amara.

I glance to my side when Eden stops next to me and smirks in my direction.

"Thank you," I say around a long breath while still watching Gigi and Amara.

"You don't have to thank me." Eden gently squeezes my shoulder twice. "I love Amara."

I scratch my cheek. "Thank you for also convincing Dante to let Gigi stay here."

She sighs. "You risked your life for me once. I'm only returning the favor."

"You returned the favor with Amara. You're doing much more than that for me, and I appreciate it so damn much."

"We're family, Antonio. Families don't keep score of favors." She angles her gaze toward Amara instructing Gigi how to properly spin. "Plus, Amara and I like Gigi … and you *love* her."

I remain straight-faced. While I trust and respect Eden, I never reveal my full hand to anyone.

"Daddy!" Amara calls out, her voice and face animated. "Watch our dance!"

My body relaxes as I anchor my gaze on them. I laugh at Amara's unclear cues and Gigi trying her hardest to follow them.

When they finish, they take their bows while Eden and I cheer with whistles.

I pull my phone from my pocket when it vibrates.

"Let me call you right back," I tell Damien, answering his call. My stomach knots with disappointment that I can no longer watch them. I end the call. "I'm sorry, but I have to leave for a few hours. I'll be back soon, okay?"

Amara pouts out her lower lip. "You promise it won't be too long?"

"It won't be too long," I assure her, refusing to promise her that because I might break it. I peer at Gigi. "Can we talk for a sec?"

Gigi follows me into the foyer, and I turn to face her, taking her by surprise. When she nearly falls into my chest, I grab her elbows, but don't bother releasing her when she's stable.

"I'll be back later," I say, releasing her arm and caressing her cheek. "Please, for the love of God, don't do anything that'll piss me off."

"I'll stay away from all electronics *as long as* you promise me something," she whispers, palming my cheek.

I glance down and meet her worried gaze. "What's that?"

"Promise me you'll be back later." Her raspy tone is desperate.

"I'll be back for my girls." I kiss her forehead.

"You won't promise." Her hand on me shakes.

"You know I can't make that promise, baby." I rest my forehead against hers. "What I will promise is that I'll do everything I can to come home to you."

When I raise my head, our eye contact remains unbroken.

The air is thick with a potent blend of fear and passion.

Death always casts a shadow on our doorstep. I'm scared it'll never go away.

40

GIGI

My heartbeat slows to a crawl, a heavy sense of dread weighing it down when I watch Antonio leave. I settle my back against the stair railing and press my hand to my chest.

Before he left, I read the expression on his face all too well. I've seen it on my father countless times, each time etching a lasting memory inside me. It was the kind of goodbye that left you unsure if there'd be another hello.

Amara is teaching Eden dance moves when I return to the living room. She's adorable with her messy hair tied back in a red ribbon. Her shirt says *Dance Princess*, and she's wearing star-printed leggings. I see so much of Antonio's features in her. It's also clear that he attempts to create a sense of normalcy and conceal his violence from her. Even though we just met, I want to make sure it stays that way.

"Gigi! It's movie time!" she says when I catch her attention. "Aunt Eden will make popcorn with M&M's and nuts!"

"That sounds amazing!" I squeal.

Eden leads us into the kitchen for drinks and snacks. She hands me a bottle of water and Amara a juice box. Like Amara, Eden radiates kindness, but something about her tells me life hasn't always returned that gentleness to her.

We grab soft blankets, sinking into the plush couch cushions, and Amara snuggles between Eden and me. The movie starts, and I keep my attention divided between the screen and Amara. I relax as I watch her squeal in excitement over a cute character.

What a perfect life this would be.

I shut my eyes, hoping we can do this again someday but with Antonio by our side. We'd have a family—a haven of happiness and sanctuary from the chaos.

This is my dream life.

One with Antonio, Amara, and me.

And possibly another future child.

"I'm taking a bathroom break," I tell Amara and Eden, grabbing my empty water bottle and tossing it inside the recycle bin on my way out of the theater room.

After using the bathroom, I return to the kitchen for another water. As I round the corner, I jump when finding Dante sitting at the island, sipping on a Starbucks.

While Dante isn't as menacing as most men I know, his facial expression makes it clear he's not fond of me being in his home. He's dressed in blue scrubs, his name tag swaying from a lanyard, and his brown hair is neatly swept back.

"I was just, um … grabbing myself a water." I point toward the fridge.

For a moment, he studies me as if I were a patient he was attempting to diagnose. "I'm only doing this because my brother loves you." His voice is direct. "I'll always protect Amara. She's family and means the world to us, but you? You're someone from a life I've always wanted to distance myself from."

I wrinkle my nose, unsure how to reply, and he maintains

that same expression until I do. "I can go somewhere else. Really, I don't want to burden anyone."

"How about you return the favor?" His request doesn't sound manipulative. It's coated with desperation.

"What do you mean?"

"Don't let your father kill Antonio." He gestures toward the kitchen. "You're welcome here, but I need you to do that for me. Keep him alive, Gigi."

"Would you have done the same for Vinny?" I step forward. "Protect him?"

"God, no," he says without hesitation. "Vinny hardly cared about my existence, and I always wanted to keep it that way, but then I needed help."

"Help with what?"

This time, there's a delay before he answers. "It doesn't matter, and it's not my story to tell."

"Gotcha." I draw out the last word. "I respect that."

My nosiness just needs to figure out whose story it is.

He taps the kitchen island twice before tossing his cup in the recycling bin. "Have a good day, Gigi."

When Antonio gets home—and he'd freaking better, or I'll raise hell myself—I have a long list of questions he needs to answer.

I hang out with Eden and Amara for the rest of the day, and before bed, Amara requests I read her a bedtime story. We spend nearly an hour in her bedroom—which is directly across from ours—chatting and reading.

Now, I'm in the guest room watching TV and waiting for Antonio's return.

Ugh, I wish I could call him.

I bite my nails, ruining my manicure, as vivid scenarios parade through my mind.

What's leaving him out so late?

Three hours and a hand of chewed-off nails later, he returns.

"What did you do for Dante?" I ask the moment he shuts the door.

He halts. "What are you talking about? Did Eden or Dante tell you something?"

"Eden didn't."

"Dante did?" he asks in surprise.

I tap my toes against the sheets. "He started to, but then immediately stopped himself."

He sits on the ottoman, sighing, and unties his shoes. "When Dante met Eden, she was working as an escort, and after a year, he convinced her to quit and marry him. One of her clients had developed an obsession with her and was unhappy about her leaving the business. He started stalking her and making death threats." He sheds his blazer. "Dante decided to kill him and reached out to me, asking for advice on the best way to do it without getting caught. However, when I met with him, it was clear he couldn't do that. So I told him I'd take care of it, and I did. Dante was meant to save lives, not take them."

I press my hand to my heart.

Aw. Big brother helped little brother.

Okay, I'm definitely on the same crazy street as Antonio, but it's heartwarming to hear about Antonio caring about Dante like that.

Antonio sets his shoes to the side and stands, the smell of his cologne lingering in the air. "From that point on, Dante and I formed a friendship, if you can call it that. They occasionally watch Amara for me, and when my father fell ill, Dante reluctantly helped care for him."

"Poor Eden," I say wistfully. "Does she know what you did?"

"Dante tried to keep it from her, but she knew something

was eating at him. So he told her. She gifted me a bottle of bourbon and a thank-you letter for it."

That explains my intuition about her. She's strong, resilient, and now, I understand why.

Even though I complain about it, I've lived a privileged life. Some women, like Eden, weren't fortunate enough to have that luxury. I wish I could go to her bedroom and hug her, but Dante would definitely throw my ass out and ban me from their house.

Antonio unbuttons his shirt, allowing it to drop to the floor. "Were you good today?"

My mouth waters at the view of his bare chest, and I rub my thighs together. I roam my gaze down his chest.

Abs so sleek that they could cut glass.

A chest as smooth as marble.

I want to run my tongue down his stomach, tease him as he does me, and then pleasure him with my mouth again.

I perk up and cup my face while cheerfully grinning. "I was a good little hostage."

"That means I must keep my word." He steps to the bed, helps me out of it, and then strips my pajamas off on our walk to the bathroom.

Then he rewards me for being his good little hostage, just like he said he would.

41

ANTONIO

I've trailed enough people to know when someone is following me. I sense him growing closer with each step I take.

He won't kill me.

Not yet at least.

He needs something from me first.

I wait until we reach the back alley of Viego's Sandwich Shop and grip my pistol inside my waistband when turning around. The sun setting and the flickering sidewalk light limit my view of him.

"Don't you ever doubt my ability to find someone," Cristian says, standing inches away from me. He slowly withdraws a Glock with a silencer on the end from his black peacoat.

"You've been on my tail all day." I remain straight-faced while keeping a level tone. "And considering you didn't immediately put a bullet in my head means you won't."

I left before Gigi woke up again this morning, but I plan on coming home to her tonight. Which means I need to persuade her father not to blow my brains out. The moment I realized he was following me, I knew I wouldn't return to Dante's until he was gone. No way am I leading him straight to her.

"Where's Gigi?" He stands in a wide stance.

"Safe," I reply, maintaining my composure.

He keeps his gun raised. "Where exactly is safe?"

"You know I won't tell you that."

He plants the gun against my skull, but I don't move, blink, nothing. "Give me a fucking address, Lombardi."

I inhale a deep breath. "Are you really going to shoot your son-in-law?"

He adds tension to the gun, tightens his grip on the handle, and snarls, "You forced her hand, motherfucker."

"I might've forced her hand, but had you given Gigi her freedom, we'd have married a long time ago." I tsk. "How do you think Gigi contacted me so easily when Natalia went missing? You don't know the extent of my history with your daughter, so I'm asking for your trust."

"I don't trust anyone."

"Gigi is smart. If she were in true danger, don't you think she'd have figured out a way to escape me? Once Sonny is dead, I'll release her. Then you and I can return to being on good terms."

"After what you pulled, we'll never be on good terms."

"Our families have lived harmoniously for years. We can do it again." I hear the click of his gun.

Gunshots fill the air, and we instinctively duck to dodge them. Cristian's surprised face confirms the shooter isn't one of his men. I take off running, and when I round the corner, I spot Leo poking his head out the window of Damien's SUV. He's gripping his gun and shooting where Cristian had me cornered. Damien comes to a sudden stop, and I hastily open the passenger door before diving inside. He slams his foot on the gas, and we speed away, leaving Cristian in the dust as he shoots at us.

"Yeah," I say, catching my breath as Damien weaves through traffic. "Shooting at my father-in-law will definitely put me on his good side."

"The man wants to kill you either way, but we have bigger

problems," Leo says behind me before turning on the interior light.

I shift in my seat to find him with a beat-up man next to him.

"One of Sonny's men flipped," he says mockingly, staring at the man and raising a dark brow.

Flipped, my ass.

The motherfucker's hands are bound, his eyes swollen, and blood is seeping from his stomach through his shirt. He chokes a few times while inhaling gasps of air to mask his pain.

Leo presses the Glock against the man's head. "Tell him what you told me, and do it fast."

His face tics. "Sonny knows where your daughter is."

42

GIGI

Just like my father, I can sense danger.

Okay, minus the time Antonio abducted me, but your girl was off her A game for a minute. Blame it on the excitement of meeting my baby brother.

I'm in the kitchen, refilling my water glass, when I hear a faint voice coming from the window overlooking the backyard. Unease washes through me when a shadow passes the walkway.

As carefully as I can, I settle the cup on the island and run to Amara's room, where she's reading bedtime stories with Eden. I round the corner so fast that I have to grip the doorframe to avoid stumbling.

"Eden," I say in a hushed tone, "did Antonio ever tell you where to hide if there's trouble?"

My heartbeat is racing so fast that I'm waiting for it to explode.

Her face pales, and she drops the book in her hand.

"Yes," she says, peeking at a confused Amara.

"Where?"

"The basement." She casts a glance at the doorway as if we're already doomed.

Not that I blame her. It's on the opposite side of the house. If someone is outside, they'll see them going there.

I search the bedroom for the best hiding spot, but we have limited options. Most people don't have the luxury of hidden passageways in their homes like I'm used to. My bedroom alone has two secret exits in case enemies ever breach the mansion.

The closet and underneath the bed are the only choices.

And the most obvious places for an intruder to search.

Amara flings off her blanket and jumps into Eden's lap when a crash echoes through the house. She whimpers, tears falling down her cheeks, and Eden gently presses a finger to her lips.

"*Closet*," I mouth to Eden before helping them off the bed. "*Now*."

Eden holds Amara tight as I open the door and slide clothes down the rack to provide them with enough room. I push them inside and gulp as footsteps grow loud.

I dip my head into the closet. "Does Dante have a gun here?"

She attempts to pull me inside with them. "Come on! We can all fit."

We can, but it'll take too much room, and we won't be able to shut the door.

"The gun?" I say, ignoring her efforts.

"Get in here, Gigi," she snaps.

I shake my head. "The gun, Eden."

She blows out a defeated breath. "There's a safe in his desk drawer. The lock combo is one, two, four, five."

A gun means hope. My father started shooting lessons with me when I was eight and makes me take refresher classes every six months.

Amara whimpers, and I caress a hand over her teary face.

"It's okay, sweetheart," I tell her. "Please just be as quiet as you can for me, okay?"

She nods while holding back sniffles.

I return my attention to Eden. "Keep her ears covered."

I shove the clothes in front of them and shut the door. Before I leave the room, I kick the book under the bed, turn off the lamp, and half-ass make the bed. The room needs to look like no one has been here.

"Please be my father," I whisper as I peek around the corner.

I inhale a breath, softly close the door behind me, and scramble toward the office. Just as I'm about to reach my destination, someone grabs me from behind. A hairy, scarred arm wraps around my waist, jerking me backward.

"Oh no, you don't, cunt," he grunts in my ear.

This man definitely doesn't work for my father.

None would dare to ever speak or touch me like this.

My heart rattles in my chest. I kick my foot back against his ankle, but he stops me. When I try to elbow him, he curls his arm around my shoulders. Lowering my head, I bite into his hand, sinking my canines in as deep as I can.

"Fucking bitch." He pulls his arm away and shoves it against my throat, putting me in a headlock. "Help me out here, Savi!"

I gasp for air and desperately attempt to fend him off. The pressure on my windpipe eases when another man—Savi, I assume—joins us and helps him restrain me.

"Damn, Billy," Savi says to the man holding me. "Can't fight off a whore yourself?"

I keep resisting them while they drag me into the living room, where Sonny and a woman are waiting. I've only seen Sonny a few times, when he spoke with my father, but the sight of him makes me sick.

"Gigi Marchetti," he says in satisfaction. "It's so nice to officially meet you." He licks his lips as if I were the dinner he was ready to devour.

Or like he's about to gut me like a pig.

Sorry, asshole. No way am I becoming bacon today.

The woman, dressed in stilettos and a Chanel tweed blazer, definitely didn't get the memo to dress for the occasion. She steps forward as if someone summoned her.

"Where's my granddaughter?" she asks, glancing around.

When I refuse to answer, she walks toward the bedrooms.

"Amara, honey," she calls out, her voice filled with fake warmth. "Come out to Grandma. I'll protect you."

My mouth falls open in revulsion when it dawns on me this is most likely Antonio's mother and she's betrayed him. There's not a chance in hell I'm letting her near Amara.

"Yeah, little girl," Sonny taunts. "Come out."

Antonio's mom stops in her tracks and glares at him over her shoulder. "You promised not to hurt her, baby."

Sonny sighs in annoyance like she asked him to take out the trash. "I told you I wouldn't hurt the little brat, didn't I, Marsha?" He licks his chapped lips. "Now that we have the Marchetti bitch, we can use them both as bait."

My skin crawls at him so casually referring to Amara as bait. *Well, and me.*

"Amara isn't here," I say, gawking at them. "Antonio didn't want us in the same location. He said it was too risky."

"Where is she, then?" Marsha rests her hands on her hips.

I shrug. "Antonio wouldn't tell me. In case you're unaware, he's holding me against my will here."

"It sure doesn't look like you're trying to escape," Billy says, his voice dripping with sarcasm.

"I already called my father," I lie. "He's on his way here now. I had to wait until Antonio left. So you'd better leave before he gets here and kills you."

My lie can either help me or backfire. Sonny could kill me now or take me to dodge my father. Best-case scenario: he leaves without me, fearful he can't outrun my father.

Sonny narrows his beady eyes at me, staring with mistrust. "I don't believe you." He makes a show of turning in a circle, looking around. "Where's Dante and his whore wife?"

"I'm here alone. They left because they knew it was too risky and were scared my father would kill them. Because that's what he does … kills people who hurt me." I smirk at him.

"What's all the fuss with you anyway?" Billy asks. "Why are all the Lombardis so obsessed with you Marchettis?"

I stand tall, digging my bare toes into the rug. "You lay a hand on me, and my family will slaughter you and everyone you love."

"Oh, I'll do whatever I want with you," Sonny says gravely, inching closer to me while drawing a pistol from his jacket. "Imagine my reputation if I was responsible for the death of Monster Marchetti's daughter." He stops when we're toe-to-toe and slightly digs his loafer into my bare feet. "People will fear me, knowing I had the balls to make it happen."

He runs his hand along my cheek, and I recoil.

"But maybe, I'll play with you first."

"Take your grimy hand off me," I spit. "Or I'll kill you."

He chuckles. "I'd love to see you try. I could have so much fun, touching you, raping you."

I spit in his face.

A sharp pain shoots through my head when he backhands me. Billy keeps me restrained, and Sonny jams the muzzle of his pistol against my cheek. The gun's sharp edge cuts into my skin.

"You do that again, and I'll blow your fucking brains out and send them to Daddy in a water bottle." He backsteps away from me and stares at Billy. "Zip-tie the bitch. If she tries anything, bash her fucking head in."

I snarl at him, "When my father finds you, I'll tell him to do just that to you."

Sonny uppercuts me, and I double over in pain.

I need to keep his attention on me so he doesn't look for Amara.

"While you're at it, tape her smart-ass mouth shut," Sonny adds, shaking out his fist. "Marsha, make yourself useful and look for the girl. It's time to have some fun."

43

ANTONIO

Damien races down the road toward Dante's while I frantically call Eden. I'm sweating harder with every unanswered ring. Leo interrogates Sonny's man, but he's as clueless as the boy in the strip club. Sonny used them as protection—that's it. I attempt to log in to the home cameras, but they're offline—most likely Sonny's doing.

"He told us to keep you alive," the idiot in the backseat tells me. "The same for the Marchetti daughter."

My uncle wants me at his mercy.

I want him at mine.

May the best man win.

When we arrive at Dante's, everything appears normal. The only difference from when I left earlier is the blacked-out sedan in the driveway. I clench my fist, ready for whatever violence is coming.

Damien lowers his speed and parks down the street in case anyone is monitoring the area. Dante doesn't have too close of neighbors, but they're not distant enough not to hear outside gunfire.

Damien snatches the 9mm from the cupholder while I withdraw my Glock.

Is this a trap?

I step out of the SUV and look at Leo. "Stay in the car with him."

He salutes me and then elbows the guy in the face.

We charge toward the door while glancing in every direction, making sure Sonny doesn't have his men waiting for us.

The front door is unlocked, and Damien follows me inside. I head straight to the living room, where I hear voices.

"There's my favorite nephew," Sonny cheerfully greets like I'm a long-lost relative, not someone who wants to murder his ass. "I've been waiting for your arrival." His plump face brims with wicked eagerness.

I move deeper into the room to see him surrounded by Billy, Savi, and my fucking mother.

Disgust swirls in my stomach.

When my gaze cuts to the couch, I find Gigi tied up, tape over her mouth, and her face red. I charge toward her, and Billy snatches her up by her hair. He drags her away before I reach her, clamping his hand around her throat as he arrogantly smiles at me.

I move closer, but Savi steps between us and directs his pistol at me.

Damien points his gun at him.

I raise my Glock toward Billy, keeping my eyes on Gigi. "Let her go, Billy."

Gigi attempts to squirm free, but he only tightens his hold on her.

I've never felt so powerless as I do now, watching him hold her.

Vulnerable.

But I quickly contort back to fury.

My nostrils flare, and the burning rage inside me intensifies, turning into an all-consuming inferno when Billy presses a gun against her head.

Gigi's face doesn't have a trace of fear, but I know my

princess deep enough to understand it's there. Cristian taught her to hide it well.

I want to massacre Sonny and all his men.

And I fucking will.

Gigi's eyes are wide as they collide with mine, and I hope to God she can read the promise in them that I'll save her from this.

Keep my wife protected.

Even if it means my life.

A flutter of worthlessness slithers through me.

This is my fault.

I made too many wrong moves.

Now, it's time I fix them.

"Calm down, nephew," Sonny says, heaving out a sigh. "He won't kill her."

"Where's Amara?" my mother asks.

If I wasn't adamant on keeping my eyes on Gigi, I'd stare at her coldly.

The air in the room is tight with betrayal and violence.

"I can take her to safety," she continues.

If she's looking for Amara, that means no one has found her. I need to make sure it stays that way.

"Stay the fuck away from her," I sneer, my jaw ticking. "You're a disgrace to the Lombardi name. Both of you are."

Gigi has stopped fighting while she listens to our conversation.

Billy's gun is still on her, but he isn't applying the pressure he had moments ago.

"No, I'm a survivor," my mother corrects. "It's in your best interest to surrender to Sonny. He'll help you slaughter the Marchettis, and then you can lead the family together."

Even with her mouth covered, Gigi immediately starts talking shit at the mention of her family, but no one can make out her words. When she realizes this, she does a weird version of flipping my mother the bird while also tied up.

I shift my gaze to Sonny, staring at him in repulsion, and ignore the gun pointed at my face. "Let Gigi go. This is between you and me."

"Oh, nephew, did you forget *you and me* are at war with the Marchettis, the very person you're trying to protect right now?" Sonny asks. "You kidnapped Cristian's daughter, for God's sake, Antonio. Why do you care what I do with her?"

A chill runs through me.

Enemy or not, Gigi has tucked herself into my heart.

Consumed me.

Even if I tried to remove her from it, I'd die anyway.

Sonny smirks at my silence. "Oh, that's right. For those who don't know, Antonio is obsessed with the Marchetti cunt. He didn't only take her as revenge against our rival family; he took her because he wanted to fuck and keep her as a little pet. Isn't that right, nephew?"

All my self-restraint is gone.

Fucking perished.

I move my gun, pointing it at him now.

His smirk drops before he grabs my mother and plants his Glock against her skull—the same way he did in her kitchen the night I learned she was a traitor.

"What the hell, Sonny?" my mother yells, waving her body from side to side to break loose. "This wasn't part of the plan."

Sonny laughs at the fact that he played her again. "You never knew the real plan, bitch." His attention slips to me. "How about we play a game, nephew?"

"You know I'm not one to play games, Sonny," I grit out.

"Put your gun down, and I'll tell you the rules."

"Fuck off."

"As you can see, there's a gun on your mother's head and another on the woman you love," he explains like we're on a game show. "I'll shoot one in the head in the next two minutes and allow the other to live another day." He flicks his finger through the air to gesture back and forth between my mother and Gigi. "You choose who dies right now."

My gaze pings from my mother to Gigi.

Gigi remains stone-faced, but the longer I stare at her, the more I see right through it. She knows the rules of this life—family over everything—and is scared I'll break my promise to her.

But what my princess should remember is that she's also my wife.

Do you choose your wife or mother in a situation like this?

My mother whimpers.

"Pick one," Sonny shouts.

Savi moves so his gun still faces me.

Damien does the same, keeping his on Savi.

"If you or your little rottweiler pull your triggers, *both of them* will die," Sonny says. "Don't be stupid, nephew."

Fuck, I want to destroy him.

Annihilate his entire world.

Sonny, like most of us, doesn't just find murder enjoyable. We love the psychological manipulation that comes with it. It's like a drug, a high, a reminder that we carry no morals.

But unlike Sonny, I don't kill innocent people.

"The Marchetti cunt or your whore mother. Pick now, Antonio."

I can shoot Sonny.

But he's right. If I do, his men will do the same with my mother or Gigi.

Or both.

I need to make the right move.

Sonny might like to play games, but I'm better at them. Smarter.

Because I'm the motherfucking boss of the Lombardi family, and it's time I make that known to every bastard here.

I raise my pistol, so it's better pointed at his head.

I can already imagine the satisfaction I'll feel when I see his brain matter splatter all over the walls.

"Antonio," my mother cries out, all her confidence from earlier dissolved, "I'm your mother. That girl, she means nothing to you."

"She means everything to me," I bite out without taking my eyes off Sonny.

"And that's why you're too weak to lead," Sonny taunts. "Me, on the other hand? I'll kill anyone who gets in my way to be king. Wife, kid, anyone. Pick one, or I'll hold down the Marchetti bitch and let my men fuck her until you make a decision." He points toward Billy with his chin. "Let's see if she feels as good as she looks."

Gigi's body goes tight, and I follow Sonny's movements with my gun while he walks to her. She recoils when he rubs his fingers together before drifting them down her cheek while staring at me. My mother attempts to pull away from him, but he somehow manages to multitask, holding her still. He has too much confidence while lowering his hand toward Gigi's chest.

And I lose my fucking shit.

It takes me a second since I don't want to hit Gigi, and I pull the trigger.

Let the mayhem begin.

44

GIGI

Everything happens so fast.

Antonio squeezes the trigger, and I swear, I hear the whiz of the bullet as it comes toward us. Billy shoves Sonny aside, causing the bullet to only strike his arm.

Ugh.

I so wanted it to blow his head apart.

Jesus. I sound too much like the men around me.

Sonny howls in pain when he's shot again in the leg. Billy throws me aside, skillfully tosses Sonny over his shoulder, and runs to the back door.

"Get him!" I attempt to scream through the tape.

I also try to point, but the restraints are making it too difficult.

My ears ring as gunfire reverberates through the house.

But it's not only Antonio firing off his weapon. More men have joined, but I don't take my eyes off Antonio. He starts following Billy, but jolts backward. When he holds out his arm to run a hand over it, his palm is covered in blood.

I struggle to break free of the zip ties, freaking out more than him, desperate to help him. He wipes the blood on his pants as if it were spilled juice and flees in the path Billy disappeared.

My heart thuds when someone sneaks up and captures me from behind—*again*.

Jesus. I need a camera on the damn back of my head.

I attempt to fight them off, but they're stronger.

"Gigi, it's me, Luca," a male says as he carries me to the side, hidden from others, while shielding me with his body.

I gasp for deep breaths when he rips the tape off my mouth.

"Sonny!" I rub at the stickiness on my lips. "He went outside. You need to find him!"

"My job is to protect you." Luca shakes his head. "Your father and Benny will handle him."

I squeeze my eyes shut, and dizziness and nausea crash through me.

My father and Benny are here.

Now that they've found me, they'll want to kill Antonio.

My father won't sleep until he marks both men off his kill list.

When the gunfire stops, Marsha crawls out of her hiding space and straightens herself. I jump when a bullet coming out of nowhere hits her. She violently falls back against a bookshelf, knocking items off. Turning my head, I search for the shooter.

My father stands a few feet away with his pistol aimed in that direction. When blood pools from her forehead, he lowers his gun. Luca helps me to my feet and cuts off the ties on my wrist with a pocketknife.

When my father sees me, he rushes in my direction, yanking me into the tightest hug we've ever shared. His hug feels safe ... *like home*.

"Giana," he says into my hair, running his hands down it. "Are you okay?"

"I'm fine," I reply, squeezing him.

He steps backward, settling his hands on my arms, and I realize I'm shaking. Benny comes forward to hug me next.

Then Bruno.

My hug-a-thon stops when my father says, "Lombardi."

Antonio appears in the room with a busted lip, and blood completely covers his sleeve. Leo and Damien stand to his left.

Benny drags me behind him. Antonio lifts his arms as if waving a white flag.

"Amara?" Antonio asks me, out of breath and in what sounds like desperation.

I walk around Benny, resulting in a glare from him. "She's hiding in her closet with Eden."

He glances up at the ceiling, as if silently thanking God, before nodding toward me in gratitude. But even though he knows Amara is safe, no tension has left his face.

Understandable.

He now has to deal with my father.

"My father won't hurt her," I assure him, and my dad rolls his eyes in annoyance.

No one says a word as Antonio's gaze wanders to his dead mother.

"It was me," my father says, making sure to get the credit. "She wanted my daughter dead, so for that, she needed to die. If I were you, I'd want her dead, too, especially with how she betrayed you." A cold smile crosses his face when he points his gun at Antonio. "And now, it's your turn."

Leo and Damien, standing behind Antonio, immediately draw their guns.

So do my brother, Luca, and Bruno.

"Please," I whisper to everyone in my family, "don't do this here. His daughter is here."

"I don't kill children," my father says, furrowing his brow while keeping his eyes on Antonio. "I also try to prevent them from seeing their parents murdered. So I'll give you the courtesy of that, Lombardi. You instruct your men to back off, follow me, and I'll make sure your daughter goes somewhere safe."

"What?" I croak out, tugging on my father's blazer. "Dad, please."

Antonio clenches his jaw. "I'm not going anywhere with

you." He points toward the floor. "Kill me right here, right now, if that's your wish. But if you want to kill Sonny, then I think it's in our best interest to set aside our differences for a second and focus on him." He holds up a finger. "But I want to make it clear: my daughter is off-limits and will always be off-fucking-limits."

"But mine wasn't?" my father fires back. "I don't like double standards, Antonio."

"Dad—"

He raises his hand to stop me from speaking. "No one is asking for your input, Giana. I'm actually concerned for your fucking sanity that you're asking me to let him live. To teach you some sense, I should give you this gun and force you to shoot him. He fucking held you hostage."

"Please," I whisper, never feeling so helpless in my life.

"I'm not a forgiving man." My father stares at Antonio with disdain. "You should've learned that when I murdered your brother."

My mouth drops open. This is the first time I've heard him admit to killing Vinny. It was always obvious it was him, but he tends to stay quiet about his crimes. Not today, though. He wants Antonio to know it was him so he loses control, giving my father further reason to kill him.

But Antonio stays composed.

"He never hurt me," I say, my throat scratchy. "I promise."

"That's enough, Gigi," Benny barks.

"Don't talk to her like that," Antonio tells him icily.

"How fucking ironic." Benny sweeps his arm toward Antonio. "The man who abducted my sister thinks he can tell me how to speak to her."

Tears gather in my eyes, but I'm trying to remain calm.

"Come on, Gigi." Benny points toward the foyer. "Time to go."

I cross my arms. "I'm not leaving if you plan to kill him."

"Jesus Christ." Benny scrubs a hand over his face. "Just shoot him so we can be done with this shit. She'll get over it."

I plant myself between my father and Antonio. If he wants to shoot him, the bullet will go through me first. I'm facing my father, my back to Antonio, because I want my father to truly see me.

To see the pain he'll cause if he harms Antonio.

How it'll rip me apart.

I know if he wants to kill Antonio, he eventually will.

But not right now.

God, not right now.

He stares at me in distrust.

Then sensitivity.

Not for Antonio. *For me.*

It's killing him to hold back from hurting Antonio, but he's doing it for me.

The skin around his eyes bunch while he studies me like I'm a stranger he's trying to read. I've never tested him like this, and I don't know how he'll take my insubordination.

I wish I could see Antonio right now, but I won't turn my back on my father.

"Gigi," my father finally says, "I'm only offering you this one time. If you leave, right now, with no fucking back talk, I'll walk out of here without killing Antonio. But this offer only stands for two seconds before I have your brother blow his brains out behind your back. I hope, after today, you've learned no one will protect you like I do."

Nausea swirls in my stomach like a hurricane, and I'm sure I look as defeated as I feel, staring at him.

"Now, Gigi," he yells when I don't answer after two seconds.

I briefly glance at Antonio with tears in my eyes.

His gaze is tortured when it meets mine.

"Okay," I tell my father weakly, "I'll go."

45

ANTONIO

My pulse throbs against my neck as I watch Gigi leave with Cristian. As badly as I hate to admit it, right now, she is safer with him. Until Sonny is dead, no one is safe around me.

I failed her.

Failed Amara.

Failed fucking everyone.

I never wanted the don role. Countless times, I gloated, happy I had been born the second son. I should've considered that eventually, there was a chance I'd be the only alive one.

What happened today further proves why I never wanted that responsibility.

A dullness thuds in my chest.

It could've gone worse, though.

Gigi and Amara are safe.

Just as I think that, I'm reminded of my dead mother on the floor. A heaviness hits me, guilt weighing down my body.

So many lives lost.

For what?

Yet none of those lives are Sonny's. I need to fix that, pronto.

"*Riposa in pace,*" I whisper, kneeling at my mother's side to shut her eyes, careful not to get blood on my shoes.

When I glance up, I find Damien stepping toward me.

"I'll take care of her body," he says as I rise to my feet. He doesn't pay her one glance.

"Don't throw her over a cliff." I'm not joking.

His face fills with disappointment. "No disrespect, but she doesn't deserve a decent burial."

I scrub a hand over my face, smearing blood along with it—a reminder that I was shot.

My brain is so fucking scattered because who doesn't remember a bullet hitting them?

Bruno shot me while I was following Billy and Sonny, but that didn't stop me from chasing them. Unfortunately, the bastards got away.

Today wasn't the first time someone shot me, and I'm sure it'll happen again. The bullet was a simple graze, nothing serious. I just need to be bandaged up.

"Have Julian take her to Harold," I instruct Damien. "Get a blanket to cover her up and then get her out of here ASAP. I don't want Amara seeing her."

Harold is the city coroner, and since he owes the casino debt, he agrees to all favors asked of him.

Damien salutes me and drags his phone from his pocket.

I speed-walk toward Amara's bedroom, wiping my hand on my blazer while calling her name. Since the day she was born, I swore to shield her from the depravity of this world. But now, I've thrown her straight into it—when it's more dangerous than ever.

"In here," Eden calls out from the closet.

I open the door to find them squeezed in the corner, surrounded by a tipped-over basket and clothes. The hairs on the back of my neck stand at the sight of Amara. My sweet girl's face and eyes are puffy, and her cheeks are tearstained. She jumps out of Eden's hold and straight into my arms, clinging to me. I've never held her so tight in my life.

"It's okay, sweetheart," I say, rubbing her back with one hand

and cupping her head with the other. "You're safe. I promise, and I'm sorry. So, so sorry."

She sobs into my shoulder, her tears soaking my shirt alongside the blood. I frown, realizing I didn't change my clothes before coming to her. But she was my top priority. I needed to see my daughter safe and sound.

My gaze lowers to Eden while she crawls out from the closet.

"Thank you," I tell her.

She runs a hand over her hair and sighs loudly. "I need to call Dante."

When Amara finally releases herself from me, I tenderly wipe the tears off her cheeks.

I drop to one knee so we're face level and collect her hands in mine. "I need you to stay in here until I tell you to come out, all right?"

A flash of panic crosses her face, and she grips my hands tighter.

"It's okay, Amara," Eden says. "I'll stay in here with you, okay? And let's change into some clothes that don't have the red paint Daddy was using while he was gone."

I squeeze her hands and bring them to my lips. "I'll be right back. I promise."

"Okay," she whispers weakly around a fit of sniffles.

Dragging her back into my arms, I give her the longest hug of my life, wishing I never had to let her go. That feeling of failure in my stomach hardens.

I kiss the top of her head and help her to the bed, mouthing another, "*Thank you*," to Eden as I walk out and return to the living room.

Everyone turns their attention at the sound of the door suddenly slamming. All of us reach for our weapons. Dante storms around the corner, dressed in scrubs.

"What the fuck happened to my house?" he yells, looking from the bullet hole in his couch to the covered-up dead body on the floor. "I've been trying to call Eden for an hour, and the cameras were down. Where the fuck is my wife?"

I hold a finger to my mouth. "She's in Amara's bedroom with her."

"Are they hurt?"

"No, but I'm trying to hide this from her."

He scoffs. "Antonio, this is getting bad. You need to leave the country with Amara and never come back." A groan leaves him while he scrubs a hand over his face. "I came as quickly as I could, but it seems I was too late."

"Eh, I wouldn't consider that," Julian comments. "I mean, you could've been shot."

Dante shoots him a death glare. "All of you, out of my house *right fucking now!*"

"I'm sorry," I say, shame filling me.

I told him it wouldn't come to this, and I broke my word again.

It seems that's all I do anymore.

He inches closer, blinking at me. "You're dripping blood all over the floor."

I hold up my arm and inspect it. "Yeah, I'm sorry about that too."

"You need medical attention!"

"Good thing you're here, then."

Thirty minutes later and post Dante tending to my gunshot wound, I'm driving Amara, Eden, and Dante two hours away, ready to cash in a favor. Jerry, a six-foot-nine retired football player who moved off the grid, told me there's always an invite if I need it.

Well, *after* I persuaded the governor to override the city regulations that were stopping him from building on his property. He has a guest home, and that's where they're sleeping until the morning, when I can fly them out.

Leo is on a flight to Chicago so he can bring Clara back to New York. After that, I've chartered a private plane to take them to Italy to stay with family.

Dante waits until Amara is snoring in the backseat before asking questions. "What's your plan with this, Antonio? Let Sonny be boss, or whatever you call yourselves, and leave with Amara. You're too good for this life."

I pay him a glance while merging on the highway. "I'm definitely not too good for this life. Sonny will die for this."

Eden pokes her head between us to join the conversation. "I vote on killing Sonny."

Dante winces at his wife's nonchalant tone. "You aren't spending time with him anymore." He glowers at me. "You have her thinking she's some mob wife now."

"Sonny wants to kill you too," she tells him, chomping on gum. "You're also Vincent's son, another man in the way of him being boss. And I think I know how to get him."

I jerk back to briefly glance at her. "Tell me more."

46

GIGI

"Don't you dare cry over a Lombardi," Benny grits out. "They aren't worthy of your tears. They deserve to bleed out."

My father hasn't said a word since we left Dante's. He's waiting to speak with me privately.

I fight to control my emotions. Drawing back my shoulders, I examine my nails and ignore Benny. His hatred toward the Lombardis is justified. Even though Antonio didn't order the hit on him, he was still guilty by association. Then he had to complicate the situation by kidnapping me.

I scowl at Benny and swipe tears off my cheeks as if they personally offended me. "I was safe with him."

"Please don't start some Stockholm bullshit." Benny snatches my hand and glares at my wedding ring. "You can take this off now too."

I tear my hand away from him and tuck it under the right one. He'll have to cut my finger off if he wants it removed.

Silence takes over the SUV as we drive to the mansion. My father helps me out of the seat and walks alongside me to the front door. Benny trails us. The door swings open as soon as we reach it. Natalia greets me with a constricted hug so tight that I'm worried my spine might snap.

She clings to me, crying. Tears weigh down my lashes, and they're salty as they escape and drop down my cheeks. We pull apart, and she wipes her thumb along my cheek in a silent *everything will be okay.*

I grip her hand tight in mine, and she interlaces our fingers while leading me inside. She's never seen me broken like this. No one in my family has. I've always been well equipped with an attitude. This is my first time experiencing and showing true heartache.

And, ugh, I fucking hate it.

I'm ready to throw this stupid thing in my chest away.

"The office—now, Gigi," Benny demands, slamming the door shut behind us.

Natalia peers up at my father, silently asking him to award me patience.

"Benny, give her a minute," he says.

I nod a silent thank-you to him and then Natalia. "I'm going to shower … freshen up."

No one replies while I pass them, trudge up the stairs, and disappear into my bedroom. Cold air surrounds me when I step inside. Less than a week has passed since Antonio took me, but my room feels almost unfamiliar now.

I'm sore from Sonny's violence as I shower, and my thoughts drift to Antonio while water cascades down my body.

Antonio chose me over his mother.

I almost died.

He almost died.

He was shot.

My father showed him mercy.

Temporary, but hey, mercy is mercy at this point.

I cross my fingers, hoping he's okay after being shot. It's fucked up that I don't even know if the man I love is okay.

After taking the longest shower of my life, I clip back my wet hair, dress in my pajamas, and return downstairs. It's time I speak to my father without anyone else.

His office door is open, like a monster luring me in, and he's already waiting for me. As I stand in the doorway, he signals for me to join him. I shut the door behind me, and he directs his full attention on me as I sit.

"I want every piece of information from when you were with Antonio," he says sternly. "Everywhere he took you, what he did and said, every fucking detail. And I want it *now*."

"He didn't hurt me." That's the only detail I provide. "Dad, please don't kill him."

I jump when he slams his hand on the desk.

"Excuse me?" He harshly pushes two fingers against the side of his head. "Do you hear yourself? This man kidnapped and forced you to marry him." He stands, circles his desk, and sits on the edge. "His uncle threatened to rape and kill you. Whether you stupidly believed you were safe with Antonio, you weren't. So at this moment, you don't get the privilege of making requests. Anything you had with him is over." He inches closer, and something more than anger flashes across his features. *Pain.* "Do you not remember what they did to Natalia?"

I wince and am careful with my words. "Antonio would never hurt me like Vinny did her."

I so badly want to tell him Antonio loves me.

And I love him.

It'd only make the situation worse though.

"He forced you to marry him, goddammit," he roars before shooting me a questioning glance. "Did he do anything beyond that?"

Did he rape you?

That's what he wants to know.

I wince again. "He only married me to hurt you."

"No, Antonio married you because he desires you. As much as I want to believe it's because we're at war with him, it's not. He wants you as his wife, and it seems he'll go to great lengths to achieve that." His voice softens to land whatever blow is coming my way. "That's why I have to kill him, Gigi."

"Dad, please." My voice breaks at the end.

"If I don't kill him, Sonny will. He's at war with two powerful men. Two against one. He's outnumbered." He leans back and crosses his arms. "Until then, you won't leave the mansion."

"Oh, so now, I'm a prisoner here?"

"This is *your home*. You're never a prisoner in your home."

"What about your promise to Mom?" I wipe a tear off my face. "You swore to her you'd let me choose my husband. What if I choose Antonio?"

"I made your mother many promises." He starts counting them on his fingers. "I won't select your spouse. I'll allow you to attend the high school she attended. And I'll always keep you alive. The last one is the most important. I will break any others to ensure the third happens."

"What if you teamed up? Killed Sonny together?"

He shakes his head. "His father ordered a hit on your brother and shot Neomi, among other things. We'll never have an alliance with a Lombardi again. I'll have your uncle Santos draw up annulment papers."

I pull myself to my feet and turn to leave the room when he says, "Oh, and your little burner? I have it now, so don't waste your time looking for it."

I whip around to face him. "I'm a grown woman. You can't make these decisions for me."

His pulse throbs in his neck as he strokes his jaw. "Then right now, consider me your keeper, just like Antonio." He raises a brow. "You seemed to understand him abducting you. Give me that same respect."

I place a hand over my chest. "You're breaking my heart."

His voice turns quiet and even. "I'm sorry, Gigi. If that's what needs to happen to keep it beating, so be it."

If one thing can comfort some of the sadness inside me, it's finally meeting my baby brother.

At no point am I biased when I say Enzo Fredrick Marchetti is the cutest baby to ever exist. I can't wait to be the best big sister ever. He'd better get ready for all the kisses, gifts, and cuddles.

I play with his tiny hand in mine while cradling him. Even though I desperately wanted to meet him last night, I wasn't mentally there. Enzo needs calmness around him. I won't exactly consider myself *calm* now, but it's improved.

Well, correction: I'm doing a better job at faking it.

Natalia sits next to me, and we laugh when Enzo releases a tiny burp. Seeing her as a mother fills my heart with so much warmth. She's absolutely glowing. Just for an instant—and I hate myself for it—a twinge of jealousy hits me.

I'll never have this.

Gigi Marchetti—forever the aunt, the sister, the daughter.

Never the wife or mother.

Earlier, when my father brought Enzo down, my anger toward him briefly faded. He resembled a completely different man from last night.

There was a softness, a relaxation while he held Enzo.

Monster Marchetti showing tenderness.

I recognized the vulnerability while he stared down at him compassionately.

It's how he also looks at me and Natalia.

Like he'll die before allowing anyone to hurt us.

But then all my anger resurfaced when I remembered he wants to kill the man I love.

He gently passed Enzo into my arms, introducing us, and then kissed my forehead before wishing me good morning. He pressed a kiss to Natalia's lips, promised her he'd be home soon, and left.

"Hi, little man," I say to Enzo, running a finger over his

chubby face. "Sorry it took me so long to meet you. I was kinda, sorta taken hostage."

Natalia throws her head back and laughs.

I rock him in my arms.

"I can tell he already loves you, Gigi."

I snuggle him closely. "And I love him."

Enzo has a head full of thick black hair, the Marchetti nose, and a major case of gas. He's perfection, wrapped in a snug baby-blue blanket.

I hold him as Natalia fills me in on life while I was gone—her labor, how my father insists on changing diapers when he's home, and how she's already told Enzo story after story about me. My chin quivers as I remember how excited I was, driving to the hospital to meet him. If I hadn't told Bruno to stay home that day, everything would've been different.

Some people believe I have this super-glamorous lifestyle, but if only they knew the reality, where it relentlessly drains me until there's nothing left to offer.

As if she knows where my mind is going, Natalia rests her head on my shoulder and whispers, "Everything will be okay, I promise."

Thirty minutes later, Neomi and her sisters arrive at the mansion. We migrate from the living room to my mother's rose garden in the backyard. The space is my favorite part of our home. It's where I go whenever I need to clear my mind. I've traveled all over the world, but nowhere puts me at ease like here. The vibrant hues of pinks, reds, whites, and yellows create a beautiful landscape for us, and the smell of roses is like a scented candle you never want to burn out.

We make ourselves comfortable on the black patio furniture I chose two years ago when we remodeled the area. As Natalia breastfeeds Enzo, Bria uncorks a bottle of merlot and pours three glasses—one for her, Isabella, and me. Alcohol is exactly what the doctor ordered for my imprisoned self.

"And there's my future husband."

Isabella's voice breaks me out of my daze, and I glance up to find her waving at Luca, who's passing by us.

I grip my wineglass and lean toward her. "Wait, what did I miss? Is something going on with you and Luca?"

"I wish," Isabella says, blowing out a long breath before grabbing her bag and pulling out a tube of lipstick. "But a girl is manifesting over here."

"Why don't you try manifesting for someone else?" Neomi insists. "Someone more realistic."

"The *only* way Luca would ever marry is if my father forced him to," I say.

Which, one day, could happen.

"And unfortunately, we already have a contractual marriage with your family." I squeeze her wrist and offer her a gentle smile.

Isabella returns her lipstick to her Chanel bag. "All right, now that we've crushed my dreams, are we allowed to talk about the elephant in the garden?"

"The what in the what?" Bria asks, pulling her straight black hair into a ponytail.

"You married a Lombardi," Isabella tips her wineglass toward me. "The somewhat sane and hot one."

Chills rumble through my body.

My head spins, and it's not from the wine.

The smell of roses suddenly makes me feel nauseous.

"Oh my God, Isabella," Neomi yells, and I've never heard her voice so stern as she stares down her sister. "I told you not to go there."

"*And* since when do I listen?" she asks before shifting her body to face me. "Plus, considering you haven't removed that ring, I have a feeling you don't hate your husband."

Looking away from her, I down my wine and hold out the glass toward Bria for a refill. She pours it until it's nearly spilling over the rim.

The Cavallaro girls are my new favorites to drink away misery with.

"You love him, don't you?" Isabella whispers.

I gulp, debating whether to lie.

But right now, this is the closest thing to therapy I'll ever get.

And, dammit, I need some fucking therapy.

"I do," I croak out, my voice cracking.

"Aw," both Bria and Isabella say.

Natalia covers her face with her hand, clasping it tight, and the pain is clear on her face. As best friends, if one is hurting, we're both hurting.

Bria looks at Neomi. "Maybe you can talk to Benny?"

Neomi shakes her head. "In case all you traitors forgot, a Lombardi *shot me*. Hard pass on having one in the family." She holds out her hand. "No offense, Gigi."

"His father's man shot you. Not Antonio," I correct, feeling protective of my captor-slash-husband. "Antonio had nothing to do with it. In fact, he stopped his father from doing it sooner or harming more of us."

Everyone turns quiet.

Natalia carefully hands Enzo to Bria, then sits next to me, and pulls me into a hug. "I'll talk to your father, okay? We'll figure this out."

I swipe at my eyes, hating that I'm getting emotional in front of so many people.

I'm not a crier.

Marchettis don't cry in public.

Ew.

I stare down at my ring. "Will I be considered a widow when my father kills Antonio?"

My body turns cold at my morbid thoughts.

Amara won't have a father.

I won't have the love of my life.

The Lombardi family will either be a name of the past or a terror if Sonny takes over.

I wave my hand through the air. "Can we have a subject change, please?"

Enzo, already my little sidekick, understands that assignment. He spits up and then bursts into a fit of crying.

When the night is over, everyone is gone, and I'm no longer tipsy. Reality crashes through me. My sorrow transforms into anger.

Anger toward my father for making me feel like I'm on a leash.

At Benny for suddenly becoming an asshole brother.

At Antonio because why the fuck isn't my Romeo here, fighting for me?

For us?

He stalked me, tracked me down for nearly a year, and now, he's giving us up?

I toss and turn in bed so many times that I'm surprised I haven't worn a hole in my sheets.

"Ugh," I groan, ripping the comforter off my body and rolling out of bed.

Still in my pajamas, I slip on sneakers and stomp downstairs. Darkness consumes the mansion, and it's quiet. Like my father, nighttime is my favorite. There's no chaos, just us and our thoughts.

I check each side of the foyer before disarming the alarm, opening the front door, and slipping outside. I ignore the chilly drizzle of rain while beelining toward Benny's house on the property. It's dangerous to wander around here, especially at night, and even more so now. My father has snipers stationed along the tall perimeter wall.

When I reach his porch—which is covered, thank God—I

pound on the door. Inside, lights switch on, and I'm staring down a gun barrel when the door swings open.

"Jesus, Gigi," Benny says, lowering his gun. "What the fuck?"

I swat wet hair away from my eyes. "We need to talk."

"It's three in the damn morning."

"And?"

He motions for me to come inside. "If this is about Antonio—"

"It is, and for once in your life, can any of you listen to me?"

Benny snatches a throw blanket from the back of the couch and drapes it over my shoulders. Water from my hair drips on the travertine tile, but we ignore it.

I push my thumb toward my chest. "I'm a Marchetti just as much as you are. Sure, I might not be a violent, murderous psychopath—no offense."

He nonchalantly shrugs as if proud of my insult ... compliment ... whatever the hell he considers it. "None taken."

"But I should have some control in my life."

"You can have control in your life when you're smart about your decisions."

He reminds me so much of my father when he pulls back his broad shoulders and confidently strolls toward the bar in the corner of the room. Running his fingers along two bottles, he selects one. He pours an expensive bourbon into two crystal tumblers and passes me a glass.

I gulp back the liquid in a single swig—hardly savoring the smoothness of the liquor—and hold it out for a refill. Benny repours my glass, returns the bottle to the cart, and signals for me to sit on the plush leather couch.

"Antonio fucked with your head," he says, taking the chair across from me as I make myself comfortable. "Even though you believe it right now, you're not in love with him. He played you, Gigi."

I shake my head violently. "I was in love with Antonio before he kidnapped me."

He attempts to appear as comforting as he can. "He's a master manipulator."

"I wasn't manipulated, Benny."

"Look, right now, we have too much family shit going on to worry about your love life."

"I'd consider this *family shit.*"

"Natalia just had a baby. Neomi is pregnant. We're at war. That's family shit."

"Wait." I hold up my glass. "Neomi is pregs?"

He scrubs a hand over his mouth. "We're keeping it hush-hush for now, so don't tell anyone."

I cross my heart, and he tips his head forward in appreciation.

"I never ask you for anything," I tell him. "But please, do this one thing for me."

"We're going to kill him, Gigi. Find another favor."

"Antonio risked his life for me. His mother's life. It's only fair that I do the same."

He sighs, rests his glass on a coaster on the end table, and stands. "Be right back."

I sip on my drink, and when he returns, he's holding documents and a pen.

He drops the papers on the coffee table, clicks the pen open, and sets it on top. "Marriage annulment papers. Sign them." He taps his foot on the floor, making himself more annoying than I thought possible.

My face burns as I glare at the papers and cross my arms. "I'm not signing."

"Give it up, Gigi. He's on the kill list of many men. Why would you want to be his wife?"

I stare at him, waiting until our eye contact is strong. "Because I love him, Benny."

His dark gaze drifts from annoyance to understanding.

To pity.

Few people can drag compassion out of Benny, and right now, I'm one of them.

For a moment, he becomes a loving brother.

Not a cruel mobster.

I blink away tears.

He snatches his tumbler and drains his drink. "Love doesn't solve problems or end wars, Gigi. In fact, most of the time, it causes them."

As I tilt my head back, his words sink in deeper, and he settles himself on the edge of the couch, pulling me in for a hug.

"I'm sorry, but you'll move on from this," he tells me. "You of all people know nothing is promised in this life."

We separate when his phone rings, and I dab away tears as he fishes it from his pocket.

He listens to the person on the other line and clears his throat. "I'll be there in fifteen. Make sure he doesn't leave." Ending the call, he looks at me. "I need to get to Seven Seconds. Your soon-to-be ex-husband is there, asking for us."

47

ANTONIO

The past twenty-four hours have been hectic.

We chartered a private flight for Amara and Clara to Italy. They're out of the city and safe. I should've done that when this war started and sent Gigi there along with them.

Even though I begged them, Eden and Dante refused to leave with them, hell-bent on helping me kill Sonny.

And thank God they did.

Eden made some phone calls and learned Sonny frequents the brothel she used to work in and has a favorite escort, Candy. She and Eden are friends, and she connected me with Candy.

Candy agreed to set up a night with Sonny in exchange for a hundred grand and help leaving the brothel. Once Sonny dies, she'll be under our protection.

There's still the possibility Candy is setting me up.

That she's working with Sonny, but I trust Eden and her judgment.

I'm also done playing cat-and-mouse games with my uncle.

At this point, one of us needs to die ASAP.

It's dark when I park down the road from the brothel and cut my headlights. I have a good thirty minutes to prepare before Sonny is scheduled to arrive. I've never been so thrilled to kill someone. I'm already excited at just the thought of the life leaving his eyes.

God, what a great world it'll be without that stupid motherfucker living in it.

"Are you sure you want to go in alone?" Damien asks from the passenger seat.

I hand him the car keys. "It's time I end this."

"Antonio, it could be a setup."

"A risk I'm willing to take."

The Cabaret brothel is sketchier than Luna's.

Less protected.

Better for me to murder someone in.

The refurbished motel has a separate outside entrance into each mini suite. No bodyguards watch the coming and goings happening.

I tuck my gun inside my blazer, grab my bag, exit the car, and walk to the brothel. Keeping my head down, I take two stairs at a time to the second level, a rush of adrenaline spiraling through me with each step. Candy answers, dressed in lacy black lingerie. She grants me access inside, and I lock the door behind us.

The room is cramped and poorly lit. The couch in the sitting area looks worn and stained—like it's seen too many cum shots —and a separate doorway opens up to the bedroom. When I turn around, I find Candy leaning against the door with her arms crossed, pushing up her cleavage.

"Hi," she says, her face revealing a slight nervousness as she puckers her pink lips.

"Hey."

"Sonny texted me." She inches her phone from under her panties. "He'll be here in fifteen minutes."

I grin.

Come to me, rat.

"I expect you to honor your word," she says, her tone all business.

Sonny did well in selecting his whore. A beautiful brunette in her twenties. But I easily see through her beauty. This life has drained her.

"I always honor my word."

"What if we marry?" As if convincing me it's a good decision, she arches her back against the door and opens her legs, showing me a sample of her wet pussy. "I've heard men in your world marry women to protect them all the time."

Raising my hand, I show her my ring. "I'm a married man."

She cocks her head to the side. "Every married man needs a mistress, then."

I adjust my collar and smirk. "I guess I'm not your typical married man then. Not only do I lack any desire to touch anyone other than my wife, but she's also fucking insane."

"Oh, come on, all men say their wives are crazy."

"My wife is a Marchetti. It's practically a well-documented fact in history that they're batshit crazy."

My stomach curls, and a pain shoots through it.

Fuck, I miss my wife.

I love her.

I can't wait to get her back, and this time, there'll be no sneaking around.

No safe houses.

I want to be the perfect husband for Gigi and for us to have a real marriage. And I'll do whatever I have to in order to make that happen.

She smiles, all fake sultriness now gone. "Lucky woman."

"Nah, I'm a lucky man."

She clasps her hands together and steps away from the door. "So what's the plan?"

"Greet Sonny as normal, bring him to the bedroom, and I'll handle the rest."

"And you swear I'm safe? I might be a hooker, but I don't want to die for this."

"You're not just a hooker, Candy. If anyone else tells you that again, tell me, and I'll kill them."

Like I told her, I keep my word.

Unless Candy ever turns on me, I'll make sure she's well protected.

We start preparing for Sonny's arrival. Candy lights candles that smell fucking nauseating, and I enter the bedroom. It's as sleazy looking as the living room, and I'd allow someone to slit my throat before I lay naked on the bed. I drop my bag on the stained carpet and wait for my prey.

My blood already hums in anticipation of seeing him.

I crack my knuckles when Candy says, "Sonny, baby. I've missed you."

"Put on that outfit I like," he grunts to her, already sounding out of breath, most likely from climbing the stairs. "The strait-jacket number. I'm in the mood to get frisky."

"Yes, Daddy."

I hold back the urge to vomit all over the bed.

He smacks her ass and grunts again. When I hear footsteps approaching, I hide behind the door. As soon as he steps inside, I slam the door shut, trapping him in. He trips forward, losing his balance, as I flip on the light and flick the lock.

He's close to naked, wearing only holey, stained boxers. His hairy belly hangs over his waistline, and he stares at me, wide-eyed. When he attempts to charge forward and flee, I shove him. Unless there's a weapon up his asshole, he's completely defenseless.

"Candy!" he starts to yell, but I punch him in the face mid-scream.

He groans and stumbles backward. When his thighs connect with the bed, he topples over it, landing on his back. He nearly rolls into a ball while cupping a hand over his nose to catch the blood from my punch.

He's so busy fucking with his nose that he doesn't notice me gripping the syringe in my fist. I jam it into his neck and don't stop until it's empty.

"What the …" he cries out, swatting at his throat when I pull away.

"Pavulon," I say, referring to the drug that causes muscle paralysis.

He stares at me, panicked, fully aware that in just a few minutes, he won't be able to move.

I roll my eyes when he calls for help. And even though I relish his pleas, I don't want anyone else hearing and calling the cops. I collect the roll of duct tape from my pocket, and it squeals as I extend it. I rip off a piece with my teeth and slap it over his mouth.

He stays still, like he's already given up, and I tie him to the bed.

Staring down at him, I inhale a breath so deep that my lungs rattle. "How fucking pathetic you look."

He's a fraud.

Not a real boss.

A real boss would never fall into a trap like this.

I pause when there's a knock on the door, and Candy's voice drifts from the other side, asking if I need help.

"No," I reply. "You can go."

I won't risk unlocking it for anyone.

"Now, Sonny," I say, licking my lips, "I've put plenty of thought into how you should die. What would provide me the most satisfaction." I whistle. "Should I do it myself or hand you over to the Marchettis to gain favor with Cristian?"

It's not like he can speak, but I enjoy taunting motherfuckers.

He glares at me, and his nostrils flare as he takes deep breaths.

I move around the bed. "But do you know what my decision is?" I dramatically wait as if he'll actually answer.

He hisses underneath the tape, wincing in pain.

"I deserve to kill you more than anyone." Bending, I pat his cheek, rip his glasses from his face, and break them. "You fucked with my father. My daughter. My wife. Everything I love, you tried to destroy. Your last breath is for me to take." I click my tongue against the roof of my mouth. "And don't think I'll go easy on you."

I unzip my bag and ease the tub of crab-and-shrimp dip from it.

"Eden, you remember her? She visited the deli today and said they have the best seafood dip, so she bought me a tub. And you know what I thought? Oh, wouldn't my shellfish-allergic uncle *love this?*"

I hold his stare, giving a dramatic pause, and he shuts his eyes, the full despair hitting him. He attempts to jerk upright when I scoop out a heaping portion of the dip on a plastic spoon. I push him down, edge the tape off his mouth, and grip his chin to hold it open.

In one swift motion, I shove the bite into his mouth, pull the spoon out, and retape his lips. He closes his throat, his breaths coming out in long drawls.

I drop the tub on the nightstand and plug his nose. "Swallow, you stupid motherfucker."

He chokes, fighting it, so I edge the tape off his lips and insert my finger inside his mouth, shoving the dip farther. I collect the tub, sit on the edge, and repeat my actions until there's nothing left.

Then I wait.

My eyes are sinister, my face carnal as I casually watch his allergy kick in.

Hives pop up on his skin like little friends, and his eyes puff up.

His lips twitch beneath the tape.

His skin reddens until it's so deep that it's nearly the color of his blood.

Throwing my head back, I enjoy his choking.

But then I return my attention to him, not wanting to miss a moment of him dying.

I hear him attempt to beg for help, but he can't form words.

When Sonny is finally good and dead, I text Damien to come up.

"I've never been happier to see a deceased motherfucker," he says when he enters the room.

Neither of us bothers to shut Sonny's eyes. They remain lifeless, red, and pointed at the ceiling. Then comes the tedious task of sawing his body parts. I separate them into two bags.

One for me.

One for Cristian.

And who said I don't like sharing?

What a giving man I am.

After cleaning up, we leave the building, each of us with a bag slung over our shoulder.

"Next stop"—I glance back at Damien—"Seven Seconds."

"This time, I'm not letting you go in alone," Damien says, tightening the cap on his water as I park my car down the road from Seven Seconds. "I'm going in with you."

"No, we had this discussion." I turn off the ignition. "This is my mess and my responsibility to handle."

Before I killed Sonny, I had a contract drawn that stated if I died, Damien would assume control of the Lombardi family. He might not have the last name Lombardi, but he's more of one than anyone else born with it.

As I signed the contract earlier, something dawned on me.

I don't have a son to carry the Lombardi name.

Neither did Vinny.

Our name will die with me.

I step out of the car and feel the weight of the duffel bag on my shoulder. My steps feel heavy against the concrete as I walk to the club's back entrance. Earlier, Julian slipped the bouncer a hundred dollars and told him to deliver a message to Cristian that I'd be here.

I adjust the bag's straps as a light drizzle sprinkles on me. As much as I don't like giving my enemies a heads-up, I can't just casually walk into the club. I'd bet Sonny's limbs that every man on the Marchetti payroll knows they want me dead. If they kill me, I'm a ticket to a promotion.

The steel door swings open the second I reach it, and a tall man stands in front of me. He wipes his hand down his goatee, and his stare is frozen on me. He waits to wave me inside, similar to how Candy did earlier.

My guess is, the motherfucker wanted me to wait in the rain longer.

The door slams behind me, and he searches me for weapons. When he's done, he presses a gun to my back, shoving me forward, and guides me down a hallway. The space is quiet, not much noise, and every door is shut. When we pass one man, he curls his lips at me in disgust.

I'm brought into a room that reminds me of a car dealership waiting room. On one side, a TV plays some reality show, and along the wall is a table covered with baked goods and deli sandwiches and a stocked mini fridge.

He motions for me to sit on the black leather couch, but I cross my arms and remain standing. No fucking way am I turning my back on anyone here. He doesn't say a word before leaving the room.

They named Seven Seconds after Cristian's rumored death game. Supposedly, he grants his victims seven seconds to escape before killing them. If they succeed, he lets them live. From what I've heard, there's never been a winner.

Fuck, maybe that's the game I'm about to play tonight.

I check my watch every minute, and ten passes before the man returns.

"They're ready to see you," he says with a hint of cautiousness.

They're.

I'm not dealing with only one Marchetti.

We stop at the same door I entered when I visited Benny after my father's death and he pretty much told me to get fucked. It opens with a loud click, and as soon as I walk in, it shuts behind me.

The room is deathly quiet, the tension as thick as the list of reasons they want to kill me for. I stole something so precious, something they'd vowed to always protect, and now, they want me to suffer for it. It's time to live up to the Lombardi name and stay alive.

And also get my wife back.

Gigi is mine. She'll always be mine.

That won't change whether I'm breathing or a rotting body in the ground.

I look at Cristian first. He stands in front of me, leaning against the desk, already looking like a judge ready to deliver a death sentence. As bad as I want to continue searching the room for threats, I anchor my attention on him.

Always face the executioner first.

Don't take your fucking eyes off him.

His eyes assess mine as he waits for me to make the first move.

I toss the bag at his feet, and it lands with a loud thud. "A gift for you."

Our eye contact drops when he cuts his attention to Benny. I follow his lead to find Benny a few feet away, sipping on a drink. Unlike Cristian, whose face is heated with so much hatred that I'm shocked the room hasn't caught on fire, Benny's expression is unreadable.

No one says a word as Cristian kneels to unzip the bag. He opens it, getting a better look, and then plucks out gloves from his pockets. The room remains quiet as he withdraws Sonny's bagged decapitated head and drops it onto the duffel. It doesn't land inside the bag. Instead, it lingers on the outside, along the zipper. I squint, staring at the bag, and I'm almost positive his earlobe is stuck to the zipper.

"Glad to see he's finally dead," Cristian says, rising before removing his gloves and tossing them on Sonny's head. "Although I'd have preferred to do the killing myself." He kicks Sonny's head like it's a ball. "Now, what is this *gift* for, Lombardi? For me not to kill you and everyone you love? To release you from your father's sins?"

I stand tall. "To marry your daughter."

He scoffs. "My daughter isn't for sale."

Benny downs his drink when Cristian snaps his fingers, sets the glass down, and then swipes a stack of papers from the desk. He hands them to Cristian.

Cristian passes the papers to me. "As a matter of fact, I need you to sign these annulment papers. Your little forced marriage scheme won't work." He plucks a pen off the desk and extends it in my direction.

I flip straight to the last page. "Gigi hasn't signed."

"Not yet," Cristian replies.

"I'm not signing." I hold the papers out to him.

"I'll forge your signature then. Or cut off your fucking hand and use it to sign them."

I shake my head.

Cristian grabs the Glock from the desk, cocks it, and aims it at me. "Sign the fucking papers, Lombardi."

I won't be the one to end our marriage.

Gigi is the rhythm of my beating heart.

The peace to my chaos.

The beauty to my destruction.

She's why I'm here, willing to die. I could've easily fled the country with Amara and Clara. But now that she's my wife, I'll never let her go. Even if Cristian forged my signature, he'll be signing Gigi's happiness away. Just like I vowed on our wedding night, I'll kill any other man who thinks he can be her future.

I toss them onto the floor. "If Gigi signs them, I will." I glare at the men. "And I've never seen Gigi as *for sale*, but it seems you did when you were marrying her off to Elijah."

Cristian's finger plays with the trigger as he keeps the gun pointed at me. "It was Gigi's decision to marry Elijah."

This isn't the first time I've stared down the barrel of a gun, so I act like it's not even there.

"Gigi isn't a deal to me," I continue. "She never has been." I throw out my arms. "Shoot me if you want. I'm not signing those papers. If she wants an annulment, I'll give her one. But I want evidence she wants it first."

I just lied out of my damn teeth, but I'm not above manipulation.

If that problem arises, I'll stop it then too.

Benny steps forward, and Cristian lowers his gun.

"What makes you think you'll make it out of here alive to even see that evidence?" Cristian asks, working his jaw.

"If you kill me, Gigi will never forgive you." My gaze whips to Benny. "She won't forgive you either."

"My daughter isn't some guardian angel in your life," Cristian spits.

"No, she's my *wife*. The woman I love and who loves me back." I stare at him with the most certainty I've ever spoken between us. "I'll never make her choose between us because I know it'll kill her. That's why, for years, we kept our relationship secret—"

Cristian storms in my direction. "Excuse me?"

I don't fall back a step, and we're toe-to-toe, faces only inches away from each other. "But that sneaking around stops now."

Our breathing is hard, ragged, and I'm waiting for him to pull a Monster Marchetti move.

Stab me with a hidden knife.

Slit my throat.

At least punch me in the face.

And that's what he does.

I wince and jerk my head to the side at the impact.

Cristian shakes out his fist.

As if he's satisfied for now, he retreats a step.

I jerk my chin toward Sonny's head. "I'm not asking for an alliance or any favors. Sonny is dead. One of my wars is over. We can continue ours if you'd like. That gift is asking you to accept my relationship with Gigi. Let your daughter be happy."

Cristian cocks his head to the side, his eyes narrowing as he studies me. "You're right. Gigi will hate me if I kill you. That's why I'm letting you leave now because I have a brokenhearted daughter at home. But she won't remain married to you for long." His lips tilt into an evil smirk. "She'll be a widow soon anyway."

"Is this my seven seconds?" I raise a brow.

"This is me granting you one day on earth so I don't have to go home and lie to my daughter, but don't be confused, Lombardi. I'm sending you to hell soon."

48

GIGI

I've been waiting in the foyer for my father and Benny to return from the club for hours.

The door opens just as I'm about to *rest my eyes* for a moment. I spring to my feet and rush to meet them.

"Not now, Gigi," my father snaps while storming past me. "We'll discuss this in the morning."

"But—" I start, but he interrupts me.

"I said, we'll talk in the morning."

When he stops, there's a relief that he's changed his mind.

"Get some sleep," he says, proving me wrong. He kisses the top of my head and walks upstairs to his wing of the mansion.

I spin around to face Benny.

He holds up his hands, his palms facing me. "He's still alive, okay?"

I release a long, almost-painful breath of relief. "Sonny?"

"Dead."

I brush my hair back with my fingers. "How do you know?"

"Antonio brought us his head."

"Funny," I grumble.

"I'm not joking, Gigi."

"Oh."

The man I love beheaded a man.

That wasn't on this year's bingo card.

"Still want to remain married to him?"

I kick my foot out and scowl. "Should I go wake up Neomi and ask if she still wants to be married to *you*, a murderer who is gifted people's limbs? Because I'm sure you and Dad were over the moon seeing Sonny's raggedy old head."

He chuckles. "Jesus. Go to bed."

I start to turn away but stop mid-turn to whisper his name. "Yeah?"

"Will you tell me everything is going to be okay?"

"Everything is going to be okay, Gigi."

"Are you lying?"

"Go. To. Bed."

He leaves before I can ask him any more questions.

Sonny is dead.

We're safe … for the most part.

Well, I am.

My father still wants to kill Antonio.

I'm surprised he didn't do it tonight.

Instead of returning to bed, I slide against my father's office door until I'm flat on my ass and rest my back against it. Adjusting myself a few times, I struggle to get comfortable.

My dad said we'll talk in the morning.

Damn straight we will.

First freaking thing.

"Ugh," I groan before rising and stomping to the living room to snatch a pillow and blanket. Then I return to my spot in front of his door.

I need to know what happened.

But more importantly, I need to see Antonio.

Talk to him.

My husband fought for me so many times.

Found me in a different country.

Killed for me.

It's time I become a strong wife and do the same for him.

And even though it's uncomfortable as hell, I shut my eyes.

It doesn't take long to fall asleep.

"Gigi."

My father's sharp voice wakes me like a whip.

I open my eyes to find him standing above me. Sunlight shines through the windows, and I hear movement around the mansion.

"What the hell are you doing?"

Raising my head, I wipe the drool from my mouth. "You said we'd talk in the morning."

"Yes, but I didn't mean first thing in the morning."

He planned to sneak out of here and delay our little talk. But I'm not letting that happen.

"It's morning." I stretch my neck to work out the sore kink. Sleeping on a marble floor is not for the weak.

His face is rigid, and his eyes shift to Natalia behind him, cradling Enzo in her arms. She's still in her lace pajamas, her hair a wild mess, and Enzo coos.

She softly smiles at me before doing the same to him and resting her fingers on his shoulder. "Hear her out, Cristian."

He extends his hand and helps me to my feet. I gulp, a strong silence between us, while he gestures toward his office. I tremble as I grip the handle and open the door. He closely follows and shuts it behind us.

Instead of going behind his desk, as usual, he stands in front of it. He cocks a brow toward me while perching halfway on the edge. My knees feel rubbery as I drag my feet along his rug and sit down, facing him.

"He's not dead yet," he says simply, as if it's his first line of business.

As if that'll appease me and we can end this chat so he can leave.

"*Yet?*" Goose bumps run up my arms.

He drops his hands into his slacks pockets and extends his legs. "I have annulment papers for you to sign."

I frown at his lack of answering my question. "I already told Benny I'm not signing them."

He's calm as he says, "Giana—"

I'm not as I interrupt him, "Dad, please."

He just stares at me, unsure of what exactly I'm pleading for.

That, or he wants to appear clueless so he doesn't have to answer questions.

My father answers to no one.

"Benny said Sonny is dead." I draw my shoulders back. "The threat is gone. Can you please leave Antonio alone?"

"*Leave him alone?*" He removes his hands from his pockets to stand tall. All his calmness has dissipated into callousness. "Antonio took you as his prisoner, and you're defending him?"

I blink away tears. "Yes, because I love him."

He flinches like he smells something rotten. "Gigi, you're young."

"Oh, that's rich." I scoff as anger pours through me. "I'm the same age as your wife, so please, don't go there."

The cords stand out on his neck, and he scrubs a hand over his face in frustration. "This shit with Antonio ends *now*. A sane woman doesn't love a man who took her hostage to get back at her father."

"He also wanted to protect me from Sonny."

"Antonio is a master manipulator. He told you that to fuck with your head."

"He might be a master manipulator, *like you*, but that doesn't make it wrong to love him." Closing my mouth, I inhale a breath of courage. "Nor does it mean he doesn't love me. You got your happily ever after. Benny got his. Now, it's my turn." I wince at my voice breaking at the end.

"A happily ever after doesn't exist with him." Somehow, he manages to darken his eyes more. "He'll break your heart, or you'll end up dead."

I furiously shake my head. "You don't know that's true."

"Yes, I do."

"My heart's already breaking—"

"Sure, but you're still safe, alive, and breathing. That's all I care about. Your heart will get over this."

"Why don't you give me a chance to find that out myself?"

"Absolutely fucking not."

"Antonio would die for me."

"His manipulation wants you to believe that."

"No, he's shown me repeatedly. I'm in better hands with him than I would've been with Elijah. And unlike Elijah, or anyone else for that matter, Antonio loves me back. He doesn't see me as property, or a contract, or just some annoying wife to appease." I sniffle. "He appreciates me. Sees me. Cares about me. *Loves* me."

He turns quiet, which might be worse than him talking angrily.

"Antonio and I have history."

That sure ends his silence, and he bares his teeth. "Excuse me?"

"We weren't exactly strangers when I left with him at the hospital."

"You didn't *leave with him*," he snarls. "He held you at fucking gunpoint."

"We had somewhat of a secret relationship."

He stares at me, hard and malice, and I'm waiting for him to charge out of the room and hunt down Antonio just for that. But he stands there, focused solely on me, waiting for me to continue ratting my ass out.

But I'm done sneaking around.

Being seen but not heard.

"Please don't make me choose between you and the man I love." My lips tremble, and the tears finally break free. "Antonio is my husband, and I want you to accept that. If you make me choose, it'll be him." Tears fall down my cheeks so hard that I'm waiting for them to puddle at my feet.

"No." He unbuttons his blazer and breaks our eye contact when he strolls toward the bar cart to pour himself a drink. "Having an alliance with the Lombardis would make us look weak."

My dad is somewhat calm.

I've never seen him like this.

He's doing it for the sake of my feelings.

"You don't have to have an alliance with him." I swipe a tear from my cheek and am tempted to request he also pour me a glass.

He tightly grips the glass. "Me not murdering him means an alliance."

"You kill him, you kill my happiness. My heart." I fist my hand and rest it along my chest. "And I don't know if I'll ever forgive you for that."

What I'm asking for from my father is a lot.

It's everything he's ever stood for.

He grew up with the mentality of killing anyone who crossed you.

No guilty man goes unpunished.

He settles his untouched drink on the desk, steeples his hands together, and holds them against his reddening face.

One long breath leaves him.

Then another.

And another.

"I have to do this, Dad," I whisper.

He lowers his hands, and his scowl meets my teary face.

"Gigi," he says, running out of patience.

I hold out my hand. "All I'm asking for is your support and not to kill the man I love."

"Gigi!" He swipes his glass from the desk and hurls it across the room. His breathing is so ragged that his chest is nearly vibrating.

I don't wince.

I know my dad will never hurt me.

If anything, he'll find some poor schmuck—or Antonio—to take his frustration out on.

"It's time I act like a Marchetti and do what's best for me." I hold my chin high because even though I look like a heart-broken girl, I mean business. "I'm doing what's best for my happiness. I refuse to live a life without control. I almost died, so now, I'm choosing the life I want. The love I want."

He stares at me with a mixture of contemplation and warning.

Like I'm a man who's wronged him in the worst way possible.

In a way, I have. Even though, in the pit of my stomach, I know it's not true, this is considered turning my back on my family.

I rise to my feet, and my heart batters my rib cage as I hold out my hand. "Can I please have the burner you confiscated from my room?"

"You're not his real wife," he bites out. "You're his *forced* wife, like he bought you at the fucking store and decided you're his."

"I *am* his. And I'll take that to the grave." My attention darts to the portrait behind him, and I frown while staring at the sad girl. "The only reason we weren't married before he forced me is because you wouldn't allow it. But now, Sonny is dead, and it's time for me to return to my husband. Antonio made a mistake, but don't act like you haven't either. You used my best friend to get to Vinny, yet she forgave and loves you." Heartbreak laces my every word. "You of all people should know love makes you do insane things. Antonio is crazy—I'll give you that—but he loves me. The *real me*. And I love him, crazy and all. And I'll be damned if I let anyone—and I mean, anyone—take that from me."

His eyes remain fixed on me, and he steps over the shattered glass to open a desk drawer. He withdraws something, clenching his fist around it, and I hold my breath as he comes closer. His hand is cold as he takes mine, smooths out my palm, and gently drops the burner on top. The flip phone suddenly feels like the heaviest item I've ever held in my life.

My father isn't a man of many words, but his action just told me more than an entire book could. His silence remains unbroken as I clutch the phone and turn to leave the office. Standing in the doorway, he watches me as I walk upstairs to my bedroom.

I grab the first overnight bag I see, clumsily shove clothing and shoes inside, and my trembling hands fumble with the zipper. It takes me three attempts to close it.

All I can think about is Antonio.

I need to see him, hear his voice, and know he and Amara are safe.

Hell. A wife needs her damn husband.

My father, Natalia, and Benny are talking in the foyer when I return downstairs. Quietness falls over the room when they notice me. My father's eyes are red, but since he has a permanent scowl of angriness, it just appears that he's still, as always, pissed off at the world.

But today, I know it's more than that.

"What's going on?" Benny asks, his eyes dropping to my bag, but it doesn't take him even a second for what's happening to dawn on him. He shifts to face my father. "Are you kidding me?"

When my father doesn't reply, he steps to me.

I tense when he attempts to snatch my bag from me and jerk it away.

"Let her go," my father demands, and Benny freezes, taking a second before dropping the handle and retreating a step.

"Go where? *To him*?" Benny snaps in a way he's never spoken to him before. "She'll fucking die."

I glare at him and clench both hands around the strap of my bag. "No, I won't."

"He doesn't deserve you," Benny snarls.

"No one does." My father runs his hand along his mouth. "But we don't get to make that choice for her. I made a promise to your mother, and I will keep it." He sighs heavily, almost defeated, but his words are sharp. "But, Giana, you will not go unprotected. I'll always have eyes on you, and if you need anything, you call me. I'll be there by the first ring."

I'm sobbing, breaking down as I come to the reality of what's happening.

Natalia rushes forward and pulls me into a tight hug. "You call when you get there," she says, crying. "No, you call when you leave the driveway, then when you get there, then after lunch, then after dinner." When we pull apart, she holds me at arm's length, smiles, and brushes away a tear. "You are my best friend. No matter what, I am here. I have your best interest at heart, and right now, I know this is what you need to be happy."

I drop the bag to hug her better.

Tighter.

A silent promise that even though I'm leaving, I'm not turning my back on any of them.

Benny's eyebrows pull together, causing his forehead to crease, before he kisses my cheek and holds me tight. Unlike Natalia, he doesn't give me a speech. He and I have this unspoken sibling bond. For years, he's been one of my biggest protectors. I know that won't change.

My heart nearly breaks in two and falls at our feet when I reach my father.

This is what I've feared more than anything.

Leaving him. Disappointing him. Turning my back on our family.

No words can even express the sadness shattering through me. In order to be happy, I have to hurt those I love.

Like a filthy traitor.

And deep down, I'm terrified that's also how my father sees it.

We're Marchettis.

The notorious ride-or-die family, but now, I'm turning away from them. In my gut, I know I'm going in the right direction, but there's still that fear I'll drive right off a cliff.

My father clutches me tight, as if wanting to push common sense inside me.

A Marchetti doesn't show sadness.

We hide emotions until they become angry.

"You'll always be my little girl," he says, his voice so low that only I can hear.

"Then let that little girl decide her fate," I whisper.

He kisses the top of my head, keeping us there for another second, and then slowly releases me. I hold my hands together, clutching them against my mouth, and he becomes blurry through a world of tears.

No one stops me when I walk away.

I'm as alone as I've ever been when I enter the garage and toss my bag in my barely driven white BMW. I gulp for air through my sobs as I drive through the mansion's gates.

My home for so long.

My walls of protection, but also my shackles, stopping my freedom.

But I'm more than just a Marchetti now.

I'm also a Lombardi.

I pretend not to notice my father's car behind me.

It's just him.

No driver.

A rarity.

If my father didn't let me go like this, I'd think he was setting Antonio up. But there's no way he'd ever use me as bait.

When it starts to pour, I swerve to the side of the road, and my father does the same while still keeping his distance. I shift the car into park and sob while pounding my knuckle against the steering wheel.

Why does this life have to be so hard on us women?

Why do I feel like such a shitty person for choosing myself for once?

I unbuckle my seat belt and pull the burner from my bag. It's almost surreal as I call Antonio, praying he still has his and will answer.

Relief settles through me like a comfort blanket when he does. I unbuckle my seat belt and rest my forehead against the steering wheel as I ask my husband to come get me.

He doesn't ask questions.

Within one minute, he's already on the road.

As soon as he arrives, he jumps out of his car and runs to mine. I open the door, rain pelting my body, and press myself into his arms, shoving my face into his chest. My sobs intensify, shaking through my body louder than the rain.

Antonio strokes my hair, my back, and soothes me as I break down.

I'm not just Gigi Marchetti, the obedient Mafia princess.

I'm Gigi Marchetti-Lombardi.

It's time I chose myself.

It's time I gave my husband the same protection and commitment he's given me.

49

ANTONIO

Sonny is dead.

We've been killing his men left and right.

Amara is safe.

Gigi is with me.

All should be right in the world, but it's not yet.

Gigi provided the worst description of where she was, but I had to give her credit for trying. It surprised me she even had her driver's license since Bruno drove her everywhere.

The rain soaks us to the bone as I hold her. I'll stand here all day if it's what she needs. When she pulls away, our clothes cling to each other's body.

"My bag is in the passenger seat," she says, shivering.

I glide my hands down her arms to soothe her. "Let's get you in the car to warm up." I cranked up the heat and turned on the passenger seat heater on the drive here.

I help her into my car before returning to hers to retrieve her bag. There's no stopping me from offering a nod toward Cristian before ducking into my car, tossing Gigi's bag in the backseat, and driving off.

The only sound in the car is the windshield wipers squeak-ing. When I brake at a red light, I snatch a blazer from the backseat and drape it over Gigi's shaking body. Smiling softly, she adjusts it around herself before glancing out the window. She needs a moment to process everything before I bombard her with questions about how this came about.

She doesn't ask where we're going. The rain intensifies, almost becoming a monsoon. Her attention snaps away from the window when we approach my front gate. Vito sticks his head out from the guard booth and salutes me with two fingers, and the gate opens.

Gigi's gaze darts everywhere, taking in the exterior of my home.

No, our home.

Unless she doesn't like it.

If that's the case, I'll buy her something else. Whatever makes her happy.

She doesn't say a word when I pull into the garage, nor when I help her out of the car and lead her inside. The lights are on, a result of my rush to leave.

Damien and I were mid-convo when the burner rang in my desk. He cocked his head to the side, and my blood warmed when I answered the call. I told him we'd talk later.

Water drips from our bodies, and she stops to kick off her shoes. I do the same before shrugging off my blazer and tossing it to the side.

"Where's Amara?" she asks as I unbutton my shirt.

"Italy with my family."

She slips off her top and uses it to dry her hair. "Eden and Dante?"

"Safe."

Her lack of asking about Sonny confirms she knows the fucker is dead. When she drops her shirt to the floor, I take the three long strides that separate us. I stare at her in devotion while cradling her face in my palm.

Fuck, how I missed her.

Gigi shudders, her breathing hitching. Our gazes collide, as intense as the storm outside. She chews on her lower lip, causing mine to tingle.

I want to suck on it.

Taste it.

Bite it.

Just like every other inch of her body.

She blushes, lowering her head, and breaks our eye contact.

My wife, suddenly growing shy on me.

How cute.

I'm about to fuck that right out of her.

While still holding her face, I lift her head, and we lock eyes again. "You chose me."

"I chose my husband."

Husband.

When she calls me that, it's like a shot of whiskey, warming me from the inside out.

Sure, I've been called a husband before, but the only feeling that accompanied it was dread. With Gigi, it's like a high I'll do anything to keep getting a hit.

My thumb glides along her lips, tracing the perfect curve, and I whisper, "I love you, baby," before pressing my mouth to hers.

And that's all it takes for her to become my Gigi again.

She reaches around, gripping the back of my head, and draws me closer. Her touch sends shivers up my spine as I suck in a breath and desperately kiss her back.

Our kiss is manic, depriving me of air, but I don't give a fuck.

Suffocate me, princess.

I lift her, and she wraps her legs around me.

Gigi might've been my prisoner, but fuck, I've been hers for years.

I didn't touch or lust for another woman after having a taste of her.

Gripping her ass cheek, I carry her down the hallway,

ignoring the water trail. I nip at her lips while cupping her head and deepen our kiss with my tongue.

"God, I love you," she moans.

Hearing her say that puts me on top of the world.

My everything loves me.

I open the door with my foot and hit the wall switch. The room lights up, and I beeline to the bed, dropping her on it. It's not gentle, but it's not as rough as I usually am either.

I've never been a tender lover.

I fuck rough, raw, and dirty.

And that's how my princess likes it.

But tonight, I'm giving her more than that.

We're going to experience what it feels like to make love.

I back away a few steps to soak in the view of my wife in our home, in our bed.

And what a sight she is.

Her hair, wet and dripping on the sheets.

Her lips, already swollen from our kissing.

She unsnaps her bra, her perfect tits bouncing forward, and I lick my lips. Her nipples, already perky, are ready for me to suck on them. My cock jerks in my pants, begging to fill her pussy, when she lifts herself, resting her elbows on the bed. My sneaky little wife grins, teasingly rubbing her thighs before spreading them in invitation.

My plan to take it slow with her is gone.

Out the motherfucking window.

She rises to her knees and unbuckles my pants when I reach the bed. As soon as she pulls them down, she immediately lowers her head and starts sucking my hard cock. I groan, tilting my head back, and clutch her damp hair as she moves me in and out of her mouth.

"You suck my cock so good, wife," I praise while thrusting my hips forward.

I don't allow her to keep my cock in her mouth long before stopping her and lowering her on the bed. My patience dwindles as she shimmies out of her panties, so I tear them off her body.

I pin her down, straddling her, and sink my lips on her neck, groaning loudly. "I fucking love you so much." I suck her skin hard, as if I want to merge myself inside her.

She angles her head to the side, allowing me to run my tongue along her neck and bite down with my teeth.

"Yes, husband," she gasps, dragging her heels across the sheets. "Make love to me."

Drawing back, I firmly hold her face and attack her lips, pushing her face away while pulling it closer—our kiss moving from gentle to intense over and over again.

I kiss her hard and dirty to make sure this is real.

That Cristian hasn't murdered my ass and I'm in some dream.

When my cock grazes her thigh, she shifts her hips, ready for me to enter her.

"Not yet, princess. I'm taking my time with you tonight."

I devour every inch of her wet body.

My thumb traces her right nipple before I take it in my mouth.

Then I do the same with the left before flattening my tongue across both of them. It's never felt so real with Gigi as it does right now, and I want this to last forever. My hands are wild as I lower them between her legs and scissor my fingers between her clit.

She arches her back, so I do it again.

Then again, but this time, I add a flick of my tongue.

Repeat.

Repeat.

Making sure I taste every inch of her.

I shove my tongue inside her pussy. It's hardly been a few days, but I've missed her sweet taste on my tongue. She calms, slowing down as if she wants this to last forever.

I rest my chin between her legs to stare up at her. Her eyes are slammed shut, her lips pinched together as little whimpers escape.

"Ride my face," I tell her. "Slide your wet pussy against me and suffocate me."

"Goddddd," she groans before driving her hips forward and doing exactly what I asked. Her eyes are hungry and intense when they meet mine. She slides her body against the sheets and uses her heels to give herself more momentum to fuck my face. "More, more. Antonio, I need more."

"More of what, princess?"

"You inside me." She squeezes her thighs together and pleads. "Fuck me, Antonio. Fuck me, *husband*."

"Aht, aht," I say with a tsk. "In order for my wife to have my cock, she has to come on my face first."

And she fully accepts that challenge.

I eat her pussy while plunging three fingers inside her.

Four.

Just as I'm about to add a fifth, she falls apart beneath me.

Moaning my name. God's name. Jesus's.

I'm waiting for her to name a goddamn president.

Her entire body trembles.

"Challenge completed," she says, the words coming out between labored breaths.

I grip my cock, jerking myself a few times, and just as I press the tip against her entrance, she shuts her eyes.

"Don't you dare close your eyes," I demand. "Look at your husband as I enter your sweet pussy."

She peers at me with glossed-over eyes.

I smirk at her, running my hands along her thighs. "That's my good wife."

I slide inside her until I'm only inches from completely filling her. I halt, rotating my hips a few times, and then slam my entire cock inside. Her body jerks up the bed.

As I start to fuck my perfect wife, she pants, "I love you."

"I love you, and I will love you even when I'm in my grave," I sneer while pumping my hips. "You are mine, Gigi *Lombardi*."

I press her into the bed like I want her to stay there for the rest of my life. I've never been so deep inside anyone before. I need to feel every inch of her.

We start slow, but it grows more intense.

Our wet bodies slap into each other, and it's the best sound I've ever heard.

Gigi is in my bed.

No sneaking around.

No kidnapping.

Just us.

I turn her, rain kisses down her spine, and lift her ass in the air. I slap it once, twice, three times. She moans louder with each one.

I throw my head back and groan while entering her from behind. She arches her back, sticking her ass higher, and fucks me back so damn good.

Nothing feels better than this moment.

Being inside my wife is better than killing Sonny.

It's fucking heaven.

It's hell.

It's every fantasy I've ever had.

And I can never go back.

She's inside me.

A part of me.

And so deep that you can't cut her out if you tried.

She comes on my cock as hard as she did on my tongue.

The bed frame slams against the wall as I pound into her. She cries out when I circle my hand around her waist, dragging her closer, and I go wild until I groan deep and release inside her.

She tries to fall forward when we finish, but I don't allow it.

I hold her there, making sure she gets every drop of my cum.

I want to drown her pussy in it.

My body jerks a few times, and I slowly move inside her before finally pulling out. Her body gives out, and she collapses on her stomach.

I tug her into my side, holding her tight, in fear she'll get swept away from me at any second.

"All mine." I slide my hand between her legs and push any last traces of cum inside her. "My wife. My everything."

I grunt when she presses her hand against my stomach, applying pressure to flip herself over. She rests her chin on my chest and smiles.

"My husband." She traces her hand over my face. "I'm going to put you back together and create the perfect life for us."

I grab her hand on my face and press a tender kiss to the palm. "As long as I have you, I have the perfect life. I love you." I give her palm another peck before bending forward to meet her lips.

"Remember when you said you'd rip my heart out of my chest if I tried giving it to another man? You said you'd take it and never give it back."

I rub away the sweat on her forehead. "Yeah."

"I think at that moment, that's exactly what you did."

50

GIGI

Rays of light streaming through the blinds wake me. As I stretch out in the king bed with soft black sheets—the color will definitely need to be changed—I replay yesterday's whirlwind of events.

Every day, my life takes a different route.

Mafia princess stuck in her castle.

Italian princess.

Antonio's hostage.

Antonio's wife.

And a former tenant of the Marchetti Mansion and now living with Antonio.

I swear, it's like I'm just pulling *what is life today* cards from a hat and just going with it.

I never planned for the office visit with my father to go the way it did. My goal was to at least convince him not to kill Antonio. Never in a million years did I imagine he'd let me leave. In fact, I was prepared for him to lock me in my room, install bars on my windows, and murder Antonio to spite me for my disobedience.

Under some eyes, what I've done is disloyal.

Turning my back on family.

And no man survives doing that to a Marchetti.

Not even other Marchettis.

But my father will always spare my life.

When I pad to the bathroom, I find all the necessities waiting for me on the counter. I brush my teeth and my *I was fucked too many times* hair. My bag is on the white leather chaise in the closet.

A very impressive closet.

I run my fingers along the line of Antonio's blazers hanging on the top rod, the Italian fabric soft between my fingers, and unzip my bag to get dressed. I leave the bedroom and scan all my surroundings, taking in my new home.

When I walk in, Antonio is alone in the kitchen, drinking coffee and typing on his MacBook.

He smiles when he notices me. Stainless steel appliances, a massive island, and tall cabinets surround us.

"Good morning." I can't help but timidly smile at him.

What happens from here?

The war with Sonny is over, but he and my father have no peace treaty.

"Morning." His voice is husky as he steps to me and brushes his lips against mine. "How'd you sleep?"

"Not bad. Although waking up to an empty bed was a bit disappointing."

"Sorry." His brows furrow, and he places a tender kiss on my nose. "I don't sleep much."

"Like all the other men I know."

Sleep deprivation is basically a required skill on the Cosa Nostra résumé.

Thank God that isn't expected of me. I can barely do my eyeliner without a good eight hours of sleep, let alone murder people and commit felonies.

Antonio scrubs a hand over his face in an attempt to hide the stress, but it's so deep that there's no masking it. "I wish I could stay with you today, but I can't."

"It's okay," I say gently. "I understand."

I might've fallen for the wrong man, but I'm not completely naive. There was no expectation of a romantic honeymoon with him where we lay in bed, bingeing cheesy reality shows and eating too much sugar. Antonio still has a binder-sized list of problems on his plate.

"We can arrange for you to get more things from the mansion." He digs his hand into his pocket, drags out his wallet, and places a black Amex on the counter. "But anything else you want, you buy it."

I swallow, shaking my head. "I can't take your money."

His eyes grow heated. "You're my wife."

I'm about to tell him I have my own money—independent woman over here—but then it hits me. That's not *my* money. It's my father's. Not that he'd ever cut me off.

Antonio taps two thick fingers against the card. "And you use this, not your father's. Do you hear me?"

"Okay," I whisper.

For once, there's not that need to argue with him. He has too much going on. If my husband wants me to spend his money, then spending his money is what I'll do. Although he might regret this when he realizes I have a little shopping problem.

But it's for the economy.

That's what I told my father when he found out I'd bought a twenty-thousand dollar Hermès bag and then matched that amount for my favorite charity the same day.

"Back up your contacts when you get a chance," he says, his voice sounding more businesslike with each word. "I'll get you a new phone on my plan. As for cars, I can buy you a new one or hire a driver."

"But I have Bruno." I immediately shut my eyes, a pang of regret forming in my throat that I didn't tell him goodbye in person. I hadn't expected everything to happen so fast.

"Bruno works for your father," he points out. "Not me."

"Can *you* hire him then?"

His lips twitch into a slight smile. "Good luck convincing Bruno to work for a Lombardi, princess."

My shoulders slump. "Good point."

Bruno would probably never speak to me again if I suggested the idea.

Antonio shakes out his wrist and fidgets with his Rolex. "But for now, I'll have Damien escort you." He sucks down the rest of his coffee.

I don't know Damien well. We've never even carried on a conversation, but everyone knows he's Antonio's right-hand man.

I tap my nails along the counter. "I get to officially meet your bestie."

His handsome face pinches. "He's my most trusted man, Giana."

"Your *bestie*." I smile. "It's okay. I have one too."

Our moods aren't lining up as well as our genitals did last night. But I need to be understanding. Sure, a large weight was lifted off my shoulders, but Antonio's fight isn't over. He still has a family to run and stresses.

"I wish I had the time to fuck that little morning snark out of you," he says, settling his mug in the sink. "But I don't."

He sighs as if he just gave away his favorite childhood toy, and just as I think he's leaving, he shifts in my direction, wraps his arms around my waist, and lifts me onto the counter.

The stone is cold and rough against the skin my shorts don't cover, and goose bumps roll over my body. A slow smile builds on Antonio's face as he lowers his head, nuzzling his nose against mine, and steps between my legs. I hiss when he lowers his hand down my panties.

He freezes, his face softening as he pulls his head back. "Are you sore, baby?"

"A little." I curl my hand around his wrist to stop him from moving his hand from my panties. "But please, don't stop."

He stares at me, as if giving me a moment to change my mind.

I tilt my head and whisper, "I'm already soaked for you," in his ear.

He tilts his hand in my panties, finding the perfect angle, and fingers me. His hand work doesn't last long. It's awkward with my shorts on. So he rips them and my panties down my legs and spreads me out on the island as if I'm his breakfast.

He doesn't *fuck the snark* out of me.

He eats it out of me.

And when he's finished, he licks his lips and says, "Welcome to your new castle, princess."

"Ugh, I already miss you," Natalia tells me over our second FaceTime call of the day. "Tell Antonio we have to share custody. I mean, technically, I am your stepmother."

"Funny," I grumble, flipping her off. The motion causes my hand to bump the phone, and I have to save it from dropping off the counter and onto the floor. "And the only reason I'm not throwing something through the screen at you is because I'm convinced you played a large part in my father allowing me to leave."

Pre-Natalia Cristian Marchetti would have never.

"Yeah, he's kind of pissed at me for that." She rolls her eyes and applies moisturizer to her hands. "But if blaming me is what he needs to have some fucking emotion, then so be it. I'd rather him do that than behave like a concrete block who only eats, sleeps, and plays Monster Marchetti."

Before Natalia, that's pretty much what his life was.

"I guess all monsters are capable of emotion," she adds. "Which means he'll come around with you and Antonio. It's only been a day. Men need, like, five to seven business days to get their heads out of their asses."

"Come around enough to invite Antonio over for Christmas?"

"Only if you request your father make you a widow." She carries her phone with her from the bathroom to the bedroom. "Your father, he isn't used to this. It's a power struggle. When he wants to kill someone, he kills them. Unfortunately, the man he wants to kill just so happens to be your husband. And on top of that, he doesn't see it as a legit marriage. Antonio did kind of force you to marry him."

Just as I'm about to argue, she continues talking. "But, hey, thou shall not judge because your father pretty much forced me to marry him, too, and look at us. Married. A baby. Happily ever after over here." She smiles. "On a serious note, I'm here for you. I already informed him that Enzo and I will be visiting you. I need to come see your new house and bring you a house-warming gift. Oh, and maybe a wedding one too."

My father might've listened to Natalia as she told him that, but I'll believe it when I see it. Sometimes he likes to just entertain shit to appease people.

But I'd love for her to come over. After Antonio left this morning, I took a self-guided tour of my new home. As I walked down the hallways, I remembered Neomi hating Benny's home when they married. Not that I can blame her. His bachelor pad reminded me of a marshmallow.

Not even a toasted one that tastes delicious on a s'more.

No, a dull, dry marshmallow that makes you want to chug a glass of water after eating it.

So Benny built her a new house.

Luckily, I don't have to deal with that problem with Antonio. My new home already provides so much of what I love. It's spacious with a comforting warmth to it, and I love the evidence of family sprinkled throughout.

Framed photos of Amara and her drawings on the fridge.

Toys stuffed in a toy box in the corner of the living room.

My favorite part of the house is the patio nestled in a sea of colorful flowers. It reminds me of my mother's rose garden, and I know I'll spend a lot of time there.

So far, I've only come across one cold item in the house.

And it goes by the name of Damien.

He acted like he'd rather babysit a fire-breathing dragon than me.

"I'll be in my wing," he told me after Antonio left.

"The dude has a wing?" I asked myself under my breath.

That's how I learned Damien also has ears like a hawk because he turned around and said, "Yes, I do."

So far, I'm 1-0 in loving the roommate situation. But as soon as Amara returns home, I know that'll change. Maybe she'll lighten Damien up for me. The girl could drag sweetness out of Hannibal Lecter.

Perhaps I should send her to my father to smooth things over between our families.

Enzo crying snaps me out of my thoughts.

"Dinnertime," Natalia says while walking to Enzo's crib. "Call or text later, okay?"

I blow Enzo a kiss, say good night to Natalia, and collapse in bed after ending the call.

Today was draining, filled with talking to people nonstop.

Most via call or text.

I texted with Bruno, who said he had no problem being my bodyguard but confirmed he'd only accept payment via my father. So now, bodyguard-wise, I'm down to no one or Damien.

And Damien isn't looking too great.

I also talked with Aunt Helena, Aunt Celine, Benny—who asked if I'm ready to come home a good ten times— Neomi, and Luca.

Just as I'm about to plug my phone into the charger, it vibrates with a text from my father.

It's a single red-heart emoji.

Since when does he use emojis?

He once claimed emojis were banned from all group chats because he found them *fucking ridiculous* and said they were for people who were too lazy to type out an actual response. I'm also certain he's salty they changed the gun emoji to a squirt gun.

I reply with a heart-hands emoji.

If my father can warm up to lazy texting, maybe he can do the same with Antonio.

It's time for this princess to end the war.

I'm woken up by arguing from the other room.

"Fuck you, Damien," a feminine voice screams. "I wish I'd never met you, let alone allowed you to touch me."

"I'm warning you, Pippa."

"Or what?"

The anxiety that stirred in my stomach dissolves into curiosity now that I know the situation isn't with a murderous mob boss. From what I hear, it's a heartbroken, scorned woman ready to rip a man apart.

As she should.

Since I'm a nosy shit, I step out of bed, shove my feet in my slippers, and creep out of the bedroom toward the living room. My slippers squeak against the floor, so I kick them off, realizing they don't make great sidekicks for eavesdropping.

I peek around the corner to find Damien and a petite woman arguing. He has her pinned against the wall, his hands on each side of her face, as he dips his face to her level. His massive body blocks off most of my view of her.

She lifts up on her tiptoes to better square off with him, but is still nowhere near his height. Damien is tall and massive as hell. Men would fear for their lives, challenging him like this.

"And I want that GPS you planted—*without my permission*

—removed from my car right fucking now," she screams in his face.

Damien scoffs cruelly. "Not happening."

She groans, attempting to push at his chest, but he doesn't flinch. "Fine. I'll sell my car or gift it to my cousin for your wedding with her."

Oh shit.

Excitement bounces through me.

A live-action soap opera.

Damien just got a little more exciting.

I'll add *marrying his ex's cousin = entertaining drama* to my list of pros of him being my bodyguard.

I lean against the wall, making myself comfortable while rudely watching them.

Damien jerks his hand back and then slams it back against the wall.

This time, she's the one who doesn't flinch.

She's not scared of him, but she's sure as fuck pissed.

"Watch your mouth," he warns.

"Why? Does the truth hurt?"

Now, I do wince at the chill in her voice.

The girl has some balls—that's for sure.

Sure, I got snippy with Damien earlier, but that's because I am who I am.

But other people? They don't give men like Damien an attitude.

So whoever this woman is, I already like her.

Hell, sign her *up as my bodyguard.*

From what I'm gathering, Damien deserves every lashing she's giving him.

"Who should I bring as my date to your wedding?" she taunts. "You know what they say? Weddings are the best places to find one-night stands."

"Stop while you're ahead, Pippa," Damien bites out.

"Maybe he'll fuck me better than you."

Jesus. She's gunning straight for his soul.

The room turns quiet, like when you mute a TV and the subtitles aren't working, but the show still plays. I sneak nearer. They're staring each other down but not muttering a single word. If I wasn't playing creep, I'd ask them to continue their regularly programmed arguing.

"He had no choice, Pippa."

Everyone turns at Antonio's harsh voice.

My gorgeous husband strolls into the living room, looking like a freshly sculpted man of my dreams, and takes in the scene in front of him.

Damien steps back, and a flustered Pippa stares at Antonio, wide-eyed. Her face is red, and dried mascara lines her patchy cheeks. The heartbreak on her face forms a pit in my stomach, as if I were experiencing the pain with her.

"Everyone has choices, Antonio." Pippa inhales a shallow breath and releases it slowly in an attempt to calm herself because no way will she speak to Antonio like she was with Damien. "But men like you and him love to lead us women to believe otherwise." Her voice hardens, and I'm shocked she's sticking up for herself like this to him. "I didn't leave this life behind because I was stupid. I left it because of this very situation, because I'm *smart*."

"Maybe if you didn't, I'd be marrying you instead," Damien yells, inching up closer behind her.

She flicks her hand through the air. "Good thing I did then."

He shakes his head, and even though his voice is as loud as a speaker, he lowers his mouth to her ear. "You left because you're a fucking coward."

"That's enough," Antonio barks when he notices me out of the corner of his eye. "Pippa, go home."

Pippa pushes herself away from Damien while staring at Antonio suspiciously. "Fine, but I don't want one of your men—"

"It'll be them or me," Damien interrupts.

She flips him off without bothering to turn to look at him.

He snatches her wrist, gives it a twist, and turns her to face him. "Flip me off again, and I'll hold you against the wall and shove that finger inside your pussy until you stop with your fucking attitude."

I step back, placing my hand to my chest, and blush as if Antonio hasn't said ten times dirtier shit to me.

Pippa jerks from his hold and pushes him back. "I hate you."

Antonio walks toward them, and Pippa storms past him, headed for the door. Damien attempts to follow her, but Antonio stops him.

"Leo will trail her," he explains. "We need to talk in my office."

Damien scans the room and glares when he notices me. I perform a two-finger wave before turning on my heel and high-tailing it back to the bedroom. I jump into bed, this newfound drama like an upper to my nervous system.

Maybe Damien isn't as boring as I thought, and I can't wait to ask him one hundred questions about it tomorrow.

From what I witnessed, their relationship reminds me of the beginning stages of Antonio and me. Although there's more to them. They have history—I'm sure of it.

Instead of going back to sleep, I make myself comfortable and wait for my husband.

51

ANTONIO

Had any other man created that kind of scene in my home, there'd have been severe consequences. But I had known this would happen when Pippa learned of his engagement with Riona. It was a fuckup on my end, but desperation always comes with fuckups.

Or maybe it's fuckups that lead to desperation, which then leads to more fuckups.

Yeah, I think that's better.

Damien is making an enormous sacrifice for me.

I'm not one of those bosses who will force their men into marriages.

I'll suggest it.

But ultimately, it'll be their decision.

It's a grace I wish my father had given me.

"Do you want me to break off your engagement?" I ask when we enter my office, and Damien shuts the door behind us.

He massages his temples, grinding his knuckles into the skin as if he wants to create pain there. "We can't. Koglin isn't a man you want to break contracts with."

That's true, but right now, the Lombardis are looked at as

connivers anyway. I can keep that name up if it means Damien doesn't resent me for having a shitty marriage later.

"We're trying to get back on our feet." He says the words I should be saying. "If we break this contract, we'll have even more enemies."

I pop my neck while walking to the bar cart. Bottles clank against each other as I grab two tumblers and pour us double shots of whiskey. As soon as I hand Damien his, he drinks it in one gulp. I do the same and lick my front teeth as the liquid burns my mouth, giving me a sense of satisfaction. Instead of pouring us refills, I offer Damien a full bottle.

"You're off for the rest of the night," I say, pouring myself another glass. "Stay here. Leave. Do whatever you want." I want to forbid him from going to Pippa's, but I know that's exactly where he'll go. "But if you leave, wait to finish the bottle until you return."

He holds up the bottle in a silent thank-you and leaves the office.

I take one shot.

Then another.

"I don't get a fucking moment of peace," I say while leaving my office and venturing toward the bedroom.

My wife, always one to eavesdrop.

And it seems she's not discriminatory on her snooping.

Murder.

Torture.

Fucking relationship problems.

I'm sure she'd listen to someone's fucking medical records if she had the chance.

I'll need to fuck that nosiness out of her.

Or just tell her to pay more attention to my cock and less to the love lives of my men.

Gigi is in bed with her back resting against the headboard.

She looks so fuckable in our bed.

My cock twitches, loving her in it.

Her eyes follow me as I close the door and move through the room while undressing.

"What was that about?" she asks as I place my pistol in the nightstand drawer.

"Pippa is Damien's ex, and he's marrying her cousin via a contract we recently signed for a weapons deal."

Her shoulders slump. "Poor thing. No wonder she's pissed." As if something dawns on her, she squishes her brows together. "They didn't want you for marriage?"

I hold up my hand, showing off my ring the same way I did with Cernach. "Polygamy is illegal in New York, princess."

"Even if it wasn't, I'd shoot your dick off with that gun if you ever tried to have another wife."

"That's not a problem you'll ever have to worry about."

I sit on the chair and untie my shoes.

"I'm pretty sure Damien hates me more for eavesdropping."

"Damien doesn't hate you."

"Well, he sure doesn't like me."

"He has trust issues."

"And apparently, an *I'm marrying my ex's cousin* issue as well." She frowns. "I wish our marriage had been arranged forever ago."

"That I agree with. Unfortunately, I had to resort to forcing you to marry me via gunpoint."

"There's never been a sexier wedding." All of a sudden, her demeanor changes, and her face pales.

I kick my shoes aside and move to the bed, reaching across it to sweep a strand of loose hair from her face. "What's wrong?"

"I'll never have a real wedding," she says, all the playfulness she had now gone.

"We can have another one." I caress my thumb over her cheek.

Her face relaxes in my hold. "I don't want a wedding where my father doesn't walk me down the aisle."

Fucking Cristian Marchetti.

I need to get him to stop acting like such a pain in the ass.

"We'll figure something out, okay?" I tip my head forward to brush my lips over hers. "Maybe I'll send him another dead body or something that'll make him happy."

She laughs, sniffling away a tear. "That or he does like cash."

I chuckle, and this time, it's my change of demeanor. "No sleep paralysis lately?"

She shakes her head. "It seems I have a husband who kills everyone who tries to hurt me, including spirits in my imagination."

"And I'll keep slaying every single one."

"My murderous Prince Charming."

52

GIGI

ONE WEEK LATER

"Has anyone ever said you give them anxiety?" Damien asks. "And this is coming from a guy who's hardly ever anxious about anything."

I stop in my tracks to peer at him. "My anxieties have anxieties, so absolutely."

Since I've always enjoyed being a social butterfly, meeting people has never scared me.

Would I trust them? No.

But I love socializing.

Today is different though.

Antonio is picking up Amara and Clara from the airport. I haven't seen Amara since Dante's house, and I'm still upset at my father for not giving me the chance to tell her goodbye. We started forming a bond, and then I just … left.

I've yet to meet Clara—except for saying hi on FaceTime calls. She's always been kind, but I don't know her thoughts about me living with them. From what I've heard, she's very protective of her granddaughter.

Damien relaxes in the leather chair, checking his watch. "My first suggestion: stop fucking pacing. It's annoying."

"Why should I take advice from a man marrying his ex-girl-friend's cousin?" I swing my arm to gesture toward the area I was pacing. "Would you like the floor? It seems like pacing might be better suited for your problems."

He glares at me.

I smirk.

Fuck around and find out, Damien.

So far, the time we've spent together hasn't been a good one.

I'm so used to Bruno who—albeit a snitch at times—cracked a jokey joke sometimes.

All I've learned about Damien is, he's incredibly loyal to Antonio, has *keeping it in the family* problems, and doesn't fully trust me.

He's also attractive. Not as hot as my husband, but I can see why Pippa's cousin wants to marry him. He has a solidly built body, created from genetics and plenty of time in the gym, and brown hair trimmed on the sides yet longer on the top. His eyes are a shade of yellow-green I've never seen before.

Oh, and he also takes care of Ace the snake. I almost lost it when Antonio told me they had to transfer Ace to Damien's wing after Amara tried sneaking him into her bed so they could snuggle at night.

Damien flicks his hand through the air. "Go back to your anxiety before I shove you in my trunk and roll you out of it like old luggage at the Marchetti gates." He throws his head back. "Amara is much better company."

"What's your plan with the *marrying Pippa's cousin* problem?"

Yesterday, I asked him to invite Pippa over. That's probs why I'm so high on his shit list.

"What's *your* plan with *your father wanting to kill your husband* problem?"

"Maybe I'll ask him to take you instead."

"If that puts an end to your questions about my personal life, I'll take it."

We're interrupted by the alarm firing off, and Damien rises to his feet. It shuts off seconds later, and Amara bursts into the room. One of her sandals flicks off her feet when she runs straight into Damien's waiting arms.

"I've missed you, sweet girl," Damien says, his gloomy mood gone with her.

She hugs me next and jumps up and down. "Gigi! I'm super-duper happy you're here!"

"I'm super-duper happy to be here," I reply.

My head spins. I didn't eat all day since my stomach has been a ball of nerves. Amara and I had a good time at Dante's, but I want her to like me.

When we separate, I find Clara standing next to Antonio and walk toward them. Antonio lowers his head and brushes a kiss to my lips. I extend my hand toward Clara, but she shakes her head.

I stare at her, panicked.

That panic doesn't last long since she embraces me in a hug.

Her hug isn't as tight or warm as Amara's, but it sure beats a handshake.

"It's so nice to finally meet you, Gigi," she says, and her eyes are misty when she pulls back.

Leo rolls their luggage down the hallway, and Clara takes hers before walking to her wing of the house. As Antonio takes Amara's, she flops down on the couch. Damien snags the remote and turns on cartoons.

"Watch a movie with me, Gigi." Amara taps the cushion next to her.

I nod, and a flicker of a smile plays at Antonio's lips when I join her. She scoots closer when I sit down.

She doesn't last a good ten minutes before she dozes off, snoring louder than the TV. Damien leaves, and I watch the TV until Antonio comes in, asking if I want takeout for dinner. We order Chinese, eat in the kitchen, and then I shower while he gets Amara ready for bed.

As I walk past Amara's bedroom toward the kitchen, I pause when I hear her ask Antonio, "Are you in love with Gigi, Daddy?"

I flatten my back against the wall and press my hand against my chest, waiting for his response.

"Yes, sweetie. I'm in love with her."

"I'm in love with her."

Words I never thought I'd hear a man say.

I was the Mafia princess, trapped in the castle, destined to have a lonely future.

But then my brooding prince came.

He didn't care about the danger.

The risk of death.

He only cared about me.

It might be a dark version, but this girl is living her own fairy tale.

"Can you and Gigi have babies so I can have a baby brother or sister?" she asks, almost sounding pleading.

"I sure hope so," he replies.

My body feels lighter as I exhale a deep breath and walk away. The last thing I want is for Antonio to think I'm eaves-dropping on them.

I mean, technically, I was.

But for a good cause, obvi.

When I enter the kitchen for a drink, I find Clara pouring steaming water into a mug.

"Tea?" she asks, returning the teapot to the stove.

"Sure."

"Is lavender okay?"

"That'll help me sleep, so absolutely."

She retrieves a mug from the cabinet, lowers a tea bag into it, and adds water.

"How's your sister?"

"Better. I keep telling her to take her diabetes seriously, but she can't stay away from Reese's Cups."

"I mean, Reese's Cups are pretty good." I smile at her.

She chuckles. "That's why I confiscated all of hers—for *health reasons*, of course—and brought them home with me. I made sure to replace them with sugar-free ones though."

Clara moves around the kitchen in rubber-ducky pajamas and a messy French braid.

I take the tea from her when she's finished. "Thank you."

She leans back against the counter, observing me. "You know, you aren't as intimidating as I thought you'd be. When I heard Amara was with Cristian Marchetti's daughter, I had someone completely different in mind. I won't lie and say I wasn't nervous."

"Understandable." I take a sip of tea. "I hope you don't find me intimidating at all as we get to know each other."

People hear the Marchetti name and immediately think, *Monster Marchetti.*

Like my father speaks for every single one of us.

Reaching out, she takes my hand in hers. "I'm excited for us to become friends." She pauses as if something hit her. "No, I'm excited for us to become *family.*"

A tear slides down my cheek.

Family.

I'm not ashamed to admit that I'm on the tipsy train. I drag my hand along the wall to keep my balance as I walk to the bedroom. The door is closed, and I open it to find Antonio leaving the bathroom, wearing only a towel wrapped around his waist.

Goddamn. My husband is fine.

I stand there for a moment, admiring the view of the most perfect man I've ever laid eyes on.

"Baby, you want to shut that?" he asks, breaking me out of my eye-fucking-him trance.

I stumble while doing so and catch myself by collapsing on the chair.

Rather, the chair catches me.

I knew it was a good idea I rearranged in here yesterday.

"I wondered where you'd ventured off to," he says, shuffling his hand through his damp hair. "It seems you found the liquor cabinet?"

My gaze travels down his bare chest, to his six-pack, to his waist. I can't help but notice his cock already hardening beneath the towel.

"Clara had the bright idea to add tequila to our tea," I explain.

He chuckles. "Sounds like Clara. She enjoys a good spiked tea from time to time."

"I like her."

"I'm glad."

"Butttttt …" I attempt to make my voice sound sexy but am sure it comes across more as slurring, "I came up with a great plan."

"Oh, yeah?" He raises a brow. "What's that?"

"Let's make a baby."

"I think that's something you should decide when you're not plastered."

Oh, my husband.

A man who pretty much stalked me.

Shoved his cum into me numerous times.

Kidnapped me.

Forced me to marry him.

Now has morals.

I mean, you gotta love a man who supports women's rights though.

"Oh, I've thought about having your baby pre-plastered, mid-plastered, and now post-plastered. It's fair to say, I've made up my mind that we should have a baby."

Our eye contact is intense as I make a *come here* motion with two fingers.

I don't have to ask him twice. He takes the three short strides to me while untying his towel, and it drops to the floor at our feet. His cock, now throbbing and craving attention, is eye level with my face. My mouth is nearly salivating with the need of having him inside it. Leaning forward, I nuzzle my face between the base of his cock and his stomach before licking up his length.

He shudders, and his dick twitches. Opening my mouth, I hollow my cheeks and take him fully inside.

"Like that, princess," he grunts while controlling my pace as I suck him. "Suck my cock like the good wife you are. Suck it like you want me to fuck you until I give you a baby."

And that's exactly what I do.

I suck.

Lick.

Slurp.

Tease.

His fingers are in my hair, pulling.

He tightens and then eases his hold repeatedly.

And just when I feel his cock swell inside my mouth and I know he's close, he pulls it from my mouth.

"If you want to have my baby, then I'm saving all this cum for your pussy."

Grabbing my thighs, he jerks me to the edge of the chair and rips my pants off, along with my panties. Spreading my legs wide, he places himself between them before bobbing his head forward to spit on my pussy. Every nerve in my body lights up as he rubs the spit along my clit with the head of his cock.

I moan, my thighs trembling, and he covers my mouth with his hand to quiet me.

He takes his turn teasing me while he nudges my clit with his cock.

Then my slit.

He slips the head of his cock in a few inches before pulling out.

Every move he makes is slow and torturous.

But thankfully, he doesn't tease me as long as I did him.

With one quick thrust, he pushes his cock inside me. My legs are already sweaty as he holds me up, my ass hovering over the chair, and pounds in and out of me. He fucks me so hard that my teeth chatter, and drool is practically dripping from my mouth.

"Oh my God, oh my God," I chant underneath his hand.

And like he knows so much about me, he knows when I'm ready to come.

He reads my body so well.

He tightens his grip on my mouth, closing his hand around my cheeks as my orgasm shatters through. His fucking grows more intense.

My husband, so wild as he fucks me.

He says my name before throwing his head back and moaning. His hips jerk once, twice, three times as he comes. While we're still connected, he lowers us to the floor, holding me down as he continues pumping his hips. His cock never fully leaves me as he makes sure I don't lose any of his cum.

He drags his mouth to my ear and licks the lobe before answering, "I will fuck you this hard every day until there's a baby in you." His lips trail kisses down the sensitive skin of my neck.

I turn my head to brush my lips over his. "To us making *babies*."

He smiles against my mouth. "That's my princess."

53

ANTONIO

TWO WEEKS LATER

"Unfortunately, we've run out of Sonny's men to kill," Damien informs me over the phone.

I shift my car to park and pop my neck. "Very unfortunate."

The traitors who sided with Sonny—whether by choice or chance—are now burning in hell. It didn't take long to do that either. It's also a massive relief I don't have anyone challenging my control of the family.

Many of his soldiers begged us, expressing weak apologies and pleading loyalty to me, to spare their lives.

I made sure they suffered longer in their deaths.

Don't attempt to win me over with false allegiance.

It only pisses me off more.

I think Damien is more disappointed than I am that our Sonny murdering spree has ended. He's been on a rampage tour, as if running for the record of killing the most Cosa Nostra men in the city. Sonny's actions are the reason Damien signed the marriage contract, so he's unleashing his anger on anyone who helped with that.

I'll need to talk to him tonight.

Find him somewhere else to direct that energy.

He can focus more on the casino. Not only did I promote him as my underboss, but I've also given him part ownership of Lucky Kings.

My life will never be perfect, but it's getting damn close.

All the women I love are safe.

I go to bed with my wife every night, and she fucks my brains out while we try for a baby.

Happy wife, happy life, right?

But there's one thing holding back that complete happiness for her.

Her family.

"I'll meet you at the casino in an hour," I tell Damien. "I need to take care of something."

"Please say you're not where I think you are," he says. "It isn't a good idea."

"I'll get it worked out." I massage my forehead.

"I guess if the Marchettis kill you, it'll give me more people to kill."

We end the call, and I turn a corner, driving, until I arrive at the black iron gates with a large *M* engraved on each side.

"Oh, hell no," the beefy guard wearing too much cologne grunts when he approaches my car. "Not a fucking Lombardi."

"Tell Cristian I want to speak with him." I grind my teeth.

He chews on a toothpick. "You must want to die today."

"I'm married to his daughter." I jerk my head toward the radio clipped on his jacket. "Call him."

He narrows his eyes at me skeptically while backing away. The guy next to him lowers his gun, aiming it at my head, while the other speaks into the radio.

The man returns, whistling, and says, "Rest in peace, man," while waving me through the entrance.

I don't say a word while driving past him. Adrenaline pumps through me as I enter a place normally reserved for only those tightly associated with the Marchetti family. It's well known that

Cristian rarely welcomes visitors here. It's like sacred ground to him.

The mansion stands tall and imposing, but I'm too busy to take in the architecture as I exit my car and approach the front door. Just as I raise my fist to knock, it swings open, and Cristian comes into view. He waves me in with three fingers, as if summoning me to my death, and I clear my throat while taking the first step inside.

He doesn't say a word as he continues walking until we reach a doorway, and I follow him through it. I stand tall, not showing one sign of weakness, and straighten my cuff links as he shuts the door behind us.

"What can I help you with, Antonio?" he asks, straight-faced, while leaving a gap between us. He wants to make me uncomfortable, but is confused about who he's dealing with.

"I need you to put our problems aside for the sake of Gigi."

"Any issues she and I have are between us."

"I'm her husband."

"You forced her to marry you." He scoffs. "I hardly think you can refer to yourself as such." Walking around the desk, he opens a drawer, pulls out documents I recognize as the annulment papers he offered before, and slaps them on the table. "I'm giving you another chance to sign. Quit wasting my daughter's time."

"As I said before, no. Show me those again, and I'll carry them to your gate and shove them down your guard's throat until he fucking chokes to death."

"You didn't even give her a real wedding."

"That's why I'm here. I want to give her the wedding of her dreams, but she refuses to have one where you aren't walking her down the aisle."

"I'll never willingly give my daughter to you."

"I don't need your blessing. I need you to let your daughter get the marriage ceremony she deserves." My fingers itch to grab the annulment papers and rip those fuckers to shreds. They shouldn't even exist.

"If I attend your nuptials, it'd appear as if I was approving your marriage."

"You should give your approval."

"God, how I wish I could shoot you in the head."

At this point, with how stubborn he is, I'd like to do the same with him. But I need to remain calm and reasonable. This is for my wife.

"I've tried righting family's wrongs," I go on. "I love your daughter and will always protect her. If my actions haven't proven that, then I don't know what else can. Me being here, risking my life, so I can give her a wedding is proof enough. I'm not your enemy, Christian."

"Anyone with the last name Lombardi is an enemy."

"Did you fail to realize your daughter is now a Lombardi?"

He winces and clenches his fist. When I push my hand inside my blazer, he tenses before reaching toward his drawer again. Before he can grab a gun, I extract three photos.

A photo with Amara, Gigi, and me.

Another with us and Clara.

And then one with Amara and Gigi.

I drop them on the desk the same way he did the annulment papers. "This is what you're missing out on. I don't want anything from you. No money, weapons, deals. I have a broken wife who misses her family, and her heart doesn't deserve to suffer for the actions of bloodthirsty men."

He works his jaw and ignores the pictures. "I haven't killed you because I love my daughter."

"She needs more than that." I motion between us. "Father to father, I know you feel the pain of losing Gigi. Don't let too much time pass. The longer it does, the more damage it inflicts." I jerk my head toward the photos. "You can keep those."

I turn and leave his office.

While Monster Marchetti gives no fucks about hurting people, Gigi doesn't fall in that category. The same with Natalia.

It's the same situation with Benny. He isn't sparing my life out of kindness. He's afraid of losing his sister if he acts on his anger.

But the Marchetti men know she's safe with me. Deep down, if they thought I was a threat to her safety, they'd slaughter me, not caring if she hated them for it. There's no way in hell Cristian would've let her come to me if he didn't trust I'd put my life on the line for her.

And just like them, I won't kill them because I love her. I don't want a war with the Marchettis. I hope we can go back to how things were before Vinny's antics. When we coexisted in the same city with no animosity.

54

GIGI

I grab my phone and text Natalia.

> **Me:** Hurry up and get here!

She and Enzo are coming over today. I can't wait to introduce them to Amara and Clara. Natalia has been on my father's ass to visit me, but he continues to refuse.

He was persistent that I see them at the mansion.

To which I refused.

No way am I giving him the opportunity to hold me hostage there.

But surprisingly, yesterday, he agreed.

That, or Natalia threatened him with divorce.

> **Natalia:** Be there soon! Enzo needed a last-minute diaper change.

Five minutes later, the doorbell rings, and I dash down the hallway to answer.

The door swings open, but it's not Natalia.

I stand face-to-face with my father.

There's a moment of hesitation.

Confusion.

Either he killed Antonio's men at the gate or someone gave him access.

And from how everything is calm, I'm guessing the latter.

"Gigi," he says before stepping forward and squeezing me tight in his arms.

I press my face into his shoulder as the tears come within seconds.

Does this mean he's back in my life?

Or is this a onetime thing?

Either way, he's here now, and I've missed him so much.

He might have a heart of stone, but little do people know, there are a few hidden pockets where it beats with warmth. Even though I moved into a new home, that doesn't stop me from missing the comfort of the first.

And that's my father.

"Can I steal you for lunch?" he asks. "You can see Natalia when we're back."

I sniffle, drawing away to shout to Clara that I'll be back. She comes into view with concern etched on her face.

When she notices my father, her eyes widen, and I mouth, *It's okay.*

But from the way she's digging her phone from her pocket, I know she's calling Antonio as soon as we leave.

He walks me outside, where I find Bruno waiting by the Suburban. I run into his arms, hugging him, and that comfort of my first home intensifies. I'm a sobbing mess by the time I slide into the backseat, him doing the same behind me.

The SUV is quiet as Bruno drives to my favorite brunch café—a place I always invited my father, but he refused to go. In his defense, he's not an *out to brunch* man. Bruno stays in the Suburban, and I make my father wait until I clean the smeared mascara from my cheeks before we go in.

All eyes are on us as we follow the hostess to a table on the front patio.

"How have you been?" he asks after we sit.

Other than the occasional text to make sure I was still breathing, our communication has been nil.

"Good," I reply while spreading the cloth napkin across my lap. "Happy, but missing you guys like crazy."

"I'm sorry for that. I should've kept better contact, should've allowed Natalia to visit you."

Whoa.

My father never apologizes.

"It's okay. I know this whole situation is difficult."

"Difficult or not, you're still my daughter. I'm a father above being a boss."

The server interrupts our conversation to take our drink orders.

I order a sangria. He orders nothing.

He rests his arms on the table. "I know I've been unfair and overprotective, Gigi, but it was always in your best interest. You're my daughter, and if something happened to you, I'd never forgive myself. My life has always been comprised of death and violence, and I can't stop myself from always thinking the worst."

I nod in understanding.

"But it seems protecting you has also resulted in hurting you," he adds.

"I know you had good intentions." *At least with me.*

He extracts a card from his pocket and slides it across the table to me. I pick it up and read it.

Rita Eiken

New York Wedding Planner

I gulp. "What's this?"

"She's the best wedding planner in the city. I've hired her to give you the perfect ceremony."

I trace my finger along the embossed letters of her name. "My wedding with Antonio, right?" The question slowly trickles out of my mouth.

I'm not easily fooled. Apology or not, my father is still Monster Marchetti. Given his manipulative nature, it wouldn't surprise me if he arranged another marriage for me. He's always resourceful in getting what he wants.

"Yes … with Antonio." His face pinches together as if he tasted something rancid.

"And …" I'm afraid to ask because the answer terrifies me. "You'll be there?"

That sour expression relaxes. "I'd never miss anything so special."

Luca's Suburban is in the driveway when we return from lunch.

My head feels dizzy.

What is life right now?

It's like I'm in some new world where the Marchettis don't want to kill the Lombardis.

Luca steps out of the SUV and gives me a tight hug. "I've missed you, troublemaker."

I smile while pressed to his chest. "Did you come here to hang out with Antonio?"

"Fuck no." He waits until I pull away from him to glance at my father. "Natalia and Enzo are inside."

A sudden adrenaline rush zips through me like I chugged fifteen energy drinks.

"Luca is driving me. Bruno will stay with Natalia and Enzo until they're ready to go," my father tells me before brushing a kiss along my forehead. "The wedding planner will contact you tomorrow."

Bruno follows me into the house, where we find them in the living room with Amara and Clara.

"Gigi!" Amara says, grinning from ear to ear when she notices me.

We've developed a close relationship these past few weeks. Every morning, we have breakfast together, and I usually spend the rest of the day with her either watching movies or doing crafts, and I help Clara with her homeschooling.

Natalia gives me a side-hug while holding Enzo, and when I extend my arms out, she passes him to me.

"Oh man, you've gained some weight, you little chunky boy," I say, cradling him while moving to the couch and sitting. "He looks so much like my father."

Natalia works out a tangle in her thick hair, compliments of Enzo's curious fingers. "A spitting image of him and Benny."

"I've missed you." I tenderly play with his hand and glance at Natalia when she makes herself comfortable next to me. "Did you know about my father's plan today?"

"At first, no. But he stopped me before we left and told me everything." Her voice softens. "He's coming around, Gigi."

I draw a deep breath.

It's like I woke up today and I'm getting all I've ever wanted. Salty tears hit my lip, and I sniffle.

"Do you know what changed his mind?" I smile when Enzo coos.

"Antonio visited him at the mansion last week."

"He did what?"

"I have no idea what was said, but whatever it was, it changed Cristian's mind."

My smile grows.

"I love seeing you in love." Natalia's voice is consumed with emotion. "You deserve it so much."

She's also come around with Antonio.

Neomi has, little by little. It's just taking her a while to process since she was shot.

I rest my hand on her shoulder. Bruno stands against the wall, rigid like a board, as if on full duty. Clara occupies Damien's usual chair, casting suspicious glances at Bruno.

"Can I show baby Enzo all my friends?" Amara comes into view with stuffed animals shoved in her arms.

She drops them to the floor, and we spend the next hour listening to her introduce all her stuffed animals to Enzo. Clara eventually warms up to our new guests and volunteers to make dinner.

When Antonio returns home, he doesn't look surprised at the scene. He has cameras in the house, so I'm sure he's kept constant surveillance on us. Not to mention, Clara has kept her phone in her hands, randomly texting—my guess, providing him updates.

Antonio offers Bruno a head nod and says hi to Natalia.

"That's Enzo!" Amara announces, pointing at him. "Is it my turn to hold him yet?"

"Yes, but be careful," Natalia says as Antonio helps Amara off the floor and guides her to sit on the couch.

"Lord knows Cristian will definitely kill me if there's even a scratch on that kid's head when he leaves here," Antonio mutters.

After we get Amara and Enzo situated, Antonio smacks a peck on my lips and tells me he'll be in his office if I need him.

"I can't wait until I get a baby brother," Amara says.

"Same," Antonio calls out over his shoulder while leaving the room.

"Are you happy, baby?" Antonio asks while joining me in bed.

I yawn loudly, exhausted from the day. "You went to my father."

"I went to your father." He tenderly pulls me into his arms, fitting me there perfectly.

I raise my head to meet his gaze. "Thank you, Antonio."

He smooths his hand along my jaw and whispers, "Baby, you never have to thank me for anything."

I softly brush my lips against his, and he lowers me to my back.

Then he proves further how much he loves to make me happy with his mouth between my legs.

GIGI

TWO MONTHS LATER

The sun is overcast, and fresh air breezes by me as I stroll toward the courtyard.

I've enjoyed wedding planning with Rita, and I also love that Antonio has helped with decisions as well. Not many husbands do that. Since we were on a short timeframe, I did have to settle for some options.

One decision that wasn't negotiable?

Having our wedding at the courtyard where I'd snuck away with Antonio at the masquerade ball.

I love that it's different this time. We're not wearing masks or hiding from the crowd.

We get to show off our love and have a real wedding.

Inhaling deep breaths, I concentrate on my feet. I'm no stranger to wearing heels, but no bride wants to fall and face-plant on her big day.

Although I'm pretty sure the award for Most Traumatic Wedding will forever go to Neomi.

Natalia and Aunt Celine trail me, carrying my gown train. It took two Italy visits to create my dream dress. *The one* is elegant with lace, off-the-shoulder swag sleeves, and a laced corset back.

My heart swells with happiness when I spot my father waiting for me. Benny stands next to him. The initial plan was for Damien to walk Natalia down the aisle, but my father put a stop to that real quick.

"Over my dead body will the Lombardi underboss touch my wife," was what he said before completely shutting down the idea.

So Benny is now on maid-of-honor walking duty.

The orchestra rendition of "Isn't She Lovely" plays across the courtyard. I peer past Benny to find Amara gracefully parading down the aisle as the flower girl in her bright pink dress with butterflies. She's been practicing her walk for weeks.

"You look amazing," Benny tells me as Natalia loops her arm through his.

"Thank you," I say.

Natalia smiles at me and blows my father a kiss, and Benny leads her toward the altar. Aunt Celine remains behind me to continue the role of train duty.

My father, dressed in a black tux, turns to face me. "You make a beautiful bride, Giana."

I blush and say, "Thank you," for what seems like the twentieth time today.

But this time, the compliment hits deeper. He was so against Antonio and me marrying, but he let that go for me.

He changed his every rule for the sake of my happiness, and I'll always appreciate that.

"You deserve this love," he adds in the softest tone I've ever heard him speak. He captures my hand in his while we look at the sky. "Your mother is here with us today. I can feel it."

I blink away tears.

Why can't he make me emotional after *the wedding so I don't ruin my makeup?*

He places a tender peck on my palm before linking our arms, and I choose not to mention the slight wetness in his eyes.

And people claim Monster Marchetti bears no humane feelings.

The "Bridal Chorus" begins, and I've never felt closer to my father as he escorts me down the aisle, taking his time. Family and friends—both Marchetti and Lombardi—surround us. Black and red roses are scattered along the pathway.

Rita worked a miracle, creating a seamless flow through the courtyard despite its twists and turns. My father's unlimited budget also helped.

When I raise my gaze, I lock eyes with Antonio, stationed at the altar.

I've never felt so loved.

The two most important men in my life are putting their differences aside for my happiness.

There's no better way to prove you love someone than that.

My gorgeous husband's eyes overfill with emotion as we grow closer. He's dressed in a vintage Italian tux I found in Italy during one of my dress-shopping trips. Many women in our world doubt their husband's love, but that'll never be a problem in my marriage.

Antonio has sacrificed for me.

He stole my heart when I was reluctant to give it to him.

Showed me that, yes, a Mafia princess can find love.

My father pauses and turns to kiss my cheek when we reach Antonio. Even though I made it *very* clear he would shake Antonio's hand when this moment came, my father doesn't offer his hand. He groans when I softly nudge him. Pretty sure I'm the only person ever allowed to pull something so bold with him. No one reprimands the bride on her day.

My father extends his hand, and Antonio takes it, respect etched on his face. All eyes are on them. There's been so much talk about my father approving our marriage, and he just gave it to us.

Two rival families brought together by a love story.

Only a woman could conquer such a thing.

My father takes his chair in the front row beside Benny. My brother has come around just as much as him. He won't be making BFF bracelets with Antonio anytime soon, but they're coexisting within the same space.

Damien is standing behind Antonio while Natalia is practically squealing inches from me. Aunt Celine releases my train, and I stand before Antonio.

My love.

My everything.

He steps forward to raise my veil, cups my face, and caresses my cheek. As if all eyes aren't on us, he lowers his mouth to my ear.

"My breathtaking princess," he whispers, his voice sending shivers down my spine. "I have never seen a more gorgeous sight." He groans. "I can't wait to take this dress off you later, baby."

I squeeze my legs together, my clit throbbing.

He reaches for my hands, clasping them tight, and presses them against his chest.

"I love you," I say, only loud enough for him to hear.

"You are my everything."

I gasp, startled, when the priest clears his throat.

Antonio shifts backward a few inches as I finally cut my gaze to the priest.

He's not the one who married us the first time.

Pretty sure that one retired after his dealings with us.

"Let's begin," the priest says in a rumbling voice.

Antonio lowers our hands, a bond that'll never break, while reciting his vows.

My breath catches in my throat as the glossiness in his eyes grows more noticeable with each word.

My villain doesn't hide his emotions—even if we're surrounded by murderous men.

A tear slips down his cheek, and he uses his arm to wipe it away.

That doesn't stop another from escaping.

When it's my turn to say my vows, my eyes are wet. He smirks and mouths the words along with me.

As I slide the ring on his finger, I pause to admire my initials tattooed on his ring finger. A month ago, I pouted over him having to remove his ring for some of his, er … *dirtier* jobs. The next day, he came home with the new ink. So no matter what, I'm always marking him.

When we kiss, it's like I've forgotten every nightmare I've ever had.

The sadness, the chaos, and the rough history it took us to get here.

The loneliness I lived in the mansion, the times where I felt I'd forever be alone, all of it brought me to this moment.

All of it was worth it.

Because now, I have my love story with the villain.

In our version of *Romeo and Juliet*, there's no tragedy.

In the end, we have a beautiful life.

Visiting Italy is different when you're married.

The birds chirp louder.

The sun hotter.

The romance stronger.

My body is alive with just the lust for Antonio.

I can also blame that on his annoying antics during our drive. My pain-in-the-ass husband listed the dirty things he plans to do with his mouth during our honeymoon. At one point, I slid my fingers down my panties and touched myself as he spoke.

Antonio possesses the power of a nun when it comes to my

safety, considering I begged him nonstop to pull over and fuck me, but he claimed it was too dangerous.

My husband, always paranoid.

Killers know killers.

"I did it, Mom." I twist my wedding ring on my finger while standing on the terrace and staring up at the clear blue sky. "I found the dream you'd wanted me to have." I press a kiss to my fingers and raise them forward. "I love you."

I allow the sun's heat to pour over my skin for another second and then return to the cottage.

Aunt Aida and Uncle Felice are on vacation, so we have plenty of privacy here. She even left us a honeymoon basket with my favorite treats on the bed.

Antonio exits the bathroom while drying his wet hair.

My mouth waters as I stare at his bare chest, sprinkled with water droplets. I hitch a breath, eye-fucking him as my gaze descends to his six-pack.

He plays with the knot on the towel around his hips. "Is there something you want from your husband, princess?"

"Yes." I chew the edge of my lip, waiting in anticipation.

He doesn't loosen it. "We've come full circle, baby. I went from stalking you here to sleeping in your bed."

"You did way more than just stalking me here, *husband*."

I yelp when he wraps his arm around my waist and drags me toward him. He rotates me in his hold so I'm facing the bed. I shudder when he clutches me against his chest, his mouth grazing my ear.

"Mmm … my baby remembers all the dirty things I did to her here," he says, sucking on my earlobe.

I roll my head to the side as he showers my neck with kisses, and goose bumps crawl over my skin when his cock twitches against my ass.

"You have no idea how often I stroked myself, thinking about it," he groans against my skin.

I turn in his arms and tenderly place a kiss to the small scar on his arm from when he was shot at Dante's. "You said you'd teach me a lot in Italy. Did I learn well?"

"Exceptionally, but I think you need to show me you haven't forgotten."

He groans when I release his towel, and it collapses to the floor, draping over our bare feet. I wrap my hand around his hard cock, teasingly stroking him.

His mouth finds mine, and he nips my lips while walking me backward to the bed. Clutching the top of my head, he pushes me to the edge. His cock is situated inches from my mouth, begging for me to suck it.

I open wide, inching closer, but he plants his palm against my forehead, stopping me.

"Did I tell you to suck it?" He tsks, staring down at me with half-lidded eyes.

I run my tongue against my front teeth and shake my head.

"Stroke it," he demands, but then stops me after one jerk. "Other hand. I want to see that wedding ring when you touch my dick, baby."

I switch hands, jerking him off, and he pumps his hips in a steady rhythm. He hisses in a breath when I lower my hand, cupping his balls and playing with them.

"Gigi," he groans before retreating a step, and my hand drops from his cock. "Take off that dress, get in bed, and spread those legs for me."

He doesn't have to ask me twice.

I toss my dress across the room, make myself comfortable, and open my legs wide. He joins me, almost predatory, assuring me there's no sweet intention in his mind.

Settling between my thighs, he licks up my stomach, my neck, and then crushes his lips to mine.

Our kiss is wild.

Animalistic.

"Warning, princess," he says, sinking his canine tooth into my lip while trailing his hand downward, moving the same route his tongue did. "This body will be sore as fuck by the time we return to New York."

When I attempt to thrust my hips forward, he presses his hand to my stomach, restraining me. I don't fight his hold as he finger-fucks me, and his mouth attacks mine.

He devours my entire face.

And I allow him to do anything he wants with me.

He stops, his lips wet. I pant, my eyes half open, and wait for his next move. Thankfully, it's everything I desire.

He raises my ass up from the bed and teases my entrance with the head of his cock before shoving himself in me. Even though he's taken me dozens of times, my body always has to adjust to his large size.

His eyes fixated on me, he's almost out of his mind and entranced.

"I intend to fuck my wife all the ways her sweet pussy needs it," he says, holding my waist tight while keeping himself inside me. "I want to rip you apart and then put you back together."

Italy Antonio is back.

His dirty mouth.

His wild fucking.

And I can't wait for more of it.

Hell, maybe we should move here.

When I close my eyes, he curls his hand around my cheek, placing his thumb on my eyelid and holding it open. "You don't look away from your husband when he's fucking you unless he gives you permission."

"Yes, husband," I whisper.

"That's my princess."

His body falls on top of mine as he thrusts inside me.

Over and over again.

Sweat blankets our bodies as we slide against each other.

I go insane, not even remembering what my name is when he interlocks our fingers and pushes our hands above my head.

That simple movement helps his cock sink deeper, hitting my G-spot like it's the golden key to everything he wants.

Then stroke by stroke, his pace slows.

He rears back, his eyes praising as he stares down at me. "I'm going to fuck you slow now, baby."

I glare at him.

He chuckles. "Does that mean my wife wants me to keep fucking her hard?"

"She wants you to fuck her like the villain you are."

He practically growls in my ear and pounds into me.

The bed frame rams into the wall so hard that I'm worried it'll cause damage.

Swear to God, he's fucking me so damn wildly that I'm waiting for the entire cottage to collapse.

I almost feel like a rag doll as he jerks me up, whips me around, and presses his cock back inside me.

One hand digs into my hip while the other smacks my ass. I fall forward, unable to hold my weight, while he pumps in and out of me. I grip the top of the mattress to hold myself up. He's fucking me so hard, and it's a struggle to gasp in breaths.

He's controlling our every move.

And I fucking love it.

He whacks my ass again. "I will put a baby inside you before we leave here."

"Yes," I moan, throwing my head back.

"There won't be one drop of my cum wasted." His pace turns more frantic. "All of it is going in your pussy."

"Oh my God." My entire body trembles, and my heart pounds so hard that I'm sure I'm suffering a heart attack. But no way am I asking him to stop.

"I fucking love you, princess."

"I love you," I say between gasps … pants … whatever is happening.

"Me and only me, baby." His hand finds my ass again before he completely flattens me against the mattress. He covers my entire body with his, nearly every inch of us touching, except for when he hitches his hips forward to keep his strokes level.

I love how dirty my husband is.

How he doesn't care about boundaries.

With me, he's not the ruthless Mafia boss.

He's my lover.

My nurturer.

My version of a happily ever after.

Everyone thought I was crazy for falling in love with the enemy.

But what's love without the risk of falling?

Without risking it all to find happiness in the end?

Now, the gorgeous villain belongs to me.

And I'll forever be his princess.

ALSO BY CHARITY FERRELL

MARCHETTI MAFIA SERIES

Gorgeous Monster

Gorgeous Prince

BLUE BEECH SERIES

(each book can be read as a standalone)

Just A Fling

Just One Night

Just Exes

Just Neighbors

Just Roommates

Just Friends

TWISTED FOX SERIES

(each book can be read as a standalone)

Stirred

Shaken

Straight Up

Chaser

Last Round

ONLY YOU SERIES: A BLUE BEECH SECOND GENERATION

(each book can be read as a standalone)

Only Rivals

STANDALONES

Bad For You

Beneath Our Faults

Beneath Our Loss

Pretty and Reckless

Thorns and Roses

Wild Thoughts

RISKY DUET

Risky

Worth The Risk

ABOUT THE AUTHOR

Charity Ferrell is a USA Today and Wall Street Journal best-selling author of the Twisted Fox and Blue Beech series. She resides in Indianapolis, Indiana. She loves writing about broken people finding love while adding humor and heartbreak along with it. Angst is her happy place.

When she's not writing, she's making a Starbucks run, shopping online, or spending time with her family.